D1422274

BARKING & DAGENHAM
906 000 000 74574

PENGUIN BOOKS

City of Gold

Anton Gill was born in Ilford, Essex, the son of a German father and an English mother, and grew up in London. He was educated at Chigwell School and Clare College, Cambridge, and worked in the theatre (especially at the Royal Court Theatre in London), for the Arts Council and for the BBC before turning to full-time writing. His work includes both fiction and non-fiction, where his special field is contemporary European history. Non-fiction includes *The Journey Back From Hell*, *An Honourable Defeat* and *Berlin to Bucharest*. In fiction, he has written a series of thrillers set in Ancient Egypt, featuring the world's first private eye, the scribe Huy, which has been published worldwide. More recently, he published *The Sacred Scroll*, a Jack Marlowe history-mystery, with Penguin. He is also the author of two biographies, on William Dampier and Peggy Guggenheim. When not working, Anton Gill enjoys travelling, art and playing the clarinet (badly).

City of Gold

ANTON GILL

PENGUIN BOOKS

PENGUIN BOOKS

Published by the Penguin Group
Penguin Books Ltd, 80 Strand, London WC2R 0RL, England
Penguin Group (USA) Inc., 375 Hudson Street, New York, New York 10014, USA
Penguin Group (Canada), 90 Eglinton Avenue East, Suite 700, Toronto, Ontario, Canada M4P 2Y3
(a division of Pearson Penguin Canada Inc.)
Penguin Ireland, 25 St Stephen's Green, Dublin 2, Ireland (a division of Penguin Books Ltd)
Penguin Group (Australia), 707 Collins Street, Melbourne, Victoria 3008,
Australia (a division of Pearson Australia Group Pty Ltd)
Penguin Books India Pvt Ltd, 11 Community Centre,
Panchsheel Park, New Delhi – 110 017, India
Penguin Group (NZ), 67 Apollo Drive, Rosedale, Auckland 0632, New Zealand
(a division of Pearson New Zealand Ltd)
Penguin Books (South Africa) (Pty) Ltd, Block D, Rosebank Office Park, 181 Jan Smuts Avenue,
Parktown North, Gauteng 2193, South Africa

Penguin Books Ltd, Registered Offices: 80 Strand, London WC2R 0RL, England

www.penguin.com

First published 2013

001

Typeset in 12.5/14.75 pt Garamond by Palimpsest Book Production Ltd, Falkirk, Stirlingshire
Printed in Great Britain by Clays Ltd, St Ives plc

PAPERBACK ISBN: 978–0–405–91081–1
OPEN MARKET ISBN: 978–1–405–91082–8

www.greenpenguin.co.uk

To
Daniel and Matthew
&
Janie and Jean (with thanks for the sanctuary)

When they are anointed all over, certain servants of the emperor, having prepared gold made into fine powder, blow it through hollow canes upon their naked bodies, until they be all shining from the foot to the head; and in this sort they sit drinking by twenties and hundreds, and continue in drunkenness sometimes six or seven days together. The same is also confirmed by a letter written into Spain which was intercepted, which Master Robert Dudley told me he had seen. Upon this sight, and for the abundance of gold which he saw in the city, the images of gold in their temples, the plates, armours and shields of gold, which they use in the wars, he called it El Dorado.

Sir Walter Raleigh, *The Discovery of Guiana*, 1596

PART ONE

I

Rio de Janeiro, the Present

He couldn't see the famous statue of Cristo Redentore spreading its arms from the impossible vertiginous stump of rock which is the summit of the Corcovado because the mountain was veiled in mist, a heat mist in the humid city. It was close to thirty-eight degrees today, and the yellow cab's air-conditioning was making a poor job of battling the sweltering temperature.

The plane from Schiphol had arrived at Carlos Jobim only an hour late, and there was still plenty of day left to get over the jet lag before the meeting, though Gerrit de Vries, despite his fifty years and long acquaintance with world travel through his work, felt too keyed up to be particularly tired. A new city, for him, hemmed in by thickly wooded, dramatic hills, with a notorious reputation, a lagoon and a great crescent of beach – all this *and* what looked like the deal of his life in his pocket. These were exciting prospects.

As the cab weaved its way through the cacophonous traffic south down the Avenida Presidente João Goulart, past Cidade Universitária to the right, he looked out of the grubby windows of the taxi at the city, smelling it – the usual gas and pollution of a big place, but garlic and scented dust and coffee and the ghost of cigars too; getting his first feel of it. Such things were important to him. As de Vries's cab drew into the tighter streets of the Centro and battled the traffic on its way south through it, the Dutchman watched the Cariocas on the sidewalks, jostling past shops that were already beginning to tout World Cup and even Olympic souvenirs in their windows. Tower cranes dotted about confirmed the building rush, and the city looked glitzy. But Gerrit's neighbour in Club, a Carioca himself, who'd been over to Amsterdam to buy diamonds, had told him gloomily word was that the spanking-new rail link between Rio and São Paulo wouldn't be ready in time, that it'd gone from an original estimate of 8 billion reais in '97 to breach 55 billion now, and that despite the chrome-and-glass pzazz Gerrit would see in the flash parts of the city, the economic miracle was a house built on sand – and anyway, the favelas haven't gone away, have they? Some things you can't sweep under the carpet.

All this de Vries found a little hard to believe as he drove south through the crazy, beautiful city towards Leblon, where his hotel was. He hugged his briefcase tight, careful of its contents. He'd even been scared during the short walk from the airport to the cab rank – you never knew these days: thieves everywhere, and worse since the Crisis.

He hadn't let the briefcase out of sight or reach since

he'd locked his apartment door on Prinsengracht sixteen hours earlier.

He'd be glad when the meeting was over and he could relax. He'd been lucky, being able to time his trip to coincide with Carnaval like this. In a couple of days he'd have only himself to please, and the Cordão do Bola Preta beckoned already through brochures and clips on YouTube. Carry this one off, boy, and you'll deserve a bit of a treat, Gerrit told himself. And if the clients had insisted he bring the thing all the way here personally, what of it? The money they were spending, they had a right to verify before parting with it, and they'd paid for his trip, all expenses, without a murmur, and the deposit they'd already transferred had entered his business account as smoothly as silk, despite the roundabout route his clients had chosen to take. But the very rich liked their privacy, and de Vries was used to that.

He wasn't worried. He knew it was genuine.

He opened the window a crack and lit an American Spirit, glancing at the driver to see if he'd object, but no snarl came and de Vries drew happily on the cigarette, his first since the enforced purdah of the airlines had imposed itself back home, where even the hash cafés were bowing to Nanny Statism and closing down. Rio felt like a place where you could still loosen up. And he intended to. No one at home to worry about him – not since that bitch Bob had swanned out last November, taking three of the best early Waldseemüllers with him, damn him to hell.

But not before the deal was tied up. The LGBT beaches he'd read about on Wikipedia would have to wait.

A hot wind rushed through the slit of open window and the driver made some remark about the air-conditioning, so de Vries wound the thing up. By the time he'd finished the cigarette (still, miraculously, no objection), they were drawing up at the blank, modern façade of the Sheraton on Avenida Niemeyer. Bellhops rushed to his aid as he stepped out into the baking heat and wafted him, as soon as he'd paid his fare, into the seriously air-conditioned comfort of the skating rink of a lobby. His suitcase followed him, though he resisted all attempts to relieve him of his briefcase.

He scattered a handful of dollar bills as tips as his escort bore him to reception, where a sleek woman smelling of gardenias took his passport details.

'*Boa tarde*, Senhor de Vriezz. We've given you a south-facing room. Towards the sea.'

'*Obrigado*.' Gerrit meant it. He'd read a review of the hotel which told him that if your room faced north you might hear gunfire from the favelas. That, he could do without: he wanted Rio without its warts.

He filled in the necessary forms, took the plastic card-key and noted the floor and room numbers, but as he made for the lifts, his way was courteously blocked by a slim woman, mid-thirties, in a business suit.

'Herr de Vries?'

'Indeed.'

'My name is Moraes – Fernanda.'

'Senhora.'

She had a haughty face, beautiful, if you were interested in women, but she was no hotel hooker, so Gerrit wasn't surprised when she said, 'I am here to greet you on behalf of Dr Louvier. We have a car scheduled for you at' – she glanced at her watch – 'nineteen hours. I trust that will give you enough time to freshen up and rest.'

'Thank you.'

'Dr Louvier hopes your business may be concluded swiftly.'

'As do I.'

'Good. I will meet you here five minutes before, if that is agreeable. In the meantime, if there is anything you need' – she handed him a card – 'I will not be far.'

De Vries watched her as she made her way across the lobby towards the doors. They are certainly taking care of me, he thought, turning towards the pinging lifts and the porter waiting with his valise, feeling suddenly more tired than he'd believed and clutching his briefcase to him.

An evening meeting. He'd hoped to get a night's sleep in before confronting his clients, but he shrugged off any worry. The whole thing should go through without a glitch, if everyone was civilized about it.

He was ten minutes before time, cleaned and pressed and in a formal suit, his briefcase in his hand, standing in the lobby, unaccountably a little nervous, but still confident of the outcome. It shouldn't take more than twenty-four hours for his principals to verify the merchandise. After that, he'd relax for the short time he'd allowed himself before returning to Amsterdam and, recharged, use the new money to get his affairs back into some kind of order, after the chaos Bob's departure had left them in.

Fernanda Moraes was already there. She hastily interrupted a call when she saw him.

She greeted him with a warm smile and led him outside, where, right on cue, a blue Cadillac drew up smoothly. Its chauffeur ushered them into the car's cream leather interior, and de Vries was treated to the sight of a slim knee and slender thigh as Fernanda slipped into the seat beside him. Not deliberate, he decided, thanking God anyway that he was impervious. Life was complicated enough without women. Fleetingly, de Vries wondered if he shouldn't have warned someone of where he was going. But Dr Louvier wasn't the first client to have insisted on a degree of secrecy; deals of this magnitude sometimes made them nervous, and he respected that. Still, he was glad he'd left a little insurance concealed in his hotel room. And it wasn't as if he didn't know where he was being taken. All this had to be above board.

They made their way east, past the Lagoa into Copacabana, finally drawing up at a house in a tree-lined street near Rua Souza Lima. The white building was set back from the street and surrounded by white, two-metre-high walls. An electric gate swung open silently to admit the Cadillac, which deposited its passengers before a wide run of shallow steps which led up to a veranda. The front door stood open and a warm light issued from within. This looked like the kind of place that could only be inhabited by people well able to pay his price, thought de Vries, pleased that his instincts had not let him down.

Fernanda led him through an icy marble-and-gold hall into a room whose white furnishings reflected discreet opulence. Nothing was out of place, but there was nothing either to indicate any kind of personality. This might have been a room in a film set or a grand hotel. The paintings on the walls were tasteful abstracts that lacked any originality; the magazines neatly stacked on the glass coffee table were insipid glossies, and the bookshelves contained neat rows of leather-bound, respectable volumes that looked unread.

At one end of the room, by a window whose panes were hidden by heavy silk curtains, there was a large table. Its surface was bare, and well lit, though not too brightly. That's where they'll examine the goods, thought Gerrit, walking over and depositing his briefcase on it.

'Champagne?' Fernanda asked.

'Afterwards, I think.'

'They'll be here directly.' She gave him her smile again, thinner this time, and left him alone. Her footsteps had hardly receded when an inner door opened to admit two men and a woman.

The bulkier of the two men, and the woman, wore

dark suits, and bland expressions to go with them. The man had the disquieting air of a bodyguard, though he lacked the boneheaded look; the woman was a redhead and finer featured than Fernanda, but might otherwise have been her clone. The other man, about Gerrit's age but enviably slim, was dressed less formally, in jeans and a white polo shirt. His face was open, eager, relaxed, but his pale-blue eyes were hard, and Gerrit noticed that it was only his mouth that smiled. Well, never mind that, they were hardly friends: this was a business meeting, and there was a lot of money involved.

'Herr de Vries,' said the man, approaching and extending his hand. Gerrit recognized the voice from the phone. 'Good flight? I'm sorry to have rushed you into a meeting on the day that you arrived, but you can understand how keen I am to see it at last.'

Gerrit smiled self-deprecatingly, shaking his head: no problem.

'Fernanda said you wanted no refreshment, but you must allow me to twist your arm. Kristof, if you please . . .'

The other man crossed the room to a walnut cocktail cabinet which opened to reveal sparkling bottles and a small fridge, while the first continued: 'As you have probably gathered, I am Ambroise Louvier; this is my associate Drita Agoli, and that is Kristof Struna.' Gerrit shook hands with the woman and exchanged nods with Struna, who was rattling glasses. 'I'll have my usual, please, Kristof, and I guess Drita will have a Sancerre.

And you?' A courteous eyebrow was raised in Gerrit's direction.

'Gin on ice, if you insist.'

'Oh, I do.'

Struna busied himself with the drinks, taking a beer for himself, pouring a large Tanqueray 10 over ice cubes that looked like pieces of crystal, for Gerrit.

Once they had toasted each other, Louvier allowed his gaze to rest on the briefcase.

'And here, I presume, it is?'

'Yes.'

'Excellent.' Louvier paused with that irritating confidence, Gerrit thought, the mega-rich have: the confidence brought by the knowledge that all you have to do is convey by a glance what you want, and you'll get it. 'Well, I can hardly wait.'

De Vries didn't usually drink at all before business had been concluded but this time he was grateful for the reassurance the perfect gin gave him. He took a long sip, nodded, unlocked and opened the case.

He took it out carefully, undid the ribbons that attached its wooden binders around it, then put on a pair of cotton gloves before removing the protective paper. He had brought spare pairs of gloves, still in their cellophane, but as he looked round he saw that the others had already donned latex gloves of their own. They crowded in on him.

De Vries would have preferred them to use his own gloves.

'Ah,' Louvier said, as the last sheet of tissue was

removed. He all but shouldered de Vries aside as he bent over the map.

He was leaning in too close: he shouldn't breathe on it before it was his, Gerrit thought, but was unable to intervene. Louvier took out a watchmaker's glass and screwed it into his left eye to peer at the faded brown ink, the pale contours in green and yellow, the traces of ancient pencraft. He followed lines with his finger, smiling, though he didn't touch the surface of the parchment. His examination continued in silence for half an hour, during which de Vries finished his gin and, feeling beads of sweat break out on his forehead, accepted a refill, noticing now a faintly metallic taste as he drank. Must be the jet lag.

At last Louvier straightened. 'And this is the only example?' he asked.

'It is the only one. No plates were ever made for this, so there are no copies.'

'Made by Thomas Hariot? You can confirm that?'

'In 1596, or early 1597 at the latest.'

'But he had something to work from, hadn't he? The map drawn up on the expedition itself?'

'Something must have existed, yes. But it was lost long ago. My searches have been exhaustive.'

Why was it suddenly so inexplicably hot?

'So have mine,' Louvier replied.

There was something in the man's tone that de Vries didn't like, but he couldn't put his finger on it. He said, 'I imagine you'll want to verify finally before we conclude. If you would send your representatives to my hotel . . .' Gerrit was feeling an increasingly urgent need to get out of that room, that house. He wanted to get up, pack the map and go. But his will seemed to have deserted him.

Louvier waved a hand. 'No. I don't think that will be necessary. We have been following your research closely and we have double-checked what we felt we needed to. I am enough of an expert to see that the thing is genuine. What is important is the authenticity.' He placed a hand on de Vries's meaty shoulder. 'Thank you, my friend. You have played your part.'

De Vries was nonplussed. 'Then – that's it?'

'Yes.' Louvier smiled. 'All we have to do is conclude our business. But first, let's get this out of harm's way.'

He slid the map to one side and motioned de Vries to a chair as Agoli produced a notebook and a pencil from a drawer in a side table and turned to face the Dutchman. He could read nothing in her face.

'We just need a couple more details,' said Louvier, his voice reassuring. 'Then we'll give you the money. As you requested, nothing through any tiresome books – straight open bonds on Schollendorf's in Zurich, correct? And two million was the sum agreed.'

'Less your advance.'

'Oh, you've done so well, Herr de Vries. We'll call your advance a bonus.'

'Very generous of you.'

'If only we could be sure of your absolute discretion.'

'You have that.'

Louvier made a gesture of regret. 'More may hang on this transaction than you imagine, Herr de Vries, and I fear so much is at stake that we cannot afford to take any chances.'

The heat was oppressive now. Gerrit felt the sweat running into his eyes. He tried to get up but found himself pinioned from behind. Struna, he thought. The metallic taste in his mouth was stronger, his head swam and the room seemed to belong to a dream as Agoli approached, the pencil held like a dagger in her gloved hand.

With great precision she drove its point into his left eye just above the orbit, and with the flat of her hand pushed it down until it had disappeared fully into de Vries's brain. She held it there firmly while Struna kept down his flailing hands. Louvier had bunched a handkerchief and pushed it into de Vries's mouth, stifling his screams, before stepping back in distaste.

There was very little seepage. Once the body had stopped jerking, Agoli calmly dressed the wound.

'They'll be suspicious when they find him,' Struna said. 'A pencil in his eye? They'd use a gun or a knife in the favelas.'

'It kept him off his guard,' Louvier said. 'I thought it was a nice touch.' His tone hardened. 'Just to be sure, douse him with petrol when you dump him, and burn him. If they ever bother to identify him, there'll be nothing to link him with us.'

'His hotel room?'

'Fernanda's already dealing with that.'

Louvier turned away, back to the table. He took the map and held it up to his eyes, smiling.

The key was in his hands at last.

2

The Orinoco River System, South America, 1595

'Another cauldron of a day,' Sir Walter Raleigh wrote in his notes, the sweat streaming from his brow and on to the already moist page he balanced on his knee. But the Virgin Queen had at last looked kindly on this expedition and spent some money on it. If he were to get back into her favour, he'd have to succeed. Succeed for England where Antonio de Berrio had failed for Spain. And to do that, he'd have to go on. He paused to slap another of the damned insects that swarmed attendance on him and settled obstinately and unceasingly on his neck, his wrists, his ankles, biting even through the thick hose he wore to protect them, despite the heat.

The crew half sailed, half rowed against the sluggish current. When the slight wind dropped or the oarsmen's arms could do no more, they drifted back. The air was dense with heat and moisture, suffocating them. Even the silence that hung over them was oily, opaque.

'Another cauldron of a day – 20 May in the year 1595 on some tributary in the labyrinth of tributaries of the Rio Orinoco, as I estimate four hundred English miles now from our base at Trinidad, and God in His wisdom knows whether or not de Berrio was lying to me, as our goal is not reached yet and I begin to despair. A hundred rivers, de Berrio said, run into the Orinoco from north and south. They twist and turn and wrap themselves around islands in the stream, and all the islands look alike, and every bend in the river looks alike, and the shrieks of unseen creatures at night in the trees and the flapping carnival of coloured birds in the day are all the same. I talk to our Arwacan guide about when we'll get to the next village, and he nods and grins and says, "Soon".

'We are far south of the main river now. Far from where my first – bad – information told me was truth. Pray Master Francis Sparrow draws the map well, or we will never get out of here again. But he has a steady hand, and loves adventure.

De Berrio hinted at six hundred miles upriver. I kept that knowledge from the men, or they would never have agreed to the venture. As it is, I wonder if we'll make it. Are we lost?'

Raleigh left off writing and looked from his barge across to the other four. They were a sorry collection, worse now: the old galego he'd had fitted out like a galley, two wherries, and a ship's boat taken from the *Lion's Whelp*. Perhaps the hundred men he'd brought with him were too many – not all of them would return, he was sure of that. What with the sun and the rain, and having no cabins to shelter in, only the hard boards of the boats to sleep on; food and drink brought for a month now running out fast. The boats were cluttered, untidy, a sure mark of low morale, bits of equipment all anyhow, and the gunpowder damp.

He slapped another biting insect. Demons in hell couldn't be worse, for all the minute size of these tormentors. Now he knew what the horses back home in Dorset felt like in summer. Cooking on board, what they did of it, left its stink and grease, worse because they were driven ever more to eat river fish, and the smell of the waste got into your nostrils and stayed there. He thought of his soft bed at home and of Bess in it, Bess his wife. His marriage had meant the Queen's displeasure and jail, but Bess was worth it. Why the hell had he left her? Why not just stay home and quiet and look after the estates?

Too late now. He breathed in the smell of the brown river-water and the wet clothes and the sweat of many men and the rotten-fish waste and thought that even the Tower had been more comfortable than this – and he wanted no more of the Tower. The trees loured from the banks, and their long branches reached out as if they'd like to strangle him. He'd set a small group on land to reconnoitre, and they'd never come back. Later, they'd seen the heads of Ned Barker, Samuel Foote and Dick Hemming on spits by the bank, three of the five sent, some magic set on them before they died, heads shrunk to a quarter size.

Didn't do much for the men's morale. They only stuck it now because there was no help for it. Unless fear got the better of greed and glory and they mutinied, turned back. But who'd lead them then? Who'd get them back? First sign, he'd kill Sparrow and throw the map in the water. They'd be swallowed up by the labyrinth, or run up against them that'd done for Barker and the rest. Back at base they'd wait till year's end and then go home. Not much of a prospect.

Raleigh scanned the thick woods that shouldered right up to the banks an arrow shot away on either side and hemmed in the view, limiting it to their green, prison-like monotony. No direct attacks yet, but he knew they were being watched. All the time. And the Arwacans they'd taken on board had to be watched too, though they would be friendly and helpful and loyal as long as the payment of hatchets and knives could be eked out to them. The Indians were their lifeline. All the compasses told you was that you were going round in circles, but that time was past. With the Arwacans aboard, there was hope.

He fed the men with the tales de Berrio had told him. Gold plate, eagles of gold, images of men and divers birds, beasts and fishes – all in gold, some life-size, some greater. A land unsacked and mines unwrought. But de Berrio's men had been ambushed and killed, and though he had yielded much information to friendly persuasion, Raleigh remembered his warnings:

'The river systems are treacherous and shallow, Englishman. You'll never navigate them with the boats you've got. Even our canoes, which draw no more than twelve of your inches, ground on the sand often. And the natives are not friendly unless you can buy them.'

'You have turned them against white men with your greed and plunder. We shall not show them such a face.'

'They may not be disposed to give you a chance.'

And so it went on, but *we* went on, all the same, and proved the Spaniard wrong. We treated the locals fair, and got no trouble.

Until now, when there are people in the woods who do not wish to make friends. Who watch us.

Until now, when my doubts begin to move in on me.

But I cannot allow them to.

I must succeed.

The people in the woods are protecting something, and that something gives me hope. I even believe that we are closer to our goal than I thought.

'When do we get to the next village, Ferdinando?' Raleigh asked the Arwacan again, thinking of fresh fruit and fresh water, and a change to dry clothes, even a chance to clean them. And maybe a woman or two if the price was right and no one would be offended.

'Soon.'

'We'll call this river the River of the Red Cross,' Raleigh told Francis Sparrow later, with no village in sight and the sun dipping low over those accursed trees. 'Ferdinando has no name for it, and we are I think the first Christian men ever to sail on it.'

'I'll mark it down.' Sparrow, the map-maker, was a young man, wiry, with a lean scholar's face hard-bitten by wind and weather, and a thick crop of brown, curly hair matted with dirt.

Raleigh's own scalp crawled as badly as his groin, but he tried to make light of his discomfort as he encountered the hopeful, questioning looks in the eyes of his men which had replaced blind optimism and would soon give way to resentment. He'd talk to his captains. No doubting Caulfield or Gifford; and most of the other officers seemed sound. Though if the men rose up as one . . .

He looked across at the left bank wearily. Then his eye caught something a few yards inland but already more than half hidden by branches – something that flashed yellow-bright in the rays of the dying sun. Breastplate? But were there still Spanish outposts – forts even – this far out?

Whatever it was didn't reappear, but the bushes along the bank shuddered as if a sudden wind had stirred them. Raleigh called out a warning, which rang out across the river to be echoed by Caulfield and Gifford where their boats lay sagging in the oily water. The men scuttled to their stations, gathering muskets and cutlasses, but not before a rain of hissing bolts had shot from the left bank, hammering into timber but also into flesh.

Five men hit. Raleigh could see that one had caught it in the throat, but the others had minor wounds, to leg and shoulder. The rowers strained towards the right bank, away from the fire, only to run into a second ambush.

It didn't take them more than a few minutes to get midstream, where they rowed like madmen away from the attack. But a curious thing happened to the wounded. They went into a St Vitus's dance, flapping their arms and bending their legs as if devils possessed them. Their faces grew black as their breath halted in their gullets, they struggled against unseen attackers that seemed to fly close to them, and one by one they flopped to the bottom of their boats, like puppets with their strings cut.

3

New York City, the Present

Jack Marlow stuffed the copy of *Moby-Dick* he'd been reading on the subway into an already occupied outer pocket (penknife, cigarettes, matches), pulling his battered leather jacket further out of shape as he paused for a moment to look up at the discreet town-house hotel that concealed his place of work behind its elegant façade.

He was edgy. They'd put him out to grass for a while to undergo a psychological reaffirmation programme, but now, suddenly, he was back – recalled a fortnight before time. The cipher message from Sir Richard 'call-me-Dick' Hudson had been high on urgency, low on detail.

Dick by name . . ., thought Marlow, who didn't have much time for psychological reaffirmation. He'd spent the leave he'd been granted after that in Santa Lucia, chartering a small yacht to coast round the neighbouring islands, drinking a little too much rum and enjoying an uncomplicated fling with a delightful French brunette who was convalescing after her recent but lucrative divorce from a billionaire software developer.

But now it was back to business. He walked briskly

through the lobby, nodding at one or two of the staff as a regular guest who'd been absent a while might do. One or two smiled back at the tall, untidy, irregularly handsome man who looked, the girl at Number 3 Desk thought, like an academic played by an actor. Brainy, but dashing. She smiled, but he was already past her.

Making his way through the door at the back marked PRIVATE, he ran the gamut of new, improved Security (which beeped at his penknife) and took the lift to Section 15, Room 55, and his new boss.

New boss, but familiar company. Laura Graves had his old job now; but he'd accepted his masters' decisions, recognizing that a step down didn't mean a step backwards. Laura was more of a line-toeing type anyway, and he felt freer than he had for a long time. The shrinks up in INTERSEC's so-called summer camp outside Montpelier in Vermont had scratched away at what they saw as his 'issues' and he'd given them enough to amuse them, keep them busy; but he had to admit that the enforced leave in the golden autumn countryside had given him something he really needed: a breathing space to patch himself up. Paris and Istanbul were now distant memories; the appalling blonde and Su-Lin de Montferrat just so much scar-tissue. So much misjudgement. All you can do is learn and move on. Needing to draw a firm line in the sand, he'd also left his NYC uptown apartment for a new one in Greenwich Village: a minimalist, all-white modern flat that was now transformed – full of Jack's untidy clutter of books and art.

Now, he was ready again.

The suite of white rooms which made up Room 55 were pretty much the same, though Leon Lopez's section had expanded to make space for fresh equipment. Bulky stuff, for he was using old machines – the only ones capable of decoding the seventies and eighties material he was working on. The tall West Indian, who had not lost his bookish stoop despite his wife nagging about it, came out to greet Marlow, explaining:

'Cold War stuff, Jack – academic really, but now that Putin –'

Jack nodded. 'It never hurts to be sure.'

'Right.'

'Family?' Jack was looking round the room as he talked. The central desk was neat and clear, a blue bomber jacket slung over the chair by it.

'Mia's fine. Lucia's got a new best friend. Alvar is adolescing and he's a pain in the ass.'

Marlow nodded again. 'Where's the boss?'

'Laura's already upstairs.'

'With Hudson?'

'Yes.'

'Nothing changes.'

'Come on, I thought you'd squared that.'

'Oh, I have.'

'Then let's go. They're waiting.'

Sir Richard Hudson's office hadn't changed either, though these days the man himself had decided expensive colognes were vulgar in a man of sixty-plus, and there was no odour of Havanas any more either, as his doctors had told him to quit. But the Savile Row (or wherever he got them from) suits were still on his back, and he retained his stagey English imperturbability perfectly. He was doing it now, as Jack and Leon were buzzed in. He stood by the window. Over by the Kandinsky, a new acquisition that hung on the adjacent wall, sat Laura. Though she tried hard, imperturbable was something she didn't do so well, and Jack noticed the tightness around her mouth immediately. She glanced at him and forced a quick smile, but she didn't do welcoming too well either and Jack knew that being his boss was a role reversal she had yet to get used to.

'Hi, Leon,' said Hudson. 'Jack. Welcome. Sorry to haul you back before your time.' Hudson loved to think of himself as a convivial kind of guy, but it was always a struggle, and sometimes the mask slipped. He was not finding it easy now, Jack noticed; but he'd already braced himself for bad news. To his surprise, his summons had come as a relief. He needed some action, needed to flex his muscles. He didn't like rest. He didn't know it, or admit it to himself, but his dislike of it stemmed from the fact that leisure allowed his demons time to come at him.

Jack was already looking at the fourth man in the room: beefy, mid- to late-fifties, what hair he had left in a crew cut, little red wireframe glasses covering self-satisfied eyes. The sort of face that creased easily into professional affability – but change the lighting and you had a thug.

The man rose from his chair as Hudson said, 'Gentlemen, this is Mr Adams –'

'Call me Nick,' said the man, extending a hand to Jack, nodding to Leon. Close up, the eyes didn't look so sure of themselves. There was a trace of a southern accent. Carolina?

'– from the Treasury Department,' Hudson finished. 'He needs our help.'

4

The Orinoco River System, South America, 1595

Five more dead but, thank God, no wounded. Brief funerals and river burials. Too risky to moor and dig graves, no matter how close they were to the bank. Though they knew what would happen to the corpses, they tried not to think about it. The dead feel nothing, but it seemed a sacrilege.

Two days later they found the village – or *a* village, for now it was clear they were not where Ferdinando had thought them to be. The river had widened and there were many islands dotted in its sluggish stream. The village was on the shore of one they reckoned to be as big as the Isle of Wight back home. They stood off and surveyed the place. The people lining the bank looking at them carried no weapons, but they belonged to no tribe the English had seen before.

'Let me go ashore,' Ferdinando said. 'I will take my brother. He speaks the local dialect. These people are good. They will help us.'

'I don't want to lose a good pilot.'

'There will be no trouble. Let me take some hatchets. I can use them to buy food.'

Raleigh let them go, watching the canoe carefully as it covered the hundred yards or so to the shore. The people of the village did not move.

'They are sending a boat out to us,' said Frank Sparrow.

Raleigh saw the local canoe depart from the bank. It was crewed by a lean, bronzed boy and an old man, both naked except for loincloths made of leaves.

'Perhaps they want to parley.'

'Watch them.'

Ferdinando and his brother reached the shore before the other canoe reached the English boats. Then the ruse became clear.

'Look!' Sparrow cried.

No sooner had Ferdinando and his brother landed and pulled their craft up on the narrow grey slip of beach than the villagers fell on them. The canoe with the old man, sent out as a distraction, now started again for the shore.

'Cut them off!' Raleigh yelled, as he watched the fight on the beach. The villagers had Spanish knives, but Ferdinando and his brother had swords and held the people off long enough to break away and vanish into the forest that edged the clearing the people there had made for their dwellings. A group of villagers, yelling with rage, broke away and set off after them, taking their deerhounds with them. Raleigh cursed – there goes our pilot! But Gifford's men had managed to bring their wherry, which was nearer the shore, round to cut off the old man in his canoe. Maybe the villagers had sent him out because they could afford to lose him – but maybe, thought Raleigh, we can use him to redeem our pilot.

There was no fight over the native canoe. As soon as they saw they were cornered, the Indians gave themselves up and Gifford took them aboard his boat. But then the boy pulled a knife and drove it into the arm of the sailor holding him. The man let go with a howl and the boy dived into the water, disappearing for a moment and then reappearing, swimming hard towards the shore. Another sailor aimed a musket, fired and missed. Gifford swore at him, his voice carrying tinnily across the water: 'Waste any more ammunition and I'll throw you in after him.'

The people on the shore were shouting too, anxiously encouraging the boy. He had the wounded sailor's blood on him, and the piranha had scented it. You could see the water ripple as the school concentrated on its prey. The boy knew. His arms began to flay frantically against the leaden water, but he could not swim fast enough and the ripples became a churning that surrounded him as he screamed and rose half his height out of the water before being drawn back in. The water closed bloodily over him and was still.

'What shall we do, Commander?' Gifford said when his wherry drew close to the barge. Caulfield was drawing close too now, along with the others.

'Make way,' said Raleigh bitterly, 'but keep as close to the shore as we can.' The villagers were waving their arms furiously as the little fleet drew away from them, but made no move to give chase. The old man was yelling something to them – something that held them to the spot: 'If Ferdinando's survived, we may be able to pick him up.'

'We must pray that he has,' said Caulfield quietly.

'If not, we have this old bugger to redeem him with.'

'If they want him.'

The old man continued to yell.

'What's he saying?' asked Gifford.

'I can make out a little,' said Sparrow. 'He's telling them to call off the hunt. He's scared we'll kill him if they kill Ferdinando.'

'He's got that right,' said Caulfield, eyeing the old man, who returned his look with frightened eyes. 'We'll cut his head off and throw it ashore.'

They coasted for half an hour, sometimes thinking they could hear the sounds of a chase hidden in the trees along the shore. Then they saw movement at the river's edge.

Clinging to an overhanging branch was Ferdinando, his face strained and desperate.

Thank God, thought Raleigh, shouting, 'Make in to him. Close as you can!'

The sounds of the dogs and the chase were close. Gifford brought his boat in hard, five men steadying themselves and poising muskets. When he was ten yards out, Ferdinando's pursuers broke through the dense vegetation and made for him. With a despairing cry, the dogs loping silently towards him, he let go of the branch and threw himself heavily into the water. He must have got a slight wound, maybe torn himself on the bushes, for there was a trail of blood after him as he swam.

He hadn't got ten feet before the water downstream of him began to surge. He hammered against the current with his arms and the sailors reached out futilely, yelling encouragement. The people on shore stood and watched. One held something by the hair: the head of Ferdinando's brother. The dogs lay down and licked their long snouts.

But Ferdinando was safe. They hauled him aboard just in time, when the devil-fish were snapping at his heels. They thrashed around the wherry's side for a good minute before subsiding. They'd been bilked of their second feast.

Once they'd given him a change of clothes and a strong drink, Ferdinando, fighting his grief for his brother, told them:

'They were not bad people, but they have knowledge of the Spanish. They thought I was bringing more Spanish to despoil them. And' – he paused – 'and they spoke of something else, some other people, something I couldn't catch.'

'Other people who threatened them?' Raleigh said. 'Another tribe?'

Ferdinando shook his head. 'I could not catch it. Perhaps.'

The old man, still in the chains they'd put on him, mumbled something.

'What did he say?'

'They are not of the Ciawani or the Waraweete peoples. They are Tivitivas like the villagers. He said they come from the depths of the earth.'

'Question him.'

Ferdinando tried. They even threatened to cut him, to throw him to the devil-fish. But he would say no more.

'Kill him,' suggested Gifford. 'He does us no good. He is another mouth to feed.'

'No,' Raleigh said. He had noticed the look on the faces of the other Indian members of his expedition. Ten of them. He did not want them against him. He'd lost eight English sailors to attackers; another ten to disease. The rest were surly. He would take no risks.

Two days later, he was glad of his decision. They had sailed on hopelessly and lost two more men, to fever. On the wherries, Gifford and Caulfield were out of food and there was half a barrel of fresh water between them. No one on the other boats was much better off. Ferdinando tried to save face but he was under pressure, and when Raleigh put more on him, he said, 'We are lost. I do not know which route to take.' They had just reached yet another bifurcation of the river, each strand alike, each leading into the same monotonous, unchanging landscape.

The old man rattled his chains impatiently, and spoke.

Ferdinando looked at him, at first quizzically, then hopefully.

'What does he say now?'

'We must free him. If we do, he will help us.'

'Rubbish!' said Gifford, on board the barge to measure out a sack of dried fish for his men. Raleigh gave him a look.

'Your hunger mars your judgement, Mr Gifford, and you speak out of turn.'

'Commander.'

Raleigh gazed at the split river ahead. 'Release him.'

They did so. The old man rubbed his wrists and ankles, mumbled and grinned, but guardedly, and pointed then at his mouth. Taking the cue, Raleigh took a piece of fish from the sack being prepared for Gifford and offered it to him. The old man hesitated, took it, sniffed it disgustedly. For a moment they thought he would throw it over the side, which would have meant his death, for Gifford, drawn and exhausted, had read that thought too, and his hand was already on the pommel of his dagger. But the old man nibbled and gnawed the fish, moistening it with his mouth, and ate.

Then he pointed. The left fork.

Raleigh's tillerman looked at him, and the commander nodded assent. 'We might as well take the left as the right,' he said to himself.

'The old man knows these parts,' Ferdinando said later. 'He was born here and has lived, he thinks, through two hundred and forty seasons in this swamp.'

Raleigh looked at the man's leather face.

'What is his name?'

Ferdinando asked and relayed back a sound that

Raleigh knew he'd never be able to pronounce. 'I'll call him Essex,' he decided, smiling at the thought of his ambitious enemy and rival back home.

The going was better in this part of the river system, though the stream had narrowed. No hidden people threatened them. Raleigh suspected a false dawn, but days passed and there were no attacks. There was game from time to time, monkeys and a curious, tree-dwelling, slow creature, half dog, half bear, but small like a dog, face of a badger, up in the high branches, which could easily be brought down with a bow and arrow, and whose meat was just about stomachable, if you were hungry enough. There were also butterflies the size of birds and brilliantly blue, and birds that decked the trees like living jewels, but whose meat was dark and foul. They left the birds alone.

Occasionally there was an unwary deer, but generally the deer were too quick for them. And once, at dusk, they saw a big, spotted cat drinking at the edge of the bank.

There were bad days. As they grew further from his home, Raleigh saw Essex hesitate, and twice he made mistakes and took them up branches of the river that were not branches at all but creeks which petered out in muddy swamps where the little biting flies with their dreadful whining buzz massed and tortured them until they got out of there. Only tobacco kept the flies at bay, and there was little of that left.

But on they went, passing upriver with its flood and anchoring at its ebb, and the men's spirits, as Raleigh wrote in his log, revived. There was a sense of going somewhere again, as the river broadened once more. Free of the trees, for a time the air cleared. Officers and men took turns at rowing.

'There is not only a sense of going forward, but of being able to get back. We are no longer lost. Essex will navigate us back to his part of the world, and Ferdinando knows the way from there. So our hope, by the grace of God, is well founded again,' Raleigh wrote. 'And Francis Sparrow, thin as a lathe but thank God keeping his health, has parchment and ink enough for his ever-expanding map.

'We still have to succeed. We still have to find it. But now I feel that we will.

'As if God had indeed heard us, we came on to a stretch of river where the jungle on either side retreated and gave way to a plain, swathed in short, green grass, with clumps of trees planted in groves as if by men. Here both good and bad fortune befell us.

'We had sent young Captain Whiddon ahead in the boat from the *Lion's Whelp*, with eight musketeers, to reconnoitre, and, while we waited, one of our men, an African, a very proper young fellow, leapt out of the galley to swim, and in front of our noses he was taken and devoured by one of the largatos that live on the banks – big lizards with massive jaws, you would not think these lumberers could move so fast when they attack and tear their prey to pieces.

'We were grieving for him when Whiddon returned, from a large village where he had traded for food, fresh bread, fish, hens and some local liquor which tasted of herbs but warmed the gut.

'Then on again . . .'

But more time passed and the food ran out again and the men became tired and impatient and wanted to hang the old man, who kept saying 'Soon' whenever they asked him if they were nearing their goal. The river closed in once more and the flies returned with the closed country crowding the banks, and more died of fever, though none of the Indians, so to make matters worse there was suspicion of poisoning. And one day in late June they were fired on again with poisoned darts. No one was hit.

The next morning Essex sniffed the air and took Ferdinando by the arm, talking to him urgently.

'We are close,' Ferdinando translated, and he had caught some of the old man's excitement.

Raleigh wanted to believe it was true but he was under pressure to give up, to turn back before it was too late and they were swallowed up by the trees and forgotten for ever. But by midday after a bend in the river they saw a wider stretch of water leading off to the south, the current there barely discernible. Essex pointed along it with a confident hand.

'At the end there is a lake. We will be there within a day's sailing,' Ferdinando continued to translate.

'We have heard that a dozen times before.'

But Raleigh looked at Essex and saw that his eyes were clear and confident and that the trouble had left them. He gave the order to change course.

The day's sailing was uneventful except that Essex grew more excited and the other Indians in the crew, with the exception of Ferdinando, more apprehensive. Raleigh made anchor at dusk, not knowing what to think.

The next morning they sailed with the breaking day. Two hours later, with the dew scarcely off the trees, the waterway broadened into a shallow bay. The trees no longer came right to the shore, there was a beach, and the beach stretched far on either side and curved round, all but out of sight to the south, to form the opposite shore of a great lake of grey-blue water, and there, on a small island close to that far shore, stood a building like a monolith, a tower growing out of a block, which in turn grew out of a larger block, and steps were carved into the building all round, and at the centre of the second storey facing them they could see a great closed gate which was the entrance. And the sun caught the stonework and the stonework flashed like the sun.

And as they looked at the beach when the sunshine hit it, the beach glittered and danced in the light like a necklace or a diadem. All around.

5

The men raised a huge cheer. There was no holding them, though Raleigh managed to maintain enough discipline to keep twenty musketeers at posts along the starboard side of the barge facing the shore as the others swarmed into canoes or ran the wherries and the *Lion's Whelp* boat on to the shore, as the two larger boats – the barge and the galego – stood off a little and sent canoes.

The men filled their hats with sand. Only later did they find out that the offering wasn't as great as they'd thought. But, in all truth, it was great enough. One grain in five was gold.

'Have you marked it well?' Raleigh said, looking at the map.

'I have,' replied Frank Sparrow.

'That map must never leave your hand.'

'It is in an oilskin pouch in my leather wallet. It never leaves me.'

'Good.'

Raleigh had other concerns, even in the moment of his triumph. Supplies were low again, and you cannot eat gold. He saw that the Indians were worried. And there was the building on the distant shore.

He was alone on the barge with Sparrow, the impatient musketeers, Ferdinando and Essex. The ten Indian members of the crew were with them too. Onshore, Gifford, Caulfield and Whiddon oversaw the men. They organized groups to take samples. A group of five hacked away at hard rocks that bordered the shore, but having nothing stronger than daggers as tools, the chips they split off were puny. Still, they shone dully, and they should be enough to convince the most cynical back at home.

'Why will the Arwaca not go ashore?'

'They fear,' said Ferdinando.

'What do they fear?'

'They say men come from the depths of the earth to protect the gold.'

Essex pushed forward, eager to speak. He took Raleigh by the sleeve and pulled him close, whispering in his ear, though the commander of course understood not one urgently delivered syllable. He turned to Ferdinando.

'There are things you must know about this place,' Ferdinando interpreted, then listened to Essex for a long time before motioning him to stop.

'He wants to tell you of the temple. You must not go to it. Take what you want here, but do not go to the temple.'

'Why?'

'Because of the city.'

Ferdinando listened again, and then went on. 'The temple is shut, but there are times – special times – when the sun strikes its doors. Then they open. He says only the sun will open them. They close when the light passes over. The temple is the entrance to the city.'

'The city?'

The guide spread his hands. 'A mighty city, all of gold. Built for the gods.'

There was a pause while Raleigh took this in. 'How often does the light pass over?'

Another brief exchange with the old man. Ferdinando turned to Raleigh again. 'Once every year.'

'When?'

Yet another quick exchange. Raleigh waited impatiently.

'In the terms of your calendar, it is early in the year – and varies by a few days. But it is close to 25 June.'

Midsummer's Day, or near enough, Raleigh thought. We are just too late. It is a pity we have no cannon. That would be a sure way of opening those doors. But he said nothing. 'Tomorrow we go there,' he said.

Ferdinando said something more to the old man. Essex looked resigned, and replied.

'He would like the map.'

Raleigh hesitated, then told Sparrow to bring it out. Essex looked at it once Sparrow had carefully unfolded it, then made a gesture.

'He wants a quill.'

'He is not to touch the map!' said Sparrow.

'He must, he says. He will not harm it.'

Reluctantly, Sparrow produced a pen and dipped it, handing it to the old man, who spread the map on a board and drew four shapes on a corner. The shapes didn't look like anything you'd recognize. One might have been the outline of a bird, another of a star, though neither was immediately identifiable; the other two were geometric but unlike anything Raleigh had ever seen in any of Thomas Hariot's books or notes back home. Might they be diagrams of constellations?

Essex drew slowly but without hesitation. When he had finished he handed the pen to Sparrow with a satisfied look. But the other Arwacan Indians had seen what he'd done, and their faces had become masks.

'He says you are safe now,' interpreted Ferdinando.

'Safe?'

'Yes.'

'Can he explain that?'

'He will tell you when the time is right. But you must not go to the temple.'

Raleigh was about to pursue this when a fight broke out among a bunch of the men on shore – as he had feared it might.

That night he had a troublemaker hanged. He had already given orders by then for the crossing of the lake the following day.

But when dawn came there was a mist on the lake, and it did not shift. The sun couldn't penetrate it. And the Arwacans had gone, back upriver. They'd stolen a canoe in the night, and some of the remaining supplies. Only Ferdinando and the old man remained.

'We'll try anyway,' Raleigh decided, against his better judgement, sensing the men's impatience.

They made their preparations. While they were busy loading the boats and fixing the sails to take advantage of the light but steady offshore breeze that had blown up (but which failed to do any more than move the dust around, making it swirl), they were attacked. It came suddenly and in force. They threw over canoes for bulwarks and hid behind them, shooting into the trees whence the poisoned arrows hailed on them. The worst thing was the silence and the emptiness. The arrows hissed but made no other noise, and the bowmen remained unseen. Two dozen sailors and marines were killed before the others could get off to the boats. Then there was a choice to make: to flee across the lake or to beat back the way they had come. His complement was all but halved by now. Raleigh decided on retreat. They could not afford to venture further into the unknown. At the moment he gave the order, an arrow struck Essex, who was standing behind him, in the neck. The old man was dead before his body had slumped on to the golden sand.

Halfway back along the waterway he gave the signal to make anchor midstream. Between then – it was about noon – and dusk, they stripped the boats for battle and prepared to make their way back in the morning. It was insanity to have got this far and to have to give up.

But the next day they found their way back to the lake blocked by a barrier across the waterway. They sent men in canoes to clear it, but they were all killed as they made the attempt, the arrows slapping into them with such accuracy that only one in five failed to find a mark. Raleigh didn't have the ammunition or firepower to retaliate, and his musketeers had no mark for their weapons as their enemy remained invisible.

'What must we do?' Caulfield demanded.

'We must go back,' Raleigh said, hiding his bitterness behind a firm voice.

They all saw the logic of that. The old man was dead, but Ferdinando lived, and they had the map. And the current would be with them all the way to Trinidad. By God's grace, they'd be back at base within two months.

'Keep good care of the map, Master Sparrow,' Raleigh said. 'It is our insurance and our future.'

All the way home he dreamed of his return. In his mind, the golden dream that would make his fortune in England for ever became a reality: a mighty city, all of gold. Ferdinando's words rang in his ears. So the old stories were true, and he had found what the Spaniards had been seeking for decades upon decades. In his mind's eye, he saw the streets, the monuments and buildings, the towers and the palaces, the artefacts. A city built for no human habitation. A city for the gods.

It had to be a reality.

It had to be.

6

New York City, the Present

'So that's what we're talking about – a rumour?' asked Lopez.

'It isn't as simple as that, or I wouldn't be here,' Adams replied sharply. 'Hear me out.'

'OK, OK.' Lopez waved an arm. 'I'm a little tired, forgive me. Something I've been working on,' he explained to nobody in particular. 'It's relearning the old systems . . .' He trailed off.

'It sounds pretty fantastic so far,' Marlow said. 'A glut of gold –'

'We're praying it's nothing, but that looks more and more like wishful thinking,' Adams said. 'We've got to put protection in place fast, and you've got to find the source and stop it.'

'Tell us more.'

Adams spread his hands. His glance flicked over their faces. 'You're right about a glut of gold, Jack,' he began, 'though that sounds melodramatic.'

'As if we haven't been through enough drama since 2008,' Sir Richard said drily. 'And it isn't over yet.'

'This would make 2008 look like a sunny day in Disneyland,' Adams said. 'This would change the face of the world and cause a power shift so abrupt the shock wouldn't be much less if the earth shifted on its axis.'

'And you say *I'm* being melodramatic.' Marlow wasn't smiling.

'I've just come from a meeting with Christine Lagarde,' Adams went on. 'The IMF is the third biggest holder of gold stocks in the world and, if they're worried, everybody should be.' He paused. 'The word is that a vast new source of gold has been discovered. News in the financial world spreads like bushfire anyway, and news like this is all but impossible to contain. People panic where money is concerned, and already the price of gold is dipping. It's being sold, but someone out there is confident enough to be buying it up. Discreetly.'

'Got any traces?' Marlow queried.

'It's very hard to crack. Whoever it is is well-organized. No one's shown their hand, and the purchasing's being done through a network of private and investment banks. So it's obscure.'

'Any idea at all who's behind it?' Laura asked. 'China?'

Adams shook his head. 'Unlikely. China's ahead of the game anyway. Sure, if they got control of new gold in return for their dollars they could go on the gold standard, and then they *would* be in a position to run the world economy.' Adams sat back. 'But, frankly – why would they *bother*? Look, they *own* the US debt, effectively, and although they're only seventh in the top-ten world gold-holders, they've got about 1,070 tonnes of the stuff – but that accounts for around 2 per cent of their foreign reserves. A tiny percentage.'

'That's a hell of a lot to swallow. What does it mean?'

'To put things in perspective: France is fifth in the world, with about 2,450 tonnes, but that represents 72.6 per cent of their foreign reserves. We are top of the list with 8,133 tonnes, but that amounts to 78.3 per cent of ours. I'm giving you broad figures – the exact stats are classified.'

'Even to us?'

'We'll let you know if necessary. The thing is, there's no gold standard at the moment – everything's pegged to the international reserve currency, which is the good old US dollar. But it's complicated. If, say, China – or anyone – went on the gold standard and controlled most of the world's gold, we'd be vulnerable: majorly vulnerable. If we lost control of world finance we'd go bankrupt overnight.'

'But it might just be a rumour,' Leon said.

'That alone might be enough. Enough to lower the price.'

'How would you respond initially?' Laura asked.

'We'd hold our hands to our breasts and we'd hotly deny it. To stabilize the price. But if the rumour was *then* found to be well-founded . . .' Adams spread his hands again and looked bleak.

'Panic,' concluded Marlow.

'Big-time. There's something about gold. Right through history. And we haven't evolved beyond it, economically. The power of any given country is determined by how much gold it physically owns.'

'And not just countries,' added Marlow. 'These days, private companies could buy the gold and pay for takeovers with it, thereby controlling world infrastructure, and then they could up their prices without fear of competition. There are precedents.'

'Can you keep it simple?' said Sir Richard.

'It *isn't* simple. What *is* simple is this: if the dollar crashed, there'd be material and social chaos like no war or natural disaster could get even close to achieving.'

'But what could motivate such a move?' Sir Richard cut in. 'World trade makes us all interdependent. You need markets, you need money flowing around, or the gears seize up for everyone. No point in controlling all the money on earth if you can't do anything with it.'

'Your job will be to *find* the motivation. But find the people, and you find the purpose.'

'Big ask,' said Lopez.

Adams nodded. 'We're trying to contain it, but our measures are limited. Christine is wetting herself. She wants us to mark all our gold – all existing world gold if she can swing it – with small doses of radiation, and only accept *that* as having value.'

'Would it work?' asked Laura.

Adams looked irritated. 'Of course not. Not now, anyway.'

'Why not?' asked Marlow.

'Let me finish!' The tension in the room was mounting by degrees. Adams had said enough to set everyone on edge. He was clearly a man used to giving orders, not receiving them, but he was now, as Marlow clearly saw, in the ocean without a lifebelt. 'Marking the gold with a radioactive trace is no real solution, because if another country – or an organization – controlled the bulk of the world's gold and the dollar went down in flames, people wouldn't care whether the gold available was tagged or not. Look, we know that India is already using untraceable gold to buy oil from the Iranians.'

'So no one knows for sure just how much gold is out there?'

'We have the official figures, but it's not something we can keep precise track of, no. The Exchange-Traded Funds collectively own as much gold as most countries, and they are private holdings, mostly in vaults in New York, London and Zurich. Try prising the lid off *them*!'

'How do we survive at all?!' exclaimed Jack.

'That, my dear fellow, is the mystery of mankind's precarious existence,' Sir Richard replied.

'What else can you do to put a brake on this?'

'Confiscate the ETF holdings or whack a heavy tax on gold profits – if we dare do either. We're checking holdings everywhere – in the Turks and Caicos, in the Caymans, in Labuan, in Jebel Ali. But that's like chopping down the pillars that hold the whole fucking house up – pardon me, ma'am.' Adams addressed this to Laura.

'So you wouldn't dare do that.'

'It wouldn't be an easy option.'

'We only think those pillars hold the house up,' said

Marlow. 'That's what bankers have wanted us to believe since the Templars invented the game.'

'We haven't got time for philosophy,' snapped Adams. 'This trend has been going on for two months now. Enough's enough.'

'Let's get some basic data,' said Lopez, pouring oil on the water. 'Some concrete idea. How much gold do you think has been discovered?'

'That's uncertain.'

Marlow scoffed. 'So you're jumping at shadows.'

'Not at all. The panic might have taken as little as two weeks, and high-frequency trading makes it even more of a white-knuckle ride than before. There're a number of hedge funds that trade based on computer programs that react to what other computer programs are trading. No human involvement at all. A while back, Rook Capital lost 400 million dollars in an hour because their computer programs hit a glitch. Almost bankrupted the company. Once a steep downward slope starts, it's self-reinforcing. Speed is so critical that these hedge funds put their computers in the building next to the ones running the New York Stock Exchange so they don't lose a nanosecond in executing their trades.'

'Still, you'd have to find a hell of a lot of gold to upset the balance.' Jack again.

'Do you know how small a space the whole amount of known gold in the world would fill if it were collected together now?' asked Adams angrily. 'Melt it down and pour it into a mould and you'd get a cube only just over twenty metres square. You could fit that into this building! But do you also know how much buying power that represents?'

The others looked at him.

'I'm glad I've got your attention,' he drawled unpleasantly. 'If you owned just that – just that little box of solid gold – you could buy every single acre of farmland in America, plus seven companies the size of Exxon, and you'd still have a trillion dollars left over to play with.'

'But we know where all the gold mines are,' said Sir Richard.

'And gold-mining's slowing down,' added Marlow. 'Isn't that right? There are one hell of a lot of other commodities to offset gold.'

'But nothing as stable. Especially since – and I shouldn't say this – the sand we've chosen to build our house on is turning into quicksand anyway. In such a climate, gold could reassert itself overnight. After all, it's had a hold on us since people came out of the forests and down from the hills to build farms and towns. It's been a symbol and a tool of power since Babylon and Egypt.'

'And if there *is* a new mine – or whatever source this new hoard comes from – and from what you say it needn't be that big –' said Lopez.

'If it's a mine, it might take years, decades or more, to get at it. But we think it's a more readily available source – easier and quicker to reach, to extract – or we wouldn't have such a problem and the markets wouldn't be in such a sweat.'

'Then why the delay? Why two months?'

'We think they need time to prepare. We're just praying that, even now, they may be jumping the gun. But we think there may be, as you said, Jack, a glut. We think someone's got a line to a source of gold bigger than anything known to exist today. If they have –'

'They can do anything they like,' Marlow finished for him.

7

'So what we need is a perpetrator,' Sir Richard summed up when Adams had packed his briefcase and gone, leaving just a slim folder for them to work with.

'And a motive,' Marlow said.

'Find one and you've got the other.'

'Perhaps.'

'What do you mean?'

'The motive might not be what we expect. The motive might not be simply a question of gaining control.'

'I hardly see what other motive there could be.'

Jack was silent, musing. Sir Richard turned to Laura. 'I'll let you get on with it, but I want a daily report, and action by the end of the week. Meanwhile, the powers that be will feed the financial press with disinformation. It's too late to smother this completely.'

After he'd gone, Laura sat down and pulled the file towards her. She put her glasses on and Marlow noticed again the tiny heart tattoo on the little finger of her right hand, next to the emerald ring she wore. He had still not found out the history of that tattoo. He suspected that to do so he would have to be in a relationship with her that was much more than professional.

'There's precious little here,' she commented, after

flicking through it. 'One lead they have sounds too fantastic even to think about.'

'Let's hear it anyway,' said Lopez, leaning against the window. Jack took a seat opposite Laura, where he could no longer see her long legs crossed under the desk.

'It's from some report the CIA intercepted several years ago about the discovery of a lake in the Amazonian jungle . . .' She skimmed the document. 'Apparently there was an island on this lake, but the European explorers who made the discovery were moved in on as soon as news of it leaked out. They claimed later that the Instituto Nacional de Pesquisas da Amazônia put a cordon round the whole area. Something more about heavy crates being shipped out of the area in conditions of deep secrecy, but there the story peters out.' She looked up. 'Looks like someone thought they might have discovered Eldorado.'

'And the Treasury takes that seriously enough to start a dossier on it?' said Lopez.

Laura flipped the folder closed. 'If you can call it a dossier.'

'But it's a start,' Jack said. 'What else is in there? Any visuals?'

She looked at him. 'The footnotes refer to some photos. And a map. But they're ultra-classified. At least, they were, back in the eighties.'

'We should get them.'

'Eighties, eh?' said Lopez. 'Let me get on to that.'

Laura checked back. 'The source is the Agência Brasileira de Inteligência. But it's old stuff.'

'ABIN? Been a while since we've had anything to do with them. No harm in looking.' He took down the details and vanished into his lab.

'A map's good,' Jack said.

'You think I'm not being thorough enough? This isn't going to take us anywhere, Jack – they're grasping at straws.'

'So are we.'

'But *Eldorado*?'

'Someone found something back in the eighties that was important enough for ABIN to get involved,' said Jack.

'They probably just didn't want a stampede.'

'A gold rush, you mean?'

'You know what people are like – especially now,' Graves said.

'People have always been greedy.'

'Money talks.'

'It's what makes the world go round.'

'I thought love was supposed to do that.'

'Spare me your dazzling Irish wit.' Laura smiled at him. It looked as if the tension she'd feared there was going to be between them wasn't going to be a problem after all. There he sat, as relaxed as he could be, smiling back, in a jacket so decayed she would have been embarrassed to give it to a charity shop, a battered copy of *Moby-Dick* sticking out of one pocket, another full, no doubt, of the usual litter he carried about. And still he managed to look like the most beddable man on earth. God, how she hated him sometimes.

'How close are we to the Brazilian secret service?' he asked suddenly, wrongfooting her, as he so often did, the bastard.

'Close enough,' she replied, pulling herself together. 'They like to keep their distance these days, though, now they're a major player in Latin America. Not so keen on Uncle Sam pulling the strings any more.'

'I thought so. But we still have friends there?'

She gave him a veiled look. 'Yes.'

'Well, depending on what Leon comes up with, it might be worth putting in a call to Brasilia. Just an informal ask.'

'Come on, they'll know what we're on to in a heart-beat. You heard what the Kentucky Kid from the Treasury said: news like this travels like wildfire.'

'I thought he was from Carolina.'

'You may have been living here for years, but you haven't got our accents down yet.'

'Serves me right.'

'You get cocky 'cos you've got so many back home.'

'Back in the dear old UK? Yes, I suppose that's true.' Jack barely gave his birthplace a thought these days. On the rare occasions he was there, he felt uncomfortable. That claustrophobic little island, still mired in its sense of self-importance. But a useful place to bury secrets. Marlow recalled a colleague once describing the UK as the Romania of the West.

'Didn't one of your countrymen discover Eldor-ado?'

'He did,' said Jack, remembering his history. 'But it

was a lie. He made it all up to curry favour with the Crown.'

'And the Crown wasn't amused.'

'You're thinking of quite another queen.'

'People are still looking for it, you know,' said Laura, more seriously.

'For Eldorado?'

'Yes.'

Jack scoffed. 'They're like people who buy lottery tickets. There is no such place.'

'The Kentucky Kid thinks that if there is a new gold source it's not a mine.'

'Like he knows.'

'If you discovered a mine, you couldn't keep it secret at all. You'd need capital, infrastructure and time to get it all going.'

'Whatever it was those explorers found in the eighties, they were seen off p.d.q. by the locals.'

'Haven't heard anything else about that, though, have we? If they'd found gold then, we'd have known about it long ago.'

'Everybody wants to find gold. End of the rainbow. I remember reading about a suicide. Drove his car into a river. When they pulled it out, there was his body, with losing lottery tickets pinned all over his coat.'

'Something for nothing.'

'But these people – and even if it is just a rumour, somebody started it for a reason – they're not after something for nothing. They have a purpose.'

'I'll get on to Brasilia.'

'Be discreet.'

'Are you forgetting who's boss now?'

'As if I'd forget.' Marlow looked grim. It was indiscretion that'd cost him the job. But he'd paid the price and learnt the lesson. Look where you're going, he told himself, not where you've been.

Leon came back with a sheaf of papers in his hand. 'Here's the stuff,' he announced.

'That was quick,' said Laura, admiringly.

'We aim to please,' he replied, spreading the photos and the map in front of her. The photos were grainy shots of a stretch of water in Eastmancolor blue out of which jutted an island covered with dense trees surmounted by vertiginous, rocky crags. The map had clearly been drawn in the late-sixteenth or early seventeenth century and showed a labyrinthine river system, coiled around a large inland sea.

'I did a superimposition of a handful of likely modern locations,' Leon went on, producing two transparent cells. 'The one that fits best' – he placed one of the cells over the map – 'is this one. It's the Orinoco system, south of the main river. But, as you can see, there's no lake there now.'

'You could be wrong,' said Laura.

'There is that possibility. But nothing else comes close. And South America is the likeliest candidate.'

'Plenty of gold elsewhere in the world,' said Jack. 'What about South Africa?'

'No similar river systems,' replied Leon. 'Then or now. And I've covered the other places, before you ask. Same result.'

Jack was looking hard at the map.

'What is it?' Laura asked.

'This reminds me of something – something we picked up on the wires from Rio a week or so ago,' he answered. 'Could be a connection.'

'Follow it up,' Laura said decisively. 'I'll contact the Brazilians. Leon, you'd better get that Russian stuff wrapped up or farm it out to Room 64. I'll get clearance. We'll need you on this full-time.'

'Got you!'

'Back here in two hours. And you'd better have something I can throw Hudson.'

But two hours later, all they'd achieved was a blank.

Laura sat across her desk from Leon, drumming her fingers on its white surface and taking out her irritation on Marlow. But she was worried for him too. She should have known better by now.

'He's late.'

Lopez shrugged unhelpfully. 'You know what he's like.'

She sat in brooding silence for a minute, then: 'The Brazilians were extremely helpful,' she ground out. Leon had always been her friend and, when things went against her, her prop. This was her first assignment in charge of Section 15. She'd hoped for a quick result, to impress Sir Richard with her acuity. But it wasn't to be.

'What did they say?' Lopez prompted her, as he knew she wanted him to.

'The whole lost-lake thing was a blind alley. The lake wasn't lost at all – the explorers told journalists that to beef up their "discovery". There *were* the remains of an ancient settlement on the island, though. The explorers thought there was some kind of treasure there, sure, but they were wrong. The Brazilian authorities established that the explorers had wanted to get out what they could and sell it abroad to collectors in the Middle East, and there was mention of a consortium who called themselves the Chevaliers d'Uriel, but they stopped that. They crated up what there was, and it amounted to a collection of what I suppose you'd call pre-Columbian cooking vessels and utensils, as well as the remains of weapons, arrowheads, and so on – nothing more. They're in the vaults of the Museu Nacional in Rio.'

'So why the secrecy?'

'They put a blanket over it back when they still thought it might be a big discovery. They didn't want outsiders poking their noses in. Then it got forgotten – you know how these things happen.'

'And the map?'

'Some enthusiastic Spanish conquistador, Antonio de Berrio, letting his imagination get the better of the facts. Or his enthusiasm. Or maybe he just thought if he made up something that sounded valuable, he'd gain favour back in Madrid. Who'd check?'

'They'd have judged by results.'

'Maybe he just needed to buy time.' Like I'll have to, she thought. Holy shit. 'Where the hell is Jack?'

'Here,' said Marlow, pushing through the opaque glass door that shielded Room 55 from the outside world. Laura was about to rebuke him when she saw the intent look on his face. Instantly, she gave way to hope. But first she filled him in on what they'd got – or not got. He listened carefully and thoughtfully, and she noticed him prick up his ears distinctly once or twice, though he said nothing. Would she ever know what precisely was going on in that mind of his?

'Your turn now,' she said.

Marlow tossed a number of police reports on to the desktop, and Laura tidied them into a neat pile, noting, as she did so, the dates and provenance of each one. There were ten in all, from all over the world, and their timeframe covered a period dating back to the beginning of the year. The most striking feature they had in common was this: each report was accompanied by a photocopy of an old map, and each map showed the same segment of the South American continent. She looked up at Marlow and started to go through the reports carefully, passing each to Leon as she finished it.

'The map we got from Adams reminded me,' Marlow explained while she read. 'Long shot, but it might lead somewhere. But you've probably got a lead yourself by now.'

'Working on it,' said Laura, not catching Lopez's eye. 'Give me more on this.'

'What you have there is just a sample, but there've been dozens of thefts worldwide of maps of Guiana,

Amazonia and Brazil – basically, modern-day Brazil and Venezuela – as they were about four hundred years ago. They're mainly Spanish, with a handful of Portuguese and English ones. God knows how many more have been bought from dealers. It's not such a huge market, thank God, or we'd be totally buggered, and there does seem to be a system here, which certainly helps us. Whoever's collecting this stuff has a specific area in mind.'

'Stolen from where?'

'Museum archives, mainly. Others from state and university libraries. The maps weren't kept under particularly secure conditions, but some of them are very valuable indeed.'

'And the dealers?'

'More problematic. Nothing illegal in buying maps, and if it's a cash deal, who needs to know about it apart from the parties involved? I'd like to suggest that Leon follow up a couple of leads to see if we can get any info from any of the buyers or sellers involved, but these people have a tendency to clam up, and we daren't make more than oblique enquiries.'

'Just give me the details,' said Lopez.

'It won't be easy. As far as I can see, a lot of the negotiations have been done through middlemen. No direct link to any client – our boys are being very careful. But a few burglaries have been from dealers – that's how I got on to this in the first place – and they'll cooperate if they think they're likely to get their stuff back. I got most of this stuff via INTER-

POL, and we can use them as cover, as usual. No point in raising stakes by playing the INTERSEC card unless we have to.'

'Forget it,' Laura said. 'It's too fantastic.'

'It's the only lead we have.'

'We're talking world finance, not Boys' Own adventures.'

'What makes you think there's any difference? The Treasury thinks there's something in the Eldorado theory.'

'They're clutching at straws,' said Lopez.

'A gigantic stash of gold, there for the taking, with no effort involved? The idea of it has stayed in people's minds for centuries. Why not?'

'No.'

Marlow shook his head impatiently. 'Listen. There's one case we can move on. It's a fresh trail and we have something solid to go on. Two months ago, in Rio de Janeiro, the police found a body dumped in an alley in Dona Marta.'

'Drugs?'

'No. The body had been torched, but enough was left to identify it. A guy called Gerrit de Vries, a Dutch print- and map-dealer. It was an ugly killing. Pencil in the eye.'

'For God's sake,' Leon said.

'His firm had a big reputation, but he'd fallen on hard times. Ex-boyfriend ripped him off, or something. But it turns out that just before he left Amsterdam he told one or two close friends about a deal he was about to close that was big enough to get him back on his feet. And that's what he was doing in Rio.'

'Details?'

Marlow shrugged. 'That's it.'

Laura looked at him. 'So we don't know what he was selling?'

'A map, that's certain.'

'Are there records in Amsterdam to back that up?'

Marlow shook his head.

'Now who's clutching at straws?'

'Except that, since then, there have been no more incidents: no more thefts, no more approaches to dealers for maps of that period or of that part of the world.'

'It's still a long shot.'

'But let's assume that whoever de Vries was dealing with has found what they were looking for. If that's the case, we haven't got any time to lose.' He looked at Leon. 'Can you dredge something up for me on these Chevaliers you told me the Brazilians mentioned?'

'I'll check the files. The old stacks will have something.'

Laura still hesitated. 'I'll have to run this past Hudson.'

'He'll back this up. Look, it's just me on a flight to Rio – it won't even dent the budget. And if we do nothing –'

'He's right,' said Lopez, gently.

'Back after two operational days, maximum,' she said. 'And God knows where you'll start. Don't get the local police involved. And don't start any hares you can't catch.'

'It's a promise.' Marlow gave her the kind of smile which at any other time would have melted her. Now, she found herself torn between anxiety for his safety and hope that he'd succeed fast – she really wanted to impress INTERSEC with this one. She had to admit she was pleasantly surprised that they'd entrusted such a big mission to her; but she also knew how closely they'd be watching her.

Marlow was already halfway out of the door.

'Going already?'

'Before you change your mind.'

Marlow's step was always lighter out of the office. He found INTERSEC, with its proliferation of in-house rules and caveats, its budget obsession and its growing tendency towards bureaucracy and compromise, increasingly suffocating – but he would never be able to leave, he knew that; just as he knew he was too valuable to them not to be allowed a little latitude when he chose to take it. But he'd made a major mistake on a recent assignment and he was still on probation, so today, after he'd swiftly but carefully read the files Lopez had sent him, he'd drawn the standard minimum kit and checked out of the building formally. No one raised an eyebrow. He wasn't requesting special equipment or one of the firm's jets. This was being billed as a light mission, a routine check.

He wasn't going to take a company Falcon, because

sometimes it's better to blend in with the crowd and travel incognito, so he went home on the subway and packed his black leather overnight bag with the scanner-proof compartment for his kit and booked a regular ticket on his own Internet connection for the 21h30 AA flight from JFK that evening to Rio, lucky to get an aisle seat near the front of tourist class. He'd finish *Moby-Dick* easily on the ten-hour flight, so at his apartment he picked out another book, Norman Lloyd Williams's biography of Sir Walter Raleigh. Why not?

It wasn't until he'd left the plane the following morning and was waiting, sticky-eyed, for his cab – he wasn't going to waste time picking up a hire car at the airport and he'd opted for no INTERSEC-designated transport – that he suddenly became alert, certain that someone was watching him.

He cast around cautiously, but there was no sign of anyone particular in the bustle and hum around him. Just a feeling that wouldn't go away, a feeling so familiar that it was comforting – as if an old friend was watching his back. It was a feeling he had learnt to trust: it had saved his life a number of times and he wasn't about to ignore it now.

The taxi arrived promptly – a bright-yellow Hyundai. New though it was, Marlow knew the local rules well enough not to slam the door when he got in – there's no graver insult you can hand out to a Carioca cabbie.

On the way into town, he checked the traffic behind

him from time to time, but not so much as to arouse the driver's suspicions.

Nothing.

That either meant he'd been too edgy, that they were very careful or that they already knew where he was headed.

But no one outside Section 15 knew that.

8

London, 1596

Sir Walter Raleigh found it hard to go cap in hand to anyone, but he was learning. The cold, white English sun elbowed its way through the narrow windows of Sir Robert Cecil's waiting room as he paced it. His deep tan had faded since his return, and his weather-beaten face, crevassed with more lines than a man in his forties deserved, was worn, though his eyes were still bright, and obstinately hopeful. But this interview looked like his last chance of getting what he wanted.

Cecil had a lot of influence. Raleigh didn't like him, but he needed him. The man was ten years his junior, and stood way up the ladder from him now. Never a favourite, but never out of favour either, Cecil was set in the dull family tradition of administrative service, Raleigh thought, half contemptuously, half enviously. Cecil's father was the 75-year-old and now ailing chief minister, and everyone knew his son would inherit the post when the old man dropped off his perch. Already he was five and a half years into the job of spymaster, navigating the capricious backwaters of England's relationship with Spain and France, while bejewelled ambassadors mouthed courtesies at each other at Court, and Gloriana believed not a word anyone said.

Raleigh itched to be away at sea again. The Court suffocated him. But to get away, he needed money.

Finally, after another half-hour's impatient wait, a flunkey opened the large oak door at the far end of the antechamber and beckoned – without bowing, Raleigh noticed angrily. But he had to swallow his pride.

He swept past the flunkey, pushing him aside. A heavy curtain behind the door was drawn closed, but Raleigh didn't hear the door shut after him.

The panelled room was spacious, though stuffy, and littered with papers. Behind an imposing desk sat a small man dressed in black with a crooked back, slicked-back hair and bulging, very careful eyes.

'Walter!' he said, smiling with well-rehearsed warmth.

'Robert.'

'What can I do for you? I'm so sorry for the wait, by the way.' He waved a hand at the paperwork. 'Always busy here. But I don't need to tell *you* that.'

What can I do for you? thought Raleigh, but he was more nervous than angry. Cecil wouldn't dare treat him like this if he'd been more in the Queen's favour. 'You've read my report?' he said.

'On the expedition? Sounds promising. Very promising.'

'There is gold there,' Raleigh continued eagerly. 'If we get to it first, there's enough to cancel the debt, refit the fleet and send Spain packing for good!'

'That's excellent news,' said Cecil. 'But how do you propose to get at it?'

It was all in the report, Raleigh thought. Why is he stalling? And his heart misgave him. 'I need enough to fit out a proper flotilla, with provisions and munitions to last three years,' he said. 'I need engineers and soldiers. Not a large force, but a well-trained one. The best men I can get.'

Cecil looked at him, and sucked his lower lip. 'Not the best time, my friend,' he said. 'You know how things stand.'

'I've brought proof back with me of what I've found!'

Cecil still looked regretful. 'I know, but, frankly, it's not enough to convince us. Your *Discovery of Guiana* is amazingly thorough and absolutely fascinating, but the evidence you've given us – a few rocks and some bags of sand –'

'It's gold! It's been assayed.'

'But how do we know there's enough of it? Digging it out and bringing it back, all that way, through Spanish territory, at a time like this? It's very high-risk.'

'You have my word.'

Cecil looked awkward. 'No one is doubting that, Sir Walter,' he said at last, and more formally. 'But we have immediate problems to face and pay for. You've heard the rumours.'

Of course he had. Following the spectacular defeat of their navy eight years ago, the Spanish were well advanced in their plans for a new Armada. Spies in

Madrid and Cadiz reported that the new fleet was nearing completion. And with the death of Francis Drake, the great combatant of Spain, that very January, Queen Elizabeth's confidence was low, and her attention was focused on the new threat. Raleigh, who had aspired to take Drake's place, was bitter. An attack on Cadiz was in the planning, but he'd heard it would be his rival, Essex, who'd command it. They'd offered him command of a landing party.

'The fact is, we have little money in the Exchequer to spend on a venture like yours just now,' Cecil went on. 'But that is not to say it could not be found – given patience, and time.'

It was Raleigh's turn to look wary. 'What do you mean?'

Cecil studied his fingernails, which were in need of a clean and even a manicure, Raleigh thought. He looked at the man's fragile, ink-stained fingers. And I have to make him my friend. He remembered the piranha in the Orinoco river system and thought he'd rather trust himself to them than to this slippery eel of a man. 'I want to give you some advice,' Cecil said. 'If you can be patient and not speak of this to anyone else – in short, you play it down – then perhaps, if we can avert the Spanish threat – and I am sure your contribution to that effort will be invaluable – then we will talk again.'

Raleigh was reluctant to play his trump card. That, he wanted to keep to himself for as long as possible. He knew he wasn't the most discreet man on earth, but he hadn't survived this long in politics without learning one or two basic rules on how to avoid the headsman. Tower Hill and the Block were not for him if he could help it. But he didn't see now how he could keep that card to himself.

'I have a map,' he said. Francis Sparrow's papers and drawings were in a strongbox in Raleigh's London house.

Cecil looked interested. 'God forbid that it should ever fall into Spanish hands,' he said.

'It shows precisely where I must go to collect the fortune that awaits Her Highness.'

'I would need to see it.'

'You shall, Robert.'

'Whom have you told of it?'

'No one but you,' Raleigh lied.

'Bring it to me,' said Cecil.

Leaving Cecil's office, Raleigh knew that, having told the spymaster of the map, he'd need someone else on his side if he were not to be outmanoeuvred. There was one person he believed he could still turn to, one person in a position to use influence without calling in favours later: a fellow member of the select group Raleigh belonged to, whose views of life they preferred to keep to themselves.

So engrossed was he in his thoughts that he didn't notice the flunkey, still at his post by the door, cram a notebook into the leather wallet on his belt and follow his departure with malevolent eyes.

9

Rio de Janeiro, the Present

Armed with the information Laura had gleaned on Gerrit de Vries's murder from the Brazilians, Marlow checked into the Sheraton, and just a little judicious influence had got him the room de Vries had occupied. He didn't expect to find anything there, but there was no question of not leaving the smallest stone unturned. Two months was a long time, but Marlow knew all about hotel rooms, and where things could be hidden in them so as not to be discovered for years.

He hadn't shaken off his instinctive feeling that someone was shadowing him, and he paused in the lobby, sliding his travel bag off his shoulder and resting it on the floor in front of him, casually scanning the area and seeing nothing to arouse his suspicions. But a fleeting look back through the entrance told him more. A slim, brown-haired girl in a cream dress getting out of a taxi. He'd noticed her out of the corner of his eye at the airport, among the people waiting at Arrivals. What made him think her appearance here was more than just a coincidence was the way her eye was drawn to him. He was careful not to catch her momentary glance, but he was aware of it. He made his way unhurriedly from the reception desk, not looking back. It was enough to know his presence had been noted, and he was pretty sure she thought she'd evaded his attention.

As he went up to his floor in the elevator the old sense of elation flooded through him – always a relief. He had work to do, something to concentrate on, which, while it continued, freed him from any other consideration. Freed him, in other words, from his darkest thoughts. That liberation was what drove him to do his job. He rejoiced in it. And when it was over he hungered for it again. He knew this was how it would continue always, until the last job, the one when he made a mistake he couldn't rectify. He was thirty-nine years old; he had maybe seven years of field service left. Then they'd give him a desk, he'd put on a suit and run younger agents. A visceral part of him didn't want to get that far.

Once in the clean, impersonal, space of the room, he made a routine check for cameras and microphones, and found none. His precise destination in Rio hadn't been known by anyone else beforehand. They knew where he was now, though. He wondered who the girl was working for – but her presence was more of a relief than anything. He was looking for a needle in a haystack: a needle he wasn't even sure was there. But someone was interested enough in his presence to have him monitored. That could only mean one thing.

He undid his bag and from the kit compartment took a pair of 30-160x70 Sunagor binoculars, specially developed in a miniaturized model for INTERSEC, opened the windows and stepped out on to the balcony. He leant on the railings and looked out at the morning, before raising the binoculars and examining the approaches to the hotel. The girl was there, though a good hundred metres away, leaning on a cream Mercedes, talking into a mobile. Her face was partly turned from him so he couldn't read her lips. It didn't matter. They'd make their move soon enough, whoever they were.

The important thing for him was that she was confident enough not to hide. That confirmed she was unaware he'd noticed her. But she might not be alone. Unwise to stay out and exposed longer than necessary. He moved back out of sight, slipped into one of the cane chairs and lit a Camel, inhaling gratefully, planning his next move, and in no hurry for now. Do nothing to alert them.

When he'd finished the cigarette he took the IR/UV scanner from his kit and examined the room. Nothing behind the walls. Nothing under the lining of the safe. Nothing slipped behind the landscape painting in its frame, or its backing. Marlow carefully lifted a corner of the carpet – again, nothing.

If de Vries had left any kind of message in a bottle, any kind of signal as insurance if anything should go wrong, somebody had been in since his departure to wipe out any trace of it. But nobody's perfect, Jack thought as he started on the bathroom.

He hadn't expected to find anything behind the bath panel, and didn't. Nor behind the washbasin mirror, nor anywhere obvious. Nowhere a pro would think of hiding the scrap of paper Marlow hoped to find.

Then it hit him.

He crossed back to the bedroom and took out the reddish-brown leatherette-covered Gideon Bible in the right-hand bedside-table drawer. Flicked through its India-paper pages. Bookmark in Revelation. The name of a street in Copacabana, and a French, or Canadian, surname: Louvier.

Marlow took his time. He planted a Bronx-registered private detective's card where it could be found with some difficulty by the curious, just in case anyone decided to check on his identity. Needing to be fresh, he showered and changed, went down to the coffee shop and ate. He remained always alert, always bearing in mind the fate the Dutchman had met. He was dealing with some rough players, and by his own choice he had no back-up. There wasn't a hint, though, of anyone watching him in the public areas of the hotel.

Returning to his room, he ascertained that no one had entered it in his absence and equipped himself with what he needed from his kit: the little Glock 28 lightweight, the Leatherman Skeletool CX, six metres of ultra-thin black nylon rope and the specially adapted iPhone 7X – indistinguishable to the untrained eye or user from any commercially available model, but capable of 28-350 photography. He wanted to keep his kit to a minimum, but he decided on the binoculars as well.

He fitted the gear to an undershirt harness and, dressed in a white polo shirt, grey linen pants and flexible trainers, left the room, picked up the Avis Chrysler that was waiting for him and headed north-west a while before re-routing east and south. No evidence of being followed, but he'd expected that, though he knew they couldn't route him through his phone. He just needed to be sure.

His ace was that they didn't know he was on to them. For all he knew, the girl was from ABIN. Had Laura been indiscreet? It was unlikely, but he knew her well enough to know that she wasn't above taking risks to get credits. Brazil was a major player these days: any friends in ABIN would be useful.

He parked two blocks from his target and went the rest of the way on foot. His senses alert, his old instinct nagging him, he still couldn't nail a shadow, neither in empty nor crowded streets. Whoever they were, they were good. His adrenaline pumped, and for what must be the tenth time he verified that the Glock was within a second's grip of his hand.

He turned into the street. He had no house number, and there was no reason to suppose that, after two months, the trail wouldn't have gone stone cold. On the other hand, the Dutchman's death had raised no smoke until now, and his killers wouldn't be the first to fall prey to overconfidence. In Marlow's experience, the slickest operators were the first victims of that.

The question was: whose side were his shadows on?

He walked down the street at an easy pace, sizing up

each edifice as he passed it, glancing at its windows. The slightest sign – a radio antenna, a CCTV camera – might be enough. The more secluded the building, the more interested he was. If de Vries had been killed in one of them, they'd have had to get the body out without being seen. He only had the street name from de Vries. No specific house name or number. He kept going.

There was another element here, and Marlow knew he was playing with fire by inviting it. Laura would never have condoned it. His shadows didn't know he was ignorant of the precise house. If they thought he was getting too close . . .

It was early afternoon and he could hear the distant hum of traffic, but here in the street it was quiet. Not a person on the sidewalk, not a car driving by. There weren't any parked cars. A few trees big enough to provide cover. Low walls.

The nagging voice at the back of Marlow's mind suddenly started to scream. He knew better than to ignore it, realizing at the same time that he was himself too exposed. A movement at the windows of one of the nearby houses caught his attention. He'd only glanced at them before; hadn't paid them enough attention. He was closer than he'd guessed. What the hell had he been telling himself about overconfidence? When the hell are you ever going to learn your own lessons, Marlow? And what the hell will you do when your guardian angel finally gives up on you?

In a split second he had stopped and turned. He had

already begun his sprint back to the busy cafés and shops of Rua Souza Lima when he sensed rather than heard the soft *whump* of the air rifle behind him. Then the bee sting of the dart piercing his neck.

10

London, Late 1596

'You should be glad. Cadiz was a great success.'

For Howard and Essex, maybe, Raleigh thought darkly, sitting in Cecil's by now familiar office. His own part in the action had passed unnoticed. Glory to the victors, sure, and the Spanish had burnt their own fleet rather than see it fall into English hands, but the triumph had gained him no personal ground at Court.

Cecil had remained cordial all year, trailing promises but always stalling, and someone from the spymaster's office, Raleigh was certain, had kept him in sight since their first meeting six months earlier. Even during the expedition to Spain there'd been somebody among the mariners.

One thing was clear, and it kept Raleigh hopeful: Cecil was keeping his options open.

There was much to consider. The Queen was getting old; she'd just passed her sixty-third birthday. There'd been poor harvests for several years, and the dragged-out conflicts with Spain continued to milk the Exchequer. There'd been plague in London. The Catholics were being leant on heavily, and the secret police were making their presence increasingly felt. Morale was low, and Elizabeth's relentlessly upbeat propaganda programme was wearing thin. Worst of all, with her longest-serving and most reliable advisors either aging or dead, she was beginning to believe her own myth.

Raleigh knew two things, and he kept them to himself: Cecil was in touch with King James VI of Scotland, a distant cousin of the Queen and the son of her old Catholic rival, Mary Queen of Scots.

And James knew all about the value of money and the cost of wars. The old Queen's violently anti-Catholic ways were waning.

Changes were in the air.

Raleigh needed to survive in these dangerous waters, more dangerous than any sea he had ever sailed, and to do so he needed to up his credibility.

'Cadiz was indeed a success, Sir Robert, and my hope is that now the threat of a new Armada has, by the grace of God, been removed, I may look forward to a favourable answer regarding my expedition.'

Cecil, elbows on his desk among the scattered papers, made a tent of his fingers. Never a good sign with him, the attitude usually presaged a negative response. But Raleigh also knew that, however distracted Cecil had been by recent events, his interest in the gold remained piqued. Raleigh was aware, too, that the two attempted burglaries at his London home during his absence in Spain had been clumsy ruses, their focus something else entirely, though a few trinkets had been taken as cover. They – and the spies set to watch him – could only be Cecil's work. Cecil wanted the map. He was speaking of it now.

'I know you have an honest tongue and an open heart, Walter,' he began; but Raleigh knew that Cecil's true opinion of him was that he was a blabbermouth. 'I have not forgotten the map you spoke of, and my hope is that you have told no one else of it.'

'It is our secret, apart from the man who was privy to its making.'

'Excellent. We may, I think, soon be in a position to do something about implementing its use, but you must be patient and discreet. Lord Essex's successful expedition has raised morale and confidence both, but it was costly.'

Raleigh inclined his head, but he could not hear Essex's name praised without feeling bitterness. He knew he still had enough pull for Cecil not to make any open move against him – yet – but he had been patient long enough. If he didn't do something now, it might still take years for him to get the permission and the money he needed; and then the credit would be taken from him. He looked across at Cecil, but it was impossible to gauge what the man was thinking. He wished he had the same knack of impenetrability.

'The name of your map-maker?' Cecil asked casually.

'He is not in London.'

Cecil didn't insist. 'As you wish. I admire your discretion.'

'It is not that I do not trust you.'

'You would be a fool to trust anyone, Walter. But,

equally, you should know who your friends are.' He leant on the desk. 'Come and see me again soon. It is always a pleasure.'

Raleigh knew the time had come to act for himself. And, thank God, he knew who his friends were.

11

Christopher 'Kit' Marlowe, poet, playwright and spy, sat confidently in the Mermaid Tavern, a mug of Malaga sack and a plate of bread and Cheddar before him. He was growing confident in the new identity he'd taken on three years earlier; he still couldn't credit its success, though with time even he was beginning to believe in it. It had been a masterstroke of his boss, Sir Robert Cecil; a decision taken at a time when Kit had risked exposure and death at the hands of agents working for Sir Edward Stafford, the former ambassador to Paris and double agent for Spain. Or so it was thought. Some in Cecil's ring suspected it was the Chevaliers who wanted Kit dead.

But despite his collusion with the Spanish, Stafford had since been brought back into the fold, no further attempts had been made, and few knew the secret of Kit's true identity.

By a most fortunate whim of providence, when the crisis hit in May 1593, another young playwright, only a couple of months Kit's junior and as alike him in looks as to pass for a brother, had been making his name in London. Up from the country and pretty gullible despite his undoubted talent, it had been an easy matter to send him in Kit's place to the meeting in Deptford that had resulted in his death – a knife wound to the right eye – the death meant for Kit himself. Since then, Kit had gone on working for Cecil, taking the identity of his murdered colleague, William Shakespeare, and continuing to write pretty good plays for Shakespeare's company, the Lord Chamberlain's Men. Shakespeare had no family in London, his wife was content to stay up in Stratford where he came from, there was nothing to tie him to Kit, who, as far as the Spanish were concerned, was dead.

But the organization that had targeted him was not one to be appeased by a simple death in London. And Kit had a mission that went beyond his brief with Cecil and the English secret service. He was fortunate that the organization's suspicions had, for the moment, been allayed.

Kit didn't have long to wait before the messenger came. He abandoned his meal and followed the boy out into the potholed roads of the down-at-heel city, through a network of streets where the light, restricted by the overhanging houses that virtually met overhead, was perpetually dim, to emerge at last on the broad thoroughfare of Fenchurch, then north, to the house at which he was expected.

Sir Walter Raleigh was waiting for him in a room at the back. It was already dusk and two candles burnt in brass holders on the shining oak table that stood against one panelled wall. The curtains were already drawn and the atmosphere was close.

The two men greeted each other warmly, for they had secrets in common which drew them together. Now, finally, the time was ripe to discuss them.

'It is the greatest cache of gold the world has ever seen,' Raleigh began, spreading the map out on the table and tapping it with his right forefinger. 'And ready for the taking.'

'You have seen it?'

'No – but I have seen where it is, and the hinterland itself yields gold in quantity.'

'You will never get the money from Cecil. He isn't satisfied with your proof, and you know what he is planning.'

Raleigh nodded. 'I have some idea. But the Queen may live for years yet.'

'That may be true, but she has no heir and will name none. She closes her mind to the future. She listens only to what she wants to hear.'

'And that makes us vulnerable.'

Kit nodded, his face set. 'We are at least forearmed,' he said. 'Cecil trusts me.'

'Which is why I asked you to come. We need this gold. You are Cecil's chief agent for our watch on the Spanish colonies. Use your influence with him.'

'We must proceed carefully. Spain is not our only opponent in this game.'

Raleigh looked grim. That was a truth he'd been reluctant to face, but if Kit could now tell him so to his face . . .

'You mean the Chevaliers?'

'Yes.'

'Do they still have a presence here?'

'They have a presence everywhere. You know that, Walter.'

'They do not know what we know.'

'The Chevaliers were responsible for my "death", I am certain of that.' Kit smiled thinly. 'Richard Topcliffe planned it. He is their new Knight Commander.'

'But they have retreated, they have returned to the Château d'Uriel.'

'They watch, and wait. We can only pray they are not aware of your discovery. You were unwise to publish that account of your expedition.'

'It gives nothing away – nothing essential. And the idea that there is unlimited gold to be found in Amazonia is not a new one.'

'Only now, it appears, it is closer to being a reality.'

'My tracks are well covered. I am not as indiscreet as you – and Sir Robert Cecil – seem to think.'

'I am glad of it,' Kit said, smiling more warmly now. He turned back to the map. 'And no one has seen this except you – and now, me?'

'Except for its maker, Francis Sparrow. Not even my captains had full sight of it.'

'And this Sparrow can be trusted?'

'Sparrow is dead.'

Kit looked at him sharply but made no comment. 'We must guard it well,' he said. 'You will entrust it to me?'

'I have a feeling it will be safer with you than it is with me. I am being watched.'

'Watched?'

'I thought you would know.'

'No – it is not us. If it was anyone in Cecil's department, I *would* know.' Kit was thoughtful.

'Were *you* followed here?' Raleigh said.

'I have men to cover my back. My coming and going will not be noted.'

'Then I will draw the fire.' Raleigh paused. 'The Spanish remain watchful.'

'Perhaps, but their teeth are drawn. Even with their wealth, they must lick the wounds we've given them.'

'King Philip is an old man now, but his wrath is implacable. However, he will concentrate on war, not subterfuge, to subdue us.'

'You are old-fashioned, Walter. And so is the King of Spain. His era, and Elizabeth's, is drawing to a close. The game is played differently now.'

'Keep the map for me. But let no one else in our Brotherhood have knowledge of it yet.'

'That may be necessary. If what I plan is to succeed.'

'Will you tell me of it?'

'Not now. Not until it is clear in my own mind. Until then, this will be as safe with me, as will its secrets, as it has been with you – safer, I think.'

'And if I die?'

'Your purpose will not die with you, Walter. I give you my word.'

Raleigh folded the map carefully and replaced it in its leather pouch. He was aware of a slight reluctance, a slight tug at his heart as he handed it over, but he and the younger man had a bond closer than blood, joined as they were in the Brotherhood.

He waited for half an hour after Kit had left, drinking a small tumbler of ale and eating a cinnamon cake while his thoughts roved without real focus over the plans that obsessed him and that at some level occupied every moment of his waking day and part of his dreams. He thought, too, of Bess, down at Sherborne with their three-year-old son. He would pay his Queen back in true gold for forgiving him his marriage to her lady-in-waiting. He would show his gratitude in such a way as never to fall from favour again.

But it was also true that Elizabeth's time was running out. He would have to look to the future too, and it was well that James of Scotland was notoriously fond of money.

He left the house by a side door opening into an alley, nodding to his attendants as he walked towards the main street; they would follow him without seeming to. He automatically checked his sword and dagger to ensure no clothing would snag them if he needed them fast.

The streets were emptying as night fell, and he noticed a watchman's lantern already lit up ahead. He was making for it when his path was blocked by three cloaked figures who'd appeared from nowhere.

He turned, to face two more who had come up behind him.

There was no sign of his own men.

12

Rio de Janeiro, the Present

The prison he awoke in was stifling and dark. He lay prone and could hear the rustle of insects by his head. Waiting for his eyes to grow accustomed to the gloom and fighting down a feeling of nausea, he automatically went over what had happened. He'd covered his tracks. He'd left nothing in the hotel room that could betray his identity. The equipment they'd have found on him would tell them the nature of his work, of course, but they'd know that anyway.

Would they use torture to find out the rest? If these were the same people who'd killed de Vries – and the probability was high – he could expect a bad time.

They'd left him his shirt and trousers, but no shoes or belt. He ran his tongue around his mouth to find that the cyanide microcapsule had also gone. Well, he didn't need that to tell him he was dealing with pros. There was no way he could communicate with base. He had to get out of here and access a phone. Even though his mission was unofficial, Laura would at least be able to claim she'd authorized it under the remit of Section 15. That might be enough. He'd have to hope it was.

They hadn't tied him. He got to his feet, scattering cockroaches, and felt his way around his cell. It was about three metres square and its low ceiling barely allowed him to stand upright. What light there was came from the edges of the door frame: the yellow light of bulbs, not daylight. He guessed the cell was underground, maybe in the cellar of the very house he'd been casing. There was nothing in it – not a stick of furniture, nor any implement he could use on the door frame. It was dirty and smelt musty.

He had no idea how long he'd been unconscious, or whether during that time he'd been taken any distance. It couldn't have been that long, for he felt neither hunger, nor, more importantly, thirst. He needed to urinate, and did so in a corner. A dull headache circled his skull, the result of the drug they'd used on him, and his legs were weak. But his mouth wasn't dry, and he sensed no other after-effects.

He needed to find a way of telling what time of day it was. He concentrated and listened. There was nothing at first but, gradually, he could make out, very faintly, the sounds of people moving – walking along maybe narrow streets where sound would be amplified – a Babel of conversation, in Portuguese as far as he could judge, and a distant growling he identified as the noise of motorbike engines.

So – it was daytime, probably the same day he'd been taken. And he was probably still in Rio. INTERSEC couldn't track him, though. He'd stubbornly refused a GPS implant. He didn't want people knowing where he was all the time, didn't think it was secure. And adversaries knew about these things. They'd search for one under the skin with knives.

He had no watch, but he reckoned they'd let him wait before they came for him. There was no way of marking the time. The dim light that emanated from the rim of the door never varied, nor did the temperature of the room. He'd expected the waiting: there was no better way to make a captive nervous. Jack had seen cases where they were simply so grateful to see another human being – any human being – that there was no need even to show them the thumbscrews before getting the information out of them. Women were tougher than men, though they'd crack too. But these were usually people who hadn't had full resistance training. He wondered just how much his jailers knew about him, and thought again about the girl in the cream dress.

The hardest thing was staying alert. After a while, your senses dulled. You began to doubt the reality of your situation. And you began to feel thirsty and, despite yourself, hungry; and unless you were very lucky you wanted to do more than urinate. The inability to satisfy these simple needs was step one of any torture technique. As time passed, Marlow braced himself mentally for the next step. The worst thing for him was the claustrophobia – the cramped space and the near-dark, the sense of being buried alive.

He calculated two hours had passed, though he was beginning to lose track – two hours in a place like that could seem like two days – before they came for him. The first sign was an alarm bell. There was none in the room and he had no idea through what sound system they fed it, but it shattered the silence with ear-splitting insistence and went on, a nagging, jangling sound that shook every pore, every muscle, for what seemed like half an hour. Then it ceased abruptly, though it was a full minute before it stopped ringing in his head, which now ached furiously, impeding his ability to think. He needed to stretch his trembling limbs, his legs especially, needed to be able to stand up properly; but the low ceiling prevented that. He forced himself to breathe evenly, but he barely had time to pull himself together and subdue panic before he heard the fast clatter of heavy boots on concrete. The door was flung open. He was too close to it and it smashed into his shoulder. Two men in black overalls, their faces hidden beneath ski masks, seized him and manhandled him out of the room into a wide corridor, not very long, bringing him quickly to another door, which a third guard, waiting by it, had already opened.

Marlow could have predicted the technique, but its effect was no less terrifying for that. The room was all white and lit with appalling brightness. It was not a clean room. Low on the walls there were dark stains and smears. Its only furniture was a heavy, wooden three-legged stool. The men in ski masks held Jack's arms while the third, similarly dressed, stripped him before seizing the stool and hitting him with it ferociously across the shoulders, thighs and stomach, bringing him to the ground. Marlow's arms were already up round his face to protect his teeth, though he recognized that the blows were calculated, for they went nowhere near his head. The guard righted the stool and the men tied him to it with thin nylon cord, attaching his wrists to the rear leg, his ankles to the front two. There was a refinement to the stool. At the centre of its seat was a round peg, ten centimetres long and two in diameter. It was greased. The men inserted the peg brutally into his anus. No movement now was possible without terrible pain.

One of the guards stamped hard on Marlow's feet, and then they left him alone, gagging, bruised, in agony, but with nothing broken; even the trampling of his feet had been calculated to cause the most pain possible without serious damage. The steel door slammed shut and the footsteps faded. The lights went out, plunging him into total darkness.

The room was warm and humid. There was silence for a while before he became aware of the whining. There were mosquitoes in there – whether by accident or design, Marlow didn't know. But these guys were good. He braced himself, kicking in the mental exercises they'd taught him when he'd started this dreadful job almost two decades earlier, exercises and refinements on refresher courses at training facilities in the Sobraon Barracks in Lincolnshire, England, and the Bulgarian-American Air Forces Logistics Center at Aitos. He started to work on his bonds, but his feet were too painful to manipulate and with every cautious motion of his wrists the nylon rope bit deeper.

The whining ceased, only to start again with maddening suddenness in his left ear. His hands twitched instinctively and, as they did, the wooden peg wrenched within him. His involuntary reaction caused the unstable stool to overbalance and he crashed heavily to the floor.

The mosquito, interrupted for a moment, resumed its investigation of his ear. Already he could feel the itch of bites on his ankles and fingers.

A mental exercise came to his rescue. Lines from a poem D. H. Lawrence had written about a mosquito. Find a shared experience. Keep the mind apart from what is happening to the body. Literally, watch yourself. Watch over yourself.

Marlow recited the lines to himself, went on with what he could remember of the poem:

> It is your trump
> It is your hateful little trump
> You pointed fiend,
> Which shakes my sudden blood to hatred of you:
> It is your small, high, hateful bugle in my ear.

This would come to an end. Everything comes to an end. They were softening him up. It was par for the course.

But the itching from the bites was unbearable, the

type of pain that renewed itself every second. And it was so simple, so primitive.

He tried to right himself, but it was impossible to move, to roll over, without intense and searing pain from the wooden peg that penetrated him.

He'd lost all sense of time when they came for him. By then his agony was so intense he could think of nothing else, except a burning desire for revenge. These people would pay for what they'd done to him, and they would pay long and hard.

Light flooded the room, and the door crashed open. Marlow's back was to the entrance, but his thumbs had started pricking the moment he'd heard the footsteps. Hard to tell how many, but different people this time, he was sure of that. Into his line of vision came a casually dressed man in his fifties who cocked his head to look at him. There was nothing in his gaze but mild curiosity. He looked like a middle-aged management consultant, fighting age with fitness programmes; but Marlow's gut went cold at the sight of him.

The man nodded to someone beyond Marlow's line of vision and invisible hands righted the stool. Marlow felt a wave of nausea, and his head swam. He knew he'd been stripped as a deliberate humiliation, but that knowledge was of little help as the man was joined by two women, who took their places either side of him. One was a tall redhead in her late thirties, cool and elegant, as out of place here as the man appeared to be. She looked as if she belonged behind a desk at Omnicom; her suit was probably from Adeline André.

The other was the slim, brown-haired girl, now dressed in jeans and a black shirt. Whereas the man and the older woman looked at Marlow impassively, he noticed that the girl avoided his eyes. A second man, the one who had righted the stool, presumably, now joined them. He was thicker set than the first, dressed in a dark business suit that fitted him as well as it would any all-in wrestler, and carried a bullwhip.

'My name is Louvier,' said the management consultant. 'Who are you?'

Marlow grinned at him. 'Isn't that what your gorilla is here to find out?'

The other man released the whip and cracked it centimetres from Marlow's right ear. The noise sang there as the man curled it again.

'Who are you?' repeated Louvier.

'A passer-by.'

'Interesting equipment you carry, for a passer-by,' said the redhead tonelessly.

'All right – I'm a private detective.'

'Since when did any private eye carry a suicide capsule?' asked the older woman.

'Where are you from?' said Louvier.

Marlow was about to pass out with pain but he knew they wouldn't kill him until they'd got their answers. He summoned the last of his forces. 'London,' he chanced.

'You're a long way from home.'

'So are you, I think.'

The bullwhip cracked again, this time stinging his shoulder; but Marlow was certain the man wouldn't use it in earnest. They wouldn't damage him before they got what they wanted.

But they were too confident. He would make use of that.

'Who are you working for?'

'That's confidential.'

Louvier pulled a pair of rubber gloves from his pocket and came close, seizing Marlow's shoulders and shaking him. The pain was excruciating.

Louvier put his mouth close to Marlow's ear. 'We don't have a lot of time, and we don't believe you're that important. You can't stop us. We just want to be sure.' He pulled away to look Marlow in the eye. 'All you have to do is tell us why you are here. Or we leave this room and lock the door. No one will come back, not in a year.'

'We have destroyed the equipment you were carrying with you,' the redhead said. 'There is no escape.'

Louvier looked at his watch. Marlow guessed this was another ploy. 'We are going to give you an hour to think things over,' Louvier said. 'Then we'll make our final arrangements. But there is no need for further discomfort.' He nodded to the man with the whip, who left the room, to return moments later with the guards. They brought a bucket and a tray with bread, water and a towel. These they placed on the concrete floor before releasing Marlow from his bonds and the murderous stool.

Then they went, leaving the stool, the bucket and the tray with him.

This time, the lights stayed on, and Marlow's first thought was that there was some way in which they could watch him; but a careful examination of the room told him there was no possibility of a hidden camera here. The floor was concrete, but the walls were stone. An old building.

It was silent in this room. None of the sounds he'd heard in his first prison penetrated here.

He examined the stool, the plastic bucket and the metal tray. The bread lay on a paper plate and the water was in a thin plastic tumbler. He looked at the door frame. Though the door itself was steel, the frame was wood and had been set into the stone surround recently. The cement which held it had been roughly applied. He ran his fingers over it. There was a chance, but he hadn't much time. He drank the water after one cautious sip. The tray was made of cheap metal, nowhere near tough enough for the job he had in hand. But the stool was a possibility. The legs were attached to the seat with nails. Mustering his strength and ignoring the pain that shot through him as he exerted his muscles, he worked one leg loose and exposed three long nails, which he worked clear of the wood of the seat. He used the concrete floor to force the nails into the leg he'd wrenched off, and was left with a primitive pick. Grasping it, he set to work on the cement.

It was hard work, but he didn't think beyond it. The main thing was that it raised no alarm. These people were too confident, he thought again. But his labour was paying off. After only fifteen minutes, he had chipped through most of the cement down the side supporting the hinges. The door opened inwards. If he could get at the hinges . . .

But then he heard footsteps. Light ones, one person, walking fast.

His heart almost stopped. He stood back from the door and to one side, holding the stool leg now as a weapon. The footsteps hesitated as they reached the door, and there was a long moment after they'd stopped outside it. Marlow held his breath, tense but cool, knowing this sensation well and feeling the odd kind of relief that always came when action replaced helplessness. He would get out of this. His pain and his humiliation were forgotten. Every nerve in his body was concentrated on survival and retribution.

He heard the key placed in the lock and turned decisively, quickly. He stood back, the makeshift pick raised. As soon as the arm came into view he started to bring the stool leg smashing down on it, and only his lightning reactions enabled him to swing it away from its target at the last minute, as he saw that it was the brown-haired girl who was entering the room. She was fast too, diving away and back from him, alarm in her eyes.

Over one arm she carried a bundle of clothes; in her hand was a small handgun, a little Kel-Tec by the look of it.

'Jesus!' she said. Her accent was curious – part American, part something else. French? Recovering swiftly, she thrust the clothes at him. 'Put these on. No shoes. Deal with that later.'

'What –?' he said, but the picture had already formed in his mind and he slipped on the T-shirt and jeans fast. They hung a little loose on his lean frame, but the jeans fitted well at the waist and were not too long. He could move easily with speed. Perfect.

'No time,' she snapped back. 'Come on.'

She led him out of the room, not forgetting to lock the door behind them, and along the corridor to a narrow flight of stone steps that led into a small, bare courtyard surrounded on three sides by a concrete wall about three metres high. The back of the yard abutted the house. A windowless wall rose behind them. There was a heavy iron gate in one of the walls, chained and padlocked shut. Beyond it, Marlow could see scruffy trees and a road. The girl nodded at the wall.

'Can you make it over that?' She glanced behind her. From back the way they'd come, they heard the sound of boots clattering on the floor of the corridor outside his cell and its door rattle and bang as it was flung open.

Following her, Marlow leapt to grasp the top of the wall and haul himself over it. They dropped down on the other side, and the girl immediately headed off left towards an alley fifty metres distant. Marlow ignored the pain as he sprinted after her. Parked in the alley was an old motorbike straight out of *The Wild One*. She tossed him the gun and fired the bike up as he straddled it behind her. The engine roared then settled to an angry hum as she hammered out of the alley and took a left down a steep hill. They'd cut it fine: the first shots jetted past them impotently from the house as they sped away from it, and Marlow heard other engines snarl into life behind them.

They were heading towards one of the favelas. Rocinha had been cleaned up, pretty much, and they'd built a cable car over the Complexo do Alemão recently, after the long-drawn-out battles between the police and the army on the one hand and the drug lords who ruled and terrorized the complex on the other. Now the cable car made the place more accessible, more open, and the drug lords, it was hoped, would have nowhere to hide. With the World Cup and the Olympics looming, the city was anxious to put its house in order. To that end, José Mariano Beltrame's Unidade de Polícia Pacificadora was being heavily implemented. But there were still 'dirty' favelas, and they were skirting one now.

They had to get off this road, he thought. It was too wide, too open, too empty. But the girl knew that too. Jack glanced behind to see a black SUV and two bikes swing into pursuit as she gunned the motor and shrieked sharp left again, just avoiding a lumbering delivery truck, into a narrower street hemmed in by walls and buildings, rising steeply into what rapidly became a dense network of humble dwellings, bars, shops and cafés. The streets were busy with people here too, who leapt aside cursing as the girl skilfully weaved her way up the hill and deeper into the favela. Marlow knew then that he had been moved from the place where they'd ambushed him to distance him from any back-up he may have had. The girl's role in all this he could only guess at.

He looked back again. The SUV had swung off – the streets here were too narrow for it and he knew it would use the wider, faster roads which skirted the district to cut them off at the top of the hill – but the bikes were on their tail. Their drivers were less careful or less skilful than the girl and, more than once, he heard, or saw, a market stall collapse amid a welter of imprecations and howls of fear and distress as the heavy machines glanced off it. Each bike carried two men clad in heavy, black leather outfits, the pillion rider clamping himself to the machine with his thighs and knees and shooting at their target with lightweight Mini-Uzis, aiming, Marlow guessed, for their machine's thick tyres. They wanted them alive. The bullets scattered and danced around them as people scrambled for cover.

Higher up, the incline increased and the road wound back on itself at the level of the flat corrugated-iron or concrete roofs of the houses just below. These roofs, grading back down the hill, at last formed a kind of rough stairway and, as they reached the top, their pursuers within metres of them, the girl thrust out her left leg and swung the bike round and down a flight of shallow stone steps just wide enough to take it. Marlow pulled his own legs in tight, but still the walls either side of the steps tore at his jeans. The bike lost its grip once and skidded dangerously, and for a moment Marlow thought they'd fall; he shifted his weight slightly to compensate and they were away again, though he'd grazed his right leg on the rough stone. Another few millimetres and his knee would have been ripped off. It had been close.

The two other bikes were still just behind them, though the girl's manoeuvre had caused them to fall back a little. Now they were catching up fast. Bracing himself, Marlow twisted round and fired straight into the front tyre of the nearest one, just as a bullet from its gunner whacked through his rear mudguard and ricocheted off the chrome engine mounting. At the same moment, the steps debouched into a small, open square with a little church on one side, another low flight of steps leading to its entrance. The pursuing bike, its front tyre shredded, skeetered out of control, falling on to its left side and skidding violently across the square, smashing the legs of the driver and rider pinioned under its weight and crashing against the low steps of the church, its momentum carrying it right up to their top, where it shuddered to a halt and burst into flames. The chaos brought the second pursuer to a confused halt.

Using the moment, the girl angled their bike out of the square through a gap between buildings so narrow Marlow couldn't believe they would make it. With millimetres to spare, they were through and out in the open, no longer with ground beneath them but sailing through the air towards the crumbling roof of an abandoned building that loomed beneath them. Marlow braced himself, and felt the girl tense too: they were too high, falling too fast: the roof would never support their weight.

Where they hit, the tyres span madly on the collapsing concrete beneath them, but they gripped just before the roof gave way and threw the bike forward, into space again, leaving a pile of wreckage behind them. Marlow turned again to see the second pursuit bike plunge into the void, the driver and pillion rider thrown clear. The first fell out of sight into the cloud of concrete dust that had once been the roof, the second, his scream of fear abruptly cut off, was impaled through the chest on a jagged iron girder, one of several which had supported the building. The metal stake went right through him and such was the force of his fall that his body rammed down it a full metre before catching on a protruding bolt and hanging like a broken doll.

All this Marlow took in as if in a dream. Reality slowed as his own bike sailed through the air, on a slighter, downward curve this time, to land on a solid roof, the girl weaving the machine to avoid washing lines and TV aerials which, at the speed they were going, would be fatal in a collision. They passed down the hill by a succession of three more rooftops, leaping the low walls which girded them before hitting a road again and curling around a series of hairpin bends back to the weird normality of traffic, glass-fronted shops, high-rises and all the usual trappings of a busy, sophisticated city. They remained on the alert for the SUV, but there was no sign of it. The girl navigated the streets until they came to a quieter district near the eastern seaboard. She parked the bike behind a high hedge in a private driveway, switched it off and dismounted.

Marlow followed her, walking fast for two blocks. Then she turned into an anonymous apartment block, where they took the elevator to the top floor. There was only one door off the landing here. She produced a key and let them into a small apartment with open views across the city to the ocean. The apartment was light and modern and in one corner was a large white desk with a laptop, phone and several books, neatly stacked. The living room, simply furnished with a low sofa and armchair positioned around a coffee table, gave on to a small balcony, visible beyond the broad living-room windows. Doors off it revealed a kitchen-diner and a bedroom, with a black-tiled bathroom beyond. The place was impeccably tidy, and there were no personal touches of occupation visible anywhere.

The girl motioned him to a seat, but he remained where he was, watchful. He was tired beyond belief, but there were things he needed to know. The first was:

'Who are you?'

She grinned. 'Someone who thought you were worth blowing her cover for.'

'You got a name?'

'Have you?'

It was his turn to smile, some of the tension draining out of him. 'I'd have got out of there without you,' he said.

She shrugged. 'If you say so.' She paused. 'My name is Natasha. Natasha Fielding. I work for the Treasury Department, and we would have been grateful to hear officially that someone else was muscling in.'

'Jack Marlow,' he replied. 'Thank you for your help.'

'You're welcome.'

'You going to tell me about it?' He was polite. He didn't know how much she knew about him, but she was one step ahead of him as far as his adversaries were concerned and he wanted to see how far she would take him into her confidence. After what they'd just been through, he was impressed that she was unflustered – it was incredible that she could be so cool after such an experience, and during it she had carried herself with a professionalism more than equal to any crack INTERSEC field operative. It intrigued him. It also intrigued him that the Treasury Department should have agents of such calibre on its staff. He wondered how much she already knew about him that she wasn't letting slip.

'I think you could do with a shower and a drink, maybe something to eat first,' she said after looking at him quizzically for a moment. 'And you can relax. We're safe now.'

'For the moment.'

'For the moment.'

He looked at her. 'And couldn't you do with the things you've just mentioned yourself?'

She grinned again, accepting the release of tension. 'First things first.' She walked into the bedroom and emerged carrying his bag from the hotel. 'Here. Some clothes that'll fit you. And the rest of your gear, hidden in there somewhere, I imagine. The stuff that survived, anyway.' She smiled again at his look of frank admiration. 'I've been working with the opposition long enough for them to trust me. I hated watching what they did to you. And it was time to break away. I've got all I'll get from them, and I need some outside help.' She interrupted the questions he started to ask by saying, 'I know I owe you an explanation. As you do me. But let's get you tidied up first.'

'How long did they hold me?'

'Forty-eight hours.'

He'd run out of time. Unless he decided to disobey orders. He would find a way to get in touch with Laura. He owed her that.

He sat next to her on the sofa and, swiftly but cautiously, they established each other's credentials, each knowing that the other was telling no more than was strictly necessary. But Natasha knew the key code words and checked out in every other way. And she had already proved her status in the game in the most obvious way possible. There would have been nothing to gain for Jack's adversaries in staging a mock-rescue.

'Where are you from?' he asked her.

'I'm a mongrel,' she replied. 'My father is American, my mother French; I was brought up in Paris and Marseilles, and my French is still better than my English. Though I have to say I think my English is pretty good!' She laughed, shaking off a little of her tension.

Marlow looked at her. She was still dressed in her jeans and black shirt. She was probably in her late twenties, early thirties, maybe. Olive-skinned, with a lithe body; a long, oval face, a strong, almost aquiline nose, the chin determined, the lips full but firm. Startlingly bright, baby-blue, intelligent eyes. As they talked, he noticed that she talked without reference to any notes, and her computer lay neglected on the desk. She spoke quickly and lucidly, though Jack noticed she glided over certain details – details he knew she wouldn't yet trust him with. Posing as an Exchange-Traded-Fund manager who'd worked for Benchmark Assets in the early days a decade before, she'd been recruited by the group six months earlier as a market assessor. They'd presented themselves as an international private holding with interests in Russia and India, and everything had seemed above board until a flurry of excitement two months ago, when she had been politely excluded from a series of meetings.

'I don't know much about those, but they were expecting someone to fly in from Amsterdam. He came and went, and it must have been successful. They started trading in gold very seriously after that, but I was kept on the outside. There's a main man here, a Dr Louvier – Ambroise Louvier – and he has two assistants, a Slovenian gorilla, Kristof Struna, who looks more like a bodyguard than an exec, and a much smoother operator called Drita Agoli. But, of course, you've met them.'

'Agoli. Is she Albanian?'

'The name certainly is, but whether she's an Albanian national I don't know. My brief was to observe, not to investigate in depth. My principals didn't want me to take the slightest risk. Agoli is someone I wouldn't turn my back on. You saw her. She's as deadly as a stiletto.'

'And Louvier?'

'Who knows? French-Canadian, I think. It's an international outfit, woolly profile, uses a private bank as its shell.'

Marlow nodded. 'What are they up to?'

Natasha leant forward, sweeping her long brown hair back from her tanned face with an impatient, businesslike gesture, and proceeded to astonish him with an array of figures and details, with dates and amounts of trades, still without reference to any paperwork at all. She spoke almost without pause, allowing him to interrupt only with the occasional sharp question, for more than half an hour.

'You've kept all that in your head?'

She shrugged. 'I'm blessed – or cursed – with a good memory. You know the old Dorothy Parker adage: women and elephants never forget.'

'A photographic memory, by the sound of things.' Marlow couldn't help asking himself if she wasn't wasted at the Treasury. Not that they'd be likely to let such an agent go. No wonder they didn't want her to stick her neck out.

And yet she had, for him.

Why?

Nick Adams from the Treasury Department hadn't

mentioned her – not unusual in itself, but it would have been professionally helpful if he'd let them know he had someone on the case already. And her mention of a man from Amsterdam chimed with the dead Dutchman, de Vries.

'Do you know what happened to the guy from Amsterdam? Who he was? Why he came over?' He was testing the water.

'No.' Her manner was straightforward and direct. There wasn't a glimmer of a suggestion in her eyes that she was holding anything back. But she was a very astute operator. Maybe she was just choosing not to tell him everything. And yet it had been the Treasury that had come to INTERSEC for help. What was Adams holding back? What was Natasha Fielding holding back?

He decided not to let her know he'd been aware that she'd shadowed him from the airport. No one except Laura, Leon and a small handful of Section 15 operational staff knew he'd been on that plane. Then she surprised him, as if she'd read his thoughts, by volunteering:

'I wasn't sure you'd made me at the airport, and then again at the hotel. My people had given me, and a couple of others, a brief to keep a watch there. Stray people who might look like a threat to their security. There's a lot of economic espionage in this business. I played a hunch on you. When I found out you'd checked into the same room as the Dutchman, it was a cinch.'

'You told them about me?'

'I needed to see where it would lead. Don't forget: I've told you everything about me; I still know nothing about you.'

'I'm on your side. Just an INTERPOL cop playing a hunch. The Treasury Department isn't the only organization interested in what's happening to gold.'

She looked at him archly but didn't reply directly. 'When I saw what they were doing to you, I knew I couldn't play along any more. And I guessed what had happened to the Dutchman.'

So she'd decided to come clean on that, at least. How much more would she open up?

'Didn't you think it was odd that they set an exec like you to do an airport-surveillance job?'

She shrugged again, an attractive gesture, her slender body moving fluidly under the black shirt. 'They liked to keep things tight. And I won't tell you how much they're paying me – were paying me.' She looked humorously regretful. 'They still owe me a month's salary. That's $250,000 down the tubes.'

'Big players.'

'Big enough.'

'Long contract?'

'Twelve months initial.'

He was silent. They *had* trusted her. 'What name do they trade under?'

'Overseas and General.' She looked at him. 'No, we'd never heard of it either.' Then she trailed off, thoughtful. 'But I did hear them use another name, twice, and I noted it because each time it was Struna who used it and the others were angry. I pretended not to notice and I don't think they were even aware I'd heard.'

'What was it? Do you remember?'

She gave him the arch look again but hesitated before replying: 'The Chevaliers.'

She'd said it casually enough, so what was it that gave him the impression she was waiting to see what effect it had on him? They looked at each other for a long moment, and neither of them could quite disguise the real thoughts behind their eyes. In that moment was born the faint beginning of a trust that was more binding than any code word or credential, and neither of them could have said why. But still, Jack, aware of where impetuousness had led him in the past, held back for one more moment before deciding to throw the dice. If she knew already, no harm done, if she didn't – well, there was no doubt in his mind now that this woman was on his side. He told her the bare bones of what he knew, and as she listened it was as if she were receiving confirmation rather than information; and that confirmation, for all she tried to hide it, excited her.

'I thought they were long dead as an organization. I've looked at some old files on them recently, though – we thought we had a lead – and those files have never been closed. They call themselves Les Chevaliers d'Uriel. They go back a long way. A very long way.' He paused, choosing his words carefully. 'Had their roots in France and Spain, grew over the years into an international group, widened their interests.'

'What interests?'

'They began life as an offshoot of the Spanish Inquisition. A fanatical offshoot, which had its roots in an abbey in Galicia, I believe.' He gave a dismissive shrug. 'But all that died off when religion and politics parted company.'

He noticed she looked thoughtful at that, though her eyes burnt. 'Uriel?' she said.

'Uriel is the fourth archangel. We only ever hear of Gabriel, Michael and Raphael. There are four more. Uriel is the one who "watches over thunder and terror".' Jack looked thoughtful himself as he pronounced those words. 'The archangel who cast out Adam and Eve from the Garden of Eden.'

'Go on.'

'Their headquarters moved to a chateau owned by the de Sade family in the Loire Valley in France. But not on the river itself. Somewhere to the south of Chenonceaux. The chateau was destroyed towards the end of the Second World War, in 1945, by an American Special Commando.'

'Do we know why?'

Jack looked at her. '*I* don't,' he said cautiously. 'But it's too fantastic. The Chevaliers d'Uriel was an old organization, a bunch of religious headcases bent on bringing people closer to God through an enforced regime of poverty and austerity. All worldly goods, all comforts, all material advantages, were to be stripped from humankind – everything that complicates life through competition and greed.'

'Everything that makes humanity function,' commented Natasha drily.

'If you like. The Chevaliers planned a return to what they saw as the Garden of Eden. But they'd stop at nothing to achieve it. They had a reputation for ruthlessness that matched their austerity. But they are long gone – a bunch of lunatics with warped ideals.'

He fell silent then, grimacing as a vicious pain shot through his feet where his torturers had trampled them. He became aware again of how dirty he was, and how tired. To fight this battle he needed to draw strength from rest, to let go of the tension that had mounted in him since his capture, which seemed like months ago. She hadn't said anything, but she'd noticed his agony. She knelt to inspect his feet, kneading them gently with her strong, long-fingered hands.

'I should have thought . . .' she said, half to herself. 'They're not broken. Can you get up?'

He tried, levering himself out of the sofa, but he was surprised at his own weakness, and did his best not to let it show. He didn't want to look vulnerable, not to her, not yet. Ignoring his protests, she pulled him to his feet. He noticed the strength of her arms. She led him to the bedroom.

There, she left him alone, and he undressed, going through to the bathroom and into the big shower cubicle. The jets of water, which came from overhead and three sides, were hot and invigorating, further easing the aches in his bruised body. He washed thoroughly but fast, not caring to have her out of his sight too long. But he need not have worried.

He was standing under the shower head, letting a

hard stream of cooler water run over his head, clearing it, when the door of the cubicle opened and she was there, naked, close to him.

'Need a shower too,' she said brusquely, to his amazement shy, yet sure of what she wanted, coming into his arms and pressing her body against his. And he realized that this was what they both needed, this was a reaction to what they'd been through together, the most natural thing in the world. The part of him deep inside that would never drop its guard remained in place, but it allowed the rest of him to surrender to her caresses as she soaped herself and then him, and he ran his hands over the smooth body that rubbed itself against him as sensually as a cat, offering no angles, just smooth curves, delicious, a silk covering of firmly muscled flesh, her hands exploring now, as his were, lubricated by shower gel, creamy under the water as their lips met and their tongues, hesitantly at first, then urgently, greeted each other.

She caught her breath and drew away from him a fraction, keeping his hand in hers as he led her out of the cubicle, the need too urgent now to turn off the water or dry themselves, across the floor of the bathroom, to the bedroom, to the bed, where they threw themselves, embracing hungrily, savagely, her hand guiding him as she slid under him, wrapping her long legs around his torso and making all the pain go away as he entered her, soft and wet, feeling her muscles down there gently clamp him in welcoming embrace as he raised himself above her and thrust, softly at first, then harder, with a need he couldn't deny or control, gasping, her hands scrabbling at his body, as she cried out, arching herself up against him to feel the full force of his penetration, '*Comme tu me fais jouir*,' and her arms around his neck now, and her legs behind his back and her breath on his neck and her smile caught flashing against her brown skin out of the corner of his eye, and the dancing light in her eye as they melted together in a universe that contained only them, only this moment, only this beyond-thought, undefinable moment of paradise. Pleasure burnt through them and engulfed them as he, barely aware, supported his weight on his straining wrists so as not to crush her and yet seemed to hurt her, impaling her on himself as she clung to him, pushing against him as if her life depended on fusing with him, her breath faster now, her eyes open but looking nowhere, his on her, lips bruising each other's impatiently, greedily, wanting the moment to come and yet delaying the pleasure they anticipated so eagerly. But at last she couldn't wait any longer and nor could he though he wanted to, and she said to him in a rush, 'Don't stop, don't stop, come to me, come to me, *maintenant*, *je te veux*, *je te veux autant* . . .' and he didn't know if it mattered to her that it was him, or if it was just that he was the engine of her appetite, her hunger, her need, and he didn't care, for now there was only this moment and it would protect them from whatever would come crashing back into their lives when the moment was past, with its memory, its promise, its . . .

And then he was soaring, his pain forgotten, and she was soaring with him alone and together at the same time for those few seconds, minutes, hours when time fuses and ceases to exist and the world soars with you and the room and the bed and the world disappear and it is just you and her and the touch and heat and smell of your bodies together and not even those any more as the mind itself stops and gives way to the soaring.

And afterwards, the heady descent, the embraces, the soft touchings, the warmth. But after reality had reasserted itself, he turned the shower off and she brought towels for them to dry each other.

'Stay where you are,' she said, when they had finished.

He obeyed, while she laid one crisp white towel on the bed before disappearing into the bathroom to re-emerge with a jar of oil, with which she gently massaged him. He allowed her to look after him, grateful for the reprieve, glad to let the stress flow out of him.

Which led, as she brought her body down on to his to caress him with her breasts and thighs as well as her strong hands, to another, more languorous entwining. At last, deliciously sated, they slept.

When they awoke, it was twilight and the first stars shone like diamonds in the velvet sky. Under them the distant sea moved like molten jet. Slowly, unwillingly, they became two people again, two people with things to do. But not yet, they wouldn't let the moment go yet, and it stayed with them while, all but silently, brushing against each other, not wanting to lose contact, they prepared a simple meal, eating it hungrily, avidly, and with it drinking an ice-cold St-Véran, too cold really, but never mind, clean and refreshing, dining close together on the sofa, nestling, feet touching and caressing, eyes shy with each other yet shining.

But the moment doesn't last for ever, it can't, it has to die before it can be re-created, and they knew they were not in paradise. Somewhere not far away in the glittering night city the Chevaliers were looking for them, intent on cutting them off before they could break free. Natasha had said they were safe here for now, but already the airport would be watched, already the harbour would be covered, already they would have to be doubly alert on the streets.

They started to make plans, and she looked at Jack appraisingly, coming to a decision.

'I haven't told you everything,' she said at last. 'But I think I am going to tell you now. Their activity was triggered after the Dutchman's visit.'

'Yes,' he answered cautiously, wanting to encourage but not wanting to sound too eager. He'd leave personal questions until later. If they ever got that far. At the moment he was assessing how quickly his body would be able to function again at something approaching normal levels. But the relief he felt helped, and he knew the damage, for all the agony it had caused him, was superficial.

'I knew they'd been looking for something, and I'm certain he had it,' she continued.

'Do you know what it was?'

'I heard them discussing a map,' she said.

13

Paris, the Present

Ambroise Louvier wasn't looking forward to the interview. At first he'd hoped he could avoid the summons from Paris, having of course sent news of his progress on from Rio at regular intervals, but the summons, though still icily polite, had been repeated, this time, with an imperiousness that couldn't be defied. Leaving Agoli and Struna to take care of operations in Brazil, with urgent instructions to take Fielding and the still-unidentified man she'd fled with alive, he'd caught a red-eye from Galeão and was now waiting in the cold early morning on a corner of the rue de Rivoli a judicious distance away from the Hôtel Meurice, where he had checked in his bag earlier. He was quite certain his movements had not been observed, but one couldn't be too careful – especially now, especially with everything to play for.

Seeing him waiting at the kerb with his briefcase, a couple of cruising taxis slowed and their drivers looked at him interrogatively, but he ignored them. He was early anyway; nerves always made him get ahead of himself. The street was slick after a dawn rainfall, now past, and still quiet on this Sunday morning. He was lightly dressed for the weather here, and shivered in his grey silk suit. When it came, the car, a new Peugeot with its taxi light turned red, flashed its headlights at him briefly from fifty metres away. He stood ready.

After it had picked him up, the car drove swiftly west before turning north and backtracking east, weaving its way through the Marais until it came to a halt in front of an imposing though faintly dilapidated stone building on the east side of the boulevard Richard-Lenoir, where stallholders were already setting up their market stands. The driver, who hadn't spoken to Louvier at all during the short journey, turned now and nodded briefly as a man dressed in a business suit emerged from the doorway of the building and nodded in his turn. Louvier, clutching his briefcase, got out of the cab and hurried towards the open door, and the man ushered him inside, closing the door behind him. The hall was cool and lined with marble and a broad staircase, again of marble, led to the upper floors. There was no lift, but the interior belied the exterior by its luxury. The money that had been spent here did not want to show itself.

Louvier, nervous despite himself, followed the man in the suit up to the first floor. Still not a word had been exchanged. The man, sallow-faced and middle-aged with a stiff brush of white hair, reached a double set of highly polished walnut doors with gilded decorations that reached nearly to the ceiling and knocked. After the briefest pause he pushed one of the doors open and stood aside for Louvier to enter.

The room was decorated in a style that would not have disgraced the Palais de Matignon. Nor would the figure who rose to greet Louvier from behind an ebony-and-gold escritoire and came forward to meet him, though he did not take the hand which Louvier had extended and now apologetically withdrew. There was – there had always been – a hauteur about the man which Louvier despised. His pride and confidence hadn't brought him down yet, and probably wouldn't, as long as the money he'd conned out of the North Koreans lasted, but Louvier had patience. He was content with his well-paid niche as lieutenant, and he had all the experience and all the contacts necessary to take over the mantle of Knight Commander when his time came, as it would – he was certain – soon. He looked at his boss now with expressionless eyes, hating the fact that the man still had the power to cow him, after all these years of preparation and waiting.

James Topcliffe, short and stout, with a mane of reddish-chestnut dyed hair and a neatly trimmed beard of the same colour, looked briskly at his Number Two. His eyes were pale amber and calculating – always calculating – under their bushy black brows. Topcliffe had been born in England, and though he'd lived most of his life abroad – recently, in Thailand – he was proud of his national heritage and his ancestry. He held his one metre fifty body erect in what he imagined to be a British military stance; pugilistic and coarse-featured, he did everything he could to appear sophisticated, cultivated the arts, was a patron of the Opéra de Paris and appeared, though discreetly, whenever possible at the top level of Parisian society. His annual St George's Day party, instigated when he'd arrived in Paris only three years earlier and was first laying his current plans, was already legendary. But he was impatient. At forty-nine, he felt he had no time to waste in imposing his will on a wayward and feckless world. In the wake of the financial crash of 2008 he had seen a means to do so, resurrected the all but moribund Order of the Chevaliers d'Uriel, and made his preparations.

He could trace his line back to Richard Topcliffe, one of the main movers and shakers in the English spy rings run by Sir Francis Walsingham and his successor, Sir Robert Cecil. James Topcliffe liked to think he'd inherited, even though four hundred years separated him from his ancestor, much of Richard's sleight of hand, and he was secretly proud of another facet of his forebear's character: the Elizabethan Topcliffe had been the administration's chief interrogator and torturer. In those troubled times, Catholics especially had feared him, the more so since he had loved his work so much he arranged for the official registration of a torture chamber in his own London home. But such barbarity belonged in the past, James Topcliffe thought. He only resorted to such methods when it was strictly necessary. However, he knew his underlings feared him, and he revelled in the knowledge. *Odiunt dum metuant* was his motto. Let them hate, as long as they fear. He rejoiced in his power, in the business acumen that allowed him to wield it successfully, and in the gift of the Order of the Chevaliers. His ancestor had been an early member of its Protestant arm at a time when it was already distancing itself from religious affiliation, and its secrets had been passed down to him in documents held by his family over the centuries. Topcliffe, a traditionalist who from the age of three had been shaped by boarding schools and a privileged though rigid education, saw himself now, in middle age, as an ascetic with a vision that, once realized, would transform the world he lived in.

He, James Topcliffe, would be the Knight Commander to achieve it.

Topcliffe returned to his desk, riffling showily through the papers there and busily summoning up more information on his computer. He disliked the modern equipment and the untidy wires – they didn't chime well with the Empire furniture he favoured – but it couldn't be helped. Under his severely tailored suit – a suit that resembled a military uniform – burnt the heart of a fanatic. Sometimes – as now – he could barely contain his energy, which was fuelled by his compelling vision of the world he wanted to mould: a world whose reality was now within his grasp. The control drugs he took secretly were nowadays barely able to rein him in. He thanked God that something in his will commanded him to be patient still. But his whole body radiated energy; he was eternally restless.

'I've been through the figures,' he said, motioning Louvier to an uncomfortable chair isolated in the middle of the room. 'We need to move faster.'

Louvier looked at him. 'The markets are already ruffled. We need greater control before we strike.'

'But we have the map. You have the funding for the expedition. What is holding you back?'

'Preparations are already well in hand. But we have to proceed cautiously if we are to maintain secrecy.'

'As long as we have the map, nothing can stop us.' Topcliffe started to say more, but interrupted himself and turned a grey eye on his lieutenant. 'You *are* sure of the map?'

Louvier controlled his impatience. It was a question the Knight Commander had asked a dozen times. 'The map has been authenticated by seven experts. In my opinion, that is already too many people even to be aware of its existence, but the experts were well paid and they will not think of it again.'

'And they don't know what it shows?'

'No one knows what it shows. We were only suspicious of the Dutchman; and you know we silenced him.'

'Those were my orders anyway. And his boyfriend?' Topcliffe, though he despised women and had never married, slaking his sexual impulses with prostitutes whom he used as casually and thoughtlessly as he would use a lavatory for other natural functions, had no time for homosexuals either, and his tone carried a note of contempt.

'He has been silenced too.'

'Good.' He returned to the subject. 'And there are no copies.'

'We have searched the world. No one could have been more thorough. It *is* the map – the only copy, made by Thomas Hariot from the lost original Raleigh had drawn during the expedition. It is flawless. Otherwise, we would not have proceeded.'

'Of course not,' snapped Topcliffe, only slightly mollified. 'And the other meddlers?'

'They know nothing.'

'But you haven't caught them?'

'The net is closing,' Louvier lied. 'But they are of no importance.'

'The girl took you in for months! How can you be sure she knows nothing?'

'She advised on buying gold. She had no hint of the plan.'

'And the others? Struna and Agoli?'

'As long as they are paid they will ask no questions. Only the Chevaliers are privy to the great scheme.'

Topcliffe let his gaze rest on Louvier's briefcase. 'You have it with you?' Only now had he deemed it safe for the map to leave Rio. He'd been sent a copy under encryption, but he had hungered to see the original.

'It is here.'

'No problems?'

'None.'

'Give it to me.' Louvier rested the case on the escritoire, unfastened its clasps and opened it. He took out a heavy cardboard folder and from it drew a delicate sheet of parchment sandwiched between sheets of tissue paper. He placed the map carefully on the desk.

Topcliffe donned a heavy pair of glasses, bent over it and lovingly traced a line across it with a stubby forefinger. He tapped the point he was looking for decisively.

'Put the expedition in motion *now*,' he said. 'It is time to unleash our power.'

14

New York, the Present

'What do you mean, he's broken contact? What the hell is he doing there in the first place?' Sir Richard Hudson's voice was hard.

Laura flinched under his anger but held her ground. 'I kept you posted. This falls under Section 15's exclusive jurisdiction. We're following the one line we have.'

Hudson didn't reply immediately, and Laura could see he was accepting his own responsibility in this. When he spoke again his tone was as suave as it usually was. He had slipped his urbane mask back on.

'I haven't forgotten his previous insubordination,' he said evenly. 'If he steps out of line again I will consider him more of a liability than an asset and act accordingly. We can't afford any loose cannon on board this ship.'

'He's our best man, and you know it.'

'Don't take him as an example, Ms Graves.' He looked at her. 'And don't disappoint me.'

'Of course,' she replied evenly. Sir Richard didn't threaten idly.

'In future, if you ask me to OK a mission, I'll want

all the details – all of them.' He paused. 'If I'd known where you were sending him I would have had to square it with the Treasury.'

'It's nothing – just a hunch he's playing.'

'Anything to do with the material they passed on from Brasilia?'

'There was a link. A faint one. At this stage we have to follow every lead.'

Hudson unbent slightly. 'Just wheel him in. As things stand, he's become a security risk. I want him back here and debriefed. Fast.'

She nodded and followed him with her eyes as he left Room 55, glad not to have told him how worried she really was herself. Christ, the man was so immaculate there wasn't even a crease in the back of his suit jacket. What a contrast to Marlow. She knew nothing about her boss's home life – no one did – but she imagined the bastard must sleep standing up. If he slept at all. But however little she knew about Hudson's domestic arrangements, she did know how his mind worked, and that he, too, took orders, was answerable. If Hudson had described Jack as a loose cannon and a security risk, she knew that, if she didn't act fast, her boss would send a team of his own out to locate and neutralize him. Sir Richard hadn't forgotten the affront his agent had served him on the last big mission he'd been engaged on, and only Jack's usefulness – which was no secret even outside Section 15 – had saved him then. To Hudson, the whole team were just tools: the minute they didn't function properly, they'd be thrown away.

But she'd learnt that the hard way, after the glamour had worn off and it was too late to back out. A fellow agent, now long dead, had nicknamed INTERSEC 'the lobster pot'. Laura knew why these days.

Putting such thoughts aside and dismissing Hudson from her mind, she snatched up the blue phone and punched a key. As she waited impatiently for Lopez to pick up, she thought about Jack. Where was he? What was he doing? Was he even alive? She pushed the last idea away as Lopez answered. He had always been her friend. Her prop. She needed to think aloud, and she needed advice.

'Leon?'

'Yes?'

'Where are you?'

'At Columbia. I told you.'

'Get over here now.'

'Can't it wait?'

'No. I need you here now.'

'I'm in the middle of a tutorial.'

'Wrap it up and get over here as fast as you can. It's Jack.'

'Has he made contact?'

'No.' She suppressed a pang that was anything but professional.

'Give me' – there was a pause – 'twenty minutes.'

'I'll send a car.'

'Not necessary – I'll get a cab and charge it.'

'I'm not in the mood for jokes, Leon.'

'Twenty minutes.'

'OK.'

She hung up and looked around the big room. There was nothing to do but wait. Those twenty minutes were the longest in her life. She looked at the little tattoo on her finger. She'd kept it as a reminder never to be such a fool again. Resisted all attempts – even orders – to persuade her, to have it removed.

When Lopez arrived he found her pacing in front of the long window that overlooked the quiet street. He recognized her concern at a glance and she gave him a brief, hard hug before motioning him to a seat at her desk. She filled him in on the situation immediately.

'Jack must be on to something,' he said when she'd finished.

'Then why hasn't he checked in?'

'Security? He's operating outside the usual parameters.'

'What if he's cut off? He knows better than to use an open cell phone.'

'Trust him.'

'There isn't time. Hudson wants him wheeled in now.'

'Is he outside the time limit?'

'Yes – just. But he hasn't contacted at all since he left. That's the most worrying thing.'

'So, what do you want to do?'

She looked a little helpless. 'I was hoping you'd tell me.' She hated herself for that; she was section head: it was her call, her decision. But Leon's very presence was helping her think more clearly.

'Send someone in after him?'

'The wider we spread this, the looser the security.'

Lopez caught her look. 'I can't go. Section 14 wants this Russian material by yesterday.'

'How far are you on with it?'

'Two more days.'

She bunched her hands in frustration. 'Why can't they handle it?'

'It's ultra-priority and the budget cuts mean they haven't the expertise. And Hudson owes them one.'

'Shit.'

'In any case, I'm grounded, remember? After my last little freelance foray?'

Laura did remember. Both Leon and Jack had operated out of line on the last major mission and they were lucky still to be on board. If they hadn't, the mission would have crashed. But that wasn't how Hudson's mind worked.

She thought hard for a moment, then came to a decision. 'I'll go myself,' she said.

Lopez raised his eyebrows. 'Are you crazy? Hudson would never allow it –'

'I won't ask him. This section is my responsibility.'

'But even if you did, where the hell would you start? He has no GPS implant –'

'I have. You can track me.'

'You've tried his secure cell, and there's nothing. How else are you going to find him in a city the size of Rio – if he's still there?'

Laura was silent. She couldn't deny the logic of what

Lopez was telling her, however unwelcome it was. But there had to be a way, and there was no time for hesitation. Throughout her INTERSEC career she had toed the line and, although obedience had got her the leadership of Section 15, she couldn't see now, having already stuck her neck out in allowing Marlow to go to Rio, how she could go much further without stretching the rules more. She needed help, and she needed it from outside her own organization – but how could she seek it without compromising the security of her operation?

It was highly risky, but she couldn't see any forward movement without taking the step. It was almost a relief. Jack would have approved. She smiled.

'What is it?' Lopez asked.

'Nothing,' she replied. 'Nothing at all.'

15

London, Late 1590s

He had fought his way out of the ambush with difficulty, but his swordsmanship had been equal to that of his assailants, and the timely arrival of the nightwatchmen, and of Kit Marlowe's own people, who'd heard the scuffle downstairs, had been enough to panic the attackers into a retreat.

There had been no repeat of the attempted ambush, but Raleigh was under no illusion that it had just been a chance street mugging. He took Kit's advice and returned to the country, to Sherborne, to the comfort of his wife and young son. The seasons followed one another and he was content to lie low, but as time passed and there was no encouraging word from Sir Robert Cecil, as Queen Elizabeth grew older and her interest in the American colonies waned, Raleigh became increasingly restless. Letters from Kit advised him to be patient, but he was not a man to rest on the sidelines, and if Kit would not help him further there were others in their Brotherhood who would. But, at last, the summons came.

The new buds were scarcely formed on the trees when he was back in the capital. He had not been in residence in his London house a day before Kit sent word. Raleigh threw a long, homespun cloak over his shoulders and made his way through rainy streets and across London Bridge, fighting his way through the throngs of shoppers there despite the weather, until he reached the more open land south of the river and the Theatre.

There were few people about here, and after looking around him carefully, Raleigh pushed his way through a postern gate in the building's wall and mounted a steep flight of wooden steps to a back room filled with musty-smelling costumes. From the stage below, through the patter of rain, Raleigh could hear the actors rehearsing. It sounded like a comedy:

'I see their knavery: this is to make an ass of me; to fright me, if they could. But I will not stir from this place, do what they can. I will walk up and down here, and I will sing, that they shall hear I am not afraid . . .' Someone was declaiming the lines. How apt they were, Raleigh thought grimly.

'One of your plays?' he said to the man in black, who leapt from his chair to embrace him.

'Who else's?' Kit replied, grinning. But then his manner became grave.

'What's the news?' Raleigh asked, noticing the change of expression. 'You've kept me waiting long enough.'

'We have made progress. It has been slow, because we've had to tread carefully. Cecil hasn't forgotten about the map. Nor has he forgotten your unwillingness to hand it over.'

'That is what they were after when they attacked me.'

'That wasn't Cecil's men. Your attackers had knowledge of it from elsewhere.'

'Who were they? The Spanish?'

Kit's look darkened. 'We suspect the Chevaliers.'

'I thought so! We should have been forearmed.'

'Do not be angry. Or impatient. They have not resumed their quest.'

Raleigh mulled over the truth of that. 'I have not been disturbed in Sherborne.'

'It may be they suspect it is already in Cecil's possession – in which case they will be biding their time. The Queen is old. The King of Spain still broods, but his third Armada was driven back by storms and Philip believes a divine providence frustrates him. Besides, he is old too, and the fire dies in him.'

'And Cecil?'

'Luckily for us, he has been too busy with the Spanish threat, but he is talking in secret to King James of Scotland. James will be king when Elizabeth dies.' Kit paused. 'He is not a warlike man, he is too fond of money. He will want peace with Spain.'

'This is no news to us.'

'It is fortunate for Cecil's clique that tempests, not arms, deterred the last Spanish attempt on our shores. Wars cost money and harden enmity.

'It has worked to our advantage too. There has been time for the Brotherhood to make preparations – to insure ourselves, if you like, against anyone else stealing your discovery.'

'It is good that the Brotherhood, at least, believes me.'

'We know you would stake your life on your integrity,' Kit said quietly.

'Where is the map now?'

'Here.'

Kit spread it on a table cleared of the costumier's tools and offcuts. Raleigh's attention was drawn to the symbols the old Indian, Essex, had drawn on its margin. He told Kit about Essex, and of the temple doors that opened when the sun's beams passed over them. That the same phenomenon occurred once every year at midsummer.

'And the symbols?' Kit asked.

'Essex died before he could explain them. We think they're a key to the opening of the doors.'

'Hariot agrees,' Kit said. 'He told me too that he believes the bird is a condor.'

'I've seen them. Great vultures. But they belong in the mountains.'

'Anything else?' asked Kit, as if seeking confirmation.

'The Indians worship them – they are linked with the sun god.'

'So – the sun.' Kit seemed pleased. The logic was tying things up.

'How does Hariot know?'

'He isn't just our great astronomer.' Kit looked at his friend. 'And don't forget that he was on the Roanoke expedition you masterminded.'

Raleigh nodded. He would never forget that disastrous and mysterious venture, and he knew Thomas Hariot well. Hariot had studied the customs and languages of the native people out in the Americas, their beliefs and the natural history of the place. He had talked long with Raleigh after Walter's last expedition to the New World.

'The second symbol, the star – Thomas thinks that is Sirius,' Kit continued.

'That makes sense. It is the brightest in the heavens.' Raleigh pointed at the last two symbols. 'And these?'

'Thomas knows they are constellations, but they are crudely drawn. He thinks he knows which ones they represent, but he is checking. For the copy.'

'The copy?'

'We plan to make a copy of the map.'

'But why? Won't that make it less secure?'

'The Brotherhood has considered that. Now you are here, we can talk fully of our purpose.'

16

The meeting in the great hall under the mansion that faced the River Thames to the west of the city was a sombre one. Those attending sat at its centre, at a round oak table on which the two maps – the original and the copy – were carefully spread. The table was pivoted at its centre so that every man was able to see and compare them. The atmosphere was tense, but every member of the School knew each other through and through. There could be no question of a security breach here, either from the Chevaliers or from Sir Robert Cecil. Nevertheless, no word of the meeting had been written down, and its time and place had been arranged at the very last minute. Their cover – for all their activities – had been conveniently created for them by a Jesuit priest who had accused them of being a School of Atheism. In fact, this closely knit group had gathered originally with no more focused purpose than the study and discussion of new advances in science, religion, philosophy and discovery. The members gathered tonight were Kit Marlowe, Sir Walter Raleigh, the writer George Chapman, the scientist-astronomer Thomas Hariot and the group's youngest member, Sir Thomas Fielding.

But it now had a more immediate, practical and serious purpose.

The copy of the map had been prepared with Raleigh's consent. He had been reluctant at first but was quick to see the sense of it. Hariot had worked on it meticulously and in conditions of complete secrecy, and now presented it in his usual brusque and modest manner, though the fellow members of the Brotherhood noted an element of pride. It was a fine piece of work, given the limited time he had had to produce it.

'We fight a war on two fronts,' he began, 'a war with two enemies: Sir Robert Cecil's network and, though they lie low, the Chevaliers d'Uriel.'

The assembly nodded gravely in acknowledgement of their most feared and respected adversaries. Once, the Chevaliers had been simpler to deal with, when they were in the pocket of the Kings of Spain. But now, with their move into France and simultaneous espousal of the still-new Protestant religion (without abandoning allegiance to the Mother Church), and their independence of Church and State, they represented a far darker, less identifiable threat than before.

'The Chevaliers may have their eyes closed,' continued Hariot, 'but they are not asleep. It may be a long time yet before they make their move, but they are men who have learnt over more than one hundred years that patience is needed to achieve any great goal.

When they strike, however, they will strike hard, and fast.'

'What is the purpose of the copy of the map?' asked George Chapman.

'It is our insurance policy,' Kit said. 'We pondered hard and long over it. We know that Cecil wants it, but he doesn't know its whereabouts and, thanks to Walter, he has not seen it. But he will not wait much longer before he makes a move. Spain will not attempt another attack on us, and we know that James of Scotland will look for peace with his Catholic cousins when his time comes. Cecil knows this too, and the map would be a very useful bargaining tool in peace negotiations.'

Raleigh spat angrily, but Kit put a soothing hand on his arm. 'Look at the copy, Walter. Look carefully.'

Raleigh turned the table so that the maps faced him, and scrutinized each one. Kit watched him anxiously, especially when he was poring over the *original*, but his face betrayed no surprise. He had not noticed any changes in it since he had last seen it – to Kit's relief. Walter, he knew, was not a man used to guarding his tongue, and the small but crucial emendation he and Hariot had made to the original passed unnoticed. Kit was amazed, nevertheless. Raleigh was an experienced explorer, but evidently left scrutiny of details to trusted subordinates. It was something in his nature, some fatal flaw, which would one day, despite his brilliance, be his undoing. Kit exchanged a lightning glance with Hariot. They were right to have taken precautions.

Hariot withdrew the original map then, and said, 'If we could concentrate on the copy . . .' He pointed to certain features on it. 'You'll see that it shows the location of Eldorado where everyone expects it to be – near the River Orinoco. Only the original shows' – another exchanged glance with Kit – 'the true site of the temple. We will keep the original close. Kit will guard it until the time comes when Walter will be able once again to put it to use.'

'And the Chevaliers?'

'They must at all costs be kept in the dark. No word of this meeting must be spoken by any of us to any other person, not even our closest and most trusted companions. Do you understand that, Walt?'

'Of course,' replied Raleigh gruffly. 'The old Indian told me of the city beneath the temple. Undreamed-of wealth. If the Chevaliers got their hands on that, there would be no bounds to their power.'

'Richard Topcliffe is a dangerous man,' said Chapman. He twitched at his threadbare coat. Poor George, thought Kit. Little went well for him financially, but he'd fared better than their colleague Tom Kyd, who'd fallen into Topcliffe's hands on a trumped-up charge and had died of his injuries after torture only a couple of years earlier.

'And his tentacles are long. But we will be ready for him,' Hariot replied. He turned to the youngest member of their group, who had been bent over the copy map, studying it with interest.

'What is it, Fielding? What have you noticed?'

The young man straightened, running his hands along his dark-brown velvet doublet to smooth it. 'I do not ask you to produce the original map again,' he said. 'But there is something missing on the copy.'

'You are observant, my boy,' Hariot replied. 'But what?'

Fielding thought for a moment. He had a fine face, crowned with rich, brown hair. He looked at Hariot with clear, intelligent blue eyes. 'The symbols,' he said.

'You have left out the symbols?' said Raleigh. 'I had not noticed. Why?'

'If they have the function we believe they have,' Kit said, 'we would not want to give our enemies that advantage.'

Raleigh nodded. If ever the enemy reached the gold, they would never depart with it.

'I can keep vigil over the original map,' Kit continued, 'and over Cecil and his minions. But we will need someone to watch the movements of the Chevaliers. Someone with a quick mind, someone who is not afraid to work alongside them, perhaps for years. Someone who will not be afraid of the consequences if he is discovered.' He paused, and his gaze followed Hariot's, to look at Thomas Fielding.

'Are you ready to take this on? This would be your first great labour for the Brotherhood.'

Fielding bowed. 'If you believe I am worthy,' he said.

The meeting broke up soon afterwards. As they were leaving, Raleigh asked Hariot, 'Who will keep the copy of the map you've made?'

'Kit. He is close to Cecil still. And we do not know, apart from James of Scotland, who else Cecil is speaking with.'

'And the map itself?'

Hariot spread his hands. 'A bone to throw the dog if it barks.'

17

Rio de Janeiro, the Present

They faced each other in the flat. Darkness had fallen and the city glowed beneath them, lights scattered across the glittering sea.

'A map?' Jack echoed, ignoring the pain as he shifted his weight on the sofa. 'Do you know if they made copies, sent it anywhere electronically?'

She looked at him, her right hand twisting the gold chain she wore round her neck. 'That is the last thing they would have done.'

Jack thought about it. 'Of course,' he said.

'I am sure the Dutchman brought it.'

'That would figure.' He hadn't yet told her what he already knew about de Vries. 'But that was about the time the gold market started to fall.'

'What will you do?'

Jack knew he couldn't seek help from the INTERSEC bureau here. Its upscale from a one-person operation in the light of the World Cup and the Olympics was due but hadn't yet been implemented. He couldn't go to the Agência, either. He was on his own until he could get back to base with the information he already had. And he didn't necessarily need this girl in tow. Cold professionalism took over as he looked at her. Liability or asset?

'So – what's next?'

'Next, you tell me all you know about this map.'

'They didn't bring me far into the loop, and there was no way I could access it, but I know it was old – very old. An antique map, and it was an original. Louvier was very excited.'

'Go on.'

'There was something else – a location they were looking for. Only that map showed it. Do you know what it signifies?'

'You must tell me what it is first.'

She was about to answer his question when something, caught out of the corner of his eye, distracted him and set every nerve alert. He was sitting with his back half turned to the window. The blinds were still up and their reflections and the interior of the room could be seen in the glass. But there was something else. A shadow that was not a reflection at all, but something outside.

A figure, swaying, hovering just above the balcony balustrade. Jack calculated quickly. Whoever it was must have abseiled from the roof. A figure in black, slender but muscular, clearly male, his head covered in a black ski mask. As Jack watched, the figure touched the balustrade with his feet and, after a moment's hesitation, pushed outwards.

Jack grabbed Natasha and flung her to the floor. 'Stay down!' he commanded, as he drew himself upright and leapt to one side, making for the windows as they shattered and the figure smashed through them, feet first and already spraying the room with bullets from the Mini-Uzi grasped in his right hand, dropping to the floor and releasing the harness attaching the abseil cable with the other in one fluid movement.

But even the most hardened professional needs a few seconds to complete such a manoeuvre and in that fraction of time Jack threw himself forward, grabbing the man round the neck with his right arm and flexing upwards and back. But before he could snap the neck the man drove his elbow into Jack's side with such force that his grip slipped, and, winded, he released. The pain in his tortured body was unbearable. The man spun round, firing, shattering the surviving windowpanes with a fresh hail of bullets. Jack dived, making for the man's legs. Behind him, he caught a glimpse of Natasha, already on her feet and ready to spring. But the man sensed this and turned, leaping free of Jack's lunge and grabbing the girl's foot as she lashed out, aiming for his throat. He seized her ankle and swung her, throwing her hard against the wall. She fell to the floor, inert.

Jack, every muscle screaming, fell on the man's back as he raised the Uzi to finish her off, and they crashed against a low unit, smashing the ornaments on it and rolling on to the carpet, already streaked with Natasha's blood, their hands like claws, slashing at each other's eyes. The Uzi was thrown clear, but Jack's assailant knew where he had been hurt and punched and pressed those points when he could reach them. Jack gasped for breath, but he was also angry. Controlling it, he used it to channel his energy and landed a harsh blow with the side of his hand to his attacker's left kidney. Cursing, the man weakened his grip. Jack rolled free, stood, and delivered a vicious kick to the same place. He followed through with a chop downwards on to the neck as his adversary staggered to his feet. The man convulsed, gagged and lay still.

Jack straightened, to see that Natasha was already on her feet, rubbing blood from the corner of her mouth with her left hand. The Uzi was in her right, pointing at the man on the floor, and she was ready to fire. But she overcame that first urge for vengeance and lowered the gun, which Jack gently took from her before stooping to pull the ski mask from the man's head.

'Recognize him?' he asked, as the head fell back on to the parquet.

She nodded. 'They call him Sasha. One of Struna's – what's the word? – henchmen?' She paused. 'How did they find this place?'

They drew the blinds and switched out the lights. The room was plunged into twilight as they worked. Jack checked the magazine of the Uzi. It was empty.

'They trusted you less than you thought. What we've got to worry about is how to get out of it. Come on, get dressed.'

'What about him?'

Jack looked again at the body on the floor. He knelt

and felt the neck with his fingers. 'He's dead,' he said. He was already moving around the room, gathering his clothes and pulling them on, as she did likewise. He riffled through his bag for the remainder of his kit: no back-up for what he'd lost, but there was a spare length of thin cord and a Fallkniven slip-joint folding knife. These he slid into the pockets of the black windcheater he'd slipped on over a black T-shirt and trousers. Natasha was also dressed by now, jeans, and a leather jacket over a T-shirt. She'd produced her handgun, the Kel-Tec P-32, and a phone.

'Is it secure?' Jack asked, looking at it.

'Yes.'

'Ditch it.'

'It's OK.' She saw his expression. 'I'll only use it if I have to, OK? They won't be able to track it.'

Jack wondered if they hadn't already. He stood by the window frame and scanned the area immediately outside the block. All was quiet. There was no sign of reaction from Natasha's neighbours either. They were absent, or thought it better to mind their own business. But one of them would have called the police by now. There was no time to lose.

He thought fast. They might make it back to the motorbike, but it was two blocks away and the chances were high that the Chevaliers would already have located it. He took the phone from her and quickly disabled it with his knife.

'Is there a back way out of here?'

'There's a service entrance which leads into an alley.'

If they had that covered, there'd be little room to manoeuvre in a narrow space. Jack was looking out of the front entrance again when he heard the distant sirens. He grabbed his bag, taking Natasha by the arm.

Outside, the landing was clear. Ignoring the elevator, they took the stairs, keeping to the walls and checking at every floor, but all was clear – there wasn't a sound, not even the muted hum of a TV – and the lobby was deserted. Beyond the entrance a small lawn planted with palms separated the building from the street. But they wouldn't have sent Sasha in alone. They'd be waiting.

But if the Chevaliers wanted them dead, what were they waiting for now? The sirens were getting closer. What the hell was their game?

'Come on,' he said, grabbing Natasha's hand and using the cover of the palms to make it to the street. Still nothing. Skirting the walls and keeping to the shadows, they headed off to the left. At the same moment, behind them, three hundred metres away, they saw the flashing lights of two police cars as they turned into the street. The sirens grew suddenly louder. Ahead, at an equal distance, were the lights of the bars and cinemas of a busy thoroughfare. But Jack noticed something else – movement in the shadows behind him.

Then it hit him. Sasha hadn't been sent in to kill them but to flush them out. A man like that wouldn't have just sprayed bullets anywhere in the way he had if that hadn't been his intention. It made sense that the Chevaliers would want them alive – for now. And Sasha was dead, but he'd succeeded in his mission.

'They're on to us,' he breathed. 'Stay down. If they've got stun darts –'

She nodded and squeezed his hand as they ducked low and ran towards the lights. They hadn't gone more than twenty metres before they saw dark figures ahead.

'Down here,' she breathed, pulling him off the street down a pathway so dark and narrow that he hadn't noticed it. 'It leads to the sea.'

Fighting his pain, Jack followed her. They ran along it in single file, pausing after another twenty metres where it widened slightly into a small square lit by one dim lamp attached to a wall and hemmed in by warehouse-like buildings. Jack listened intently, noticing that the corners of the walls by the path they'd just left had iron eyelets set into them every metre or so up the buildings, no doubt to guide ropes used for hauling stores up and down from the upper floors, where he could see barn-like doors. He took out his length of cord and, working fast, every muscle still aching with the effort, so that he had to grit his teeth to complete the task, cut it to size with the knife, using the eyelets to stretch it tight across the alleyway at about shoulder height. It took him less than a minute to complete the job. The cord was black and no more than five millimetres thick. He rubbed some dust from the ground on it to take off any shine.

'That'll slow them down. Now?'

'Straight on.'

There were three alleyways leading off the square, each plunging into darkness. But he had to trust her. He kept the knife, blade locked open, in his hand. It was short, just over six centimetres, but it could do enough damage if the need arose.

'Listen.'

The silence of the night was broken only by the distant, tinny sound of the busy street they'd been making for, and, just audible and far distant, of the sea. Then came the noise of running feet.

'Come on!'

He dived after her down the passage she'd indicated just as their pursuers ran into the trap Jack had set. The first man caught the cord across his neck and fell backwards, causing a pile-up. It took his companions just moments to get his body out of their way, but the time Marlow and Natasha had gained was precious. It would take them longer to decide which of the three alleyways to choose.

Jack followed hard on Natasha's heels. The ground beneath their feet was stonier now, the paving broken and loose, making it difficult to keep up any kind of pace. But she stumbled once, losing them vital seconds. From then on she slowed slightly, and gave warning when she came to treacherously loose pavings. At last the alley debouched into a piece of sloping open ground containing a few dilapidated buildings scattered over a stretch of scruffy grass that ended at a steeper incline. Far below, the sea whispered. To their left was a building site.

'There are steps over there,' she said.

'You've done your homework.'

'Not well enough.'

'Why?'

'The phone.'

'That's over now.'

'But we must make contact –'

'We'll worry about that later. Got more pressing things to think about right now.' He indicated where a group of dark figures had emerged, fifty metres behind them, from the passageway they'd just left.

They crouched down and ran towards the building site. It was fenced in with chickenwire but the wire was rusty and frayed and, between the metal stakes supporting it, they found a section that had curled free. Ducking through it, they dived for cover behind a stack of concrete blocks as the snapping of automatic weapons began behind them and bullets sang through the air.

Natasha took out her pistol and fired back three shots, but the range was too long. Jack pulled her to her feet and they navigated their way deeper into the site. But their pursuers were close behind, shooting, clearly, to pin them down, to wound them maybe, but not to kill.

'Did you see them?' asked Natasha.

'What?'

'They've got dogs. Two of them.'

They reached a section of half-built adjoining walls. Beyond them lay the other side of the enclosure, and Jack could see that a whole section of wire had collapsed there, near a deep trench. They scrambled behind a pile of planking covered with a tarpaulin.

'How many clips?' Jack nodded at the gun.

'Two.'

'Let them get in range of that thing before you fire. We'll have to break out over there, so get ready to run once you've loosed off the five you've got left in that clip. Don't ditch the second, or the gun – we'll need them. Ready?'

She nodded. They waited, heads down, listening as their pursuers approached, cautiously, fanning out.

'Now!'

She rose just above the tarp and saw shadows five metres distant, gripped the little pistol and steadied her right wrist with her left hand, letting off the shots in fast, accurate succession. Two men collapsed instantly and soundlessly; one more stumbled forward, retching, his hands jerking to his throat.

'Let's go!'

They dived off towards the open wire and had almost reached it when the men behind them released the dogs, which threw themselves forward with silent menace. Low, dark shapes – Ridgebacks, by the look of them. But they didn't split up. They both made for Natasha, two metres behind him: it was Natasha they really wanted, and she hadn't reloaded the Kel-Tec. He spun round and grabbed her, to get between the dogs and her, but in doing so snagged his ankle in a twisted length of rusty wire lying in the rough ground. He recovered his balance fast, but not before the dogs had reached her. Four of the men rushed him from behind. He swung at the first with his knife and gashed his forearm before the weapon was wrenched from his grip and the first blows landed. They threw him to the ground and kicked him in the ribs, the head, the kidneys, then rained blows down on him with lengths of four-by-four picked up on the site. He fought his way to his feet, blood obscuring his vision, but managing to lash out with his feet at the groins of two of his attackers.

He heard Natasha cry out, but a crushing blow to the back of his head sent him into the trench, and his ribcage bounced against the jagged rocks that lined the bottom. From far away, he heard voices, indistinct and speaking French, but he caught the gist. In the remoter distance, sirens again.

'They wanted both of them.'

'The girl is more important. We have to get out of here now.'

'What about him?'

'Be quick. Make no noise.'

Someone scrambled down into the trench, felt his body, his neck, hastily. 'He's dead.'

'Make sure.'

Jack heard a scraping noise and inwardly braced himself. The blow which came was partly deflected by a block of stone which overhung his neck. He heard the length of wood his attacker had used crack with the force of its descent. He felt blood flow. He lay still.

'Done.'

'Checked his pulse?'

His attacker laughed. 'Why? When I hit someone, I hit them good. And look at him.' The voice came from the other end of the world now. He barely heard them depart.

18

Elizabethan London

'Good,' Sir Robert Cecil said, holding the map triumphantly in his hand. 'But now we must work fast.'

He unrolled the parchment and spread it on his desk, weighing its corners down with his inkwell and a Bible. He studied it carefully.

'It is the copy you seek?'

Cecil looked at Kit Marlowe, searching his eyes. 'You are sure it is the only one?'

'I am certain of it.'

'You have done well.'

'It is ever my intention to serve the best interests of my country.'

'In the right hands, this will bring the peace we seek.'

Kit nodded. He had come a long road since the meeting of the Brotherhood, and he thanked his own good fortune that he had been able to intercept Cecil's directive to seek out and obtain Sir Walter Raleigh's map of Amazonia at whatever possible cost. But it had been a hard process. The spy instructed to take the map was a trusted servant of Sir Robert's who had posed as a serving man in his immediate entourage. He'd acted as usher at his most secret meetings, and had turned out to be a difficult man to suborn.

When that tactic had failed, other measures had to be taken. Cecil was still making enquiries into the man's disappearance, but he trusted Kit. Everything hung on that trust.

'What are your plans?'

Cecil looked at Kit shrewdly. 'It is better that I do not reveal them now, even to you.'

Kit nodded sagely, playing the game. But he knew perfectly well what Cecil's plan was.

The most important thing was that Cecil believed the map in his hands was genuine, and unique. Copying a map was a slow, expensive and painstaking business, and there could be no question of etching and printing this one.

The problem was that there were now no more bones to throw.

19

New York, the Present

Sir Richard Hudson was in his coldest, most dangerous mood. Laura knew it from the icy politeness of his manner and the ominously quiet tone of his voice. Someone had shopped her. It wouldn't have been Leon – even if she'd taken him fully into her confidence, and she'd never have compromised him by doing so, he would never have done that. So it had to be someone in Brasilia, probably in all innocence, or someone had got wind of it from the Treasury and gone over her head. Either way, the damage was done. She was learning the hard way what it was to head a section and not to have the autonomy she thought she'd been given. She thought long and hard about Jack. She expected it was a relief to him that he was out of it. But where was he now? And the thought came to her again: *what was he doing?*

She sat across Hudson's desk from him in his clinical office, the Paul Klee and the other new work, by Klee's friend Franz Marc, offering the only humanity in the room, and waited. She had been offered neither coffee nor the customary glass of white Sancerre. A bad sign – as if she needed one. Hudson made no pretence of busying himself with papers while he made her wait; he simply sat and stared at her with eyes that seemed absent. He made a tent of his fingers and sat back.

'You've been in touch with the Agência,' he said at last, flatly. Not a question. A statement.

'Yes.'

'May one ask why?'

'I'm leaving no stone unturned in my efforts to retrieve Jack.'

'I thought we'd agreed not to open this up to any third parties – apart from the Treasury, and that only through Nick Adams.'

'Yes.'

'That is to say, through me.'

'Yes.' Laura was beginning to regret having let Leon sway her and not just getting on to a plane herself in the first place. 'If I may –'

'No,' Hudson barked in a tone that came from nowhere and made her start inwardly. She had never seen this side of him before. 'You may not. I am very, very disappointed in you, Ms Graves.'

'That, I am truly sorry to hear.'

'May I remind you that, although you came to this posting on my personal recommendation, it was also, as it were, by default.'

'Sir.'

Sir Richard leant forward, earnest now, his features set, elbows on the desk and hands projected forward.

Her eye was caught by the tiniest coffee stain on the sleeve of his jacket near the wrist. Another part of his carefully constructed world gone awry. Was he aware of it? It was odd, she had time to reflect as she listened to him, how small details leap out at you in moments of crisis.

'Are you listening?'

'Yes.'

'It is hell itself containing this. We can't keep the seismic movements in the financial world out of the press, and although they are steady, thank God that only professionals will understand their underlying implications. So far we've been able to build a wall of excuses to keep the world press at bay. But they aren't fools, and they aren't without plenty of their own experts. But there'll be no lack of pundits only too happy to shoot their mouths off on television and the Internet and wherever the hell else they like to air their opinions, even in quite old-fashioned outlets like radio and newspapers – the printed kind, I mean. So we've bought what cooperation we can and, for the rest, we're fobbing them off – but it won't take for ever for them to realize there's nothing there. The only reason I am telling you this is that: one, I still think you are intelligent enough to grasp its significance, and two, I think you are out of your depth and need to face the reality of the situation you are in. You are not going to drag us in with you. Do I make myself clear?'

'Yes.'

'Now. If you want to keep your job – and you know what losing it means – you will do the following. Concentrate on the significance of this Gerrit de Vries. Use all police sources you need and get to his records. But forget about the Agência. I have already asked their chief to have nothing more to do with INTERSEC unless the contact runs via me personally. And I have issued a personal apology. He was very reasonable, and I think the day is saved, no thanks to you. But still he knows a little more than he should, and I can't excise that from his memory. We can only hope he doesn't do any investigating on his own account, though from what I can gather you gave them almost nothing to go on.' She began to speak, and he held up a hand. 'And please don't give me that crap about Section 15 having to act alone – I got enough of that from Jack, and look at the balls-up he made.' Laura nodded, noticing that Dick's language was beginning to betray his loss of cool. And she found comfort in thinking of him as Dick – it deflated him somewhat. Inside her, there was a glow she liked, although she didn't know what it was yet. She suspected it was a growing sense of independence. But she nodded meekly and continued to listen.

'And what about Jack?' she said.

'The name of the game now is damage limitation,' Hudson replied, recovering some of his frost. 'You concentrate on de Vries. Say nothing to Dr Lopez beyond what's necessary for him to help you. He's off the Russian stuff now and fully at your disposal.'

'And Jack?' she insisted.

He didn't look at her, leaning forward to press a button on his desk. 'You can leave Marlow to me.'

20

Rio de Janeiro, the Present

Rafael Antunes and Gabriel Borges arrived at the site early, well before their workmates. They'd brought a roll of new oxidized chickenwire with them in the pick-up, and cutters and wire and tags – everything needed to repair the fences that enclosed their work area, a job that should have been done weeks ago, delayed because of problems (always problems!) with all kinds of supplies, which took priority with their unloved boss, Miguel Cordoso.

The new condominiums they were working on had to be ready for the Olympics, and there was another major job to be done in clearing all the old buildings and the labyrinth of alleyways between the site and the nearest section of the city proper to make way for a park in which the luxury dwellings would sit. Hard to believe that millionaires would one day in the not-too-distant future lounge here. The place looked like some muddy battlefield, like the ones you saw on the History Channel.

'Let's deal with the worst first,' said Rafael, pointing over to where a huge section had pulled away near a deep drainage trench that had been opened up the week before.

'OK,' replied Gabriel. 'Let's go for it.'

They drove as close as they could get and lugged the gear the rest of the way. But before they started they took out a Thermos and salgadinhos wrapped in foil, lit cigarettes and drank thick black coffee with plenty of sugar. It was then they heard the noise.

'Jesus, what was that?' said Gabriel.

'Rats in the trench?'

'What would they find to eat there?'

'Let's look.'

The two men approached the edge of the trench with caution. Just in time to see the man dragging himself into view. They looked at the battered figure in its torn clothes, and went forward to pull him out. He could stand only with an effort, so they guided him to a building block and sat him down. Gabriel poured coffee and Rafael handed him a couple of their salgadinhos.

Jack Marlow ate and drank with gratitude.

'What happened to you?'

'Got mugged,' he replied, inventing a handful of details in a mixture of Spanish and broken Portuguese.

'*Here?*' asked Gabriel, but Rafael silenced him with a look.

'We'll call for help,' he said. 'An ambulance.' He reached for his cell phone.

'I'll manage,' Jack said. He checked his pockets. 'I've lost my glasses. I have to look for them.'

'Of course. We'll help.'

'No – I'm OK now.'

He managed to get to his feet and, bracing himself, found that, after a few steps, he was able to walk unaided. Nothing broken, and his wallet, passport and knife were still with him, though his watch was smashed beyond repair. But he was – and he savoured the word with a keen sense of irony – operational. Searching for the non-existent spectacles, he scoured the ground around the attack for any clue indicating Natasha's fate. There were the marks of many footprints, signs of a scuffle and the pugmarks of the dogs, but everything was inconclusive except for a set of shallow furrows. Heel marks, which ended abruptly. They hadn't been able to bring a vehicle close, so they'd clearly dragged her some distance. The heel marks were scuffed at first, as if Natasha had kicked and struggled, but then the furrows were even. They must have hit her, or drugged her, for there was no resistance after that until the furrows ended. Then what? Had they lifted her? Carried her some distance to where a car or a truck was waiting?

He made his way back through the alleyways they'd run down the previous night. In the little square, three workmen were carrying boxes out through the doors of one of the buildings which faced it and loading them on to a little van, no more than a motorbike with a body built on top. A vehicle narrow enough to drive down one of the alleys, the first one, which was wider than the others, as Marlow clearly saw, now there was daylight. The one that led back to the main street.

The workmen looked at him curiously. He exchanged nods with them as he paused by the place where the alley entered the square and examined the ground. There were tyre marks here, but too intermingled to be of any use.

Then he noticed a dark stain in the dust, a large one. He stooped and touched it. All but dry. Putting his finger to his nostrils, he could just detect the scent of blood. And there was something which glittered near the edge of the stain, though it was half buried in dust. He picked it up. Natasha's gold chain.

But where to find her now? He knew they wouldn't have killed her, but he remembered their methods of extracting information – and they had barely started on him.

He showered at the little pension he'd found, where they'd ask no questions as long as the money was good, and changed into the clothes he'd bought off a stall in a street market nearby, with a flashy gold watch that would probably work for a couple of days.

Once he was ready, he made his way downstairs, thinking about his next move and the options available to him. Natasha Fielding weighed more heavily on his mind than she should have done.

But Marlow was out of time. Laura couldn't stall for him for ever, and he knew what Hudson's reaction would be when he learnt the truth. He couldn't ignore the possibility that a squad from Section 0551 might already have been dispatched. And looking for Natasha in Rio now would make looking for a needle in a haystack seem like a walk in the park. The one chink of light was that the Chevaliers would have called off their watch on Rio's airports and docks.

And what about other surveillance? He considered his options as he sat in the shabby vestibule of his *pensão*. On the counter of the reception desk stood a telephone. A landline. An ordinary landline. It was worth the risk. But calling Laura was out of the question.

He checked his watch. It should be the right time in New York for the man he wanted. Not at INTERSEC. At home.

He drained the glass of cachaça at his elbow and stood up.

After a quick word with the clerk, he picked up the phone and dialled Leon Lopez's home number. It was a chance he had to take.

21

London and Paris, early 1600s

They stood in the shadow of the Tower of London as the sun began its slow descent behind them to the west.

'The ship leaves tonight?'

'From Tilbury. Evening tide. It is safer than Deptford. More secure.'

More secure. That was the nature of the beast. For that reason they had opted for the overland route.

'Good.' Cecil had the map with him, in a soft leather pouch specially made to fit it. He wouldn't usually have undertaken this mission in person, but it was of the utmost importance, and he hadn't felt able to trust anyone, not even Kit Marlowe, with it. Now, he felt a reluctance to hand the pouch over. The map had a strange pull on him – it was the key to so much. But he shook off such ridiculous feelings and passed it to Juana de Prieto, together with another parcel.

'These are letters for the Duke of Lerma,' he said. 'They must be delivered into his own hand, together with the map.'

'I am aware of my instructions,' she replied stiffly. 'The ambassador has apprised me of them.'

'Good. And Lerma will present them to the King?'

'Lerma has built a strong wall around the King, but he is biddable.'

'And you are ready?' Cecil could not disguise his nervousness. He glanced at the ten riders who waited a few paces distant. 'You have a good escort.'

'These men will ride with me to Tilbury. The carrack is already docked and ready. It only awaits these.' De Prieto, a cousin of Lerma's and chosen for this mission by the Spanish ambassador, held the two packets up in her hand for emphasis.

'They are our pledge of peace.'

'They will be taken so.'

'Then – may the wind be in your favour.'

She gave him a tight smile and a formal bow before mounting her horse and riding away from the Tower with her bodyguard, breaking into a gallop as soon as the cluttered thoroughfare allowed them to. Behind Cecil, watching her, the sunset bathed her in a golden light.

'Go well,' he said. It was unusual for Sir Robert Cecil's heart not to be still, but much was riding on the despatches sent with the Spanish condesa. His hopes for a lasting peace, for advancement under the man who would soon – it could only be a matter of two or three years – be King of England, and for further riches of his own, rode with her. It had not been easy to get the map, and Kit Marlowe had done well.

Kit had assured him, too, that a replacement copy, indistinguishable from the one now riding eastwards in the saddlebag of the Condesa de Prieto, had been successfully placed among Raleigh's possessions. If by unlucky chance the mariner were ever granted permission and funding for another voyage to the New World, Cecil would see to it that the Spaniards were made aware of the sailor's treachery. As far as the Spaniards knew, Raleigh had surrendered his only copy to Cecil in good faith, as a token of his commitment to peace. King Philip III was not as wily a man as his father had been, and his valido, the Duke of Lerma, trusted his cousin de Prieto. How comforting it was that some sense of honour still existed in the world.

Everything had worked out well. But he did not like to think of the fate that would await the condesa if she fell into the hands of their adversaries.

Cecil watched the riders out of sight and turned back to his carriage. With the illness of the Queen, he had much else to think about. It was fortunate that Elizabeth's popularity had declined in recent years. There would be no problem in persuading the Council to announce as her heir the man he had chosen. But so preoccupied was Cecil that he had not noticed the horseman who had ridden in pursuit of the condesa, who would overtake her party on the Tilbury road, and be crossing the Channel in a light pinnace before she had even embarked.

It was close to dawn when Juana arrived at Calais. Her coach stood ready and waiting in the inn yard. She wasted no time in the little port, which still showed enough evidence of its recent Spanish occupation for her to feel at ease, and paused only to breakfast under the shadow of the Tour de Guet and to pray in Notre-Dame.

She set off again a little after 6 a.m. Fresh horses were already waiting at staging posts along the way. If they rode through the night, they should be in Paris by dawn the next day.

'If our reports are correct, she'll be here tomorrow.'

'When does Don Carlos arrive?'

'Later today. As soon as our messenger got word to us I sent couriers to him. He has already left the Château d'Uriel.'

Two of the people in the large room in the mansion overlooking a private courtyard off the rue des Francs-Bourgeois watched as the third, the planner, bent over a large map spread on the table in the centre of the floor. The map showed the city of Paris and its principal gates.

'They will head south,' said the planner. Audric Ballin prided himself on meticulous attention to detail, and took his time as he tapped a long, chalk-white forefinger at certain points on the map. 'They will leave by this gate, and take the St Jacques road.'

'Are you certain?' said the Director. Zora Ruzic, plump and black-haired, with apple cheeks and expressionless pale-blue eyes, looked at him keenly. 'We cannot allow this to misfire.'

'They have no other option. If they took any of the

smaller roads, they would be open to attack by highwaymen, and they would lose time.'

'But we are certain they suspect nothing.'

'I can vouch for that,' put in the third member of the group, the latest recruit, admittedly, but a man who'd already proved himself. The executive, Thomas Fielding. 'Our intelligence is impeccable.' But with the recent turn of events, Fielding had had to think fast.

'I hope so, for your sake,' said Ruzic evenly, her lips curled back just far enough to reveal her brown teeth.

'For all our sakes,' replied Fielding in an equally neutral voice. 'Don Carlos will not select just one of us to make an example of if we fail.'

'And they are travelling incognito?'

'They have a royal warrant, but they will not use it. The condesa has, however, a strong escort – the ten English horsemen she brought with her from London, and there will be another ten Spanish joining her here in Paris,' said Fielding.

'Fielding has done *un beau travail*,' Ballin observed. At thirty-eight, he was the oldest member of the group, and commanded respect. He looked at Ruzic admonishingly. 'You should congratulate him, not threaten.'

She shook her heavy jowls at him and attempted a smile, which her pronounced under-bite rendered grotesque. 'I do not threaten. I am by nature suspicious, as you should know by now. Thomas. Forgive me.' Her eyes were not smiling at all.

'There is nothing to forgive.' But Fielding felt a cold

hand close on his heart. He knew that Ruzic was a master-torturer, and that she enjoyed the work. He looked away from her dead eyes.

Ballin tapped the map, drawing their attention back to it. 'There is a slow curve in the road just here.' He pointed to a place some twelve miles south of the city, where a village flanked by a wood was marked. 'It is a safe place for us. The road runs between a channel carved out of a hill. We will use the wood to gain an element of surprise, and we can trap them in the channel.'

'They'll have outriders,' said Fielding.

'Then we'll set crossbowmen to kill them,' Ruzic replied. She turned to Ballin. 'How much time do you need?'

He gave a self-deprecating smile. 'All is prepared.'

'Then make all ready. They will not spend long here. Their mission is too pressing, and they will not want to draw the attention of the French to what they are doing. Be in place by dusk tomorrow. We will send you word as soon as the hour of their departure is known.'

'And where will you be?'

She looked at him. 'Ballin will be here with Don Carlos. As for me.' She paused. 'I will accompany you. It is fitting that I bring the map back personally to Don Carlos. And, besides, it is a while since I witnessed slaughter. It may be that I bring the condesa's head back to Paris myself.'

She doesn't trust me, Fielding thought. This must be a role I play convincingly.

*

The little village of St-Adalbert, grim and muddy, with a population of one hundred and nine, squatted just east of the St Jacques road, protected from the wind by its wood (which also provided its fuel) on the slope of the mutilated hill the road cut through. The hill was patchworked with strips of field, and here and there bony cattle grazed and a few sullen pigs rooted among the stumps of felled trees at the border of the iron-grey road. It was raining that morning, and that made the road muddier, and heavier going. Thunder growled as great ships of cloud rolled towards them from the north, and over distant Paris the sky brightened now and then with the eerie, ephemeral glow of lightning.

The villagers minded their own business and paid little attention to the traffic that passed along the road so close to their forlorn community. Life was hard enough without meddling in the affairs of others. But one or two did raise their heads when the shining black carriage, with cloaked, armed riders behind and ahead of it, lumbered past, its coachman urging his struggling horses to keep going through the clinging mire as the animals sought footholds on the stones that bedded the road and were meant to make it passable in all weathers.

'State business, looks like,' one farmer said to another.

'Then it's none of ours,' came the dour reply, and the men, sacks tied to their backs, turned back to their trench-digging.

One hundred yards south, where the gentle curve in the road had hidden them from sight, the vanguard of outriders, emerging from the channel cut through the hill, fell lifeless from their horses as the deadly iron bolts, fired by the crossbowmen hidden in the trees, found their targets. The rain made accurate aiming hard. Some of the men were merely wounded. Some of the horses were hit, too, and it took another round of fire to finish off both men and beasts. The crossbow men worked hard to complete their task, but it was still a mess and they had to clamber down the slippery grass slope from the wood to the road, daggers drawn, to silence the men who were still moaning, the horses that were still screaming. As they worked, they glanced up the road in the direction the coach would come. But it didn't come, and they relaxed a little. They knew the rearguard had been ambushed in similar fashion, and the coach, now, was . . .

Dimly through the sound of the rain they heard sporadic musket fire; but crossbows were more certain weapons in the wet, and they were all but silent. There were fifty men hidden in the wood on either side of the cleft the road ran through. They'd be descending on the coach now.

Thomas Fielding was the first to its door. The driver had already been felled by a crossbow bolt, but the guard at the rear of the box was slashing down at him with his sword, and he had to lunge upwards to kill him with his own blade. Waving at the men behind him to cease firing, he seized the handle and tore the door open, swinging to one side to avoid the ball which sang past his left earlobe as the Condesa de Prieto fired her first flintlock from within. He reached in and seized her wrist as she prepared to fire the second, twisting the gun from her grip. She spat in his face and tore at it with the nails of her free hand, but he warded her off and pulled her close to him. He could do without her blood on his hands. Enough had been shed already, and hers – the blood of a member of the Sandoval family – must be spared, if possible.

'I am going to throw you clear,' he hissed. 'They will not shoot until I give the order. Get to the other side of the carriage, and run. Head south. The rain will hide you.'

She looked at him hard for a moment, then nodded.

'But drop the map first,' he said. Not waiting for her reply, he felt roughly under her dress and pulled the pouch from its hiding place, quickly verifying that it contained what he sought. He transferred it to his own soaking doublet, cramming it down.

It had taken seconds, but already he could hear Ruzic's voice, a loud, insistent yell across the hammering of the downpour. He released his grip and she sprang forward and past him with a speed he would not have credited. He watched her through the cords of rain, thanking God for it, until she was halfway up the slope and heading away from the ambush. Once she paused to rip her skirts with a knife so she could move more easily. Our Saviour alone would know if she could save herself, but he knew she was a resourceful woman; they had been colleagues once. He had little time before the others arrived. He took the unfired flintlock – a brand-new kind of weapon he was unfamiliar with – and, bracing himself, fired it at his left forearm, taking care to make the shot cut only his flesh, well above the bone. He howled and dropped the gun, but he still had a few seconds left.

He rummaged in the cabin of the coach, retrieving the packet of letters. The first of his men had reached him now – with Ruzic close behind them, a long dagger in her hand.

'Where is she?' she asked, her knife ready. 'Is she dead, or must I finish the job?'

Ignoring her, Fielding shouted at his men: 'She's escaped.' He pointed northward up the opposite slope. 'That way!'

'Have you no men posted there?' snarled Ruzic.

'The woods grow too thick to fire from there,' he replied. 'The slope is too steep to descend fast.'

'Tend to his wound,' Ruzic said to a man who was already unpacking strips of cloth and a thin-bladed knife. Turning to him again: 'Do you have it?'

He waved the packet in his hand. 'Here are the letters.'

'Fuck the letters!' she hissed, seizing them and trampling them to a pulp in the mud in her fury. 'Where is the *map*?'

'It is not here,' he said.

She was still for one second. Then she screamed. So loud and so unearthly was her scream that the hard men around her trembled. The noise of the rain had blunted the rest of the conversation for them, but they were hired men, not privy to the aim of the ambush. But the scream they could understand, and they feared it. The woman was a witch, and they were afraid.

She raised her head and made fists of her hands and screamed again, the rain streaming over her. This harpy must be destroyed, thought Fielding. And the map must not fall into the hands of the Chevaliers. Whatever happened, they had to believe it was the true one, and they had to be made to continue to search for it. *They must waste their energies in the search. If it takes them centuries.*

But Fielding could not be certain which map he had, pushed down into his doublet. He hadn't been able to look at it. He had to be sure, and for that he needed time.

The woman in front of him collected herself, though her eyes were blazing as they turned in the direction Fielding had pointed.

'Get her,' she said, her voice calm now, though she was still furious. 'You will pay for this with your life, Fielding.'

'So that you can take credit for the map?'

She glared at him with pure hatred.

'We are wasting time,' he continued, and barked orders at the men. Some of them obeyed him and stumbled unwillingly up the slope in the direction they believed the condesa had fled. They were soon lost in the rain. Fielding looked around. He knew that many of the other men, already paid and their work done, had simply melted away. As he had expected they would. But Ruzic did not know this.

'She will not have gone far,' she said. 'They will bring her back, and then . . .' She fingered the heavy basilard still in her hands, and unsheathed it.

Fielding watched her. Only one small knot of men

remained, a short distance away, under the heavy, dripping branches of the trees. His own men. But Ruzic did not know this either.

He turned to them, and as he did so something happened for which he was not prepared. Behind him, he sensed her tensing, saw the faces of the men in front of him change. He moved swiftly, in time to prevent the long, double-edged blade of the basilard from plunging into his neck. He felt it strike his right shoulder blade and slide off, making a long gash in his back, the force of the blow throwing him forward. He staggered, gasping, reaching for his own riding sword. It had a well-tempered Hounslow blade and had saved him many times before but now, as he drew it, it stuck in its sheath: the sodden leather had tightened. Keeping low, he swung round to face his attacker, seeing out of the corner of his eye his men preparing to fire at her but uncertain of their aim in the rain. She was coming towards him, her mouth open, a gash of red in the monochrome grey. But her fury had got the better of her, and her second blow, a downward stab at his face, missed completely and she lost her balance, unable to compensate for her own force.

He stepped back and let her fall past him. He had wrenched his sword free now and stood over her. He watched as she scrabbled in the mud, trying frantically to stand. He poised his blade to strike, but could not. He told himself this was not a woman but a lethal animal who would tear him apart at the first opportunity, but he could not drive his sword into the back of a helpless creature, however necessary it was, however hard his every rational sense screamed at him to do it.

She was getting to her feet now, staggering and slipping in the mud, a yard from him, her black clothes sodden and hanging heavy with the clinging clay. Her dagger was still in her hand, and her mouth formed a jagged red wound of rage. Her dark hair straggled over her broad face as she came for him again.

And then she stopped. Stopped as if she had hit an invisible wall. Her body arched back and her face came level with his, the expression now one of crazed astonishment. She jolted then, as if a mule had kicked her, and her body was thrown forward against him as a third crossbow bolt hammered into her. She fell against him, her face raised to his as if for a kiss, and he took the lifeless weight of her body in his arms as the basilard fell from her grip. Inches from his eyes, the dark point of a crossbow bolt gleamed as it emerged from her mouth like an iron tongue. The last shot must have cleft her spine at the nape of the neck and that had been enough to arrest the bolt, but not before its work had been done.

Nervously, Fielding's men advanced. He ran his tongue over his lips. Only now did the pain in his wounded shoulder make itself felt as a keen ache. He allowed the sergeant-surgeon who had dressed the flintlock cut to stitch the gash and dress the wound. The others awaited his orders.

'You did well. She wanted to take the treasure for herself,' he told them. 'But she was an important person, and there will be questions. Bury her here. Church rites can wait. Then make yourselves scarce. I will return to Paris and speak for you.'

'Shall we not accompany you? You cannot travel.'

'They are flesh wounds and there are horses still. It is not a long ride, and the rain ceases.'

It was true that the storm was passing. The rain had reduced to a gentle patter, and the thunder was grumbling at a distance now, the grey ships moving in the direction of Chartres.

He could see that the men would be happy enough to go. The battle and the ambush would be cleared up by the villagers. They would want no trouble, and the abandoned weapons of the dead would be useful to them.

He had the men bring him a good horse and tested its saddle. It would serve for the return journey. Then he dismissed them, and, leading the horse, made his way towards the little stone church of St-Adalbert. It was an old stone building with round arches flanking its nave; a stocky, fortress-like edifice whose interior was dark and cold.

It was deserted, and that did not surprise him. Finding a wooden bench illuminated by a shaft of pale sunlight – for the sun had by now crept back in the wake of the storm – he pulled out the map and inspected it, breathing a long sigh of relief as he recognized it as the copy Thomas Hariot had made. But it would not be expedient to take it back to Paris. He would hide it until he could report to Kit Marlowe and the others of the

Brotherhood. Something he could not do easily or frequently without risking the deep cover he had established within the Chevaliers d'Uriel. He thought for a moment, without pride, at the things he had had to do to gain their confidence, and told himself, as he always did, though always with a lessening conviction, that his ill deeds served a greater good.

He would hide the map here. It was a small church, but it was nondescript and it was within easy reach of Paris. If he could return for it, as and when might be necessary, he would do so.

He looked around. The tabernacle in this humble place of worship was no tabernacle at all, but an aumbry, a stone niche cut into a half pillar on the right of the altar and closed off by a walnut door with iron fittings. He opened the latch of the door and took out the Holy Vessels carefully. He removed the slender fillet of stone that formed the back of the little cupboard with his dagger, working carefully. He placed the map in the narrow space revealed there and then replaced the stone, working the crumbled mortar around its edges back into place. But it would always be dark at the back of the aumbry, and who would ever look closely? He regretted not having time to make better preparations, but he counted on being back to retrieve the map soon. That was all he could hope for, he told himself, as he replaced the Sacred Vessels and closed the latch.

The water dripped from the branches as he untethered his horse from the tree and mounted, swinging it round and heading for the St Jacques road again, to make his way back to the city.

Behind him, the villagers emerged from the huts and hovels they'd been watching him from. They made their way to the church and searched it thoroughly. They found nothing.

'He was praying,' their priest decided. He was a village man himself and only lettered enough to read the Mass. A clerk came monthly to manage the records. It was as much as the priest could do to remember the births and deaths, and the Plague had been bad lately. Of this incident he would make no account.

Don Carlos Alvarez took the news impassively. He liked this young, brown-haired Englishman. You could trust the English, he thought. They were good fighters, and uncomplicated. Thomas Fielding was like that. With God's help, they would retrieve the map. The politics of Europe were shifting, its leaders preoccupied. Their interests were here, not overseas. The Chevaliers had time on their side. Don Carlos was not, however, going to give that impression to his henchmen. Their Order had suffered a severe setback, and the Knight Commander would expect speedy rectification.

Richard Topcliffe, he knew, was sailing for Calais the next day, and would be at the Château d'Uriel by the end of the week. That gave him time to prepare a story good enough to pacify his chief, and lay contingency plans.

He paced the oak floor of the upper room in the

mansion on the rue des Francs-Bourgeois reflectively. The pale light from the mullioned windows caught the silver embroidery on his black doublet as he moved. His right hand drummed the basket-hilt of his sword.

'You have done well, Thomas,' he said at last.

'The mission was a failure. I take full responsibility.'

Alvarez raised a hand to silence him. 'I welcome your candour, but the real fault lies with the Director. The planning and the execution of the operation were beyond reproach.'

'If there were mistakes, Madame Ruzic has paid for them with her life,' Ballin said.

'The condesa's men shot her in the back with cross-bows as she was fighting the condesa for the map,' said Fielding. 'I arrived too late to save her, but, as you see, only by a miracle did I myself escape with my life.'

'It is, perhaps, God's will that she died attempting to recover the map from de Prieto,' Alvarez interrupted. 'Her punishment for failure would have been the same. In trying to prevent the condesa's escape, Ruzic has redeemed herself in part.' He lapsed into silence and continued his pacing. 'But escape she did,' he added, half to himself, biting his lower lip.

'What shall we do?' asked Ballin.

Alvarez came to a halt and leant on the table. He looked at each of the two men carefully. 'Now you must show me how truly dependable you are.'

'We will do anything to set things aright,' Fielding said, though his heart was racing with relief.

'Continue the search for the condesa,' said Alvarez.

'She will be making her way to Madrid with the map, and we must cut her off before she reaches her goal. The map must not fall into Spanish hands. Use all the men you need. The funds will be advanced to you.'

'The condesa has been sighted at Tours,' Fielding lied.

'Good. Then get after her. If you move fast, you should stop her well before she reaches Bordeaux.'

'If she takes that route.'

'I leave it to you to judge that.' Alvarez drew himself up. 'I will leave you now. Report to me at the chateau. Do not fail me, Sir Thomas.'

Fielding bowed slightly. There was something in Alvarez's conscious use of his title that carried the hint of a threat.

'And I?' said Ballin, fingering his collar nervously as if to reassure himself that his head was still attached to his neck.

Alvarez looked at him. 'You will find a new Director,' he said.

22

New York, the Present

It was 06h00 but the city lights still spangled the darkness beyond the windows. Laura Graves had not slept for twenty-four hours. Her head ached and her eyes were gritty, she was nervy from far too much espresso, she felt as if she'd been wearing her clothes for a week and she was in bad need of a shower and some hot food. But she was smiling as she turned to Leon Lopez and said:

'I think we've got it.'

She'd done some hard bargaining with her boss. Sir Richard Hudson had agreed to give Jack a reprieve before he sent a neutralizing unit after him, but only on condition that she produce something concrete for INTERSEC to throw the Treasury Department as proof that they were on track concerning the downward trend in the gold market, which continued in its slow but steady decline. Whoever was behind them was proceeding with caution, but the development was inexorable and financial centres worldwide were now waiting for some kind of demand to be made. It was getting that close. Looking out at the city, Laura found it extraordinary and frightening that it could go on functioning so happily, unaware of the great axe ready to fall on it – as it surely would on sister cities across the globe. So it wasn't just to save Jack's life that she had worked. But she did need him here now. She needed his positive outlook and his ability to look at things laterally.

'Tell me,' said Leon. Jack hadn't spoken for long on the phone, just long enough for them to make the arrangements necessary to get him out of there. If Jack could make it to the airport, there was an open, first-class, fully flexible ticket waiting for him at a VIP desk few knew the existence of, ready to bring him back to New York. But until he surfaced, Jack had sworn Leon to secrecy. Leon reckoned that Jack had guessed what Hudson had in mind for him.

'Gerrit de Vries buried his records deep, and there's no way I can get to his principals, yet,' Laura was saying, 'but I know all about *what* he was selling.'

Leon looked at her searchingly. 'Can you tell me?'

'I want to. I need to run it past you before I take it upstairs. It needs to be watertight.' She looked at her watch. Her time would be up in thirty minutes, and Sir Richard wasn't known for stretching deadlines. He knew that if she wasn't in his office by 06h30 he'd be picking up the yellow phone to 0551. He wouldn't call down to check first.

'OK.'

Working fast, she arranged a multi-page display on the large computer screen, two metres by one, which, defying budget strictures, she'd had installed on the far wall of Room 55 soon after she'd taken over as section head. She pulled a number of printouts towards her on the large white work table, and pushed others across to Leon as he took a seat opposite her. She snapped a button on her console and told her desktop Mac: 'No calls, no interruptions – unit condition: ultra-secure.' Then she turned to her colleague.

'This is it.' She referred to pictures and documents, onscreen and off, as she rapidly brought him up to speed with the results of her marathon research project. 'Gerrit de Vries sold a map of Amazonia to clients in Rio a little over two months ago and wound up dead, presumably because they didn't trust him to keep quiet about it – especially once he woke up to how they intended to use it.'

'Why's that?'

'Look at this picture. It shows the location – as far as I can see – of a lost city somewhere on a lake, or on an island on a lake which must be underground, or otherwise hidden, but which – and everything points to this – is Eldorado. The city of gold people have been looking for since word of it first reached European ears five hundred years ago.'

'It's a myth!'

'That's certainly what everybody thought – until now.'

'Go on.'

Her fingers skated over her keyboard and a fresh set of pictures appeared on the screen. 'The map I think he sold has an interesting provenance, and de Vries was meticulous. It was discovered in a church in a village just south of Paris when it was demolished to make way for a new one in 1750. It went into the private collection of a local aristocrat and stayed there for a century, before his heirs finally sold it. Various private collections in France and Italy since then. De Vries acquired it a couple of years ago at an auction at Hagelstam's in Helsinki.' She paused, checking through her notes. Leon watched her in admiration as her lean fingers flicked through the pages. She took off her glasses and looked at him keenly.

'Any competition at the auction?'

'Good question. No – nothing fierce.'

'Go on.'

'The map was made by the mathematician and astronomer Thomas Hariot in 1596 or 1597; Hariot was closely linked to Sir Walter Raleigh and Christopher Marlowe – they were members of a kind of semi-secret fraternity – and actually travelled on one of Raleigh's expeditions, but not the one we're concerned with.'

'Fraternity?'

'Humanists, freethinkers. They were accused of atheism. Marlowe was engaged in espionage, but there's nothing to link any of the others with that.'

'Where does all this lead us?'

'There would have been an original map, one actually made on the expedition. I can't trace it, so I don't know if it still exists. But –'

'But it's possible that de Vries sold the original, and not the Hariot copy?'

'That's the clincher. De Vries's records don't contain any picture of the map he sold.'

'Does it make any difference? I mean, if Hariot made a faithful copy of the original . . . ?'

'It does if the Chevaliers d'Uriel were involved. If they were after the map . . .'

Leon remembered the information he'd researched for Jack. 'Have you read up on them? They're a defunct group.'

'Are they? I'm beginning to wonder.' Laura looked at the wall clock. 'Shit. Gotta go. Study this, and then shut everything down before you lift the ultra-secure bar. I'll talk to you later.'

'How much of this are you giving Hudson?'

'As I said – I'll talk to you later.'

Leon watched her depart, wondering if he should have given her the news about Jack now. He decided to tell her after her meeting with Hudson. There'd be time enough then. He looked at the clock. He knew about the deadline. Christ, she'd be only just in time. *If* she managed to convince Hudson and buy some breathing space. He thought about Jack. He knew he'd be on his guard, but would that be enough?

What he didn't know was that, after the meeting, Laura was going back to her loft apartment to pack her bags. She had a flight to catch early the next day.

23

Paris, the Present

He gazed out angrily at the ornate sandstone buildings that lined the street, grey now under an overcast sky, but James Topcliffe's fury was tempered by a mounting sense of panic. He had a meeting with the North Koreans at Fontainebleau at 18hoo – six hours' time. Now this.

'It's a setback,' Ambroise Louvier, watching the Knight Commander and knowing his moods, ventured carefully, 'but it's not irredeemable.'

'Not irredeemable? It's the wrong map. Can you suggest something to tell the Koreans?' Two months' work wasted, Topcliffe thought, furiously. And years of preparation before that. He blanched at the thought of his own frustrated ambition. No – he would not fail! He would triumph yet!

Louvier wondered if his chief had taken his medication that day. The control drugs were meant to be a secret, but Louvier had means of finding things out. He also wondered how long Topcliffe could go on. There was little point to a Knight Commander who couldn't control himself. The Chevaliers might yet find the need to stage a coup within their own ranks. But not yet. Topcliffe could at least be useful to them if a scapegoat were needed.

'We must retrench now. Stop the operation,' Topcliffe continued.

'Why?'

Topcliffe looked at him angrily. 'If we don't have the gold, we will have depressed prices for nothing. Our whole enterprise is threatened.'

'Not as long as no one knows we don't have it. My advice is to continue the operation at a reduced level. That way, we may lose time, but not the initiative. The world is used to crashing markets and mortgaged economies, apologetic governments that don't know what to do, advised by banks that don't know what to do. Everybody is uncertain. There will never be a time as ripe as this again.'

Topcliffe considered this. The failed Amazonian expedition which had just reported back had proved that the map was useless. A huge expense – for nothing! But everything pointed to the existence of the place called Eldorado.

'There has to be another map,' he said, remembering something in the archive of the Chevaliers, which he reminded himself to read properly at the first opportunity. 'If this one is a forgery, or deliberately falsified, it must exist for a reason.'

'If another map exists, we must find it,' Louvier finished for him. 'We *will* find it. We must simply be aware that we may no longer be alone in the quest.'

'Are you talking about the girl?'

'Yes.'

Topcliffe was silent for a moment, biting his lower lip so hard that the skin turned almond-white. Then: 'I'll talk to the Koreans,' he said.

'Be nice to them. Butter them up. We are going to need a lot more money from them to finish this.'

Topcliffe didn't need to be told that. He was pretty confident the meeting would go well, if he could at the same time appeal to their greed and flatter them successfully. It's not hard to lull people into trusting you once you've convinced them you have a sure-fire winner to share with them. But explaining away the failed expedition would be a tall order. In the meantime . . .

'Where is the girl now?'

'She's in Rio. Struna and Agoli have her,' Louvier replied. 'She is quite safe.'

'Have they damaged her?'

'As far as I know, she is intact. I gave orders that no force was to be used until I cleared it with you. But she is a tough little bitch and she will need breaking.'

Topcliffe thought for a moment. 'Get them to bring her here. Use the Cessna. Struna and Agoli must fly with her in person. I am closing Rio down. We'll operate from here from now on.'

'No one else knows about her. The man we took with her is dead. We checked on him. A private detective with an office in the Bronx. He was her back-up. Unimportant.'

'Someone will wonder that she hasn't reported. She wouldn't have used some crummy gumshoe.'

'We think she was working alone.'

Topcliffe looked at Louvier in surprise. 'That cannot be.'

Louvier was about to shrug, but desisted, fearful of increasing his chief's ill-suppressed rage. 'We thought she'd be Treasury Department. We've nothing to link her to anyone. There are no trails we haven't followed up. We've found no passport, nothing.'

'But you haven't tortured her?'

'As I said, they haven't touched her. Agoli wanted to apply just a little pressure, but –' Louvier shrugged, but it passed unnoticed.

'I want her here now. I'll squeeze the truth out of her.'

'She's very high risk.'

Topcliffe opened a drawer in his desk and reached inside to stroke the choke-pear he had just acquired as an addition to his small collection of antique instruments of torture. It was brass, made in Augsburg in the fifteenth century. It was oiled and cleaned, and in perfect working condition. The price of $500 had seemed very reasonable.

'We'll dispose of her when we're done,' he said.

24

London, Early 1600s

Well, it was over. It didn't matter about the map any more. Raleigh could keep it. Not that it would do him any good in the Tower.

It had been an eventful twelve months, Sir Robert Cecil reflected, after the diplomatic hiccup following the ambush by highwaymen of the Condesa de Prieto on the St Jacques road. They'd written ballads, though, about her daring escape and her journey back to Madrid disguised as a pageboy; she'd turned up at her cousin's *palacio* three months later, where the duke gave her an affectionate welcome. A search had been made for the missing map and letters, but had been without success. It was a pity, because the Spanish remained suspicious of English double-dealing and an alternative gesture of good-will had to be found.

The opportunity had come when, a scant four months after his coronation, a plot to dethrone the new king, James of Scotland, was uncovered and its principal conspirators – all men of rank – unmasked. The plot, investigated by the Lieutenant of the Tower of London, Sir William Wade, threw up a handful of people Cecil found it useful to sideline, but the cherry on the cake was Sir Walter Raleigh.

Cecil smiled at the recollection. Of course, some evidence had to be cooked up, but what a delicious dish to serve Philip III and his sidekick, the Duke of Lerma. And now, Raleigh was in the Tower and likely to stay there for ever, James was doing what he was told, and it was easy to keep him happy as long as he was left alone to enjoy his two current passions: bedding young men and hunting witches. Cecil would keep an eye on him but, so far, he seemed a compliant ruler who'd keep the Catholics in their place. Above all, he had no bellicose ambitions, and liked to keep a tight purse.

There was no more talk of expeditions to the New World either, except from that stubborn bastard Richard Hakluyt. But his ambitions were manageable.

Cecil poured himself a generous glass of Bordeaux. Things were working out perfectly.

25

Rio de Janeiro and New York, the Present

Jack Marlow knew where to collect the ticket – if Leon had been able to place it there. He had no way of confirming this, but he had no choice. He left the *pensão* at dusk. The first flight available to him was on TAM at 23h14. He'd be in New York, if all went well, at about 07h00 the following morning.

If all went well. Leaving the pension, he paused to smoke a Camel before walking two blocks, and then let three taxis go before he hailed one. Looking around one last time, consulting every last, instinctive nerve, he got in and gave the driver his destination.

From then on, things went smoothly. At the airport, he made his way to the VIP desk and gave the code name Leon had agreed with him.

'Samuel Crowe?' said the desk clerk.

'Yes.'

'Travelling with?'

'My sister, Charlotte.'

The clerk nodded. Code exchange accepted. First hurdle jumped. Jack looked at his watch. Plenty of time. Maybe too much. But he hadn't been able to wait it out at the pension in town. He had to be on his way. Among people. Safer that way. He waited as the ticket printed. The clerk handed it to him. 'We can get you checked in and through to Departures now, if you like. But you have a long wait.'

'That'd be best.'

'Regular boarding won't start for a while yet.'

'I'll buy a book.' He'd had to abandon the life of Raleigh he'd brought with him from New York. If anyone had found that, and put two and two together . . . Well, too late to worry about that now.

He waited while the clerk completed the formalities. Fifteen minutes later, he was in the departure lounge. He went to the bookstore and bought a copy of the *New Yorker* and a paperback novel, *Samba-Enredo*. He found a bar and ordered a Jameson on the rocks, settled himself in a booth with a view of the entrance, and opened the magazine. But he couldn't read. His thoughts kept turning to Natasha.

He told himself the best way of locating her again was to get home and use the resources of INTERSEC, but the idea of abandoning her to her fate in this city nagged at him, despite the professional rationale which told him he was doing the right thing. They wouldn't have killed her, he told himself again, trying not to think of the other things they could have done. But INTERSEC would have to find her, because she was a link they needed. The sooner he was at his desk and able to use Leon's help – and Laura's, God willing – to set things in motion, the better. The ten hours of flying time that stretched ahead of him seemed like an eternity.

He shook the magazine and tried again to concentrate on an article that had caught his eye, something about Afghanistan. He'd seen service there in the early days – and what a waste of time that mission had turned out to be. These days, he tried not to question what he did too much, not to think about the why of it all. In his darkest moments, it seemed that he had lost control of the tiller in his life, or as if his career had just been one long crawl further and further into a lobster pot. But wasn't it like that for most people? Hadn't Thoreau said that most men lead lives of quiet desperation? Here he was, a well-paid little boy with his finger in the dyke, aware now only that the dyke wall was cracking all around him and there was nothing he could do to stop it bursting. A well-paid little boy of thirty-nine in a profession where life expectancy was generally thirty-five and they turned the volume down on you, via a long period of psychological debriefing, at the age of forty. The ones who lasted longest were the admin boys, the Richard Hudsons of this world, who moved the pieces around the board but had never experienced what it felt like to be one of them – knight, bishop, rook or pawn – out in the field, taking and being taken.

But there was no more time for such thoughts. He had read three or four lines of the article, taking none of it in, and now, as his eye wandered from the page to the concourse beyond the bar, he stiffened.

The concourse wasn't particularly full, and the travellers milling about it were nothing out of the ordinary, not even the heavy-set, balding man with a crew cut and dressed in a green check shirt and grey slacks. The man was with a thin, elderly blonde in a short-sleeved blue blouse, her hair tied in a black velvet band. Just an ordinary couple of mid-Western tourists on their way home.

But Jack watched them as they moved slowly across the black-and-white-speckled tile floor towards a departures board. Only once, for a fraction of a second, did the woman turn her head towards him. Then she was saying something to the man and, for another small moment, they paused in their walk. It was enough.

There'd be a third agent somewhere out there, too. Jack knew all about 0551's way of working. He'd had Leon hack into their files some time back, as insurance, and he'd familiarized himself with the faces of their five operatives.

Of course their nickname was common knowledge: The Cleaners.

That bastard Hudson.

The question was, where would they strike?

They hadn't made any kind of move at Galeão, but Marlow hadn't expected them to. He took his first-class window seat, noting that those immediately around him were unoccupied and wondering how much of an advantage that would be to him or to them – but 0551 wouldn't be that obvious. He wasn't surprised to see the couple board the plane a short time after he had, the woman leading the man. They didn't even look at him as they passed down the aisle. They would have seats close enough to make a move if the need arose. He kept a discreet eye on the rest of the passengers, but the only likely third member of their party was a tall, hefty young man with a stubble beard whose face didn't match any of those Jack had seen on file.

'Enjoy your flight . . .' Jack caught the trail of the purser's announcement. As soon as he could, he ordered another whiskey, but when it arrived he barely touched it, and waved away the meals when they came, to the surprise of the cabin attendant. His book lay neglected and he ignored the in-flight entertainment, keeping his light off, staying alert in the half-dark. One of them could stick a hypodermic in his wrist as they passed, and in the sleeping silence of an all-night flight it could be hours before he was discovered – a heart-attack case.

He spent the long hours concentrating on where to focus his search.

New York was one hour behind Rio. Jack was seated on the left of the plane and it was a relief to see, through the windows on the other side of the fuselage, the pale fingers of dawn grabbing the edge of the eastern horizon. He stretched, and eased his feet in their shoes. Christ, but it had been a long night. He took a sip of his neglected whiskey. It tasted brackish, and he waited for them to serve coffee. The coffee, when it came, was very good.

Jack disembarked at the head of the handful of first-class passengers and moved quickly along the air-bridge once he was off the plane. They'd missed – or chosen not to take – their opportunity on the aircraft, and he wondered now if they were deliberately holding off, waiting for an execution order to come through. There would still be ample time at JFK, on the way into town, or at his apartment. He resisted the impulse to look behind him as he went through Arrivals, through Customs and on to the main concourse. But even there he could not afford to relax. There had been plenty of successful assassinations which had used crowds as cover.

And despite the early hour, it was already busy. He moved steadily through the crowd, hesitating before approaching the taxi ranks. It would have been too risky to get Leon to arrange a car. None of his pursuers was visible. But, as Jack hesitated, he saw someone coming towards him, someone with a look of pure astonishment on her face. Astonishment – and relief. He recognized her with equal surprise as she rushed through the crowds towards him.

'What the hell are you doing here?' said Laura Graves, throwing her arms around him and hugging him as if her life depended on it.

26

Paris, the Present

Natasha Fielding tried to take stock.

The room they'd put her in was large, well lit and opulently furnished. Heavy yellow curtains draped the tall windows, and a soft yellow light bathed the Empire tables, sofas and chairs with which the room was furnished. Landscapes by Corot and Constable adorned the white walls.

Nobody had spoken to her since they had taken her. Not the men who drove her back to the house and locked her in a basement room, nor those who had come afterwards and manhandled her to the floor before injecting her with a drug that rendered her unconscious. She had a hazy memory of travelling, in a car, in a plane, in a car again, at times when it always seemed to be night, but when she once regained consciousness she felt a sharp pinprick and sank back into oblivion again.

Since they had allowed her to recover, she had been confined to this room. Two silent attendants, a man and a woman, wearing hoods and latex gloves, had visited her once, to bring food and water, and a third person came to monitor her blood pressure and give her another shot. From its effect, she guessed it was an anti-depressant. There was a curtained-off chemical WC in a corner of the room. She had been escorted to it once.

She had only her body clock to tell her how much time had passed, and that told her: not long. She was heavily chained at the wrists and ankles. Her wrists were fettered in front of her and gave her only enough freedom to pick up the supermarket sandwiches and the beaker of water. They had watched while she ate and drank, to ensure that she did. At first, she'd refused. The man forced her jaws open while the woman crammed the food into her mouth, which they'd then held shut. The water, Natasha needed.

They hadn't harmed her yet, but she knew why she was there and she couldn't get the memory of what they had done to Jack out of her mind, so she was in a state of constant and growing apprehension that she couldn't shake off, even though she knew that was exactly what they wanted to induce in her.

On the fourth visit, they undid her chains and stripped her to her underwear before manhandling her into a heavy chair which they had covered in the kind of thick polythene sheeting builders use as dust-covers. The chair already stood on another polythene sheet, and there was a plain table near it. They strapped her to the chair using heavy duct tape. Silently, they produced and laid on the table three small artefacts. The first was an implement with a metal body, a turning-screw at one end and four spoon-like sections at the other; the second was an iron object that looked like a vice; and the third an iron carding-comb, its teeth filed sharp. All looked old, but they were clean and oiled and had been meticulously cared for.

They let her look at them for a full three minutes before covering her eyes with duct tape. She had recognized two, and her brain shrank from them.

Then they left. She heard them gently close the door behind them. There was no sound of a key in the lock.

How long she sat there she didn't know. The chair's upholstery was hard and the polythene sheeting slipped under her whenever she attempted what little movement she could, but after her initial struggles, she realized escape was impossible. The two objects she'd recognized – the carding-comb and the thumbscrews – were instruments of torture that had been in use for centuries. The pear-shaped implement was not familiar to her, and she could not stop herself wondering what it was. Her psychological training should have kept her calm in situations like this, but it had all been a long time ago and possibly not of the best. She had never felt so alone or more terrified. She didn't know whether the waiting was worse than what would come at the end of it. She knew only that the waiting was part of the torture.

But it ended at last, as all things do, and she breathed faster as the door opened. Two sets of footsteps, but still not a word was spoken. She heard someone – a man – breathing close to her, and smelt him: a smell of cologne overlying another, musky odour. She heard metallic sounds as one of the instruments of torture was picked up from the table. She felt cold metal as someone attached the thumbscrew to the fingers of her left hand and tightened it so the jaws fitted snugly.

'I think you know what this is, Natasha,' said the man. A voice she did not recognize. 'It is from my collection. You'll have noticed the carding-comb too. Very primitive, but also very effective. I believe they were made red-hot before the inquisitors used them to tear the flesh of their prisoners. I imagine the method usually produced the answers they required.' There was a pause before the voice continued crisply: 'But you may not have recognized the third tool of the trade. It is called a choke-pear. Some have called it the pear of anguish. I will explain how it works. I insert it into your mouth and, when I turn the screw, the leaves open, forcing your mouth apart. You will only be able to nod assent when I use this on you. But if I am obliged to do so, you had better make up your mind quickly, before your jaw is forced from your face. You will not be able to speak at all after that.'

There was a long pause. 'Do you understand?'

'*Va te faire foutre.*'

'Natasha, it is foolish to be brave. Your bravery will resolve nothing. But I have no wish to injure you. You have not been here long, and I have other business to attend to. You have caused problems, which I must solve. But when I return, I will expect your cooperation. In the meantime, you will be left alone. No one will come to you.'

A gloved hand stroked her skin, near her breasts. She tried in vain to draw away from it.

'It would be a pity to ruin such beauty,' the voice said, as the hand moved from her breasts to stroke her cheek, the thumb roughly grazing her lips.

27

London, in the Reign of King James

It had been a long imprisonment, but now he was free. It had been a long wait, but he had never given up. The death of Sir Robert Cecil four years earlier had given him hope, but the hope had been dashed, and he resigned himself with patience to his fate. But now, everything had changed. Now, as the spring buds appeared on the trees, a new dawn and a new start were presenting themselves to him.

Kit greeted him warmly. Both men were older and heavier set, but the fire hadn't gone out of their eyes.

'Who have I to thank for my release?' Raleigh said.

'You have never been forgotten. There are those who have never tired of trying to secure your release. But we have a new ally: the King's most recent favourite, George Villiers. We organized a little gift to his brother – of £1,500 – and he's shown his gratitude.'

'Thank you.'

'There's more good news,' Kit said. 'But we have to move fast – the King may change his mind.'

'What are you talking about?' Raleigh asked, but already he thought he knew, and hope was beginning to rise in his breast.

'A new voyage,' Kit replied. 'That is – if you still want it. If you are up to it. We are no longer young men.'

'Want it? It is the thing I would most happily give my life for.'

'That is the answer I expected!'

'You still have the map?'

'Yes.'

'It has been a long wait.'

'But the fruit has ripened at last.'

They met Thomas Hariot at a house by the river in Chelsea, just beyond the western borders of London. The place had been chosen for its seclusion, and Raleigh noted the number of guards discreetly stationed around it as they drove up in the coach through the rain which fell, as it always fell, relentlessly, on the English capital.

The initial greetings between the men assembled in the great chamber of the house were warm, but once they had been exchanged the company drew round the fire which blazed in the massive hearth to discuss the tremendous venture which lay as close as ever to Raleigh's heart. On a table near them lay the map.

'We have long since solved the problem of the four symbols on the map,' Thomas Hariot began. 'The dog and the condor we have established. The other two, as I thought, represent constellations, though they are represented in a way I have never encountered before. But, without any doubt, they represent what we call

Canis Major and Lepus. The Greater Dog and the Hare.'

'Orion's hunting dog, one of the two which chase the hare across the heavens,' Raleigh said. 'I have steered by Sirius often enough to know them, though I would not have recognized them from what is pictured here. But old Essex was in haste when he drew them.'

'Why are they there?' asked Kit. 'Do we know?'

'They are emblems of speed. Perhaps drawn from the speed at which the sun's light crosses the portals of your temple as it crosses them.'

'The time is right for you, Walter,' said Kit. 'But do you think you can reach the temple in time?'

'Midsummer's Day, or close to it, is the time. If I make haste now with our preparations, I should succeed, if it be God's will.'

'We have other things to consider as well as time,' Hariot said, as he drew the map to him. 'Where is Sir Thomas Fielding?'

'He is expected.'

Kit and Hariot looked at each other. 'He is late,' said Hariot.

'He has been an officer of the Chevaliers for many years now. If they doubted his loyalty, they would have exposed him by now.'

'They have been sleeping. Ever since the copy disappeared.'

'We should have retrieved it.'

'No – it is safe where it is, and we may have need of

it again. We must concentrate our forces now on the job in hand.'

'But –'

'This is the original? The one drawn by Francis Sparrow?' Raleigh, who had been examining the map closely, interrupted them. 'It is years since I have seen it, and my eyes are worn. But the map is incorrect.'

Kit looked at him keenly. 'In what way?'

'Something is missing.'

'Where?'

'Here – close to where the temple lies. The location –'

Kit laid a hand on his arm. 'It is well,' he said. 'All is as it should be. I will explain.'

Hariot smiled, and, taking a square of paper from a pocket on his belt, laid it on the map. 'Is all clear now?'

'It shows what is missing,' said Raleigh. 'But –'

'This is our insurance. The Chevaliers d'Uriel must never have this key. Keep it safe, and apart.' Hariot handed Raleigh the paper, then rolled the map carefully before giving that to him as well.

'I have disguised the true location of the temple on the map. Or rather, I have concealed it,' Kit said. 'The square of paper shows it. If the map falls into the wrong hands, they will never know the location, though it is still hidden there. The paper is the key. In case of danger, destroy it. Otherwise, use it well.'

'I will outrun the Chevaliers!'

'Walter, you will. But you must keep a steady mind.'

There was a noise in the hall outside, and Thomas Fielding hurried into the chamber a minute later, brushing the rain from his cloak and sweeping his cap off his head. His leather jerkin and breeches were stained with mud, and his features were drawn and weary. All turned to him.

'What is the news from Paris?' asked Hariot.

'They know Walter is set free,' answered Fielding. 'They are on the move.'

'Then we must hurry,' said Kit.

'You must take heed, Kit,' Fielding said. 'The Knight-Commander has ordered your death.'

'Then he will be disappointed,' Kit replied, though he felt a shadow passing over his soul.

There had been twelve years of peace, and it was no longer easy to raise money for expeditions of the kind loved by Queen Elizabeth, but somehow it had to be found. Efforts in the City were questioned by Ambassador Gondomar, and King James had to listen, as he was eager to arrange a Spanish marriage for his son Charles. But at last the business was concluded, to the embarrassment of nobody, and by that time a ship, paid for on credit, stood ready in Phineas Pett's yard.

Raleigh took the title of general of his expedition, and set sail on the *Destiny*, with his son as her captain.

Several who watched him depart with his little fleet thought he would turn pirate and never return.

Thomas Hariot prayed he would. Since their preparations had begun, the Chevaliers had struck at them, and struck hard. It was a miracle that Raleigh was sailing at all.

28

New York, the Present

'You didn't *tell* me?' Laura shouted.

'It was better to keep you out of the loop,' said Jack.

She didn't reply, because she knew the real reasons. She had two to choose from. One was that they didn't want to compromise her credibility with Sir Richard. The other was that they'd been afraid she'd tell Sir Richard. She couldn't blame them for that – she'd done it once before, and that had cost Jack his job and given the leadership of Section 15 to her. But it rankled.

All that, however, was more than compensated for by the fact that Jack was safe and back in the fold, and that they'd been able to get the dogs of Section 0551 called off in the nick of time. And the meeting at the airport had saved her a trip to Rio which would have been difficult to explain. It was hard enough keeping her own deep-seated reasons from Jack. But the air had been cleared and there was enough to do to prevent anyone from dwelling on her actions.

'We've established the existence of a second map. The map the Chevaliers bought from de Vries – the Hariot copy – was deliberately inaccurate,' said Leon, making his report. 'I've sourced archives worldwide and everything points to a lost original, probably made by a guy called Francis Sparrow who was with Raleigh on the expedition of 1595.'

'But how can we be sure that the Chevaliers don't have that original?' Jack asked.

'Because the gold market has slowed. If they were sure they controlled enough of the stuff to break the hold gold has on world economies, they'd have continued purchasing at the same rate as before. They must be at panic stations,' Laura said.

'But they won't give up?' queried Leon.

'They must be in up to their necks. And they must have backers to fund the purchasing.'

'Of course. And once they've got the gold –'

'– they'll have total control. They can twist money values any way they like. They'll probably do it through a rogue nation or a complex combination of multinationals, but they'll be the ones pulling the strings,' said Jack.

'To what end?' Leon asked.

'Throughout their history, they have been committed to bringing society back to a moral and ethical Square One. A kind of international Year Zero,' Laura said.

'Yes, but that is perfectly insane.' Leon again.

'Their thinking hasn't evolved since the days of their involvement with the Inquisition. As the world has become increasingly materialistic, increasingly focused on short-term profit, at the expense of the environment, at the expense of any moral or ethical considerations, so their outrage has increased. It's insane, but isn't what angers them insane too? What has happened to world economies since 2008 has given them a perfect opportunity to take action. After centuries of waiting,' Jack explained.

'A perfect opportunity is right,' said Leon.

'They've probably been plotting this for years. Imagine how much money and what kind of infrastructure you'd need to set this sort of operation up,' said Laura.

'They've been planning this one since 2007,' Jack said. 'When the first rumblings of the financial crisis began.'

'But what gave them the Eldorado idea?' asked Leon.

Laura said, 'I spent twenty-four hours straight on this. The Chevaliers have known about the Eldorado story as specifically linked to Raleigh since 1595 – the time of his expedition. The Order may have lain dormant for decades, even centuries, at a time, but it never disintegrated, and its core idea was passed down from generation to generation. Its leaders saw their chance in the financial crash, they knew the history of the expedition, and that woke them from their long sleep. They moved heaven and earth to find the map which was the key. When they thought they had it, they became over-confident, they overplayed their hand, just like any bank might – it's ironic, really – and now they must be desperate to get hold of the original.'

'Raleigh's discoveries were discredited,' said Leon. 'It's well known he played up what he'd found to curry favour at home.'

'Discredited for a reason,' Jack said.

'To bury the secret?'

'Exactly.'

'Jesus!'

'The most important thing for us to do now is find Natasha,' said Jack.

Laura looked at him. 'I know you've briefed us on her, but is she really so important?'

'She's the one key we've got.'

'How can you be so sure? She doesn't check out with the Treasury Department. They don't know anything about her, and they have no reason to hold out on us.'

'All the more reason.'

'But we don't know who she's working for.'

'The important thing is that we know *what* she's working for. She's on our side. If it weren't for her, I wouldn't be here now.'

'So she's kind of the flip side of a damsel in distress.' Laura ignored the warning look Leon shot her. 'I can't justify resources on a rescue mission based on flimsy grounds.'

'Lose her, and we'll lose the trail.'

'But we don't know where she is – where even to begin! For all you know, it may be too late already.'

'They won't kill her until they're sure they've got the information they need out of her.'

'But they won't wait for ever.'

'They may believe she knows the location of the true map. If she does, we need her.'

'Pretty big "if".'

'Did Sir Richard give you clearance to contact our representative in Rio?' asked Jack.

'Yes,' she replied reluctantly.

'We gave her the information on the place you were held,' Leon said. 'She checked it out.'

'And?' Jack said quickly.

'She says it's closed up.'

'Since when?'

'It was like that when she got to it.'

'She's sure of the place?'

'Everything you told us, we gave her.'

Jack nodded. 'It makes sense that they'd move base. They'll have taken her with them.' He paused impatiently. 'But where? Here? London?'

Leon said, 'I think we should try Paris.'

Jack looked at him.

'I got something through on that old story from the Agência,' Leon said. 'You know, that lost-island stuff from the eighties? The Chevaliers d'Uriel were mixed up in that.'

'Where does this lead us?'

'Their traditional base was in the Château d'Uriel in France, you remember?'

'Yes, but it was destroyed in the Second World War.'

'But not their Paris base.'

'Go on.'

Leon drew a file towards him and withdrew a print-out. 'There's a large building, an old mansion, behind the rue des Francs-Bourgeois in the fourth arrondissement. I've tracked back on its history and, in around 1600, it belonged to a Spaniard, Carlos Alvarez. It was in his name, anyway. Alvarez had connections to the Spanish Court, but also to the Inquisition, and to a breakaway group of some standing.'

'The Chevaliers?'

'Maybe.'

'Why didn't you bring this up before?'

'We hadn't made a connection. But don't get your hopes up.'

'Why the hell not?'

'Because it's been leased for some years to a company with a business address in the Aleutian Islands. Overseas and General.'

'Natasha mentioned that name to me.' Marlow was already grabbing his coat. 'Give me the address.'

'You can't just go –' Laura protested.

'It's our only shot, and there's no time to bugger about.'

'You'll need authorization.'

'This time, you'll get it. But I'm not waiting for it. Tell Hudson to stop farting around if he wants this job done. Leon –'

'Yes, Jack?'

'Get on to the map. The real one. Pull out every stop. The Chevaliers will already be looking for it.'

'Where to begin?'

'Your problem. Just do it!'

'Jack!' Laura cried. 'For God's sake, you haven't debriefed from Rio yet. Christ, you've only just got off the *plane*!'

But the door was already swinging shut behind him.

29

London, in the Reign of King James

It had taken place before Raleigh sailed, and neither Hariot nor any of the other members of the Brotherhood had been able to prevent it.

'What was Kit doing in Stratford?' was Hariot's first question.

'We all know his secret. He'd taken over that playwright Shakespeare's identity, and we know it worked. But after Shakespeare died, Kit made one or two visits up there. It was where Shakespeare was born. Something to do with maintaining the cover,' George Chapman replied.

'How did it happen?'

Hariot was seated with Thomas Fielding and Chapman in the long gallery of the Brotherhood's London base. The pale-grey light typical of the city poured through the tall windows and spread over the panelled walls.

'He was off guard,' said Fielding.

'Not like him.'

'I warned him. But after I'd managed to dispose of the map the condesa was taking to Spain, I think he felt entitled to relax a little. He had been under much strain before he gave the true map to Walter.'

'They killed him because they thought he still had it?'

'That is all I can assume.'

'How did they do it?'

'Poison.'

Hariot shook his head sadly. 'Poor Kit.'

'Everyone thinks Kit Marlowe died years ago. Now, he will not even lie in a grave that is his own,' Chapman said. 'In Stratford, they think it is Will Shakespeare who has passed away.'

'And the Chevaliers?'

'They continue the search,' said Fielding. 'We must ensure that no harm comes to Walter before he embarks.'

'But he still has much to prepare before he sails,' Chapman said.

'Raleigh must not be told. We know his weaknesses. Keep a close watch on him. Alert the others,' Hariot said. 'Thomas – return to Paris with all speed. And may God watch over you.'

30

Two Years Later

It was not an auspicious return. All through the long voyage home, Sir Walter Raleigh had dreaded it. He felt his years for the first time in his life, and the weight of failure and disgrace lay heavy on him.

It had been a disaster. He had not got close to Eldorado, and now all was lost. All.

In his London house, he awaited the worst, and considered the foul cards Fortune had dealt him. The first, and worst, had been the ill-considered attack on the Spanish outpost of San Tomé. It had happened accidentally: a stand-off and a few chance shots fired without his authority. He had not even been there, but nothing could excuse it, and nothing now could be a worse punishment for him than the one meted out to him there, for in the attack his headstrong, twenty-five-year-old son Wat had fallen.

When news of the action had been brought to him at his base further down the Orinoco, he knew there could be no escape. He would have to return home and die.

Back home, those fears and convictions were confirmed in the hour he spent closeted with Hariot, who delivered another blow when he told Raleigh of the murder of Kit Marlowe in Stratford-on-Avon.

'Why did you not tell me of it before my departure?'

'You would have delayed. You would have sought vengeance.'

'I had made an undertaking to the King.'

Hariot laid a calming hand on his arm. 'Walter, you know King James hates you. Only your popularity with Parliament saved you – that, and your reputation. But the action at San Tomé went against all the agreements you signed before you sailed not to engage with the Spanish under any circumstances. Your actions –'

'They were not my actions! I did not order the attack!'

'But you are blamed for it. You are declared traitor. It is you who must bear the responsibility.'

'My son is dead!'

Hariot nodded. 'A harsh blow, and I grieve for you. But there is little time. We must think of our survival. The King is in close collaboration with the Spanish ambassador . . .'

'The Conde Gondomar?'

'Yes.'

'But Gondomar knows Alvarez in Paris!'

'Gondomar would deny it. But Fielding has sent us word of his links with the Chevaliers.'

'Then he will seek my death.'

'He has already demanded it. As a condition of a continued peace between England and Spain.'

Raleigh bowed his head. In his mind's eye, he already saw the Block before him. He sighed. Soon he would join his beloved son. 'I have had a long and good voyage,' he said.

'It has not been without its storms.'

'But now I am in harbour at last.'

'They will arrest you soon,' said Hariot. 'And I have no words of comfort, though the Brotherhood will do what it can to aid Bess and your family when it is over. No harm will come to them.'

'King James is not worthy of the crown he wears!'

'He is not the old Queen. But the world has changed. It has become – more pragmatic. We intercepted letters. James sent word to Gondomar in October: *His Majesty is very disposed and determined against Raleigh, and will join with the King of Spain in ruining him.*'

'Then it is over indeed.'

Hariot looked at his friend closely. 'Where is the true map?'

Raleigh turned a face of great sorrow towards him. 'It is *lost*.'

'What?'

'After the action at San Tomé.'

'It fell into Spanish hands?'

'I do not know. Perhaps it is destroyed.'

Hariot thought fast. 'But what of the key – the slip of paper we gave you, which alone could show the true location of the city of gold?'

Raleigh smiled. 'That, I still have.'

'Give it to me!'

The urgency in his friend's voice startled Raleigh, but he hastened to open a small, brass-bound casket with a key taken from a chain around his neck. From it he withdrew the piece of parchment with the criss-crossing lines of tributaries and the island marked on the lake at their confluence. Hariot all but snatched it from him, and instantly held it over a candle, holding it there until the last ashes floated into the air and the flame burnt his fingers.

'*All* may not be lost,' he whispered, half to himself. He knew Kit had lied to Sir Robert Cecil about placing a copy of the false map among Raleigh's possessions. And Fielding had dealt with the one carried by the Condesa de Prieto.

Nothing remained but the true one. And it retained its secret.

'What do you mean?' Raleigh said.

Hariot stood. 'My friend, I must take my leave. You will understand that I have matters of the utmost importance to attend to.'

At that moment they heard a commotion in the hall below the chamber where they sat. Soldiers.

'They have come for me,' said Raleigh. 'Already.'

'The King wishes to lose no time in your dispatch. I commend you to God, my friend. Do not betray our cause.'

'For the sake of my life?' Sir Walter laughed. 'Thomas, I wish you well. Look after Bess for me. And get word to Fielding. If anyone can find the map, it is he.'

Hariot left the room and sought the back stairs, leaving by a gate which led into a cobbled alleyway. A thin rain had begun to fall.

31

Paris, the Present

Jack Marlow knew Paris well, but had already lost six hours through the time difference between New York and the French capital, and as he drove through the broad boulevards south-eastward towards the narrower, older streets of the Marais district, he both fought his impatience and prayed that they were playing the right card. It was early morning, and the sun shone brightly on the pale stonework of the stately buildings, glinting on the bright-green leaves of the trees that lined the streets. There were few people about yet, and little traffic, and, despite everything that had happened to him in the City of Light, Jack still felt a tug at his heartstrings at having left it. One day, he told himself, his ghosts would have faded and he would be back, and though part of his mind told him that was only a dream, another part told him he had the power to make it a reality.

But now he concentrated his thoughts on Natasha. He had brought the lightest kit possible with him, prepped himself on arrival in one of the restrooms at CDG, and was now dressed in comfortable black trainers, close-fitting black jeans and T-shirt, and a black Gore-Tex bomber jacket over a lightweight body-harness. The Paris INTERSEC bureau was on red alert, but it had been agreed to keep the operation low-scale; he would handle the initial search alone. Too much activity risked drawing attention, and no one knew what level of counter-surveillance the Chevaliers operated.

He turned left off the long rue des Francs-Bourgeois north into the rue Elzévir, at a well-remembered corner on which one of his favourite café-restaurants, the Camille, stood under its red awning, and parked the Audi rental a short distance along the narrow street. He walked back at a steady pace and turned left, passing the leafy courtyard of the Musée Carnavalet before he slowed, looking up at the buildings above the glass fronts of the fashion boutiques. The huge portes-cochères of the address he sought were closed, but a small door was cut into one of the high, wooden gates – designed originally to allow coaches to pass through – and, next to them, a metal keypad was sunk into a block of stone at shoulder height. You gained access by tapping in a four-digit code, which he did not have, but there was another plain button at the bottom of the pad which, during working hours, bypassed the code if pressed. Usually.

The day was sufficiently advanced for it to be activated, and he tried it, but the door didn't budge. Looking quickly up and down the street, he took a thin sheet of specially treated tissue from his wallet and placed it over the keypad. He breathed a sigh of relief – he hadn't believed it could possibly work when the Equipment Unit at INTERSEC had explained it to him, but there were the faint grease marks which betrayed the buttons most frequently used: 1-5-9-5.

He heard the soft click which told him he had access, and gently pushed the door inwards.

The grey courtyard beyond was deserted, but he kept close to the wall inside the arch, and from there scanned the tall windows that looked down on him from three storeys. They were without curtains, and the glass reflected blankly back at him.

He could see a CCTV camera halfway up the opposite left-hand corner of the courtyard, and assumed that there would be another, out of his line of vision, on the right. At the centre of the facing wall there was a glass-fronted double door, and he could see another in the same position to the left. A third would be to the right. The cameras were fixed-position installations, and he knew that, pressed to the wall inside the entrance arch, he was out of their range, but he could not rule out sound monitors. He waited, but nothing stirred in the building that brooded above him.

But within the archway was another door: very small, scarcely more than a hatch. It was as old as the building itself, made of thick wood bound with iron, and its lock was massive and forbidding. It looked as if it hadn't been used for many, many years. Still keeping close to the wall, he bent down to examine it, reaching into his harness to produce the titanium multi-tool he'd need for his task. But as he crouched he heard a creaking sound, followed by a whirring as the main gates started to swing open. He flattened himself against the wall and froze as the right-hand wing, with its heavy, iron bosses, moved closer and closer to him.

It stopped five centimetres from his chest. If it had opened flush to the wall, he would have been a dead man. Forcing himself to breathe evenly, he looked to his right. Through the gap between the gate and the wall he could see part of a large white car swing into the courtyard. He heard the driver walk round to the car's right side to open the rear passenger door, and this he could just make out. From it emerged a short, stout man, middle-aged, with reddish hair and a beard. He was followed by another, taller man of about the same age whom Jack recognized instantly as Ambroise Louvier. Louvier carried a slim, black briefcase. The men disappeared from Jack's line of vision in a moment, but he heard the central door of the courtyard open and close.

His right foot was jammed against the hatch, and, testing it with his heel, he felt a slight give. He hadn't long before the gates would close again, and he had no idea whether or not the driver had remained with the car. Bracing himself against the wood of the open gate, he pushed hard with his heel against the hatchway and felt it give more. One more effort, and his heel swung backwards into space. As the gates of the porte-cochère began to close again, he slid backwards and downwards into the open hatchway, banging his knees and elbows on the stone stairs that led down from it. He had just time to push the hatchway door closed behind him as he heard the main gates clang shut.

He was lying prone on the flight of stone steps. The darkness was total.

He gave himself a moment, then twisted his body round and stood up gingerly. He could just stand under the low arch that coved the ceiling of the staircase. There was blood on the left knee of his jeans, but he felt the wound and tested the leg. Just a cut. He'd live with that. He descended some way before he took out the small Maglite LED. Its light showed him that the stairs ended at the mouth of a dusty, stone-lined area that smelt of mould and long disuse. In one corner, he could pick out a couple of crumbling wooden crates, and, beyond them, another archway framed the start of a corridor. It was low, but relatively broad, and stone-lined. It must have dated back to the convent that had stood here centuries earlier.

Jack advanced along it, trying to gauge its relationship to the building above. He estimated that it led below the west wing.

He walked for fifty metres until the corridor came to an end in a large, square hall that marked one of the corners of the building. To his left, dimly illuminated in the torchlight, were two more narrow archways. One led to a continuation of the corridor. Within the other, he could see a stairway leading upwards.

He took a moment to check his equipment and to ensure that his pistol and his attack knife, a Randall Airman, lay within easy reach. Then he started up the stairs.

32

North-western Europe, 1620

Sir Thomas Fielding finally slowed his horse near a copse on the heath and guided it into the safety of a spinney by the roadside. They could not be far behind him, but he had to rest his mount, and there'd be no chance of a fresh animal before dawn.

He had been hunting the map now for two years. Two years since he had stood in the crowd at Old Palace Yard, watching the executioner strike Sir Walter Raleigh's head from his shoulders, two years since he had been in his native land. But that was nothing. He had lived so long in France that now, as age crept up on him, he acknowledged the beginning of nostalgia for England. But he would never return to live there. He thought and dreamed in French, he counted in French, and when he needed to express a complicated idea to English companions, he found his mind turning away from his native tongue to French in order to do so.

But now he was experiencing a certain relief. After so many years working undercover, he was relieved of the need to do so. He had escaped from the circle of the Chevaliers d'Uriel, and he knew what they would do to him if they caught him – but more important than his life was the safety of the map he carried in the pouch beneath his riding-coat.

He was the last member of the Brotherhood still active on the Mission of the Map. Thomas Hariot was dying, and George Chapman, old and broken, was eking out his years in poverty and debt in London, his fires quenched. The mantle of leadership had fallen on to his shoulders, but the company he led was reduced both in power and in scope. It was as well, he thought, that he was used to ploughing a lonely furrow through the field of his life.

Those two years searching for the map, still under cover of working for the Chevaliers, had taken him to Madrid, to Spanish Amazonia and back, and had brought him at last to his own doorstep: the Países Bajos Españoles, that part of the Low Countries controlled by Spain under the governance of Philip III's half-sister Isabella in Brussels. It was the archduchess's Court librarian who had unwittingly led Fielding, who had been posing as an antiquarian from Paris, to his find.

'I will show you a room of papers which are unsorted and spoilt by seawater, though I doubt you will find much of interest there,' he had said.

'How long have you had them here?'

'Two years now. But they are nothing. Bills of lading for cargoes long forgotten. Accounts from San Tomé and other outposts. The papers of dead sailors who couldn't be traced. They came with a galleon from the Caribbean which put in at Calais to be overhauled.'

'Allow me to look,' Fielding had replied, sweetening his request with a purse bulging with gold coins. His heart had started to beat faster at the mention of San Tomé.

'As you wish,' the librarian had replied, taking the purse. 'But you are wasting your time.'

Fielding had spent the rest of the day working his way through several wooden chests of papers, most stained, some so waterlogged they were beyond repair. It was the seamen's personal effects that interested him most.

Sailors know how to protect things from the ravages of the sea. It was evening, and he had already lit a candle, when he found a packet wrapped in waxed canvas. If this was what he was looking for, he would soon be on the run. It wouldn't take long for the Chevaliers to notice his disappearance, recognize his betrayal, and send men to bring him back.

He knew they would never abandon their quest.

He held the packet in his hands, and his fingers trembled as he undid the string that tied it.

He tethered his weary horse and let it graze. He had come many leagues south of Brussels already, but the road to Heidelberg in Bohemia was long. He knew he was obeying the orders of men who, long since, had lost their ability to enforce them, but he remained true to the beliefs of the Brotherhood. It was better for the world that it remain ignorant of the great cache of gold in Amazonia, of the great underground city that slept beneath the temple in the impenetrable jungles far, far to the west. He had buried one map, and now he would bury another. But not destroy it, for that was not the aim of the Brotherhood. The map still held secrets from any finder ignorant of how to reveal them. Its future was for Destiny to decide.

Heidelberg was safe. The King of Bohemia was married to a daughter of King James of England. The university there had a library large enough to lose the map in. It was in territory alien to the influence of the Chevaliers.

If only he could reach its safety in time.

Fielding slept fitfully until dawn, protecting himself as best he could from the damp ground on which he lay with his cloak. He rose at first light, saddled his horse and took the onward road south.

33

Paris, the Present

The stairs ended in a narrow room. A trapdoor was set in the ceiling, low enough to reach by means of a stone step built just beneath it. The door was festooned with cobwebs and encrusted with the dirt of years. A rusting iron bolt held it shut.

Using his multi-tool to free it, Jack slid it back cautiously, and the movement caused the hoops which held it to fall away to the ground. He waited on the step, not breathing, listening to hear if the slight clatter they'd made had created any reaction above – but no sound came. He placed his fingers on the door and carefully pushed upwards.

Still nothing. He pushed further and, drawing his gun, raised his head and shoulders into the void above. An abandoned room, once clearly a serving station or scullery, and long since disused. Its door had not been used for some time, and was unlocked. It opened at the far end of a grimy corridor with whitewashed walls and a wooden floor that ran about ten metres or so to a landing where dim daylight filtered through from somewhere above. He made his way towards it. At the landing, a spiral staircase led up towards the main part of the house. Far above, a skylight marked its top.

From the landing, there was a door that had to lead to the main part of the house, but it too showed signs of long disuse. Jack made his way up the staircase. On the second floor he paused. The door here, when he gently tried it, was locked, though the lock was old and rusty. But, beyond it, he could hear movement.

He identified two voices: male, speaking French. Gritting his teeth with impatience, he listened. The voices were indistinct, but he picked up enough of what was said:

'Where is she?'

'Third door.'

'The Knight-Commander will start the interrogation in fifteen minutes. Follow me.'

Relief flooded Jack's mind, followed by a racing sense of urgency: he was in the right place, but he had so little time. As soon as the men's footsteps had receded, he set to work on the lock, forcing himself to work steadily, not allowing panic to cause him to make any false moves. The mechanism was fouled with rust and dirt, and he broke one blade of the multi-tool, but at last he heard a reluctant click as something inside the lock finally gave way. The rest was easy. He turned the lock and heard it move. The door was open.

An instant later he was in the corridor, knife ready to kill anyone who might be silently lurking there. But he was alone. A burnished parquet floor. The wall to his right ran the length of the middle section of the building, punctuated by five white-and-gilt doors at regular intervals. On the left, a metal railing, black and gold, overlooked a broad, open stairwell. Huge chandeliers bathed the ornate interior in warm light. From the floor below he heard muted voices.

From whichever end you counted, the third door was the central one. Jack made his way quickly towards it and reached it just as a tall man, built like a wrestler, emerged. Jack recognized Kristof Struna instantly. The man's face registered surprise and then rage, but in the moment of surprise Jack caught him off guard and drove his knife hard into the left side of Struna's neck, dragging the blade with a sawing action down across the throat, and catching the body with his left arm as it slumped. Marlow hadn't been quick enough to prevent Struna from yelling out a warning, but the door to the room was ajar. He stepped inside fast.

Natasha was conscious, but barely. Her hair was tangled and her clothes torn off. A thumbscrew was clamped to one of her hands, and on a table by her lay two other instruments of torture he recognized: a choke-pear and a carding-comb. And it looked as if Struna had been making preparations: close by were a large bucket of water with sponges and cloths, two pairs of rubber gloves, and two sets of paper overalls of the kind used by decorators.

She flinched as she sensed him draw close.

'It's Jack. Keep steady,' he whispered. Working rapidly,

he undid the thumbscrew and threw it from him, then gently pulled the tape from her eyes before swiftly cutting through the rest of her bonds.

'Take the rest off. Hurry,' he said, as he crossed the room and drew back one of the curtains a crack. The windows reached almost from floor to ceiling, and there was a narrow iron balustrade outside them. The windows were locked shut, but there was no metal grille. He craned his neck to look down. He could see a second, much smaller, courtyard and, beyond it, a narrow street. Two floors below. But there was a projecting half-roof about two thirds of the way down that had to cover another entrance to the main building from the second courtyard.

'Jack?' Her voice was little more than a croak. Her wrists and ankles were bruised and blistered.

He lifted her to her feet, but she could barely stand. She leant on the table by the chair and flinched again as she saw the choke-pear and the comb. He made his way to the door and listened for a moment before dragging Struna's body inside – there was nothing he could do about the blood – and closing the door. There was a key in the lock, and he turned it. There was no time to make any kind of barricade.

He came back to Natasha, and was pleased to see she'd rallied a little.

'Thirsty . . .' she said.

There was nothing but the water in the bucket to drink. 'Soon,' he said. 'Put these on. Quickly, now.' His ear was cocked for danger as he handed one of the sets of overalls to her. He could see that she was willing her body to obey her as she stepped into the overalls.

'Can you walk?'

She wasn't connecting with him. She was looking down at herself. 'They cleaned me,' she said. 'Agoli – she came in here and cleaned me. She told me what they were preparing me for.'

Now he could hear footsteps running up the stairs, footsteps approaching, angry shouts – and then blows started to rain on the door. He took her by the wrist, shaking her. 'Come on!'

She nodded, and stumbled in the direction he indicated, towards the window. He threw aside the instruments of torture and picked up the table, using it to smash the panes and wooden frame, as the first shots hammered through the door. Grabbing Natasha, he threw himself out, breaking their fall on the half-roof, and bringing them both into a paratrooper's roll as they hit the courtyard. Pulling her to her feet, he half carried, half guided her through the archway and into the street. By now there were enough people about for them to blend in with the crowd, but they had to move very fast, and Natasha was weak and disoriented. He walked her through backstreets until he reached the rue de Jarente, turned left at its end into rue de Turenne, took another left there, and finally doubled back to rue Elzévir via rue du Parc-Royal. They regained the Avis Audi and, jamming it into gear, Jack roared north to pick up the route to the airport.

On the way, he rang ahead to make the necessary

arrangements. This would have been his shortest visit to Paris ever, but they had to get out of there fast.

He cupped her knee in his hand and squeezed it. They looked at each other for reassurance, and laughed in their relief. It was only then that her tears came.

34

Heidelberg, 1795

Alexander von Humboldt had long dreamed of travel. He was already making a name for himself as a geologist and botanist and, despite his relative youth, at twenty-six he was also a diplomat of some standing in the Prussian hierarchy.

But travel was his aim and, now, he had the chance to do it.

The work he envisaged involved exploration and natural history, but he was interested – who wasn't? – in the myth of Eldorado. He knew all about Sir Walter Raleigh's travels and explorations, but he had always been at once cynical and fascinated when it came to the story of the city of gold. But it wasn't that which had brought him to the ancient university of Heidelberg.

Now he sat in a room in the massive *Schloß* on its hill overlooking the red-roofed city on the Neckar, a scattering of packets and papers from the university's archives around him. After several weeks' work, he had homed in on a selection of documents dating from about two hundred years earlier and dealing with the northern territories of South America – areas in which he had a special interest. One map in particular drew his attention. It was not sophisticated, but its detail was minute.

On closer scrutiny, Humboldt thought he knew what it was. He looked at the four symbols scrawled in the margin and immediately recognized them for what they were. His excitement grew as he realized what the map showed – but far to the south of where anyone else had suspected!

Perhaps the myth of Eldorado was not a myth at all.

Humboldt wasted no time. He sought an audience with Prince-Elector Karl-Theodor, and came away from it with permission to keep the map for his own personal use and study.

'But you will return it the moment you have no further need of it,' the prince-elector stipulated.

'Of course, *Hochverehrter*.'

Humboldt returned home in triumph. Months of work, he knew, awaited him. But then . . .

35

The Present

They'd been fast-tracked at the airport and were now flying west over the coast of Brittany. But they knew they weren't safe yet. The pursuit would be as relentless as it was inevitable. Using a regular flight had been risky in itself, but there'd been two considerations. First, it was faster than having INTERSEC's own European Falcon flown from its Geneva base. Second, the Chevaliers would still be scouring Paris and, though Jack knew they would certainly be checking lines of escape from the city, they would take time to ascertain the route he'd taken, and his name and Natasha's were not on any airline computer's passenger list.

They were drinking Taittinger, but they were far too preoccupied to taste it.

'Do you know whose favourite champagne this was?' Jack asked.

'No.'

'James Bond's.'

'How old would he be now?'

'He was born in 1920, apparently.'

'Here's to him.'

Jack watched her as she sipped her drink. Already,

dressed in the clothes they'd picked up for her in haste at CDG's Galeries Lafayette, she had recovered some of her self-assurance, but he knew it would be some time yet before she overcame the trauma she'd suffered. A little small talk sometimes calmed, which was why he'd introduced it, and that was having its effect, but he didn't want too much of it. The flight would gain them six hours, but there wasn't a minute to waste if he was – as gently as he could – to get at the kernel of truth within her. There was a lot unspoken between them, and much had happened in the short time they'd known each other. But of course they didn't really know each other at all.

'Do you want to talk about what happened?' he asked.

'No.'

'I think you owe it to me. We are on the same side.'

'I can't think what they would have done to me if you hadn't –'

'That's over now.'

'I would have cracked. I think I would have cracked before they started.'

'It's what they wanted.'

'I think he would have gone ahead anyway. He wanted to. Just for the pleasure of it.'

Jack was silent. He knew she was right.

'Why don't you tell me?'

She shifted in her seat and shook her head, but he pressed her. He glanced round at their fellow passengers, but, if anyone had been paying them any attention, they would have thought this was some kind of intense conversation about their relationship.

'You don't work for the Treasury Department, do you?'

'No.'

'Then who?'

She ignored the question, but said, 'The Chevaliers think they can find the real map through me.'

How much did this woman know? 'And could they?'

'You know it exists, too?'

'My organization believes so.'

She smiled. 'I know you aren't an INTERPOL cop. But I'll let that go for now. I think I'm going to find out soon enough.'

'You didn't answer my question.'

'I'll answer that when I know who you really are. But I'll tell you this. De Vries didn't know he wasn't selling them the right map. They made a bad miscalculation. Now they're in panic. They will do anything to realize their plans now that they feel so close to achieving them.'

'And they'll be properly on track this time.'

'Without any chance of confusion.'

'So we must get there first.'

'If you don't want the whole economic foundation of the world to collapse. I don't have to paint a picture of the consequences for you.'

Jack nodded grimly.

'So you'll have to trust me.'

'If you think you have the advantage, why do you need me at all?'

'Because I know now that I cannot do this alone.'

'Then you'd better tell me everything.'

'This first,' she said, snuggling into his arms and kissing him passionately.

He returned her embrace, feeling his energy surge back as their tongues enlaced. But this was not going to be the moment either of them joined the Mile-High Club.

'I think we'd be happier saving this for later,' she breathed.

'Not much later.'

'But it's good to have you back.'

She nestled against him, and he smelt the light apricot smell of her hair. When she'd changed into her new clothes at the airport she'd managed to take a quick shower too, and she looked so fresh and neat you wouldn't have believed anything had happened to her.

But Jack was also aware that, delightful as it was to have her back, and delightful as it was to know that their first sexual encounter was one she wanted to repeat, she had also, for the moment, robbed him of the initiative. Well, he'd let her rest. The time for hard questioning would come soon enough.

36

New York

'It's confirmed,' Leon said, coming in from the lab.

Laura, Jack and Natasha were already sitting in Room 55, around a central table cluttered with books and papers, computer printouts and copies of several maps – except where they were neatly stacked in front of Natasha. Since their return and after a short rest and the necessary debriefing, Jack had spent most of his time in the room; Natasha, all of hers. Laura, hunched over her own Mac terminal, took off her glasses and rubbed her red-rimmed eyes.

'Good,' was all she said, as Leon pulled up a chair. But relief replaced the tension on Natasha's face. She'd been subjected to a Class AAA debriefing, the toughest on INTERSEC's scale, followed by hours going over material with Laura. Guilty until proven innocent, though Laura had been impressed, despite herself, with the accuracy of Natasha's recall and memory.

'Everything checks out,' Leon continued, leafing through the file he'd brought in with him, before looking at Natasha. 'Congratulations. You're cleared.'

'Nevertheless, you told Jack you worked for the Treasury,' said Laura, still unconvinced.

'He told me he was with INTERPOL,' Natasha retorted. 'And you know for a fact that neither of us would be sitting here now if it weren't for the other.'

That had weighed in her favour more heavily than anything else – that and the fact that she was more useful under their wing than anywhere else. Indeed, it was essential now that she also remained under their eyes.

She'd undergone stringent lie-detection tests, conducted by Leon using fMRI. There'd hardly been a single trouble spot. Those few might have been stress-related, though Leon had reservations, as Natasha's self-control was way above average.

The interviews had been exhaustive and focused, and had yielded more information than Jack and Laura had hoped for. There were still grey areas, but there was enough for them to commit to action.

'You'd better tell us more about this theory of yours,' said Laura.

Natasha took a notebook from the top of her well-regimented papers. 'Most of this you will know,' she began, 'but there are several possibilities.' The others leant forward attentively as she continued. 'We all know which countries and which organizations are officially the big gold-owners in the world today. But there are plenty we don't know about. President Roosevelt made it illegal to own gold privately in the USA, of course, but that has long since ceased to be the case, and there are emerging countries, like India, where activities are hard to police.'

'So which way would a major influx of gold on to world markets take us?' asked Jack.

'I'm sure your pals in the Treasury would have a whole raft of theories,' said Natasha. 'I can only give you mine, but I think they cover most of the bases. No country in the world is on the gold standard today, and the US dollar is the world reserve currency. But that could change. So the first possibility is that whoever controls this new source of gold could sell it to China in return for their enormous holding of US dollars.'

'And then what?' Leon asked.

'China could then go on to the gold standard and control the world economy.'

'And the world!'

'Naturally. If they wanted to do that. At the moment, they control markets pretty much anyway, since most industry is centred there. Short-termism was always going to be the downfall of the West.'

'And what would happen if China got that far?'

Jack said, 'Logically, if China went on to the gold standard and controlled the majority of the world's gold, the USA would be totally vulnerable –'

'Exactly,' Natasha said. 'The dollar would cease to be the world reserve currency. As things stand at the moment, that means, effectively, that you guys can print money. But if that changed, with your debts, you would go bankrupt overnight, and the nation – or organization – holding the majority of gold stocks would automatically control world markets.'

'There's another possibility,' Laura said. 'The Chevaliers could just leak rumours – as I imagine they have been anyway – that gold stocks were up, just to lower the price. They've been successful in that so far. And we know the Treasury is taking the obvious defensive course of denying the rumour, in order to keep the price up.'

'But once the bluff is called,' Jack said, 'and people find out that it isn't a rumour at all –'

They looked at each other.

'Panic,' said Natasha concisely. 'And it's a rich mix. Exchange-Traded Funds own as much gold as most countries, even though they are private companies. They have vaults in London, New York and Zurich. And there are two ways governments could react.'

'Confiscate their holdings –' Laura suggested, not liking Natasha to control too much of this conversation, though she knew her expertise was greater than her own.

'Yes, or slap a hefty tax on profits on gold trading.' Natasha looked around the table. 'But these days, does the US really still have the clout to carry such things off? And, as we've agreed, if China bought the gold from the Chevaliers and went on to the gold standard, it would become the world's most powerful nation because it would *control* the gold standard – simply by virtue of the fact that the yuan would be backed by owned gold.'

'Because the economic power of any given country is determined by how much gold it physically owns?' Leon asked.

'Precisely. It's pretty simple, really. Brutal, but simple. We haven't moved on at all from the days of the Templar or Florentine bankers.'

'If it *is* China,' Jack pondered. 'But why would they want to? They effectively own the US debt already, and although their gold holdings are – what? – one eighth of US stocks, they're a tiny percentage of their total economic worth, whereas in the States it's a huge one.'

'And don't they need markets that can pay for their product in order to grow?' asked Leon.

'For as long as it suits them,' replied Natasha drily. 'But you're right: it needn't be China. Why would any country want to wreak havoc on the world? The banks are the pillars that hold up the roof of society, worldwide. That's why we pussyfoot around them when they behave like shits, like in 2008. We've created a world society that can't function without a firm international economic infrastructure underpinning it. Take that economy away, and it's not only money that goes into free fall, it's everything. The only thing holding everything together now is that creditors like China need markets for their manufactured goods, and those markets lie in the countries of the debtors. So they choose not to call in what's owed. But that gives them power, and the debtors, who *used* to have the power, get nervous.'

'But we've already sailed pretty close to those rocks without the help of the Chevaliers,' said Laura. 'You mentioned short-termism, and that seems to be what is fucking up the world on a number of levels now: we're undermining the ecological balance of things, but we still don't believe it – or don't want to believe it, as long as there's a profit to be made. We're treating the environment like a student might treat their first bank account, spending against an optimistic guess at what's left to draw on.'

'Could it be that, instead of a country, large private companies might purchase this new gold and pay for takeovers with it? That way, they could control the world's economic infrastructure. Once they did, they could up prices for their product without fear of competition,' Jack suggested.

'It's possible, but that's been tried, and it's failed. Besides, for that to work you still need a customer with money. In fact, that's what's kept things in balance throughout the economic history of the world,' said Natasha. She paused, thinking. 'And that's the bugbear, too. The real bugbear. The Chevaliers could drive the price up again by buying it, and in so doing make their hoard more valuable, but who the hell would *profit* from that, if all the gold were finally theirs anyway, except them? They'd be like a kid with all the toys and no one to play with.'

'What if that didn't bother them?' asked Laura.

They sat around in silence then.

'Let's look at the possibilities that scenario might lead to,' Natasha continued. 'What the Chevaliers certainly would have is power. Almost unlimited power – until someone came up with a means of countering it. But it'd be such a body blow that they'd have plenty of time to make themselves impregnable. They'd have to deactivate the USA so that the States was powerless to move against them or their base country militarily. I mean, I know the West has been starting wars at the drop of a hat in recent years, but you couldn't just go and bomb the hell out of Brazil – or China, or North Korea, or wherever the Chevaliers might be using for protection. And the States is still, in a like-it-or-not kind of way, the world's cop on the corner. Corrupt maybe, fallible maybe, but still the arbiter of order, and historically respected. Remove that cop, and the looters can run free.'

'These Chevaliers would have to be pretty united among themselves to pull that off,' said Jack. 'And from what I've seen of them, they don't seem that sophisticated.'

'Oh, but they are,' Natasha said, with an authority that surprised the rest of them. 'I know them. They're not big in numbers, but that doesn't matter. Some of the most successful terrorist organizations in the world haven't more than twenty core members.'

'And look at what can grow from that, if it's given free rein,' added Jack. He was thinking of the German Nazi Party, founded nearly a century earlier, responsible for a world war and atrocities that still reverberated in people's consciousness; of the Gang of Four; of Kampuchea Year Zero; of Apartheid; and of Stalin's USSR. Make people insecure, shake them up a bit, then offer them leadership and terrorize the dissidents into silence. He looked around the table and saw that he didn't need to give voice to his thoughts.

'My guess is that they're using one of the smaller and marginalized world states to back them, but that their agenda is personal,' Laura said.

'That's possible,' agreed Natasha. The two women looked at each other. 'And what is that agenda?'

'We need to concentrate on finding the map. They don't get the gold until they have that,' said Jack.

'We're still assuming that Eldorado exists,' Laura said.

'Want to take a chance that it doesn't?' Natasha replied.

37

'Everything about her checks out – career in banking and then with Haslop-Turner Incorporated in Zurich; brilliant investment banker turning to Exchange-Traded-Fund management later on.'

'Yes, it checks out, Laura, but we still don't know what led her to work for the Chevaliers,' Jack cut in. They were sitting alone in Laura's loft apartment, on the sofa under the big clock that hung on one of her high brick walls. Glasses of Chablis and a bottle stood on the Cassina coffee table in front of them, untouched.

'How was she to know that their cover company, Overseas and General, wasn't legit? God knows I don't hold any brief for her, but –'

'– but we still haven't got a satisfactory answer out of her about why she pretended to be working for the Treasury Department. And we still don't know who she was actually working for. Hudson's followed every channel. The CIA and the FBI, and Homeland, all deny any knowledge of her.'

'I'm aware of that.'

'Then who?' Jack persisted.

'Well, we have *her* answer.'

'Yes. That she was working for herself.'

'Why not? She told us she started to look into things

as soon as she realized that Overseas and General wasn't as squeaky-clean as she had thought, and the polygraph bore all that out.'

'But' – Jack leant forward – 'what was she going to do with the information she has? And look at her – she knows how to handle herself: she carried a gun.'

'Plenty of women carry guns.'

'She needs checking out further.'

'Then we'd better do that. In any case, she's working with us, for us, now. She doesn't have a choice. And, as long as she's useful, let it ride. We haven't got time to go into her motivation, and we don't need to, as long as we keep her monitored.'

Jack nodded, took a sip of wine and lit a Camel. Laura wasn't over-fond of people smoking in her apartment, but she indulged Jack. Besides, she understood the pressure he was under. He was the one who'd have to work most closely with Natasha. She was his responsibility, and the fact that he was uneasy about her gave Laura satisfaction.

'I'll keep an eye on her,' he said. 'I'll find out why she's involved, and, in the meantime, we'll channel her energies.'

'Just as long as it's INTERSEC that's using *her*, not the other way round.'

'God but you have a suspicious mind.'

'It's what I'm paid for.'

'You're right. I'll keep her covered.'

'I know you will.' She paused. 'What about her theories on the Chevaliers' motivation?'

'We know what that is historically, but whether or not it's changed is another question.'

This was deeper water. The Order of the Chevaliers d'Uriel, especially since it had moved from under the rigid control of the Spanish Inquisition and split from its mastery and re-established itself in France, had had a chequered and interrupted history. It had lain dormant for long periods, to the extent of being forgotten, but it had never died. It was like a volcano that hadn't erupted for centuries but was far from extinct. Its declared objective had always been to reduce the world to a state of innocence, a return to square one, as close as possible to the Garden of Eden. All materialistic concerns and preoccupations were to be swept away and a new order established, which had everything to do with Christian values and nothing to do with commercialism and greed. But thinking had changed across the passing of increasingly cynical centuries, and neither Laura nor Jack believed that these could still be at the core of the Chevaliers' beliefs today.

They discussed it hard, through the rest of the bottle of Chablis in front of them, and another, until it was late. By then they had come up with a plan.

'I'll look into their background more fully. Leon is working on the missing links in their story now, and I've got a conference with him first thing. You should work on Natasha, see if you can get any more out of her informally,' said Laura. 'Anything that can lead us to the map. But know where to draw the line. Hudson's heavily on your back. You'll only last as long as he thinks you're useful, and I can't cover for you for ever.'

'You can if you want to.'

'Don't push it, Jack. He'd bring you down in a heartbeat.'

'It won't come to that.'

'I certainly hope not.'

Jack stood and reached for his jacket. A battered, dark-blue cashmere thing. 'I'll be careful.'

'Be sure you are.'

She stood too. They were very close. He gave her a kiss on the cheek and made his way to the door.

'Are you sure you wouldn't like a coffee or something before you leave?' she asked.

'I don't think so,' he replied. '"Miles to go before I sleep", you know.'

'I bet you have,' she said, watching him close the door after him.

When he'd gone, she took down her copy of Robert Frost's poetry and looked up the verses he'd just quoted from. And smiled.

But then she went back to her Mac and logged in. Took a handful of books from the pile on her work table and dumped them next to the computer. She, too, had work to do.

38

They'd installed Natasha Fielding in one of the third-floor suites of the town-house hotel above which INTERSEC's New York offices were situated. The suite had a living room – not vast, but comfortable – overlooking the park, a bedroom with the same view, and an en-suite bathroom off it. The ensemble had expensive but conservative furnishings, and the anodyne pictures on the walls were by minor nineteenth-century landscapists. It was a restful, comforting interior, and the only mod cons it lacked were a telephone (or any signal facility for a cell phone) and an Internet outlet. No one would have known that the windows were top-grade bulletproof glass and couldn't be opened. No one would have been able to begin to trace the hidden camera and microphone.

At the moment, both these, by Jack's order, were inactive.

Natasha accepted the conditions placed on her with outward equanimity.

'I know I'm better off here than out there on my own,' she admitted to Jack when he called on her after his conversation with Laura. 'And I certainly feel safer with you around.'

'I need your help.'

'I've told you all I know.'

'Are you really on your own on this? You can tell me. No one else need know.'

She shrugged. 'I had a suspicion, and I followed it up. Curiosity would have killed the cat, but for you.'

He joined her on the sofa. 'You blew your cover for me. You didn't even know who I was.'

'I knew you had to be on the same side. Maybe I already knew I couldn't go on with this on my own.'

Marlow wondered if he could believe that. 'I've been thinking about the map. The real one.'

'Yes?'

'I was wondering if you had any ideas?'

'About where it is now?'

'Yes.'

'But it could be anywhere in the world.'

'I think you could help me narrow it down.'

'I don't know any more than you do.'

But Jack had caught a flicker in her eye – a micro-expression that might tie in with the glitches on the polygraph. She did know more than he did: if not the location of the map, at least something that might point him in the right direction. Why, then, was she holding back? Was it still something to do with trust?

'If there is something, you can tell me.'

She hesitated, and then he saw that she was on the verge of tears. All this time, she'd been holding herself in, keeping herself together, but now everything she had been through was building up inside her, to such an extent that she could no longer hold up against it. 'If I tell you, you won't need me any more. You'll throw me to the wolves.'

'Why do you think that? We can work together on this. And if you want to get to the truth . . .'

'I do!'

'Then let me help you.'

She was in his arms then, and he let her cry. He well knew the feeling of letting go, the relief of throwing away all the pent-up tension and allowing yourself to depend on someone else. We all have to, in the end, however hard we try not to, and, in Natasha's circumstances, he half understood why her pride, independence and fear had conspired to keep her defences up. He wished he could find some way of reassuring her completely, but he knew that he could only do that through his actions, and that it could only happen with time.

And, at the same time, he knew that, however vulnerable she might appear now, he would still have to keep something back from her. He fought in a dark world, and it was that more than anything that sometimes made him long to leave it. But discontent is the price you risk paying for stimulation, and if you choose to live a life that involves hazard and uncertainty, you have to accept the consequences.

At last she quietened, and they lay for a while in each other's arms on the sofa. She curled closer to him, whispering, 'Do you know how long it's been?'

'Too long.'

'I need you – now. I need you to help me forget about all this – just take me away from it for a while. We'll come back to it. We have to. But not now. Not yet.'

And then they stopped thinking about anything as their lips instinctively sought each other's and their hands unbuttoned and unzipped clothing with increasing impatience until they were naked together, sprawled on the sofa. Dislodged cushions fell to the floor and their bodies followed them, rolling on to the carpet, then half wrestling, half embracing, wrapping their limbs around one another's, his lips on her breasts, his tongue caressing her nipples as her right hand sought his prick and massaged it, tenderly at first and then more and more insistently as his own hands strayed to where she longed for them to go, stroking and teasing until she groaned and he felt the soft, welcoming moistness of her. But when he made to follow with his mouth she stopped him: her need was too urgent, she needed him now and she felt him solid and warm in her hand, felt the blood in the muscles pound under her touch as she guided him, opening her legs and sliding under him as he raised himself and began to ride her, keeping his weight off her but his face near hers, seeking her lips again with his. Their mouths locked, hungrily, as he rose up inside her. She welcomed him and they moved together, and she brought her legs up to hold the small of his back with her heels and steadied herself with her hands on his taut sides as he shifted again, and moved, and she heard his voice hoarse in her ear as he moved his face aside to nestle in her hair and bury his lips in her neck, her neck where it joined her shoulder, burying his lips and his face in her warmth as she gasped and cried and lost her breath and heard him losing his breath too. One of her legs kicked free and sent something flying off a low table, a book maybe; it fell with a dull thud somewhere far, far away in the distance, as nothing was there but them and they could sense nothing but their bodies, their warmth and their smell and their comfort and their joy, and they rose and rose and pressed themselves against each other as if they were doing everything in their power to become one. She could feel him holding back, wanting to delay, trying to keep himself in check, but she didn't want him to, and she knew that he wanted to remain on the edge of pleasure still, but she wanted to feel him now and she clenched her muscles and muttered wickedly in his ear and wanted to laugh with joy and relief as he exploded in her.

And later, much later, they talked, and when she at last fell into a deep, exhausted sleep, he left her. He was almost too tired to think, but the pleasure he had found with her was real: he wanted to help her not just for the sake of his mission, but for herself.

And she had given him something he needed to work on.

He made his way through the night-lit corridors of INTERSEC to Room 55. He picked up what he needed and, getting the Corvette from the garage, drove home to Greenwich Village.

Once there, he got down to work. He had a hunch he had to follow up. He didn't know whether or not it would lead him anywhere, but his instincts told him it would. At least he knew what path to follow. He fired up his laptop and typed a name into the search engine. Nothing. He tried another. This time, he got the kind of result he was hoping for, and other leads began to open.

Encouraged, he became intensely energized, pulling old books from his shelves, cross-checking data and making notes, too busy to stop for any kind of respite. Three hours later, he sat back, weary but satisfied. Everything connected. Now he would have to put his discoveries to the test. But he had little doubt that he was on the right track.

Dawn was breaking before he got up from his desk, showered and changed into a fresh blue shirt and a black needlecord suit that was more or less pressed, drank a large, very sweet espresso, and drove the Corvette back to INTERSEC. Now, he didn't feel tired at all, but he knew he couldn't keep this up for much longer and that he'd function better when he'd had some sleep. Even two hours would be a luxury.

But he had to get this out of the way first.

*

Natasha was still asleep when he looked in on her. He left her in peace. She needed to recuperate too and, if he was right, peace was something neither of them would be getting again for quite some time.

39

Laura was already at her desk when Jack entered Room 55 at 06h00. Neither of them had had any sleep, but they were too fired up to notice. Once they'd established fully what material they had to go on there would be a time for necessary rest and recuperation, but that would have to wait.

'Have you checked on her?' asked Laura.

'Yes. She's still sleeping.'

'Good.'

Jack ignored the arch look she gave him and ran a hand through his more than usually unkempt hair. He dumped the bundle of papers he was carrying down on the central work table and produced a couple of CD-Rs from the side pocket of his jacket.

'New stuff,' he said. 'Something's been nagging me about Natasha, and now I know what it is.'

'Show me.'

He spread the bundle of papers out on the tabletop and slid one of the CDs into the side of the computer near them. 'OK. The nag was her surname. Look at this.'

He tapped a couple of keys, and the lean face of a middle-aged man with a neatly trimmed beard appeared on the screen. He wore a black velvet hat with a feather in it, and his neck was encircled by a lace ruff. Serious, sad brown eyes stared out at them. It was a quarter-length portrait, not very well done, and showed the man dressed in a plain, dark-brown velvet doublet with a small badge bearing an indecipherable emblem pinned high on the right side of his chest. The background was unfinished; the artist had simply painted in a dark-brown wall, somewhat lighter than the shade of the doublet. In the top left-hand corner a simple Latin inscription in gold had been added.

'Who is he?' asked Laura.

'This is Sir Thomas Fielding. It's a copy of a lost portrait, probably Dutch, painted in the mid-1630s. It's in the collection of the Rijksmuseum in Amsterdam, but it's not on show. It's a minor work, as you can see, and it's catalogued as "Portrait of an Unknown Gentleman". It's the only picture of Fielding in existence, but I know it's him, because I've been doing quite a bit of research at home since I left here earlier this morning, and there's quite a lot more about him that's intriguing.'

'He's an ancestor of Natasha's?'

'I think so. It was painted in Leiden by an unknown artist who may have studied with van der Helst. And if you look at these' – Jack riffled through his papers, found a sheet and passed it to Laura – 'you'll see that Fielding spent his last years in Leiden. He died there in 1635, aged sixty-four. He'd been teaching history at the university there, but he'd been retired a few years before he met his end. There's some evidence to suggest he was working on a book but, whatever it was, it's lost.'

'Where is this taking us?'

'He was murdered. He was murdered in his lodgings early one morning in September 1635. The place was ransacked.' Jack handed her a sheaf of three pages, a copy of a longhand report. 'There was an investigation, as he was a pretty eminent citizen, and a foreigner. They thought it was an interrupted burglary, but he had little of material value, and no conclusion was ever reached, no culprit ever found.'

'You *have* been busy.'

'One thing led to another,' said Jack, off-hand, 'and I'd done some preparatory work anyway. Fielding was a member of an English group when he was younger. Raleigh, and my near-namesake, Christopher Marlowe, were also members, along with the writer George Chapman and the scientist Thomas Hariot. This group was close-knit and indirectly involved, through Marlowe, with the English secret service of the time. That was a pretty sophisticated set-up, but the group worked independently of it – independently of anyone else. Their involvement with the official secret service was, effectively, exploitative. They used information from there, channelled through Marlowe, for their own ends.'

'Go on.'

'By 1635, the members of the group were either dead, or old, or, like Fielding, living in retirement. It looked as if it had died out. But when it was operational, its chief focus was to combat the activities of another group. It was totally dedicated to this struggle, its aim to neutralize, in every way possible, the activities of the

Chevaliers d'Uriel.' Jack paused to consult another sheaf of papers, and scrolled through the information on the CD to bring up fresh information. 'The worst thing about the murder was that Fielding was tortured before he died. They broke his fingers and toes, they blinded him, they forced his mouth apart with something called a choke-pear – you have to wonder who invents these things, who makes them – and they tore his flesh with hot carding-combs. They were going to use similar instruments on Natasha when I got her out. Whoever had tracked Fielding down clearly thought he had information they needed. But he either fed them false stuff, or simply didn't crack. He knew they'd kill him anyway.'

'And his attackers were Chevaliers?'

'Yes. Under a Frenchman called Audric Ballin, who'd succeeded many years earlier as Knight-Commander – as they call their head honcho.' Laura smiled at Jack's casual turn of phrase, but let him continue. 'I think – and I haven't had time to verify this yet – that Fielding was working undercover with the Chevaliers. That probably accounts for the ferocity with which they tortured him.'

'This Audric Ballin was based at the Château d'Uriel when he took over?'

'And in Paris. His predecessors were Richard Topcliffe, and, after him, Carlos Alvarez. But now look at this.' Jack replaced the CD-R with the second. 'Fielding had a son, William, who married a Frenchwoman and spent most of his life in Bordeaux working in the wine trade. That's all we know about him. But I believe – and I have to do some more digging before I can confirm this – that Thomas Fielding passed on the traditions of his group to his son. The Brotherhood, as they called themselves, didn't die out after Fielding Senior died. The tradition carried on.'

'But you can't possibly be suggesting that Natasha is working for some kind of latter-day Brotherhood!'

'Not necessarily. But she may have access to a long tradition – secret papers, arcana we know nothing of. She's an economist and a financial high-flyer. Why shouldn't she have put two and two together when the gold market started its recent sleigh ride?'

'But the question is: what's in it for her?'

'Exactly.'

'So what do we do?'

'You're the boss – you tell me.'

'That's a tad petty of you, isn't it?'

Jack smiled. 'Not at all. But whatever we do has to come from you, or Hudson won't buy it. And, if he's after my blood, he mustn't have the shadow of a doubt that everything we do is done on your initiative.' He looked at her closely. 'But I don't think you need any prompting from me.'

She shook her head. 'You've done one hell of a job.'

'There was nothing I could find to lead us to the map.'

'I'd be amazed if there had been. He'd have buried that secret deep.'

Jack stretched. Jesus, the exhaustion was catching up

in earnest now. 'I'm going home. I think I'm entitled to a few hours off. But I think now that Natasha may have an idea of where the map is.'

'Then why didn't she simply go and get it?'

'Because she had no more idea than we had that the map de Vries sold to the Chevaliers in Rio wasn't the right one. There must have been a deliberately falsified copy made to protect the real one. That copy was de Vries's map.' Jack smiled. 'But now . . .'

'We'd better keep her really close,' Laura said. 'Don't tell her anything.'

'Of course not.'

'But we can ask her – interrogate her?'

Jack shook his head.

Laura looked at him and rephrased: 'Persuade her to tell us where she thinks the authentic map is?'

He nodded his approval. 'So – those are your orders?'

'Yes.'

'Good.'

'As for the map, Leon's been working on the location. He thinks he's found a link through some correspondence he's dug up in Brussels. If he comes up with anything, we can cross-check it with whatever Natasha tells us,' Laura added. 'But we must play our cards close to our chest. She is very, very organized, and she has a phenomenal memory.'

'So I've noticed. But I don't think she's wicked, Laura.'

'That's something we have to find out,' she replied, not mentioning why she thought Jack was convinced;

but she didn't really believe he could be suckered again. Unlike the last time, he wasn't vulnerable now. Her hand strayed to her tattoo, half concealed under her emerald ring. She would have it removed, first chance she got.

'What are you thinking? That she might be a double? No – I rescued her; those guys weren't mucking about.'

'We've been hoaxed like that before, Jack. As I say, we'll keep her close. Now, go away. I'll call you when we're ready to interview Ms Fielding.'

'Good.'

'And Jack –'

'Yes?'

'We won't tell Natasha any more than she needs to know – OK?'

He smiled at her and left. Once again, she watched him go with a twinge of regret. Would she ever plumb the depths of this man? Would he ever drop the barrier he'd built round himself and let her in?

She'd had the cameras and the microphones switched back on in Natasha's suite. She didn't dwell on why Jack had had them turned off, and wouldn't mention it to him. But she'd watch what was going on between them very closely indeed.

She sighed and picked up her phone. She dialled an internal number and waited for Leon Lopez to pick up.

40

Back in his apartment, Jack Marlow sank into the red leather chair near the window and lost himself in his thoughts.

He liked to think of himself as a man in control of his emotions but, in his heart of hearts, he knew he was not. So his work involved a constant balancing act between the rational and the irrational parts of him. He knew that he was drawn to Natasha. She was a beautiful woman, and her intellect – which commanded knowledge of financial matters he could not hope ever fully to understand, because deep down they did not interest him – attracted him as well. She had rescued him; he had rescued her. When they made love, it was with a passion born of what they owed each other, the dangers they had shared, not what they knew about each other. He had been badly hurt recently enough to be on his guard, and he knew that his job made emotional involvement with anybody a perilous thing. In turn, this made him aware that he was certainly not the perfect psychological type for his profession; but he did his job well, and it satisfied whatever creative urge was in him. He knew he would never have been happy with any kind of work that offered him safety or security – though part of him longed for both, and for all the things most people seemed to achieve: steady relationships, families, and everything that went with them – despite knowing that such things were often, even frequently, an illusion, a compromise; and all were subject to the bludgeonings of chance, of fate. He had become attracted to meeting the vagaries of life head on. Fate deals the cards, and it's up to you how you play them. Some people get bad hands, and there's not much they can do about it. People think they control their lives, but they only have a limited ability to steer through the treacherous waters of existence. Why not grab life by the shoulders and not give too much of a damn about it?

He had chosen to do what he did because it stimulated him, and his own generous degree of empathy dictated that he channel that impulse in a way that put him on the side of the good guys, or at least of helping, in his small way, to maintain an order in the world without which it could not function. He knew that he lived in a world which was fracturing, a world in which human feelings, human contact, were under ever greater threat as communication became increasingly impersonal. But he also believed that humanity had within it an instinctive urge to survive, and that it would never quite allow itself to topple over the cliff into the abyss. Centuries of war, centuries of selfishness, centuries of unwise, stupid, self-centred and bureaucratic rule had not killed off people, or the societies that bound them together, entirely, however hard warped interpretations of religions and political credos had tested the survival instinct. It may be that, sooner or later, mankind would deal itself a wound so bad it would be forced to return to basics. In his bleakest moments he could see a world in which people lived in small groups, in fortified farmsteads, self-reliant and mistrusting outsiders; he could see a world in which people would once again have to do without something as simple but as crucial as electricity, and the removal of that one result of scientific discovery would wrench society as he knew it – as everyone except the last and most primitive tribes still existing deep in the last, lost outposts of the world knew it – so totally out of shape that society would have to restructure itself radically. But he did not doubt that, somehow, people could and would survive without all the icing on the cake, spread in the form of the technological revolution that had accelerated since the 1990s. So short a time since then, and how fragile its structure was, and yet already the world depended on it absolutely.

But if it were ever going to change, that change would have to occur naturally: it would have to be left to fate. If such a change was what the Chevaliers wanted, it was not their business to force it on others. If that was what the Chevaliers wanted, then they were collectively psychopathic. And he would stop them if he could. To live in a world created and controlled by them would be pointless anyway – for him at least – so he had nothing to lose by fighting.

So – his motives were simple. But what of Natasha's? And now the rational part of him took over. What were her motives? He had worked hard to prove the connection he had already been pondering – the connection between her and the Elizabethan double agent and fighter for the good guys Thomas Fielding. That Fielding's knowledge had been passed down through his son, William, was a strong possibility; but there was no evidence to suggest that there was any kind of Brotherhood still in existence to combat the Chevaliers. That would be just too fantastic to be possible. The Chevaliers had remained a coherent group, an organization that had survived the centuries, much like the Roman Catholic Church they had split from hundreds of years earlier. The Brotherhood, from its inception, had been a group of intellectuals sharing some sense of common justice, individuals with their own independent views and ideas, which would not be subjected to any slavish dedication to some fixed ideal.

Might it be that there were fractures within the modern Order of the Chevaliers d'Uriel? Modern thinking was not like that of the later Middle Ages, when the Order had been formed. Might the lieutenants of the organization have different aims from the commanders? Might there be a weakness to exploit there, if he could ever get close enough? But how would he do that, and was there time? Natasha had infiltrated the group in much the same way as her forefather had done, but she had blown her cover to save him: a real gaffe, from a professional point of view. But she was not a professional in Jack's field. She had a heart, which sometimes ruled her. He wondered whether, if their roles had been reversed back in Rio, he would have acted as she had done.

Why had she saved him? Because she couldn't get any further on her own, as he suspected? Because she thought she could use him and INTERSEC to carry her own ambitions forward? And were her goals identical with his, or did she think she could use the knowledge she hoped to gain in some other way?

Back to the question: what were her motives?

He brooded on this as he poured himself a generous slug of Jameson's and lit a Camel. He lay back in his chair and watched the narrow slit of sky he could see between the surrounding buildings. His mind started to wander as sleep began to claim him. There was a momentary image of his mother and father, who'd died fifteen years earlier, within a week of one another: they were sitting in a place he didn't recognize, looking at him but somehow also past him. There was a castle on a hill, then a face he'd rather have forgotten but couldn't forget, even after two years; then – bizarrely – a clip from an old Gamera picture, which he must have seen in France, where they reran the tongue-in-cheek Japanese monster movies from time to time on Canal Plus.

He jolted back into consciousness, saw dark clouds in the slit of sky. He thought about pouring another drink, having another cigarette; but he felt too great a lassitude to do anything about it. Where do those weird and unconnected thoughts and images come from? What tunnels does the mind go down when the consciousness is no longer in control of it?

Seconds later, he was asleep. Nothing troubled his slumber until two hours later, when the blue phone in a cabinet below a bookcase which ran along an entire wall, trilled insistently.

'Of course I didn't give them my real name,' said Natasha. 'I'm not that much of a fool. And they suspected nothing.'

'But there is a connection?' Jack asked.

'You've confirmed it.'

'Why didn't you tell us about it?' asked Laura. The three of them, with Leon Lopez, were back in Room 55.

Natasha tidied the papers and pens on the table they were sitting around, placing the pens in size order and aligning them exactly. 'I didn't think it was relevant.'

'Why not? Didn't it occur to you that it might have been helpful for us to know?' Laura again. 'And why the pretence of working for the Treasury Department?'

Natasha gave a slight shrug. 'I didn't know who Jack was – who *you* were – at first. I wasn't going to drop my guard to just anyone. And later – well, you can't blame me for keeping one ace up my sleeve. But now, effectively, you have me in your power, and I wouldn't be here at all without Jack.' She shot him a glance. 'And I was *going* to tell you. I just needed time to decide when. Meanwhile, you've found out anyway.'

'I think the Chevaliers did suspect you. I think they checked up on your background and found the link with Thomas Fielding. I think they were going to torture you because they believe you know where the real map is,' said Jack.

'It's possible. I risked a lot, getting you out of their clutches.'

Jack knew what she meant by that: her cover had been secure until she'd broken it to save him. He nodded his understanding.

'And do you know where it is?' Leon asked, after a brief, whispered consultation with Laura.

'I may have an idea, and, from the look in your eyes, you have too. So maybe you'd just like me to confirm what you think,' she replied. 'You had better tell me yours first.'

'You're not in a very good bargaining position,' Laura said.

'Do you really think that?' Natasha replied, and the two women eyeballed each other.

Jack stepped in: 'How did you get involved in all this?'

Natasha looked at him, and smiled. He just about managed to keep his professionalism in place, and she saw it. She gave him what he hoped was an honest answer, and he saw no reason to disbelieve her: 'I first learnt about my ancestor years ago. My father told me all about him when I was sixteen. It was a big thing for him. He had an old wooden chest he kept at the back of a deep shelf at the bottom of a bookcase in his library, behind a set of super-boring nineteenth-century-history books which no one can have looked at in decades. One evening, he ushered me into the room – it was a kind of sanctum sanctorum, you never went in without his express permission. Even as a teenager I was somewhat in awe of it, and of him.' She paused for a moment, her eyes distant with reminiscence. 'My father and I were not close. Blood was the only thing we had in common – or so I thought, until he opened that wooden chest.'

'Your ancestor's papers?' Jack asked.

Natasha nodded. 'Not very many. Even in those days, people in his business knew better than to commit much to paper; and little had been added over the centuries. But there was enough for me to know what he had done and who he'd worked with. Much of it was in cipher, but my father knew the codes. He told me he had wanted to wait until I was eighteen, but he had cancer and he wasn't sure how long he had left. I was his only child. He had to take the risk . . .'

'The risk of you keeping the secret?' asked Laura.

'Quite a lot for a teenage kid to handle, let alone take in. But I did keep what he told me – about Sir Thomas, the Brotherhood, Eldorado and the Chevaliers d'Uriel – to myself. To be honest, it didn't mean much to me. I knew where the box was hidden, and when my father died – three years later, as it happened – I took it from its hiding place and kept it with me. It wasn't big, and I didn't open it for years, but I knew enough to keep it safe.'

'Where is it now?'

'Safe. But I can tell you all that is of any interest. In any case, my father told me that he thought something was missing – something had either been lost, or deliberately omitted: something relating to the map.'

'But the map wasn't with the papers?'

'Of course not. I wouldn't be here now if it had been.'

Laura bit her lip, avoiding Jack's eye.

'Where is it?' Leon Lopez had kept his counsel until now, and the question came like a dart.

Natasha looked at him, and he smiled back mildly, almost apologetically. It wasn't in Leon's nature ever to play bad cop.

Jack leant forward and grasped her wrist. 'Look, you know what's at stake, and we can't afford to pussyfoot around. There isn't time! So tell us what you know, and tell us now!'

'You don't have any choice but to trust us,' Laura added. 'But if you think you can keep something back for your own sake . . .'

'It's in Heidelberg, isn't it?' probed Leon.

Natasha had seen the sense of Jack's argument and, now, any resistance within her, whatever the reason for it, collapsed. She even seemed to shrink physically, and Jack thought for a moment that this was a little-girl act designed to throw them. That made him angry, and she saw it. 'That was where he left it,' she started. 'In 1620. It found its way into the state archives. But I have no idea where it is now. I thought de Vries –'

'But he *didn't* have the real map, did he?'

'I'd intended to make for Heidelberg as soon as I found that out but I was . . . detained.'

'Well, now you'll have some travelling companions,'

Jack said. Something deep within him cautioned him. Was she still keeping something back? Laura had just told her she had no choice but to trust them, but the truth was she could choose *not* to, and he knew they had no intention of trusting her. He wondered if the Chevaliers were on the same trail. It was possible. If *he* could search for Thomas Fielding, they could too.

The internal yellow phone rang then. Laura took it, mouthed 'Hudson' at Jack, and listened intently for a minute, her interjections terse monosyllables.

'What?' Jack quizzed as she hung up.

She hesitated, looking at Natasha, undecided. Then she said, 'What the hell, it'll be all over the news in an hour. Jennings Allied has been taken over. Hostile bid, but it looks as if that was all that could save it from crashing.'

She was talking about one of the five major players in international merchant banking.

'Who's bought it?' asked Natasha.

'Overseas and General. The Chevaliers are moving up a gear.'

The ball was rolling again, thought Jack. It hadn't taken long.

'We'll get a plane organized. Now,' said Laura.

41

Amazonia, 1803

Alexander von Humboldt had long dreamed of this journey, but now, as he fought off fatigue and the constant irritation of the biting insects that danced continual attendance on them, he wished it were over. But it would be, soon.

He had been travelling since 1799 and, despite the vast satisfaction the various discoveries he had made in the Caribbean and the northern parts of the great continent of South America had brought him, he was beginning to long for the more cultivated atmosphere of Paris and Berlin. It would not be long now. After a brief stay at the White House with President Thomas Jefferson, he would return to Europe.

He was relieved at the prospect, though daunted by the thought of how he would ever transform the vast number of notes and specimens he had written up and collected into some kind of cohesive work of science to hand down to posterity. But he had, thank God, retained his health throughout his wanderings, and he was still only in his early thirties. By God's grace, he would be equal to the task he would soon have to confront.

But one thing rankled – more than rankled: disturbed him deeply. Sitting in his room in the consul's mansion in Belém overlooking the mighty River Amazon, which he had grown both to love and to hate, he thought back on the one major doubt that lingered in his mind.

Eldorado. He had consulted the map over and over, had got close to where he believed it to be located, but at a crucial moment in his exploration, the trail had gone cold.

The map was imprecise. He looked once more at the notes he'd written, and shook his head in regret at the conclusion he'd been forced to reach:

> We have shown that the fable of Dorado, like the most celebrated fables of the nations of the ancient world, has been applied progressively to different spots. We have seen it advance from the south-west to the north-east, from the oriental declivity of the Andes towards the plains of Rio Branco and the Essequebo, an identical direction with that in which the Caribees for ages conducted their warlike and mercantile expeditions.

But it wouldn't do. The doubt would not go away. He had followed the map, and it had led him to a place far from where anyone had ever believed the treasure of great gold lay, and that very difference in location had made him begin to believe in it – or, at any rate, want to believe in it – but there was nothing. He had made allowance for the fact that earlier explorers had mistaken the Orinoco River for the Amazon (a major error which he had not fallen into himself), and still nothing. No island rising from a mysterious lake; no lost ziggurat rising like a ghost from among the tangled trees and lianas.

His servant tapped on the door. It was time for him to begin packing for the voyage north to the new American Republic and his meeting with its president. Humboldt nodded to the man and withdrew to a desk in a corner of the spacious room that was piled with boxes of specimens and reams of closely written notes to draw out the map once more and ponder it. He had taken great care of the map: to look at it, you would not know it had travelled so far. He handled it delicately, and with respect. He knew already that he would never return it to Heidelberg. The political situation surrounding that town had changed dramatically in his absence and he no longer felt bound by his promise. Besides, there was something about this map, something he had not been able to fathom. It exerted a certain power which he did not understand: he knew that was why he was looking at it again, unable to let it go, though he knew in his rational mind that it simply didn't *work*. Or that it held a secret he was perhaps not meant to unlock.

His expedition to locate Eldorado had been fraught with difficulty. He had not been able to uncover the secret of the four symbols drawn on the map, though he had had no difficulty in recognizing them for what they were: Sirius, a condor and the constellations of

Canis Major and Lepus. Furthermore, his men had been attacked in the latter stages of their journey by tribesmen who had never revealed themselves, who had ambushed them with poisoned darts that left three of his company dead; two were saved only by swift medical intervention. But any attempt to pursue the attackers was futile: the Indians simply melted into the forest like ghosts. Who they were and where they came from he had not been able to discover. Locals, when questioned, would become either vague or fearful, or would flatly deny all knowledge of them.

Which added to, and confirmed, the mystery.

Humboldt looked at his notes again, while his servant supervised the enormous task of gathering up his material in order, transferring it into crates, and meticulously noting their contents.

> . . . other errors had perhaps their source in the little interest which Antonio de Berrio, the Spanish governor, felt in communicating true and precise notions to Raleigh, who indeed complains of his prisoner 'as being utterly unlearnt, and not knowing the east from the west . . .'

Humboldt went on reading until he reached his conclusion, or, at least, the conclusion he had already decided he would make public. Perhaps, after all, it was the true one. Raleigh had been desperate to regain a position of ascendancy at the Court of Queen Elizabeth:

> It seems to me difficult to doubt of the extreme credulity of the chief of the expedition, and of his lieutenants. We see Raleigh adapted everything to the hypotheses he had previously formed. He was certainly deceived himself; but when he sought to influence the imagination of Queen Elizabeth and execute the projects of his own ambitious policy, he neglected none of the artifices of flattery. He described to the Queen 'the transports of those barbarous nations at the sight of her picture'. He would have 'the name of the August Virgin, who knows how to conquer empires, reach as far as the country of the warlike women of the Orinoco and the Amazon'. He asserts that 'at the period when the Spanish overthrew the throne of Cuzco, an ancient prophecy was found, which predicted that the dynasty of the Incas would one day owe its restoration to Great Britain'. He advises that 'on the pretext of defending the territory against external enemies, garrisons of three or four thousand English should be placed in the towns of the Inca, obliging that Prince to pay a contribution annually to Queen Elizabeth of three hundred thousand pounds sterling'. Finally, he adds, like a man who foresees the future, that 'all the vast countries of South America will one day belong to the English nation.'

But Raleigh had never let go of his dream; he'd held on to it over four voyages between 1595 and 1617. After that, though, there had been nothing. Apart from a few isolated attempts, the quest for a city of gold had dwindled. Reality had taken over.

And yet . . .

Humboldt carefully stowed the map and his notes away in his personal belongings – the ones he would pack himself, and keep with him at all times.

He went out on to the balcony beyond the room and looked across the great river, its sallow waters dully reflecting the sun. He was not one to play God, but something told him that it would be best publicly to present all Raleigh's claims as the product of, at the very best, wishful thinking, and to lay to rest once and for all any sense that Eldorado was anything more than a myth.

But he would make sure the map, and the notes he would keep of his own private thoughts about it, were buried deep. Once home, he would lock them in an iron coffer he kept in his office at the University of Berlin before transferring them to the archives. There, they would have to take their chances of rediscovery. He would not destroy such important material; its fate would be better left to chance. But, for himself, Humboldt knew that any secret the map might contain would be better – for the sake of humanity – left sleeping.

42

Germany, the Present

'Nothing like this has ever happened before – not in the university's seven-hundred-year history,' said Dr Wolfgang Kuhlmey. The deputy head archivist was still visibly shaken, although the events he was describing had happened two days ago.

The archive had been broken into and one section ransacked.

'Thank God no damage was done – and thank God we recently did a full computer back-up,' Kuhlmey went on, running a hand through his leonine head of hair before shifting it to resume his habitual fiddling with his moustache. 'Otherwise we would have been in utter chaos. Heaven knows what Professor Koch will say when he returns.'

'But has anything actually been taken?' Jack insisted. This was the second visit he and Natasha had paid to the archive. On the first occasion, the previous day, the deputy head archivist had been unable to tell them anything. He knew he had to accommodate them, but he had been unwilling to be pushed around in his own domain, and Jack had quickly decided that diplomacy, rather than any more aggressive tactic, was more likely to pay off. So he had listened to Kuhlmey's lament patiently, though he was hearing it all for the second time.

Kuhlmey looked at them with a certain circumspection. If anything, though he tried hard to disguise it so as not to lessen the impact of his distress, he had an air of qualified relief, which Jack was quick to pick up on. He knew the deputy head archivist was keen to see the back of them, and that worked in their favour.

'Nothing is missing, strictly speaking,' he said at last.

It was Jack's turn to feel relief, but that was quickly crushed as Kuhlmey continued: 'But the item you seek *is* missing.'

'When did you find this out?'

'This morning. I would have telephoned, but I knew we had this appointment. So no time has been lost.' The man waved his hands apologetically. 'It's lucky we have everything on computer now. A precise search of this nature would have taken weeks in the old days.'

'Nobody's hacked into your computer?'

'Our experts assure me they have not. Why *would* anybody?'

Jack didn't trouble to answer that question; he hoped Kuhlmey's confidence was well-placed.

'In any case, that is all the information a hacker would have got: that the map was not here,' continued Dr Kuhlmey logically. 'And if they'd known that, why tamper with the archive itself?'

'Do you know who took it?' Natasha cut in.

'And when?' Jack followed up.

Kuhlmey was flustered by this short volley of questions. He certainly didn't like this pair. They didn't look as respectable as he might have hoped they would, given their unimpeachable mandate from the German government. But he knew he would have to help them as far as he could. It gave him pleasure to give them news which he was sure would perplex them.

'As to the person,' he said, 'we suspect Alexander von Humboldt.'

Natasha and Jack exchanged a glance. 'Von *Humboldt*?' Jack asked.

Kuhlmey knitted his hands together. 'Yes. But the map you want was in the collection of Prince-Elector Karl-Theodor at the time. Nevertheless, it was logged. It should have come to the university with a large consignment of other material that was transferred soon after the Grand Duchy of Baden took over the city – in 1804, to be precise.'

'And when did Humboldt come into possession of it?' Natasha asked, keeping a tight rein on her patience.

Kuhlmey smiled. 'In 1795. He never returned it. It has been noted as missing since then.' He paused, enjoying their silence. 'It's all in the records,' he went on, with a trace of pride, then added, allowing himself a tiny moment of humour: 'Mind you, no one else seems to have wanted to look at it since that time.'

'Until now,' said Jack.

'Until now,' Kuhlmey repeated, more thoughtfully.

*

They made their way back to the Europäischer Hof in silence, Natasha deep in thought, Marlow composing in his mind the report he'd have to make to Laura back in New York. Once they'd arrived, they went straight to the rooms they'd booked: adjacent rooms, one for work, the other for sleep. No one at INTERSEC knew about this arrangement.

'She wanted to come with us,' Natasha said, reading Jack's thoughts as he hunched over his laptop, making the secure connection.

'Laura? She'd have loved to. But Hudson wants her under his eye while all this is going on.'

'You can do a lot of things, Jack, but you're not very good at reading a woman's mind.'

'Nonsense.'

'If you say so.'

'What to tell her? That we've drawn a blank?'

'No.'

He looked at her. 'What are you thinking?'

'I'm wondering if the Chevaliers have made the Humboldt connection.'

'They didn't have the chance to talk to Kuhlmey, or consult the archive's records.'

'They worked out that Thomas Fielding left the map in Heidelberg.'

'And they got nowhere.'

'So far.'

'What do you mean?'

'Don't write anything for a moment.'

'OK.'

'Think Humboldt.'

'It'd be quicker if you tell me what *you're* thinking.'

'Alexander von Humboldt made a long voyage of discovery in South America between 1799 and 1804. There's got to be a connection between his taking the map a few years before he set off and that voyage.'

'That still doesn't tell us where the map is now.'

Natasha smiled. 'I think it does.'

'Where?'

'He spent a lot of time in Paris when he got back, but Berlin was home, and he worked from what was then Berlin University. It's named after him now.'

'You think it's still there – somewhere?'

'It's a lead.'

'It's the one lead we've got.'

'Then what are we waiting for?' Natasha said. 'And, as you say, we've a chance that the Chevaliers haven't made the connection.'

They packed, and checked out in haste. Two hours later, they were on their way to the German capital.

43

After a frustrating day and a half spent persuading the syndics of Humboldt University to cooperate and open the doors to some of their inner sancta without being told the precise nature of the business in hand, and with the help of pressure from the German Department of Education, backed by an increasingly anxious German government, Jack and Natasha at last found themselves in a neon-lit back room of the modern, severely functional university library building on the bleak Geschwister-Scholl-Straße. Placed on a table in front of them was an iron chest about the size of a small suitcase reinforced with iron bands and emblazoned with Humboldt's initials and crest.

'He destroyed most of his private letters and, we think, many hundreds of pages of notes,' said the academic with whom they were now confronted, Dr Günnhilde Eckhardt, a lean twenty-eight-year-old redhead from Potsdam. She was excited at the prospect of looking inside the box, which she'd extricated, dusty and a little rusty, from God-knew-where in the bowels of the building. 'Who knows what we'll find here. I don't think it's been touched since before the war, possibly even longer. Luckily, its key was attached to it.' She paused for a moment before adding, 'It's odd though –'

'What?' asked Jack.

'It took a bit of finding. Everything's catalogued, of course, but it wasn't quite where I'd expected to find it. That's why I kept you waiting a little longer than I'd hoped.'

'Any reason for it being moved?'

She shrugged. 'Could be any one of a number of reasons. We did some spring-cleaning recently, and used a handful of student volunteers to help out. They weren't supervised all the time, but they knew what they were doing. In fact, the box wasn't far from its allocated space – just a shelf along and below. Easy to get confused in the basements. At least whoever moved it rubbed most of the dust off – you can't imagine the state of some of the stuff down there.'

'Shall we open it?' asked Natasha, trying not to pick up on the slight sense of unease she was already getting from her companion. She took his hand and squeezed it gently.

'Of course.'

Dr Eckhardt pushed her spectacles back up her nose in a way that reminded Jack of Laura, untied the string holding the key to one of the handles of the chest and, with a slight sense of ceremony, put it in the lock. She had to jiggle it up and down in order to make it fit properly, and it grated as she turned it, but finally it completed its circle and she withdrew it, smiling.

'Now we shall see what we shall see.'

She lifted the lid.

Inside, a sheaf of yellow papers. Dr Eckhardt

donned a pair of cotton gloves and picked it up. The papers rustled like dry leaves under her touch. Involuntarily, Jack reached out for them, but she snatched them away.

'Not without gloves,' said Dr Eckhardt, though without irritation. 'They look as if they're about to crumble away.'

'Is there a map?'

Dr Eckhardt carefully separated the leaves of paper and laid them out. Five of them: all covered in handwriting, the brown ink faded, the paper stained and blotched. And another sheet, more recent, on which Jack instantly recognized a rubber stamp with the eagle-and-swastika seal of the National Socialist German Workers' Party – the Nazis.

44

It was easy to read the Nazi memorandum. It attested that a map of early-seventeenth-century origin had been removed for examination by the Reich Geographical Research Unit and was marked 'STRENG GEHEIM'. It was signed Martin Bormann, and dated 4 February 1938.

'What happened to this organization? Do you know?' Jack asked the archivist.

She looked grave. 'If that's where the map went, then it's almost certainly lost. But they marked their chit "Top Secret". That's very Nazi: all the paperwork impeccable. They may have put the map to some use. But if it was still in the Geographical Research Unit in 1945, you can probably forget about it. The place was bombed flat by the Russians.'

'Any chance they might have returned it to this chest at any stage?'

'It's possible, but unlikely. In that case, they would have removed this note. They were *very* conscientious about paperwork, the Nazis.'

'What's in the notes?' Natasha asked.

Eckhardt skimmed them. 'It's Humboldt's writing – that's easy to tell,' she said. 'But I'll have to get them transcribed and translated.'

'Don't need a translation,' Jack said urgently. 'Just need a copy. Fast.'

'These papers are very delicate . . .' Dr Eckhardt looked doubtful.

'Please. It's important.' Jack gave her his most winning smile.

She looked at him coolly. 'Well, I didn't imagine it wasn't, given the pressure we've been put under on your account.' She came to a decision. 'I'll try. Wait here.'

The ten minutes they waited seemed like ten years. But at last she was back. With the yellowed papers, now in a clear plastic box, she carried a set of clean white copies, which she handed to Marlow.

'And the originals?' he said.

'I'll have them restored and returned here.' She indicated the iron chest.

'No. I'll need to take them too. And the Nazi memorandum.'

'That's very irregular.'

'I believe your instructions were clear.'

'Yes.'

'In that case –' He held out his hand. After a moment's hesitation, she handed him the box.

'Thank you.'

Jack stowed the papers in the large leather shoulder bag he had with him.

'What do you think?'

'It's unlikely the Chevaliers beat us to it.'

'But not impossible.'

'We can't rule it out.'

'And now?' Natasha said when they had emerged from the building into watery sunshine.

Jack hailed a passing cab and opened the door for her. 'You get back to the Kempinski. I'll join you there later.' He gave the driver the name of the hotel.

'And you?'

'Never mind.'

He watched the taxi move off then made his way south towards Universitätsstraße and Unter den Linden, heading for the newly reopened INTERSEC offices there. The sooner the original documents were in New York, the better. Then he planned to take himself to a favourite bar in the Adlon Hotel, where he'd be able to read the notes in peace.

He was crossing Dorotheenstraße when he saw the woman on the other side of the street. She was dressed in black. He face was obscured by a wide-brimmed black hat, but he could see enough and he thought he recognized her. It was early evening, the air was keen, and there were only a few people about. He saw her raise her arm, and broke into a run as a bullet zinged past his head, missing it by a hair's breadth. She'd used a silencer, and that had interfered with her aim. But she wouldn't be alone.

He crouched low and sprinted down past the heavy stone façades of Universitätsstraße until he reached the crowds and lights of Unter den Linden, not yet bothering to pick out any other pursuers in the more crowded, lime-tree-lined boulevard. He dodged through the people, attracting angry or outraged yells when he collided with someone, and reached the cover of an arched doorway a few metres down a side street. There he took stock, hunched in the shadow the arch provided, keenly surveying the passers-by for any sign of a hunter. But there was no one.

He waited three minutes and then cautiously made his way along the street towards another turning, into the street where the INTERSEC office was. Taking refuge in a doorway, he dialled the secure number and alerted the duty agent, briefly outlining his predicament.

'Check,' said the voice at the other end. 'We'll be ready. Usual precautions.'

The line went dead. Jack knew what the usual precautions were, but he didn't like it. Two things he had to avoid: losing the material he had with him, and starting any kind of shoot-out in the street. This was a quieter street, no shops, a corner café, and little cover. The café was dimly lit, one or two people eating Hackepeter at the stand-up tables outside, under the awning, little glasses of Helles at their elbows.

He made his way along the pavement, his eyes never still, past the innocuous entrance to the apartment building where INTERSEC was located, and doubled back around the block.

No one.

He doubled back in another direction. Now, out of the corner of his eye, he caught sight of two slim young men on the opposite side of the street, similarly dressed in leather bomber jackets and roll necks. They were closing in on him.

Jack slung his pouch securely across his shoulders and shook his jacket free to ease access to the Glock in its holster under his left arm. But he wouldn't use it unless he had to. These guys were good. They couldn't have known where he was going, so they must have shadowed him well. He would take no chances, and he knew they hadn't noticed that he'd clocked them.

He approached the kerb and waited for a yellow post-van to pass. As soon as it had, he dashed across, arms wide. The two men were younger and taller than he was, but he had the element of surprise, and his arms struck each man across the throat even as their hands went for their guns, his momentum carrying them with him. They staggered backwards, and he heard the crack as their heads struck the granite wall of the building that flanked the pavement on that side. He saw blood and stepped back quickly as the two men sank to the ground.

'Hé – *Sie*!'

His action hadn't gone unnoticed. A burly man in an overcoat was yelling at him from the café, which he was passing for the third time. But the outside tables were round the corner from the INTERSEC doorway. Jack sprinted away, breathing heavily, as the other snackers outside the café started to shout as well, and others came out from its interior.

Would they recognize him again? His clothes were nondescript; he would ditch the shoulder bag and maybe swap jackets at INTERSEC. He dashed round the corner, a stitch stabbing his chest, and made it to the doorway he sought.

It opened at his touch, and a man pulled him in before swiftly closing the door behind him. Seconds later, they heard running footsteps passing outside, and there was the sound of a siren. God, these Berlin police could react fast when they wanted to.

The man who'd grabbed him ushered him into a lift, and they went up five floors, then along a narrow, dimly lit corridor to a door at the end which had a visiting card pinned to it: Freiherr von Hammerstein. The door opened in anticipation of their arrival, and the man shoved him inside.

The offices were painted grey and white and looked clinical. The neon lights drained everything of what little colour there was. But it felt like nirvana to Marlow. Another man approached, angry and drawn.

'Never do that again,' Sir Richard Hudson said.

The reason the boss was there, Marlow knew, was to check up on him. That he'd come in person meant that he didn't trust Laura. Was he sending Marlow some kind of message by that? Or was it the urgency of the situation? He didn't have time either to discuss it or think about it – for now. He tried to clear his mind of the problem Hudson presented, and handed over the original Humboldt papers with a brief rundown of what they were and how he came to have them.

When Hudson finally left him alone, he found himself a billet in a cubbyhole of an office, grey and white and glass, like everywhere else, and settled down to read the copies.

He'd been lucky, he thought. But how lucky? What was Hudson doing in Berlin? He remembered Laura's warning. The map still eluded him, too – though the one advantage he had was that the Chevaliers couldn't be any closer to it than he was.

But did they *believe* he had it? If so, he would have to tread extremely carefully.

The papers contained Humboldt's theories and conclusions about the map, and why he had decided to conceal it.

But he hadn't hidden it well enough. The map had gone, and Humboldt's notes explained why it was valuable: it was the key to Eldorado – though evidently Humboldt had failed to find the city of gold.

But the knowledge gave Jack one possible ace in the hole.

His thoughts turned to the Bormann memorandum.

PART TWO

45

Amazonia, 1938

'We are lost,' Kapitän Alfons Brandau said. He looked at the five surviving members of his team and saw that he had dashed their last hope. He looked again at the map in its celluloid folder. To protect the original, he had made this painstaking copy himself. He knew there were no mistakes in it, and he had left the original in safe-keeping at the consulate in Rio de Janeiro.

The map had led nowhere.

But he sensed that they were close – so close! Everything else, every indication on the map they had followed had worked perfectly. It was just that now, somehow, the trail had run cold. On every side, the jungle closed in on them. They would be too late to time their arrival with the sun's light falling on the temple doors.

Brandau had established himself as one of the foremost German explorer-anthropologists in the pre-war years, culminating, just three years earlier, in a collaboration with Claude Lévi-Strauss, his near-contemporary. But now Lévi-Strauss had returned to France, Brandau had joined the Navy, and the two colleagues sat on opposing sides. In addition to his native German, Brandau spoke good French and Spanish, and some Portuguese. These talents, and his expertise, had landed him his current job. Long since, he'd begun to wonder how much of a poisoned chalice it was.

Hitler was uneasy about the Navy, which had rebelled at the end of the last war; but this mission was special. All Brandau's team held naval ranks, but they were not military men. They were scientists, metallurgists, and anthropologists like himself. All were young men, however, and were experienced in jungle and tropical environments.

Brandau was not optimistic about their chances. They had lost communication with their base, and they had already fended off one attack from a local tribe – invisible assailants from the depths of the rainforest. That had cost them five men, halving their party and robbing them of two of the properly trained fighters among them. The Indians they'd encountered had been few, and most nearer the coast; but even they hadn't been friendly. They had learnt to mistrust and even hate Europeans, who had driven them further and further back into the jungle, chased them from their ancestral territories. When these men had given gifts, the gifts had been blankets infected with smallpox, and toys and beads carrying the influenza virus – diseases fatal to the Indians, and designed to free the territories they lived in for the Europeans' use.

Getting home would be a problem. But was home

the best option? Brandau was under no illusion about what he'd face when he brought the news of their failure to Hitler. Already, new prisons – concentration camps, they were calling them – had sprung up around Germany, for those who opposed or disappointed the Führer. Few who entered them ever returned.

His mind went back to the discovery of Alexander von Humboldt's iron chest and the excitement he had felt when reading the notes which accompanied the map it contained – an excitement which had overridden any glimmers of doubt aroused by Humboldt's own reservations. The great man hadn't been thorough enough, hadn't had the benefits of modern technology, had let his own conscience act as a brake on any ambition he might have had for his Fatherland. And the map itself had been so seductive, with its promise of untold riches – riches which, if discovered, might even have made the war which was looming avoidable. There would be no need to conquer the world by force of arms if infinite wealth could do the same job. Not to speak of the rewards that would fall to him personally.

But the question now was whether or not they would ever get out of this green hell at all.

Oberleutnant Günther Krantz was ill – malaria, as he knew himself, being the team's medical officer. The others helped him as best they could, but their stores – food, medicine and ammunition – were running low. They took their chances on the water from the streams and rivulets that criss-crossed their path as they cut their way with ever blunter machetes eastward through the dense jungle. Brandau was not confident that any of them would make it. Morale was low after the first attack; the flies, the humidity and the monotonous, unrelenting mass of trees and treacherous undergrowth got under everyone's skin. Tension between the remainder of his men, disappointed and tired, grew with every day that passed.

Then:

'*Scheiße!*'

It was morning, and dawn was breaking, though you'd scarcely have known from the permanent dusk here under the canopy. Brandau was woken from a fitful sleep – he'd only managed to drift into unconsciousness an hour or so earlier – by his petty officer's cursing.

'What is it, Bootsmann Müller?' Brandau was instantly alert, fearing another attack.

'The compass. Moisture's got in. It's useless.'

'We'll have to take a bearing on the sun.'

'If we can ever see it – sir.'

Brandau saw that the other two men – Matrosengefreiter Hans Schmidt and Leutnant Dieter von Langenheim, their team's metallurgist – were awake and had overheard. Well, there couldn't have been any hiding it from them. The problem was that von Langenheim was a pain in the arse, and his rebelliousness was beginning to prey on Brandau's nerves. And now that Krantz was out of the picture, he didn't have any back-up. The Bootsmann and the Matrosengefreiter, Müller and Schmidt, hung together, seeing themselves as a class apart from the officers. They were both Navy men first and foremost, and blamed the 'scientists' for setting this ill-starred expedition in motion in the first place. Not that the idea of discovering the greatest cache of gold ever recorded hadn't played on their greed, when the going had been good.

But greed was at the centre of the whole thing. Brandau, who had been interested in the anthropological aspect of the venture, along with Krantz and three of his team members already dead, had already acknowledged that he wasn't free from greed either.

And now he had to command what was left of the Geographical Research Unit's field research group, their dignity and discipline hanging in tatters, like their now barely recognizable uniforms.

They had camped for the night in a small clearing not far from the tangle of little rivers among which they had got lost. They could hear a waterfall over to the left. Brandau seemed to remember that the stream they'd been shadowing had been flowing east, probably to join up with a larger river, though they were far too far to the south for him to hope it would be the Amazon. Their weeks in the jungle had, he knew, taken them way off track.

He pointed towards the trees opposite, where he could see a faint trail. More often than not, these trails had petered out, leaving them to hack their way through until they reached a clearing. It would probably be the same this time. It was still very early, but already he was soaked in sweat. He could see that the others were too.

They drank a little water and ate what fruits and berries they could trust. They were fearful of dysentery, but they had to hang on to their glucose rations for emergencies, and everything else was gone.

'Coffee and a Hörnchen or two would be good right now,' Brandau joked. The others glared sullenly ahead of them as they crouched in a rough semicircle. They ate fast and furtively, their hands never far from the Lugers at their belts, though it had been some time since they'd used them and no one was sure whether the eternal damp hadn't affected their mechanisms. There was no oil to clean them, and the one time von Langenheim had stripped Krantz's pistol to clean it, he had dropped the mainspring into the undergrowth at his feet, where it had disappeared for ever, rendering the gun useless.

From beyond their circle, under the roughly made canopy of leaves they'd built for him, Krantz groaned loudly and twisted under the sodden grey blanket they'd covered him with. He knew he'd be better off without it, but he was in no position to tell them now, and his mind reached only occasionally into lucidity.

Müller cast a glance over at the stricken Oberleutnant. Müller was a thin, pallid man, with blond hair and a slightly receding, dimpled chin. His eyes were china-blue and devoid of any warmth. 'Better for the fucker if he died,' he muttered. 'Better for us all.'

Brandau looked at the officer's dagger – taken from one of his fellows killed in the Indian ambush – at Müller's belt and wondered if he'd suit action to his words.

He knew that the time could well soon come when they would have to do the unthinkable, and abandon Krantz to his fate. He could barely walk now, and he slowed them down. That was dangerous. He prayed they'd hit a friendly village at least, but there'd been no sign of one.

'Come on,' he said, getting to his feet. His joints ached as he carefully checked that he had the map safe before making his way over to Krantz. Behind him, the others gathered their kit in silence. As if to add deliberately to their misery, a breeze rustled in the leaves of the trees and, soon afterwards, as they'd expected, it began to rain: a soft, steady rain that bore down on you with the full effect of a Chinese water-torture.

Brandau unwrapped Krantz from his blanket, lifted him up and gave him the makeshift crutch they'd made him from a branch. It was too supple – it bent when he leant too hard on it – but it would have to do. Von Langenheim came over, his kit slung across his back, and wearily supported Krantz on his other side. Then Brandau led off.

They ploughed through the jungle for two hours, feeling the invisible sun bear down on them through the canopy after the rain had finally ceased. Now it would be the turn of the insects, Brandau thought, grimly.

He saw a pool of sunshine ahead, indicating another clearing, and made for it. They'd rest there a while before moving on. He estimated that they could do another two hours, maybe three, before exhaustion forced them to stop again for the day. He didn't dare think about how long it would take them to reach the sea. Maybe if they found a broader river, they could make a raft, and . . .

They entered the clearing and saw the remains of Krantz's shelter of the night before.

'Some fucking leader you are.' Schmidt, whose turn it'd been to support Krantz, spat the words out and dropped his burden like a sack. Krantz lay where he had fallen, curled up like a foetus in the dank leaves, whimpering like a child.

'You'll be court-martialled for that,' Brandau said evenly. 'I have two witnesses. Gross insubordination and insulting behaviour to an officer.'

Schmidt curled his lip. The other two looked down, saying nothing, but Brandau knew that von Langenheim was at the end of his tether and that Müller would close ranks with the Matrosengefreiter. Those two were stronger than the officers: Müller was wiry; Schmidt, burly. Discipline out here was to hell and gone, and of course his words rang hollow. The thought raced across his mind that he could shoot Schmidt there and then – but they might have need both of the bullet and of Schmidt's strength if it came to building and rowing a raft. He would have to let it go, even if that undermined his authority still further.

'We're fucked without a compass, sir,' said Müller, and for once his voice sounded sympathetic, as if he shared the others' sense of desolation.

Von Langenheim suddenly giggled. 'This reminds

me of a film – with Konrad Veidt – he was going round in circles in a jungle too.' The giggle developed into a laugh, and he sank to his knees. The laughter rang out even in the deadening acoustic of the claustrophobic trees, whose roots tripped them at every step, while the lianas which hung from them lashed their faces as they walked.

Then the leaves stirred again, but only to their right and left. And there was no wind.

Von Langenheim's laughter choked in his throat abruptly as the dart struck him in the front of his neck. A surprised, even offended, look came on to his face before he tipped forward and lay still, the leeches, the flies and the bone-gnawing humidity a matter of indifference to him now.

Brandau and the other two were crouching down in an instant, but Schmidt wasn't quite fast enough. He made the mistake of drawing his Luger and firing in the direction the first dart had come from before dropping to the relative cover of the undergrowth. The pistol clicked impotently as he fired, and he lost precious seconds as he checked it, unable to believe it wasn't functioning. In that moment two darts struck him: left thigh and right shoulder. He dropped down then, wrenching first one then the other out of his flesh, but too late. The poison would already be coursing through him. A third dart struck him in the face, just below the left eye, as he flailed. It was as if he were transfixed: all movement stopped and he became rigid. Then, still kneeling, he drew himself up and, with a last great bellow of rage, hurled his useless pistol towards the all-concealing trees. Then he, too, collapsed, his body writhing and jolting, until it was still.

Krantz continued to whimper, but whether it was from fear of the attack, or his sickness, Brandau couldn't guess. Perhaps he was so ill he wasn't aware of the attack.

Brandau and Müller kept low, close together, crouching on one knee, their guns held tightly in their hands, though a glance between them told them neither had much faith in their weapons.

'Pinned down,' said Müller tersely. His eyes scanned the unbroken line of trees that surrounded them.

'See anything?'

'Not a shadow.'

They waited long minutes, but nothing stirred, and there was no sound except for the distant call of birds, eerie even in daylight, and the weird, intermittent noises of the jungle. The sun shone on the gently moving leaves. Krantz continued to cry softly.

'Have they gone?' Brandau asked.

'They're waiting,' Müller replied. 'What do you suggest we do, mein Kapitän?'

Brandau looked at Krantz. He had stopped crying, and lay still, though Brandau could see he was still breathing. 'What do they want from us? We have done them no harm.'

'I don't think we have come more than ten kilometres from where the trail went cold,' Müller said. 'I think they are protecting something.'

Then the Bootsmann did a curious thing. He shoved Brandau violently to one side, making him lose his balance and crash on to his side, giving his position away. At the same time, Müller rolled away in the opposite direction, towards the far edge of the clearing, where he got to his feet and ran frantically for the protection of the trees.

At once a hail of darts swept across the space. Five hammered into Müller's retreating back. Instinctively, the thin blond man turned, his face a rictus of anger and surprise, and fired his Luger wildly in the direction of his attackers. The gun worked, the noise it made shattering the near-silence and causing birds and monkeys to set up an unbearable screeching of panic.

Brandau didn't see his Bootsmann fall. Adrenaline pumping through him, he could only think of his own survival now. His one hope was to focus on the moment when the Indians' attention would be fixed on their latest kill. Without thinking, he stood, yelling, and ran blindly into the trees. He ran for a long time, stumbling and falling but always recovering and always striving onwards, heedless of the cuts and blows he sustained as he fled. He kept going for an hour, scarcely able to believe he was still alive, until at last, by some miracle, the trees stopped abruptly and he found himself on the bank of a broad, sluggish river, its water opaque and brown.

Driven by his fear, he still did not stop, though his body screamed its exhaustion at him. Using his knife, he cut lianas to use as ropes and clumsily used them to bind together three fallen logs he found on the riverbank. He had no idea where the river would take him or how long he would survive on it. He only knew he had to get away. He had the presence of mind to cut a long branch to use as a rudimentary oar for steering, and pushed himself off. The stitch in his chest threatened to tear him apart, but he managed to control his breathing as he clambered on to his raft. It sank slightly, alarmingly, under his weight, but it held him. He gasped as he made this final effort. Then the current took him and bore him gently away.

He looked back fearfully at the riverbank, but there was no sign of pursuit. He would drift until night fell – he had a good four or five hours. Then he'd have to find somewhere to put in, and rest, and sleep. He found the thought of that soothing, and his ragged breathing slowed and became more regular. He checked his kit and assured himself that everything he needed was intact; he tried his pistol, but it was jammed and he had no way of fixing it. He would have to take his chances without it. He prayed that the river would take him out of reach of the hostile Indians, taking comfort that the tribes were extremely territorial. Once he was outside their domain, they would lose interest in following him.

Only then did he remember Krantz.

He wept silently, but whether it was from remorse or relief he could not tell.

46

New York, the Present

'Knowing the Nazis took it doesn't exactly help us. It might be lost for ever,' Sir Richard Hudson said drily. He flicked an imaginary speck of dust from the lapel of his blue pinstriped suit. He's beginning to look like a bloody banker, Jack thought, as, seated across from his boss, he rolled the ice cubes round in his glass. Hudson had decided on an informal meeting, and they were seated in the conversation area of his office, five low chairs arranged around an oval, white-oak coffee table. Leon Lopez and Laura Graves were there too. Nick Adams of the Treasury Department had just left them, distinctly unpleased with their progress but clearly too desperate to do more than bluster. China and India were expressing grave concern now, France was in a state of major panic; and, to Jack's way of thinking, everyone was running around like headless chickens. He wondered what kind of world it would be without the foundation of any kind of financial order. A new kind of holocaust.

'But I've done some research. The Nazis were very good at paperwork,' he said, finishing his whiskey and helping himself to another under Sir Richard's disapproving gaze. He knew Hudson longed for the moment when Jack's usefulness would be at an end, but did not intend to give him that satisfaction.

Beyond the windows, the lights of New York twinkled as if no one had a care in the world.

'I'll be interested to hear,' said Hudson, his voice totally arid now. 'The Nazis were also very efficient at covering their tracks.'

'Yes – they destroyed mountains of paperwork, and the Allies destroyed more with their bombs. But there were still thirty thousand tonnes of the stuff left.'

'And you've sifted through all that?'

Jack wanted to hit him, but went on instead: 'Leon has narrowed down what we need of what was left of the files of the Reich Geographical Research Unit. We found one damaged entry, which shows that the Germans acted on the map they took from Humboldt's box. They sent an expedition.'

'What happened to it?'

'Those files are missing,' interjected Leon. 'But they didn't succeed in finding anything. History would be very different if they had.'

'What about Humboldt's notes on the constellations – the symbols he mentioned? How far have you got on that?' Hudson asked him.

'I'm working on it. Blank so far.'

'And where does that leave us as far as the map is concerned? More importantly, is there any likelihood that the opposition knows what we know?'

'Unlikely,' said Laura. 'What is likely is that they'll be shadowing us, as well as putting out their own feelers.'

'Where is Ms Fielding at this moment?'

'In her suite.'

'Close watch?'

'Very close watch. If she were a double, we'd know. She can't move. And she knows nothing of this.'

'It seems to me she already knows too much.'

Laura didn't reply, but looked across at Jack. 'She only knows what can be contained,' he said. 'She believed the map was in Heidelberg. I don't think she knows anything of the connection we've uncovered.'

'And are we going to let her know?'

'It depends how useful we think she is.'

'Your responsibility,' Sir Richard said coldly. 'Have you enough of a trail to trace the map? If it still exists.'

'There's mention of a man – one of their experts, and the leader of the expedition – a certain Alfons Brandau. He held the rank of Kapitän zur Zee, but that was a courtesy rank. He was actually quite a well-known explorer and anthropologist before the Second World War.'

'And what happened to him? Eaten by alligators, I suppose?'

'Sir Richard –' protested Jack.

'It seems to me that you are wandering off track badly, Marlow. Must I remind you of the urgency of this situation? This is not the time to play out idiotic hunches about long-dead German versions of Indiana Jones.'

'The map is still the mainspring of all this,' said Laura. 'Find it, and we can assure ourselves of the city of gold. Ignore it, and we risk the Chevaliers beating us to it. We cannot afford to do that, and this Alfons Brandau is our lead.'

Sir Richard subsided. 'I ask again, what happened to this famous expedition of yours? Failure or not. Did any of them get back to Germany?'

'No paperwork is left, so we have no idea of its actual fate,' said Leon. He picked up a slim folder and drew a sheet of paper from it: a photocopy of an old, typed document bearing the swastika-and-eagle seal on the letterhead and stamped under the signature at the bottom. 'We have, however, come up with this. It's a note from the German Consulate in Rio de Janeiro dated 5 January 1939. It concerns Brandau.'

'What the hell led you to this?'

'Logic,' said Jack, taking pleasure in Sir Richard's discomfort. Laura and Leon both shot him warning glances. He wouldn't improve things by antagonizing Hudson.

Hudson snatched the paper and glanced at it. 'So – he at least got out of the jungle.'

'Looks like it.'

'And returned to Germany?' asked Hudson, dropping the paper on to his desk. 'Mad if he did.'

'That's what I think,' returned Jack.

'Where did he go, then? There's nothing in this consulate letter to say anything about that. It simply confirms the issue of a passport.' Hudson paused. 'And, wait a minute, which side did Brazil lean to?'

'The war was still nine months away, but Getúlio Vargas kept his country neutral,' Laura put in.

'Thank you for reminding me. Lucky for our friend Brandau.'

'Any clue about where he went next?'

'No. We're looking into shipping records.'

'He might have stayed in Rio – sat out the war,' suggested Leon.

'There's no record of that – though I was surprised he didn't. Maybe he was uncomfortable there for some reason,' said Jack.

'So what happened to him?'

'A German national wanting to return to Europe but not to his homeland in 1939,' pondered Laura. 'It narrows the field.'

'Does it?' asked Hudson.

'I think so.'

Hudson's desk console buzzed. He leant forward and pressed a button on it. 'OK, Sally,' he said to his secretary. He stood up. The others followed suit. The meeting was over.

Hudson looked at the three of them. 'If you track this person down,' he said, 'you'd better pray he came back with the map still on him. And you'd better work fast. And now, I have a plane to catch.'

The way he said it, it was clear he was playing for effect and hoping someone would ask him where he was going. Laura obliged. He turned a theatrically grim look on her.

'Washington,' he said.

*

'They were on to you in Berlin,' Laura said to Jack after the door had closed behind Hudson.

'Yes.'

'And you know what that means.'

'Yes,' Jack said again.

He would have to watch his back.

47

Rio de Janeiro, January 1939

When Alfons Brandau finally reached Rio de Janeiro he'd felt relief at first. By the time he reached the consulate, he felt safer. The Brazilian farmers who'd rescued him had given him new clothes, but he looked like a local peon, and it was as much as he could do to get them to let him past the gate. To make matters worse, the official to whom he'd handed the original map was no longer at the consulate. But the story he told – and his perfect *Hochdeutsch* – convinced the secretary who'd greeted him of his identity. The man asked him to wait. He waited two hours. They were probably checking his story.

Finally, a shortish, bearded man in his mid-forties appeared and shook hands. Brandau had not met him on his previous visit here, when he had left the original map for safe keeping.

The man was dressed in a white linen suit with an edelweiss badge rather than the Party insignia in his buttonhole. His manner was brisk but not unfriendly, his handshake firm and sincere, and he immediately ushered his guest through to an office whose walls were lined with copaiba wood and whose tall windows overlooked a garden full of palms but was otherwise German, down to the fussy net curtains and the lacy cloth spread on the low table near the fireplace. Armchairs with antimacassars surrounded it. Over by the window was the business end of the room: a huge carved desk in pale wood bearing a telephone, a green-shaded lamp, an imposing iron pen-set and a pile of important-looking documents, many loaded with red or gold seals and multicoloured ribbons. There was not a trace of the swastika, nor was there the usual prominent framed photograph of the Führer.

'Take a seat, Kapitän Brandau,' said the man. This was another relief. By using his rank and name without question, the official was indicating at least a degree of trust. Brandau thanked God he knew a little, at least, of how these things worked. He seated himself in one of the red velvet chairs, so solidly upholstered he might as well have been sitting in a pew, and waited while the bearded man did likewise, settling himself unhurriedly and then reaching for and ringing a little silver bell near his hand on the table. 'I expect a taste of home wouldn't go amiss,' he said, looking at Brandau through grey-blue eyes that had grown prematurely muddy with age. 'Thank you, Senhora Batista,' he continued, as a short, plump, pretty woman in her early thirties came in. She was manhandling a trolley that bore coffee, cheesecake, Pflaumenkuchen, Bienenstich and Spekulatius biscuits. In a small ice bucket rested a bottle of Himbeergeist. The woman served Brandau with a selection of cake and biscuits on a gold-edged porcelain plate decorated with flowers. Her bright brown eyes were full of laughter, and her smile was like a hug.

'I advise you not to eat too much, though. Your stomach must be pretty shaken up after your ordeal.'

How had the man guessed so much? thought Brandau, as he took the little fork and napkin he'd been given and tried each of the delicacies in turn. They stung his tongue with their sweetness. Delicious. Senhora Batista poured black coffee while the white-bearded official busied himself with the schnapps. Then the woman retreated, and the official settled himself in his chair.

'Forgive the informality, but I thought you'd prefer it,' said the official. 'My name is Schickert – Hartmut Schickert. I am the consul here, and I bid you welcome.'

Brandau had already guessed that the man held a high rank from the nature of the room he sat in, but he was surprised that he'd been greeted by the consul himself. He bowed slightly in his seat:

'Herr Konsul.'

'We are aware of your work for Geographical Research,' the man continued; and this was another surprise, for Brandau's mission was supposed to be top secret. However, he imagined that German high officials in the country he was working in would have been informed.

'However,' continued Schickert, 'from your appearance, I think you have not met with unqualified success.'

'That, unfortunately, is correct,' Brandau acknowledged.

'A pity. I think our Führer laid great store by a happy outcome.' The consul settled back as best he could in his uncomfortable armchair. 'Would you like to tell me what happened?'

Brandau was not sure that he should, but the coffee, cakes and, above all, the Himbeergeist had warmed and lulled him, and, here in this room, so redolent of home, he felt secure for the first time in weeks. He told the consul the whole story, trying to keep it short and unadorned, sticking to the facts and emphasizing that no effort had been spared to carry out the orders with which the expedition had been entrusted. At last he came to speak of his escape – the makeshift raft, the five days he'd spent drifting downriver until, exhausted and dehydrated, near madness, he'd become aware of voices near him, of arms reaching out and hauling his emaciated body into a fishing boat, of being carried from it to a small riverside town, where he was laid on a bed in a neat little house. There was a smell of fish and cow dung everywhere, and the streets were nothing more than muddy tracks between the houses. But the people – Portuguese settlers – had been friendly and kind, and the one doctor in the community had even spoken some German. The local priest had taken him to live in his house by the immaculate white church on a hill to the east of the town centre.

He had spent ten days in the town, whose name he had never learnt. As soon as he felt himself sufficiently recovered, he'd persuaded his hosts to provide him with onward transport to Rio, which, as it turned out, was only two hundred and fifty kilometres distant. He still had his pack with him. No one had rifled it during his illness. In it were his papers, ruined by damp, as was his precious copy of the map. But he still had the pouch of gold marks intended for the payment of guides and interpreters.

The headman of the township had accepted five of these and for another ten days Brandau had travelled by wagon over rough roads through ever more cultivated countryside until they reached Rio, where he was left.

'And your companions?'

'All dead.'

Schickert took the schnapps from its ice bucket and poured two more glasses. Brandau picked his up with a hand that was still shaking with emotion from his recollected tale, and downed it greedily.

'Better have no more of that,' said the consul kindly. 'Just one more thing.' He paused. 'What shall we do with the original map which you left with us?'

Brandau looked around the room. Once again he noticed the absence of the Führer's portrait and the lack of any Nazi Party insignia. 'I must take it back,' he said.

'To Germany?'

'Of course.'

Schickert looked at him evenly. 'We can issue a passport for you, and arrange passage to Europe. But you will not be travelling to a German port. After you arrive, it will be up to you.'

'Are you a Party member?' Brandau asked, lowering his voice.

The consul spread his hands. 'Of course. But I am first and foremost a diplomat.'

'Will there be war?'

'No doubt of that. I'll redecorate my office when it comes. Until then, I am in a distant, neutral country, and I trust my staff. I speak fluent Portuguese. My masters in the Fatherland will allow me my little foibles as long as I'm useful to them.'

'Is it a war we will win?'

'I don't doubt it,' Schickert replied in a neutral voice. 'But if I were you, I'd think things over on your voyage home.'

A short time later, Kapitän Brandau, dressed in a new, dark-blue wool suit, was standing at the stern of the transatlantic steamer SS *Maria Teresa* of the Italian line, watching Rio de Janeiro glittering among its green hills in the early-morning sunlight. In the pocket of the suit was a civilian passport made out in his own name, and a new wallet containing 15,000 Reichsmark.

He watched as the city receded, until it was no more than a white speck where the outspread canvas of the ocean met the lighter blue of the sky, and then he returned to his cabin.

Brandau had no need to check on the map, but he did so anyway. It was quite safe, carefully sandwiched between the new sets of clothes the consul had provided him with.

He thought over Schickert's advice. He had no idea why the man had offered it, nor what he meant exactly by 'think things over'. He did know that, if he had chosen to, Schickert could have had him killed, or kept the map, or both.

Perhaps Schickert just wanted both to be off his hands, to disappear.

48

Barcelona, February 1939

The Catalonian capital bore all the scars of the battle that had recently raged in it, the buildings pockmarked with shell- and bullet-holes, their mouldings broken and façades scarred. Only a matter of weeks earlier, General Fidel Dávila, at the head of Francisco Franco's Nationalist army, had entered the city, abandoned by its government and a large part of its population. Since then, an atmosphere of fear and paranoia had settled over the place. Old scores had been settled, the Catalan Republicans quickly brought under the Nationalist heel. The bad guys had won.

Arriving on a ship belonging to a country run by a sympathetic fellow-dictator and carrying a German passport, Kapitän Brandau didn't experience too much difficulty. Indeed, local Nationalist sympathizers who'd come out of the woodwork after two and a half years clapped him on the back and sang the praises of the 'wonderful Messerschmitts of the Condor Legion, who flew over our army and over this city like guardian angels'. Exterminating angels for the Republicans, thought Brandau, but he kept this to himself.

After his long absence from Europe, he found it a darker and more confusing place. The longer he stayed in Barcelona, the more he thought that this was what life in Germany would be like. On the surface, the city basked in its usual pleasant warmth, the sun glowing on the modernist buildings of Gaudí, Montaner and Cadafalch; the prosperous boulevards stretching north from the Plaza de Cataluña, and down from it via Las Ramblas, with its busy cafés and its opera house, to the sea. But the Catalan language was banned, socialist books were prohibited, people disappeared or were taken up to Montjuïc to be shot in the moat there after summary trials. Freedom of expression, and a whole nation's identity, were being forcibly crushed. It was not an easy place to take up residency, but, on the other hand, it was a very easy place to disappear into, especially if the new controllers perceived you to be a friend of the regime.

Brandau had decided to lie low and take stock. Finding that his gold Reichsmark went a long way here, he rented a modest one-bedroomed apartment on the fourth floor of a crumbling block in a narrow street leading east off Las Ramblas near the opera house and the market. He got a job as a clerk in the Customs House, Enric Sagnier's massive yellow wedding-cake of a building down by the port. He found it a comforting place – big enough to lose oneself in.

And then he waited. Months passed, and he found that he had made no effort to return to Germany. No one expected him to, or asked him any questions. When the tensions in Europe blossomed into war in the autumn, he found himself as if rooted to the spot.

He made few friendships, and occasional traffic with women was confined to the town whores, though he selected one favourite, but he confided little in her. He got used to his own company, and solitude became a habit.

He realized he had taken Hartmut Schickert's advice, however unconsciously. But he also became jealous of the map. He pored over it night after night until he became obsessed with it. There was a secret it withheld, he knew it, but he could not unlock it. He had been *so close*!

Brandau didn't realize that he had caught the disease of greed. If there were riches beyond anyone's dreams buried out there under the dank soil of the Amazonian jungle, if there were a temple, and if there were a city of gold beneath it, then he held the only key. And he would find the city! He would sit out this war and go back, and, this time, he would succeed.

He was secure here, he told himself, and contented. He'd made enough contacts within the local administration to ensure that no one would question his presence.

He had forgotten that the issue of a passport leads to paperwork, and that paperwork finds its way into files that unknown hands can open, unknown eyes look at. He had not reflected on the fact that the consul in Rio knew the destination of the SS *Maria Teresa.*

He thought he had buried himself too deeply to be found.

49

Paris, the Present

'We have a mission. It is one we have pursued across the centuries with a single-mindedness that has ensured our survival. Every single Knight-Commander since the split from Rome has held that one ideal sacred. And now, at last, the right time has come. The world has passed the tipping point. The train is no longer rushing towards the precipice; it is falling towards the rocks. Now is the time to take control and to salvage what we can from the inevitable wreck. To make a phoenix rise from the ashes. To control humankind, for its own good.'

James Topcliffe was speaking like a politician, Ambroise Louvier thought as he sat and listened, wondering if the Knight-Commander believed even a tenth of what he was saying. But he couldn't deny that Topcliffe was fanatically devoted to the tenets of the Chevaliers d'Uriel. Whether he would act according to them, if and when he ever laid hands on the city of gold, was another matter. But when that moment came, Louvier would be ready. And it had better be soon. Already it was late May. If they were to manage to penetrate the city of gold, they had only a matter of weeks before the sun's light would cross the temple doors and open them. But that knowledge, found in a document left in the Paris mansion by the seventeenth-century Knight-Commander Audric Ballin, would be useless to them without the map. And they knew, too, that any attempt to blow the doors open with dynamite would be fruitless.

The third person in the room, Drita Agoli, sat quiet and bolt upright in her chair. If she moved too quickly, her shirt would rub painfully across the weals on her back – the result of her punishment for having let the agent of the opposition get away in Berlin, taking with him whatever precious clues he might have been carrying. But she had taken the flogging gladly: that the Knight-Commander had not ordered her death was proof that she was still useful.

'It falls to us to do it. To me!' Topcliffe continued, his eyes burning. It was time to bring him back to earth.

'We must focus on the map,' Louvier reminded him gently. 'Without it, we can do nothing.'

'Of course. I know that.'

'And now we know that we are not the only ones interested in it.'

'But that is something our sponsors do *not* know,' Topcliffe said. He had calmed down now, and he looked around the bleak, functional office they stood in, so unlike the ornate rooms he was used to, and loved. But after the debacle in their old headquarters, they had closed the house in the rue des Francs-Bourgeois and moved to an anonymous suite of rooms in one of the modern blocks on the vast, busy and bleak Place d'Italie. Not his favourite part of Paris, but it kept him where he needed to be, at the centre of his operations, and he had moved swiftly to identify the enemy and to placate his sponsors. Fresh from a lightning visit to Pyongyang, he had returned with Kim Jong-un's personal endorsement and the promise of as much equipment and as many men as he needed when the time came, and sufficient funding to make him feel that, once the map was in his hands, nothing would stop him. Already his organizers in Brazil were busy recruiting. He did not need to reflect on the consequences of failure. The consequences of failure would be death – and death, if it had to come, would be by his own hand.

'That is to our advantage, certainly,' Louvier said. 'And our friends will lead us to the map.'

'We are sure it is INTERSEC?' Drita Agoli questioned. 'We are sure it is not the Others?'

Topcliffe made a gesture of impatience. 'The Brotherhood ceased to exist as any kind of organization years ago. The last vestiges of their power vanished during the Second World War.' He bit his lip. The destruction of the Château d'Uriel in that war had meant that much of the Chevaliers' archive had been destroyed, and all the most recent material. If he had had it now, tracing the map might have been a far easier matter.

What disturbed them all was that they did not know for sure that the archive had been destroyed. It had certainly disappeared. But the Americans had been responsible for the sacking of the chateau. Topcliffe's recurring nightmare was that the archive had been passed to the Office of Strategic Services, which later became the CIA. He reassured himself by thinking that if the CIA had it, they had certainly never used it to their advantage; and they certainly hadn't shared it with their associated organizations.

'In any case,' Louvier said, 'we have identified the man Marlow. He is an agent of INTERSEC.'

The information had been hard won. Following the same clues, the Chevaliers had dispatched agents to Heidelberg and found the same bare cupboard, but they had not resorted to violence there. That would have shown their hand too soon, and it was not necessary, so they had left a bemused Dr Kuhlmey in peace. But it was logical to follow the trail to Berlin, and they had not been surprised to pick up the irritating Mr Marlow there. Losing him had snapped James Topcliffe's never very great supply of patience. He had given the necessary orders.

Dr Günnhilde Eckhardt had buckled easily under torture and told them what she knew. It was enough. The torture had been careful, leaving no outward trace on her body, and breaking no unnecessary bones. The fire following the staged car crash on the Berliner Ring near Feldheim had burnt the body thoroughly. No pathologist would find significant indications within the corpse that the ruptures in her stomach and intestines – if they had not been obliterated – were owing to anything other than injuries caused by the pile-up.

The Chevaliers had always been aware that their enterprise would draw fire upon them. It had not been easy to discover the existence, let alone the function, of the organization that had been given the task of neutralizing them, but a hacker engaged by them in Zurich had finally located activity through a secure server in upstate New York which identified a group calling itself simply International Security – INTERSEC. The hacker had not been able to trace more than a few routine instructions and responses, but it was enough.

'Updates?' asked Topcliffe.

Louvier turned to Agoli, who, keen to redeem herself, spoke eagerly: 'Chevalier Dargent reports a sighting of the subject in New York yesterday. She adds that there is attendant activity.'

'Good. Keep her active. Reports hourly, if you please.' He turned to Louvier. 'Have we any more on the Nazis' Geographical Research Unit?'

'Little more than what we got out of Eckhardt, but we have established that the man in command of the expedition they sent was a certain naval captain called Brandau. We know he got away, because there's a trail that leads to Rio, and an old consulate note of a passport being issued to him there, but before we got any further the contact was blocked. We can't access any relevant German records now. Even Welsby in Zurich can't get in.'

'That means our friends are already on to it,' Topcliffe said. 'Inform Dargent immediately. Any move

Marlow makes, I want to know about it.' He paused. 'And eliminate Welsby. He's served his purpose.'

He looked out of the window at the busy, traffic-clogged Place d'Italie. It was wreathed in a light smog of pollution, and the trees in the island garden at its centre fought a war of pure survival against the exhaust fumes from the never-ending traffic.

He had not told his associates about the deadline North Korea had given him. No point in panicking them. And he was sure he could string his sponsors along – for as long as it took. He had no doubt that his adversaries would be looking over their shoulders, but following them was just one of the lines he was going to take. The map still existed: of that he was certain. He would succeed, and bring the world to heel, and to its senses.

He repeated the words to himself: *It is my destiny*.

He spoke a few more words to Agoli. 'And see if traces to the passenger lists of transatlantic steamers have been closed too. There must be a record of their crossings from Rio. We need those for early 1939.'

'Certainly, Knight-Commander.' She ran her hands over her thighs, and he watched her as she did so. Women with dangerous natures had always excited him – women who needed taming, needed to be subjected to his will. She had taken her beating well, but she was still wild. He would enjoy breaking her in, later, when there was a time for pleasure again.

His thoughts turned back to Kapitän Brandau. He

doubted very much that the man had returned to Germany. What better place to begin his search than at the man's port of entry on his return to Europe?

He imagined Marlow would be working along the same lines, and he hoped their paths would cross. He had plans for Marlow.

50

Barcelona, 1942

It was about 17h00 on a hot, humid day at the end of July. Alfons Brandau had just returned to his apartment after a long lunch alone in a quiet restaurant on the seafront, where he'd sat on the terrace and watched a handful of people enjoying the beach and the sea as if they hadn't a care in the world, as if there were no vicious war raging only a few hundred kilometres away to the north and east. He recognized one or two of the men as senior members of Mayor Mateu i Pla's inner circle. Their bodyguards sat uncomfortably in their suits on the edge of the sand and wore dark glasses. No one could have mistaken them for anything but gangster heavies.

The mood of the city, even now, after three years under the new regime, was forlorn and grim. But there was an active underground in which Catalan culture and its language was defiantly kept alive. Nevertheless, and despite the beautiful location of the city, Brandau felt trapped here. He missed his friends and family at home, but he had made his choice.

He lived alone and had become used to his solitary

life. Most of the time, he hardly noticed it. He had spent the first year obsessed with the map, studying it, reading every word he could find associated with Raleigh's travels and Humboldt's dismissal of the Elizabethan sea captain's claims. Not that there was much material to be found here.

He kept looking at the map, as if somehow it would reveal its secret to him. Eventually, though, his obsession waned. He decided he would wait. He was still young; he had time; he would go back when the war was over. Retrace his steps. He knew that, somehow, he would unlock the secret. But he would go back well armed and well prepared. He was not going to fall victim again to the tribe that protected the area around the location of the city of gold with such deadly determination.

He told no one of the map. This was easy, for he made few friends. There were a few drinking companions, his colleagues at the Customs House, and the whores he used when he needed a woman's company. But he had no other society and did not seek it. He avoided any relationship that threatened to become more than superficial.

The time passed quickly and easily enough. He knew that he had begun to drink too much and was spending too much time in the bars and restaurants that crowded the dark, narrow, winding streets and alleyways of the Barrio Gótico, for often the loneliness of his apartment oppressed him. He knew that he was letting himself get out of condition and that he was putting on weight. But he told himself that he would put all that right when the time came.

But his inner life was not healthy. He may have ceased to pursue the secret of the map, but its possession was something he valued greedily. He guarded it with all the dedication of the dragon Fafnir watching over the golden hoard of the Nibelung.

By the summer of 1942, however, Alfons Brandau was beginning to pull himself together. From the safety of Spain, he had been following the progress of the war closely. The attack on Pearl Harbor the previous December had brought the Americans into the war, and now Greater Germany was caught between two massive powers, Russia and the United States. The decision to advance into Russia in quest of the Ukrainian oilfields was a disastrous one. No one had ever succeeded, and Hitler should have learnt from Napoleon the impossibility of maintaining lines of supply through a vast and inimical country, especially during winter. But if Russia had unlimited oil, the USA had unlimited money, and her young men were fresh, confident and well fed. What's more, the Americans had at last decided that their mother country was worth fighting for.

It looked as if the war was lost. Indeed, Brandau knew that this had been the private thinking of some of the High Command since the very outbreak of hostilities. Hitler was a nineteenth-century anachronism. Power had begun to run from central Europe to Russia and America at about the time the Nazi leader had been born, fifty years earlier.

So now it was just a question of time. No more than another two or three years. And time passes fast. Always. Whether you are happy or sad, beaten or victorious, it always steals a march on you, and the moment is gone almost before you've lived it.

Brandau began to think about getting sponsors, raising money for his plan, without letting too much information out. It was a difficult undertaking, but greed is a great seducer, and he was making some progress.

Foolishly, he'd decided to walk home from the beach and, although he had drunk only one bottle of wine with lunch, he was feeling light-headed when he reached his apartment. Its thick walls, tiled floors and high ceilings made it a cool refuge, and he had left the windows shuttered. He bathed and changed and decided to read while he waited for the girl to arrive. One of his favourites, a pretty, stocky creature originally from Girona, she did not overcharge, and she would usually stay as long as he wanted. To her, occasionally, he poured out something of what was in his heart, knowing that she would barely understand anything of what he told her.

He poured himself a tequila over ice, lit a cigarette and settled down in his rocking chair with a battered copy of Heine's *Atta Troll.* He was expecting Dulcinea (as he'd nicknamed her) at six.

The knock of the door, soft and even timid, came at 18h15. Dulcinea was usually punctual, and reliable. Brandau had begun to feel a mixture of worry and disappointment when she hadn't arrived on the hour.

Though he was used to solitude, he knew it was not his natural state, and now he was relieved. He hadn't relished the prospect of an evening alone, and he had fretted over Dulcinea's safety. Barcelona – especially his district – wasn't the safest place in the world. He'd opened some of the shutters, and the mellow sunshine poured gently in. He'd bought wine, and ice to cool it, and chocolates. Dulcinea's fee, which he liked to pay immediately to get it out of the way, was ready in an envelope on the table by the front door. She always took the envelope without opening it and counting the money. He felt a kind of love for her for that.

So he went to the door eagerly, looking forward to the warmth of her body, to her comforting embrace.

In his eagerness, he neglected to use the door's spy-hole. No sooner had he released the latch than the door was shoved violently inwards, pushing him back into the room. He fell over the rocking chair and, in the moment it took him to regain his feet, three men had entered the room and closed the door behind them.

Two immediately pinioned him by the arms. They were dressed in police uniforms, and Brandau's first thought was that this was a question of mistaken arrest. These cops had come to the wrong place – they must have taken him for a member of the Republican resistance. He had friends in the administration through his work in the Customs House, but he knew that it would take some time for him to sort things out. He thanked God the map was securely hidden. If anyone searched the apartment in his absence, or broke in, they would never find it. Nevertheless, his heart lurched as he thought fearfully about its safety. Fafnir dragged from his guardianship of the gold. What dwarves might come and spirit it away in his absence? He felt panic rise in him but, as he started to protest his innocence, the third member of the team produced a cloth and a small brown bottle. Brandau struggled to keep his face averted from the chloroform, but it was a lost cause, and soon he lapsed into darkness. His last thought was that no one would question three policemen carrying an unconscious man to a car. People would pretend not to notice.

When he came to, Brandau realized that his abductors hadn't been police. They may have been from the Servicio de Información, but would they have bothered to disguise themselves as regular cops? And, in that case, he would have been carted off to El Hecho, or to one of Franco's other concentration camps. Instead, he found himself in what looked like an ordinary cellar illuminated by one dim bulb that hung from the arched ceiling. Dank, black brick walls, a floor covered in coal dust, and the usual junk and detritus you find in such places: old packing cases, broken chairs and forgotten domestic equipment.

His real panic arose from his situation. He was placed upright in a watertight glass tank. It was completely enclosed. Its glass top, which his head touched, had a few air holes bored into it, and above another, larger hole in one corner was a tap: a tap that dripped slowly but steadily into the tank, the drips joining the water it already contained. The water was up to his shoulders.

He was bound hand and foot, but could not lose his balance because the tank was just big enough to contain his body. He couldn't move.

There was no sound apart from that of the water dripping. In the surrounding silence, the noise seemed amplified. Brandau did not know how long he remained alone there, but he could measure the passage of time by the rising level of the water. From the time he regained consciousness to the time the door at the top of a short flight of stone steps opened, the level had passed from the top of his shoulders to the level of his chin and was beginning to creep towards his mouth. He had been starting to writhe, as far as he could, and the very fact that he could barely do even that increased the panic and fear that were beginning to unhinge him in the confined, claustrophobic space when he heard the footsteps and the creak of hinges. Two men descended the steps. They were dressed in ordinary suits and ties, like businessmen. Their faces were pale and austere. Older men, in their fifties. One ascetic-looking, like an Inquisition priest; the other burlier, a patrician. One look at their faces told Brandau that any search for sympathy or pity, tenderness or truth in these men would be in vain.

The voices when they came were a little blurred, but their sense was clear.

'Where is it?' said the patrician.

Brandau knew what they meant. He could not

imagine how they had tracked him down. He shook his head, tilting it to keep his face out of the water.

'Where is it?' repeated the patrician with a sigh. 'If you want to live, Captain Brandau, you must tell us now. Otherwise, you will drown. It will take, at this rate, one hour more. But I can increase the speed.'

'*No!*' Brandau blurted the word out before his mind engaged. But he was in no position to bargain. He would have to part with the map or die. And the map would be no use to him dead.

'Good. Then tell us.'

But again he shook his head.

'You are being very foolish. It cannot be far. We think it is in your wretched apartment. We will find it. No one will question a police search. *We* can take our time. You, on the other hand, have very little left.'

A thought occurred to Brandau. 'I can help you find it,' he managed to croak.

The patrician looked surprised. 'The map? We do not need your help for that. But you *would* save us time, and you would save your own life.'

'The city.'

The men looked at each other, appearing to consider this. They whispered together, then the patrician turned to Brandau again. 'How?'

'I have been close. So close. I know the jungle. The tribes –'

The water dripped on, the drops plashing gently close to his right ear. The very noise seemed calculated to drive him mad.

The patrician took his time, but he also consulted his watch, and, even in his predicament, Brandau could see that he was not as assured as he wanted to appear to be.

The patrician brought his face close to the glass. 'Very well. We will consider this. Now – where is it?'

Brandau closed his eyes for a moment. The water lapped at the edge of his mouth, at the lobes of his ears.

Speaking in a voice barely above a whisper so they had to crane to hear him, he told them.

The patrician grunted in satisfaction and exchanged another glance with the priest, who nodded.

'Thank you, Captain Brandau,' the patrician said. The priest reached over to the tap and made a small adjustment. The rate of the falling drops slowed. Without another word, the men made for the stone steps.

'Wait!' Brandau called out, his voice making the surface of the water vibrate.

The patrician half turned. 'Yes?'

'What about me? Aren't you going to release me?'

The patrician smiled. 'We are going to ascertain that you are telling the truth,' he said. 'If you are, we will be back in good time. If not . . .'

He let his words hang in the air. The men left.

Alone, Brandau counted the seconds between the falling of each drop. Ten – or thereabouts. Ten seconds can seem a very long time. With each drop, he knew, the level of the water rose an infinitesimal amount, but slowly, inexorably, it would rise higher and higher.

How long did he have?

Another thought struck him – too late: would they come back at all?

Then the dim light was extinguished and he was left in absolute darkness. He became aware that the water surrounding his immovable limbs was beginning to chill him. Now, at last, he knew what was going to happen. He screamed, and struggled violently, but to no avail. Then he became quiet and listened to the gentle noise of the water, drop by drop, each one separated by an infinity of time. He grew numb, and his mind, unable to accept his situation, began to wander – over his youth, his life. He thought of his parents, his friends. The greed which had brought him to this pass. And he thought of Dulcinea. She had been late. Had she arrived at last, to find an empty apartment? Would she raise the alarm? It was unlikely. He found himself shaking his head at the thought.

He knew that she had not been spared. No one would raise an alarm. There was nothing left but the darkness and the steady dripping of the water.

It had reached his fore-lip, just below his nostrils, and he was ready to give up. He let his head sink to his chin, but he couldn't meet death halfway. He jerked his head up again, craning it back, gasping, his face close to the glass top of his vertical coffin.

Then his mouth opened in a silent scream.

51

'Quickly!'

'Got it.'

The patrician, Luis Barbero, who had inherited his position among the Chevaliers from his father, had made a last effort and succeeded in heaving the large boxwood bookcase away from the wall. The books it had contained already lay scattered across the floor of Alfons Brandau's apartment. Barbero kicked some of them away to make a clear path for him to shove the bookcase to a wide enough angle to allow him access to the wall behind. It was clean there – not a trace of dust. Brandau must have hidden the map recently.

Barbero's senior, the Grand Chevalier Josep Andreu, still dressed in the long, dark overcoat he had donned to cross town, looked even more like a priest than before. His pale eyes glinted eagerly behind his thick glasses. Barbero, sweating, squeezed his bulk into the space he had made. His fingers searched the wall for the place. Under his touch, he felt the first loose brick and pulled it free, then another, and another. He felt in the alcove behind them and, with a cry of triumph, pulled out a leather-and-cellophane map case. His head felt light from the effort, but there had been no question of engaging any junior members to do this job – it was too important. He extricated himself from behind the bookcase and took out his reading glasses to verify his find. Andreu looked on impatiently, his hand already outstretched.

'Give it to me.'

Barbero reluctantly obeyed. He brushed dirt from his jacket and wiped the sweat from his face with a plum-coloured handkerchief before joining the other man, craning to look over his shoulder.

'Is this the true map?'

Andreu nodded. 'I am sure of it.'

'But the Germans had it, and failed to find the city.'

'If there is a secret locked within this map, we will find it. Brandau would not have clung to it if he had not believed in it. And our whole quest, over three and a half centuries, has been based on it.'

Barbero nodded.

'It is unlike you to show doubt,' Andreu continued, eyeing his junior with suspicion.

'Forgive me –'

'I do not need to prove anything to you. Believe that Humboldt would not have gone to so much trouble to conceal it if he had not believed it had power. Believe that the Others would not have constantly sought to thwart us down the years if it had no power. No – this is the key to the city. We have to learn the trick of turning it correctly. Nothing this important would be without difficulty. We must rise to the challenge.'

'Of course, Grand Chevalier.'

'Good. Now, let's go. The sooner this is safe, the better.'

Andreu swept the map case and its precious contents under the folds of his overcoat and made for the door. Barbero followed him down the steep staircase to the street. It was dark and narrow, so narrow that festoons of washing hung between the tall buildings on either side. The men glanced round before leaving the cover of the entrance. Andreu had elected to carry out this operation with Barbero alone, so secret was it. The disadvantage was that they had no back-up, should they have been shadowed; but Andreu had little fear of that. The Chevaliers had traced Brandau to Barcelona by checking the lists of people who'd registered in the city since its fall to the Nationalist forces three years earlier. The German chapter of the Order had dispatched his name and the broad details of his mission from the Third Reich, where they had taken care to be fully represented. At the highest level. Grand Chevalier Hermann Göring himself controlled the chapter there, though in these days his standing with Hitler was waning, and the British Knight-Commander was beginning to consider a replacement.

It had been a simple matter to follow Brandau's trail to the Customs House and from there to his private address, though it had taken patience and time. The war had been a grave disruption to lines of communication for the Chevaliers.

The important thing was to be certain that absolute secrecy had been maintained. Even so, Andreu was cautious. He had never underestimated the cunning or tenacity of the Others. He smiled to himself when he reflected on how many international secret-service organizations believed them to be long extinct – thanks to the Order's careful infiltration of those organizations.

But soon, there would no longer be any need for such secrecy. The time had come when the whole world would know the name of the Order of the Chevaliers d'Uriel, and tremble at it.

The two men turned to their left and made their way towards Las Ramblas, where they had parked the car. They'd be up in the hills beyond Tibidabo, and safe, within an hour.

It is always the descent from a mountain that is most dangerous, because it is always on the descent that you think you can relax.

It was dark by now, and the street lamps were lit. Their glow was reflected in the cobblestones, slick after a recent rainfall. Rain was still in the air, and the two men kept their heads down, Andreu hunched slightly over the map, which he held against him, protectively, under his coat. Las Ramblas was deserted, apart from a handful of dejected-looking whores on the edge of the Barrio Gótico; under the lights in the Plaza de Cataluña, away to the north, a few figures were gathered, and outside the cafés people were drinking coffee and cognac. Andreu hated the fact that the Catalan names had been replaced by Spanish ones; but, very soon, men like Franco and Hitler, who stood so proud now, would be thrown headlong into the cesspool of history. The thought warmed him.

'What about the German?' Barbero broke into his thoughts as he stooped to unlock the old Elizalde.

'No one's used that house in years.'

They climbed into the car, Barbero behind the wheel.

'Vamos,' said Andreu.

Barbero's hand was on the starter button when his head was jerked back by a thin cord flung round his neck from behind. His hands flew to it as his big body started to quiver and thrash in his seat. Andreu's reactions were lightning-fast. He reached for the door handle and was halfway out of the car, already going for his Mugica in its holster under his left arm – but the map case hindered him. A tall man wearing a Borsalino which threw a deep shadow over the upper half of his face stepped from an unlit alleyway and had a long knife twisting deep between Andreu's ribs before the automatic was halfway out. The man had removed the map case from Andreu's grip before the priest had slid to the cobblestones, the life choking out of him. His last thought, as the world turned upside-down and he slipped into darkness, was a despairing question: *how did they know?*

By now Barbero had ceased to writhe in the driver's seat, and his limp body was bundled out on to the street. His killer took his place behind the wheel as his accomplice, throwing the knife aside, joined him. The Elizalde, Barbero's pride and joy, started at the first touch of the button, and was driven off unhurriedly in the direction of Plaza de Cataluña, where it joined the thin trickle of other nocturnal traffic. It drove round the plaza and continued north, towards the hills that encircled the landward sides of the city like a bowl.

The whores, who had witnessed it all, vanished into the shadows like wraiths.

52

New York, the Present

'So Brandau disappears in Barcelona in 1942, and that's it?' Laura Graves said incredulously.

'What we've got is this,' Leon said, looking up from the MacBook Air he'd been working on steadily all afternoon, between calls on the yellow phone Laura kept in a locked closet built into the wall that contained her gargantuan bookcase. 'Keep calm, Laura. This may not be the dead end you think it is.'

'Give me what you've got.' Laura, dressed in jeans and a yellow T-shirt, her hair unkempt and her glasses on the tip of her nose, got up from the sofa. They were in her loft apartment, where the two of them had holed up to escape from Sir Richard, who'd been breathing down Laura's neck since 05hoo. Laura, Leon noticed, hadn't been able to sit still for more than three minutes – he'd timed it – before leaping to her feet again and pacing the spacious living area, from the windows overlooking Canal Street to the big clock on the bare brick wall above her front door, back to the work table with its Mac surrounded by a fortress of books, and across to the kitchen area, where she got the bottle out of the fridge and poured them both another glass of Chablis.

'Wanna sandwich?' she said. 'Or shall I call out for pizza?'

Leon knew that when she wanted food like that, Laura's nerves were really in shreds. 'Listen to me,' he said. 'And calm down.'

'In a pig's eye. Do you realize how little time we've got?'

She passed him a glass which she'd slopped full of wine, drank some of her own, plonked her glass on the slate kitchen counter and scratched at the tattoo on her finger.

'You ever thought of taking that off?' he said, going over to her and massaging her shoulders, which were like concrete under her T-shirt.

'Yes.'

'Get round to it.'

'Someday.'

'He's long gone, you know.'

'I'll have it taken off when I have time – not that that's going to be anytime soon.' She shook her head, then said, 'OK – I'm listening.'

'Brandau was an official at the Customs House in Barcelona, so when he didn't turn up for work, there was a proper inquiry. If he'd just been living in the city at that time nobody would have turned a hair at his disappearance. The other thing he had going for him in Francoist Spain, however neutral it was supposed to be, was his nationality.'

'So what have you come up with? I've tried to follow

the trail of the map and come up with doodle-squat.' She sank down on a kitchen bar-stool, only to get up seconds later and pace again, her wine neglected.

Leon, his eyes gritty from five hours at the computer, consulted the notes he'd made. He took a large gulp of the cold wine and was grateful for it.

'The Nazis went ape when they found out. There was a big inquiry, all very hush-hush, and all the German records were destroyed, early in 1945.'

'When the jig was up.'

'Yes. But the Spanish paperwork is still extant. Or enough of it to give me a sniff of what happened.'

'Give me what you've got.'

Leon rubbed his eyes wearily, put his glasses back on and picked up his notes. 'Brandau was missing for three months. Then, in the autumn of 1942, some property developer or other bought a couple of houses on a street in the Raval district of Barcelona – it's called Pintor Fortuny now.' He paused to take a sip of wine, but he needed something to quench his thirst, so he interrupted himself to take a bottle of Perrier from the fridge. Laura watched him impatiently. 'One of the houses had been deserted for a couple of years. When they went in, the surveyors found a kind of tank in the cellar. There was a corpse in it. They identified it as Brandau's from the clothing. The tank was full of water, and he was tied up. Someone had put him in there and drowned him. The cellar was half-flooded.'

'Where does that lead us?'

'Nowhere. But the first place they looked for the

map was his apartment. Everything there was in order, except that a big bookcase had been moved, and behind it was a crude hiding place – a kind of alcove. Someone had emptied it, and they knew where to look. Nothing else in the apartment had been touched.'

'They got the map?'

'It's a hypothesis. It's even likely. But what happened after that, no one knows. Except that I found something else . . . '

'Yes?'

'It's probably not related, but a few days before they started to look for Brandau, a couple of men were found dead in La Rambla, not far from where Pintor Fortuny runs into it. One stabbed, one strangled. They were both prominent citizens and supporters of the new regime, or at least compliant with it. One was Castilian, the other Catalan. There were no witnesses; no one came forward. The police set up an investigation because the dead guys were big shots, but it petered out, and, after a year or so, the investigation was shelved.'

'And they didn't find anything on them, of course?' Laura asked, without much hope.

Leon shrugged. 'Sorry.'

'Not even any motivation? Political? Anything like that?'

'Nothing specific at all.'

Laura thought about that. 'Maybe that's a clue in itself.'

'How do you mean?'

'Follow the logical line.'

Leon was silent for a minute or two, then laughed. 'You mean, they found out where the map was, took it, and then someone else took it from them? Sorry, Laura, but that really is clutching at straws.'

'What were the names of the dead guys?'

Leon didn't need to consult his notes for that. 'Barbero and Andreu. One was a banker, the other a geologist.'

Her face suddenly cleared. 'Leon, do you think they might have been connected in some way? To this whole thing?'

He looked at her in astonishment. 'You mean, were they Chevaliers?' He laughed again, a little less kindly this time. 'There's absolutely nothing to suggest that! It was probably a political assassination.'

'But what were they doing there at that specific time?'

'What specific time? We don't know when Brandau's apartment was broken into.'

'But it's likely – if he was tortured to get information out of him – that he told them where to look and they went straight there. Leaving him to die. If it was the map, they wouldn't have hung about.'

'It's too tenuous, Laura!'

'And why were they killed in two different ways? Why not just come up to them and shoot them? That's how political assassinations were usually carried out. A knife, maybe – but a gun's quicker and more certain.'

Leon did look at his notes now. 'It looks like it was a professional job. Both clean kills.'

'Someone was waiting for them,' Laura said. 'Ambush? Getting into a car maybe?'

'This isn't getting us any closer to the map.' Leon paused, undecided. 'Will you let me run it past Jack? Good to get a fresh pair of eyes on this.'

She thought about it, then nodded reluctantly.

'Where is he?'

She twisted the emerald ring on her finger. 'Where do you think? With Ms Fielding.' She looked up. 'Trying to dig more on the Brotherhood out of her. Hudson's orders, not mine.'

Leon caught her look and returned it with a sympathetic one. 'It's relevant.'

'Hudson's trying to keep Jack out of play. Out of spite.'

'He isn't that unprofessional.'

'You're right.' She hesitated for a moment. 'He doesn't trust him.'

'Does he trust Natasha?'

'Ms Fielding? No. But he still thinks she's useful.' She waved an arm listlessly. 'Go on, take what you've dug out to Jack. And then come back to me. Don't go via Hudson.'

Leon grinned. 'With you on that,' he said.

Laura watched him go, wishing she could act relaxation as well as he did. She was grateful to him for trying to put her at ease.

But her mind refused to rest.

53

Jack sent an exhausted Leon home to Mia and the kids immediately after their meeting in Room 55. He knew he should inform Hudson of his next move, but Hudson had his hands full, shuttling between the Treasury and the White House, and having a tougher and tougher time trying to look unflurried. It would be a while before Hudson had time to react, but when he did, Jack could count on Leon and Laura to field the flak for him.

He returned to Natasha's suite soon afterwards, his other decision already made. Only tell her as much as was necessary was the directive. Well, this *was* necessary. He nodded to the two dark-suited bodyguards posted outside her door. To the outside world, the 'hotel' was closed for refurbishment.

The suite was, as usual during her occupancy, so well ordered it might have been unoccupied. She had jibbed a little at first at being deprived of all telephone and computer connections; now he found her sitting at the table in the suite's living room, papers and books neatly arrayed in front of her. Prominent among them were Raleigh's *The Discovery of Guiana*, and the relevant volumes of Humboldt's massive *Personal Narrative of Travels to the Equinoctial Regions of the New Continent.*

'I've missed you,' she said.

He kissed her, but she drew away and the smile left her lips when she saw the look in his eyes. 'What's happened?' she said immediately.

Marlow told her what Leon had uncovered. She listened without comment until he had finished, then said, 'The name of this German naval officer was Brandau?'

'Yes.'

'And he arrived in Barcelona when?'

Now Jack did hesitate, but something in her expression told him he might have started a good hare. 'In 1939. He was there for three years before whoever it was caught up with him.'

'And he had the map?'

'It seems very likely.'

'Where did he come from? Germany? What was he doing in Barcelona?'

Jack realized that to get at whatever he sensed she had to tell him, he'd have to give her a hell of a lot more information on Brandau. So, in the barest outline, he acquainted her with the expedition he had led.

'And he ended up in Rio.'

'The German consulate there issued him with a new passport.'

'And he left from there to Barcelona with the map.'

'That's what we think.'

'But why would they let him take it?'

'He was the man entrusted with it. There was nothing to make them think he wouldn't return with it to Germany.'

'Didn't it occur to them that, as the leader of a failed expedition, he might be reluctant to go back to the Third Reich?'

'Apparently not.' But Jack was uncomfortable now.

She was silent for a while. It was impossible to fathom her thoughts, but he sensed that it was her turn to decide whether or not to divulge information.

'The German consul in Rio then was Hartmut Schickert,' she said at last.

He looked at her in astonishment. 'How do you know?'

'He was my grandfather.'

It took a moment for this information to sink in. 'Your grandfather?' he repeated stupidly.

She nodded. 'He spent his life in the diplomatic corps, but his other loyalty was to the Brotherhood, and when the Nazis took power he decided to resist the new regime from within it. He was a widower, he was childless then, he had nothing to lose. They posted him to Rio in 1937. It was his last position. He was supposed to coast home to retirement.' She paused. 'My father told me his story. And the map must have left Rio with Brandau.'

She stopped for a moment and, to Jack's surprise, he could see tears in her eyes. He had taken a chair near her, and reached over now to squeeze her hand. She looked up and smiled at him.

'When neither Brandau nor the map returned to Germany,' she continued, 'they sent a deputation to interrogate my grandfather. He knew what that would lead to – arrest, and deportation to one of the concentration camps they used for political prisoners. He pretended to cooperate for the first two days. Then, when an opportunity presented itself, he fled. He made his way to the US and found refuge there. He settled in Colorado, remarried – a younger woman – and, in 1948, my father was born. My grandfather lived into his eighties. He told my father his story as soon as my father was old enough to understand, and to know how to keep a secret.'

'Why did you tell me none of this before?'

'How could I possibly have known it was relevant?'

'So your grandfather knew all about the map, and – what? – he encouraged Brandau not to return to Germany?'

She nodded. 'He destroyed all his papers in Rio before he fled. Before the delegation from Germany even arrived.'

'And Brandau?'

'My grandfather knew where he'd disembark in Europe, but the Brotherhood was weak even then; it didn't have the power to counter the Chevaliers any more. No one knew that Brandau would elect to stay in Barcelona. They picked up his traces too late to save him, but not too late to save the map.'

'And what did they do with it?'

'The plan was to return it to its original home: Heidelberg – the last place the Nazis would think of looking for it. That's why I assumed, as soon as I realized the de Vries version wasn't the true one, that it must still be there. The plan must have changed.'

Jack thought about that. 'If the Brotherhood was weak, maybe they couldn't carry out the original plan?'

'Or maybe they changed it? The Brotherhood all but collapsed during the war. Nothing's known except what my father told me, and what I've now told you.'

Jack hoped she was holding nothing back, that what she was telling him was indeed the truth. 'Why didn't they simply destroy it?'

'They never believed they had the right to do so. The whole philosophy of the Brotherhood was based on containment. Perhaps, one day, the world would have legitimate need of the city of gold. But the Brotherhood knew that the map should never fall into the hands of the Chevaliers. Their plan was always to bury it deep, never to destroy it.'

'And the Chevaliers also knew that?'

Natasha spread her hands. 'They would not still be searching for it otherwise.'

No, Jack thought, and all this could have been averted. If only the Brotherhood *had* destroyed it. Perhaps, if they were still strong in the world now, they would do so. But they were gone. This girl was all that remained of them.

'The last place it was heard of was in Barcelona,' he said. 'So that's the first place to look.'

54

It was hard to get Laura to agree, but Jack managed it. Hudson was so embroiled with the mounting panic, as another two – smaller, but still significant – investment banks went to the wall, that all he said when she passed it to him for clearance was: 'Give him enough rope to hang himself.' Hudson still wanted Jack dead in the water, but evidently he didn't want that yet – not so long as he was useful, and so long as he was the only card he had to play.

But gold was slipping again, more dramatically – and Hudson wanted a few more answers before waving him through.

'Tell him this,' Jack said to Laura as they sat facing each other across the white table in Room 55 in the grey dawn of the following day. 'The Chevaliers have got subsidy – where from, God knows – and they're confident enough to be going ahead again.'

'Sounds like make or break to me.'

'If they're going out on a limb, it's because they think they're close. But let's not forget that they are probably in so deep they can't go into reverse gear now. Whoever is bankrolling them – and there must be somebody – is going to be expecting payback soon. My guess is that once they've got access to the city of gold, the Chevaliers won't care about their sponsors – they'll have their sponsors in their power, along with everyone else. But they're sailing close to the wind. Whoever's running this has got to be a monomaniac. Hell-bent on his goal.'

'Then if they come unstuck, can't we leave it to their sponsors to finish them off for us?'

'How can we take that risk, Laura? Think about it. The way things are going, the end may come – the big crash may come – just on account of its own momentum. But if we get to the city of gold and neutralize it, then it'll be business – or what passes for business these days – as usual.'

'Yeah, *if* –'

'There isn't a choice.'

After a brief pause, Laura changed tack and asked, 'Why do you need Ms Fielding on this? She doesn't know any more than we do.'

'She's the last link with the Brotherhood. She's confirmed the Barcelona connection and now we know at least where to *start* looking for the map again. If we'd taken her more into our confidence earlier –'

'That was your call.'

'This isn't the time to start passing the buck, Laura.'

'OK. Sorry.'

'There's no time to waste. Get him to authorize me.'

She looked at her watch. 'He's due here at 08h00. I'll catch him before the mandarins whisk him off to Washington again. The UN's getting ruffled feathers now, and the IMF's called an extraordinary meeting this Thursday.' She paused. 'I don't have to tell you that all this is blue-light: ultra-secure.'

'No, really?'

'Shut up!'

They looked at each other, and the tension between them broke. They laughed.

'Having a tiff,' he said. 'How mad is that?'

'Like a couple.'

'We've been together long enough.'

'First anniversary.'

That little exchange brought a whiff of the tension back.

'I'll get on to it,' she said.

'I'll get Planning to fix a flight.'

'Don't jump the gun.'

'I'm going anyway, Laura.'

'I'll pretend I didn't hear that.'

At 10h00, Jack and Natasha were seated in INTERSEC's Gulfstream C-37A as it taxied on to the runway at LaGuardia. They carried minimal kit and they were going to be operating alone. There was no longer any INTERSEC base station in Barcelona on account of budget cuts, and Hudson had stipulated that all communication be kept to zero, barring emergencies. The Chevaliers probably weren't sophisticated enough to do high-level electronic intercepts, but the risk wasn't worth taking. They all knew the Chevaliers would be following the same trail. How far they'd got along it was anyone's guess.

55

'Do you think they got here first?' asked Natasha.

Three days of exhaustive searching in the places they had taken as their starting point – the places they thought most likely that the map would have been hidden in Barcelona – had drawn a blank. The Catalan National Library and the two Catalan archives of the city contained nothing, and there was no record of the map either.

'Maybe they changed tack. Your ancestor hid the map in an archive. It found its way into another. Perhaps, in 1942, the Brotherhood decided on another hiding place,' Jack said.

'Which could be anywhere.'

'Not quite anywhere. Somewhere where it could be buried deep, but kept safe.'

'Then an archive or a library would be the obvious place.'

'Or a bank vault, or in a collection.' Jack had already shared these ideas with base.

Natasha shook her head. 'They were living in volatile times, in a volatile city. They wouldn't have had much time to pick and choose. If they weren't able to travel, to get the map out of the country, they would have had to find somewhere close, and find it fast.'

They were sitting in the room they'd taken in a modest hotel near the Plaça Reial. The hotel didn't have Wi-Fi; there were just phones in the rooms. But it was a big room, dark, comfortably furnished with old, good-quality chairs, dressing table, desk and a bed the size of a small swimming pool. They had checked in as tourists, Mr and Mrs Ross. Marlow had allowed himself one call from a public phone booth in a nearby post office to register their location with Leon in New York. Thereafter, they had kept their heads down. But they had not become aware of any surveillance, of anyone following them.

Nevertheless, Jack could not shake off the impression that their presence in the city was known. It was only a gut feeling, and he hadn't shared it with Natasha. Perhaps he was becoming too paranoid. Perhaps the stress of this mission was getting to him. Well, he would use the secure, specially adapted iPhone to alert Laura if and when the need arose. No need to draw unnecessary attention to themselves otherwise. Even the special iPhone might leave an electronic trail that could pick up unwelcome attention.

'They're here, aren't they?' Natasha had been watching him, and seemed to be picking up his thoughts. Perhaps they were getting a little too close, personally, for professional comfort. The enormous bed had already proved itself a wonderful playground.

'If they are here, they're shadowing us. If they had found the map, they would be gone.'

'Then that's a comfort – kind of.'

'But they don't know *we* haven't found it.' Jack was thoughtful again.

'Then it depends on how useful we are to them,' she said.

He knew what she meant. He'd been thinking the same thing. If the Chevaliers thought he and Natasha would lead them to the map, they'd be safe until they found it. But the Chevaliers would be running their own search, and they might think it better to get rid of the competition. Just as he would find it easier and cleaner to get rid of them – if he could find them and neutralize them. But they were in the shadows, and he was in the open.

'If they think we've got it, they'll close in,' he said. 'And our usefulness to them will end.'

'So what's our next move?'

'The longer we're here, the longer we're exposed. And we need something more specific to go on here than a hunch about where to continue the search. We're hampered because, if there's a lead from the places we've already investigated, we can't pursue it without giving our position away.' Jack hadn't told her that Leon and Laura were already tracing all possible lines leading away from official depositories in Barcelona. A Catalan archive would have been vulnerable under Franco. Under the dictatorship, such places would have been sealed. The possibility also existed that its contents might have been sold off. That would have had the double advantage of raising money and dispersing anything that would amount to a collective history and reinforce a Catalan sense of identity.

But to follow any leads they came up with, he'd have to contact them. They couldn't risk the Chevaliers intercepting such communication, and they couldn't assume that their firewalls would be strong enough to keep them out.

The best line of defence against the Chevaliers would be to draw their fire. It was a calculated risk, but if he could bring them out into the open . . .

'It's going to take too long!' said Natasha when he told her of his plan. 'We must find the map now. We must press on.'

'If we're impatient, we risk losing everything.'

'If we waste time, we lose everything anyway.' She glared at him, stood up and went into the bathroom, closing the door behind her. The room might be big, but they had been cooped up in it together and that hadn't helped the pressure, fuelled as it was by the frustration of the failed chase.

Jack shifted in his seat, then stood and poured himself a Jameson's, opened the window and lit a cigarette. He looked out across the narrow street. He'd been taken aback by the fire that had appeared in her eyes. What he didn't know was what motivated her passion. He couldn't believe that a woman like Natasha could be seriously wedded to the ideals of the group her forebears had been members of. People just didn't think like that any more. And she was the last of that group.

It had disintegrated, and the Chevaliers had not. The Brotherhood would never beat the bad guys now.

Yet she had cried when she'd spoken of her grandfather. Her own father, whom she'd described as someone she'd never been close to, had passed the mission on to her from Schickert. What *was* her motivation? And how long would she remain an asset to him? There was no room for a loose cannon. What had attracted him to her then? Was it that, deep down, he didn't believe in his own cynicism? Could it be that she really did want to thwart the Chevaliers for the good of the world? That she didn't want to use the map to further her own ends?

His thoughts were interrupted by a muted beep from his phone. Message. Had to be important. Looking towards the still-closed bathroom door, he glanced at it and immediately decoded and deleted it.

Laura. *Remain in place. Breakthrough.*

He pocketed the phone just before the door opened and Natasha returned, looking calmer, even sheepish.

'Stifling in here,' she said.

'I know.'

She came over and put her hand in his, kissing him on the cheek. The dangerous fire had gone from her eyes. They were soft and warm now. 'Can we go out?'

He relaxed a little. 'Why not?' He paused, then reached for his shoulder holster and slung his little Glock under his arm, before putting a linen jacket on over it. He looked at her. 'You'd better do the same.'

'Just in case?'

'Just in case.'

She opened her bag to show him. In an inside pocket he could see the black glint of the Beretta Tomcat he'd unofficially issued her from the INTERSEC armoury.

It was dark already and the street lamps glowed soft yellow against the dark buildings, dim light from their windows adding to the illumination of the street. Outside, the air was soft and warm, heavy rather than fresh, and the crowds and the garishly lit shopfronts and the Irish pubs added to a sense of oppression, of claustrophobia.

They made their way out of Plaça Reial and walked up to the cathedral before wandering back through the Barri Gòtic and the Ciutat Vella before turning down Carrer Nou de Sant Francesc and arriving at Los Caracoles, with its spitted chickens roasting outside. A couple who'd been walking behind them also stopped, to study the menu near the door.

'Let's go here,' Natasha said.

It was around 20h30, still very early for anyone to be taking dinner, so the restaurant had not yet begun to fill up. Its tangle of little tiled dining rooms, the walls almost invisible behind serried ranks of photographs, mainly of the great and the good who had eaten there since its foundation in 1835, were connected by corridors and staircases. Jack and Natasha walked in past the huge open kitchen with its fiery ranges and up a flight to a dining room on the first floor. A group of five Catalan businessmen, sweating in their suits, were mixing eating with business at a table against the far wall. The couple from outside, a middle-aged blonde in jeans and a dark-blue, long-sleeved T-shirt and her fat partner, a redneck in a checked shirt and beige gilet, had followed them up. The couple took their places at one of the window tables. Jack and Natasha took another. There was only a scattering of other diners in the room.

Los Caracoles wasn't an ideal place to be from the point of view of security. It was an easy place to be trapped in and a hard place to get out of, but Jack wanted to ease the mood. From the Spanish-language menu they ordered jamón serrano and navajas followed by bacalao and perdiz, with a bottle of Caligo Vi de Boira 2006 and a bottle of Vichy Catalan, almost the only sparkling mineral water you could get in any restaurant in the city.

They both hoped they'd be able to enjoy an hour or so of escape, but the tension didn't lift and most of the time they ate in silence, Jack listening idly to the blonde giving a grotesque girlish come-on to the man, whose expression Jack couldn't see, as he had his back to him; but you can tell a lot from a person's back, and its owner seemed unmoved by the prattle. He didn't speak, didn't give himself time to, as he stolidly munched his way through two plates of pa amb tomàquet, along with a massive paella.

The blonde was speaking in French. But that didn't set any alarm bells ringing. The Chevaliers were an international organization, and Los Caracoles was hardly unknown to the hordes of tourists that infested Barcelona.

But she wasn't French. Natasha confirmed that. Though she spoke the language fluently, there was a strong trace of an accent. English? Dutch? Jack felt an unaccountable sense of relief when the couple finished their meal, paid their bill and left.

His mind dwelt on Laura's message: how long would he have to wait, and how would they channel their instructions to him? And would he wait until then to tell Natasha?

Her mind was elsewhere too. He couldn't read her thoughts, but he knew her impatience hadn't subsided. And he was sure that she was still holding something back. Was that something at the root of her impatience? Was there some kind of deadline he didn't know about?

He realized that he had finished his food without tasting it. Natasha had barely eaten at all. She touched his foot with her own. The place was filling up. The five businessmen had relaxed a little, and were talking about cars and women over their cognac and solos.

'Shall we go?' she said.

Jack paid the bill and they left to have their coffee elsewhere, in one of the bars under the colonnades of the Plaça Reial.

'You didn't eat anything,' he said as they walked the short distance back up the narrow street. Plenty of people were out now, enjoying the warm May evening.

'Not hungry.'

'The waiter looked offended.'

'As if he cared.'

The cafés on the Plaça Reial were full, but they found a small place in a side street leading out of it with a free outside table. Reluctant to return to the hotel, they drank their coffee slowly.

Among the people passing by, Jack noticed the skinny blonde and the redneck. Fleetingly, he caught the blonde's eye. They both looked away again immediately, as one does when one involuntarily catches the eye of a total stranger, but something stirred uneasily within Jack. He watched the couple out of sight.

'Let's go back,' he said.

'Why now?'

'I think they're here.'

She nodded, and he left a handful of euros on the table as they got up to leave.

As they walked, she reached for his hand and entwined her fingers in his.

'It is going to be all right,' she said, and he wondered if she was saying that to convince him, or to convince herself.

They turned the corner of their street and could see the soft light of the hotel entrance up ahead. They quickened their pace.

At that moment two things happened. They saw a figure approach the hotel from the opposite end of the street. She was caught briefly in the light from the hotel's entrance as she made her way through it. A halo of blonde hair. Jack barked out a warning as Natasha broke free and started to run. He was about to follow her when someone stepped out from a dark doorway they'd just passed and a beefy arm wrapped round his neck. Jack could feel the man's belly pushing into his back, and smell his sweat, and the paella and wine from the meal he'd recently eaten on his breath.

His attacker drew his free fist back to drive it into Jack's kidneys, but he managed to twist his body away in time, and the blow glanced off his side, wide of the mark. The man was too big and had him in too tight a grip for Jack to be able to jab an elbow into his gut, but the arm in its checked shirt was just below his chin and this was no time to be squeamish. In the moment the man took to recover his balance after his failed blow, Jack worked himself free enough to sink his teeth deep into the left forearm pinioning him. He bit down hard enough to draw blood as the man wrenched his arm free, cursing wildly. In an instant Jack had spun round and, seeing his attacker bent over, nursing his wounded arm, kicked him hard in the face, knocking his curiously dandified green metal glasses off his nose and on to the cobblestones. The man staggered back, hands to his face now, but it was a feint. With a roar, he launched himself on Jack, and the force of this weight brought them both crashing down. He straddled Jack and caught him by the neck again with his left hand, blood pouring from his wound on to Jack's face and into his mouth. Jack arched his back but was unable to free himself. At the same time, the man reached round behind his belt and under his gilet to produce a broad-bladed dagger with a serrated edge. From far away, Jack heard uncertain shouts and hurried exchanges. The fight had attracted attention. But then, from further away, came the unmistakable sound of gunshots – a small, snapping sound, but loud enough to deflect attention from him. He heard running footsteps receding in the direction the shots had come from.

Jack blocked the dagger's descent with his arm and managed to wrest the blade from the man's grip. Then he drew his legs up, and, gasping with the effort, brought them forward of the man's face, scissored them and thrust the man backwards. The man released his grip on Jack's neck once more, and Jack rolled free of his bulk, getting to his feet and stamping on the man's wounded arm before he had a chance to recover. The dagger was within reach and Jack made a lightning move to pick it up; he didn't want to use the Glock and add more gunfire to the shots he'd already heard. But they hadn't attracted a crowd. Anyone who'd seen them would have thought it was a mugging and gone out of their way not to get involved.

There wasn't much time. The man was getting to his feet, breathing hard. Jack looked into the mean little blue eyes that stared back at him, ablaze with hate. He grabbed his attacker around the waist and pulled him towards him, at the same time driving the dagger hard at the left side of his neck, drawing its serrated edge across the carotid artery. He stepped back quickly before the fountain of blood could drench him. He pushed the body away from him, into a doorway, where it slumped, still jerking as the life left it, and threw the dagger away, hurrying now in the direction of the hotel. There was plenty of activity outside it, but no one seemed to know where the gunshots had come from, and Jack caught snatches of conversation in which there were already traces of doubt: maybe it hadn't been gunshots at all? Maybe a motorbike backfiring? People always preferred safe explanations if they could reach for them – it made life easier, and life was hard enough without additional complications.

His jacket had been spared most of the blood from the fight, and he had wiped his face clear of blood on his way. He made his way past the reception desk unnoticed and sprinted up the stairs to the second floor, to their room. The door was just ajar, and light from the room spilled on to the corridor.

He pulled out his gun and slipped off the safety, holding it up in both hands as he stepped quickly into the room, immediately crouching down and scanning it. He saw the blonde's body slumped across the bed, her face turned towards him, two neat bullet-holes in her head, her hair stained dark.

'Natasha?'

He made his way across to the bathroom and pushed the adjoining door wide. The room was empty. He turned back to the bedroom.

Then he saw that Natasha's bag was gone.

As he prepared to leave, the thoughts were crowding into his head. He could be gone in an instant. There was nothing that could lead to him here. In moments, he had thrown what he needed into his leather shoulder bag, opened the window and slung a leg over the sill on to the fire escape.

As he descended into the darkness he heard the first sirens.

56

'He's sent us a message,' Laura said.

Leon looked up from his work. Once again, they'd decamped to Laura's apartment. The air conditioning hummed faintly, keeping the humidity outside at bay. Laura had put on some Mozart – the *Sinfonia Concertante* – to counter the noise, and keep them calm. Mozart, for once, was fighting a losing battle.

'Incident?'

She nodded. 'Attack. But he's not leaving. He's gone into deep cover. Problem is, he's lost Fielding.'

'What? How?'

'She ran after the attack.'

'Gone over?'

'Unlikely. She killed one of them.'

Leon digested this. Natasha on the loose was a major security risk – though he doubted if she'd have more to offer the Chevaliers than they did. 'If he's in deep cover, how do we contact him?'

'One word when we go out. Rendezvous point and time.'

'Won't that be enough for them to trace him? They know he's in Barcelona, and they're already there too.'

'Have to risk it.'

'I can get Monitoring to increase block, or we'll use a proxy.'

Laura nodded. 'Get someone on to that now.' Leon reached for her yellow phone, made a brief call, and rejoined her.

'Done,' he said.

'Good. Now – how far have we got with the package?'

'You jumped the gun, telling him we were on to something.'

Laura bit her lip. 'And nothing on the constellations either –'

'I need more to go on. But we have to concentrate on the map.'

Leon sat forward in his chair. The amount of information sifted and collated threatened to bury the table by now. He surveyed it with an exhausted look.

'The map disappeared in Barcelona,' said Laura. 'Jack's search of the likeliest places there has drawn a blank. We've been over all the material twice and the trail is still cold. But it was you who told me we had something to go on.'

Leon rubbed his jaw. 'Maybe. It was something Jack said. Something I've been looking into.'

'Bank vault?'

'I don't think the Brotherhood would have had time to set one up, and besides it would have drawn attention to them. At the very least, a third party would have been aware of its existence, especially if it was a safe-deposit box.'

'What then?'

'I do have an idea.' Leon looked at the sea of papers and notes again. 'It's somewhere here, I'm sure of it.'

'What are we looking for?'

He shrugged. 'We'll know when we find it. Something to show if anything left the national archives – if they were depleted in some way – at any point between 1942 and the end of the Franco regime.'

Laura laughed. 'That's thirty-three years!'

'It's likely to have been sooner rather than later. Come on! This could be the break we're after. Something we've missed, Laura. Something that's staring us in the face.'

'This has got to be the last throw of the dice, Leon.'

They worked steadily for hours, as the light went out of the sky and the city of New York lit its own lights. Several times, one or other of them let out a cry, but what they'd found was just another false trail. They broke for coffee, stretching their aching limbs, the papers spread across the floor of the apartment in a great, confusing mosaic. They called out for a takeaway at one point, but when it arrived they were too impatient to eat. Their eyes became sore and their heads swam as they fought to focus their concentration. Words floated on the documents they held up in front of them as if they had a life of their own.

At one point – it must have been towards four in the morning – Leon let out a low moan of despair. He waved the bound set of documents in his hand and said, 'I've looked at this thing three times – *three times* – already tonight. It's a bust, Laura. We're done. Call Hudson. Get Jack back. We're never going to find it.'

'Look!'

A thin sheet of paper, yellowed with age, had been shaken loose from the set in Leon's hand and fluttered gently to the floor. He picked it up gingerly. It was a carbon copy from some forgotten typewriter, the letters brown and uneven, the few lines of writing smudged by the carbon paper that had given them birth.

'Probably nothing.'

'Read it.'

Leon squinted at it through his spectacles. 'Spanish,' he said, handing it to her.

'It's the record of a sale,' she said. 'Wait a minute.' She passed the sheet of paper back to Leon and shuffled through a stack of papers she'd already worked through until she found what she was looking for. 'I thought this was a transfer document – that they were moving a set of archives from one site to another. But I'm tired – I wasn't thinking.'

'Well, what is it?'

'Don't you see, Leon? It isn't very likely that there'd be any activity – official activity, anyway – between one Catalan archive and another during the Franco regime.'

'Because he had them sealed?'

'Exactly! A huge amount of material was simply locked up. It would have been an ideal place to hide something you never wanted found. But now I look again I see that this document isn't about a transfer at all, it's a list of material that was auctioned off.'

'Auctioned off?'

'Yes. This bill of sale relates to these lists. Look, the date's about right: February 1949. The date on the bill is the fourth. It looks as if the Nationalist government authorized the sale to private collectors of a whole load of stuff – to raise cash, to make room, whatever the reason. Old manuscripts, prints, drawings –'

'Maps?'

'Maps too – Jesus, to think we nearly let this slip away.'

'There is a god!'

'Well, there are certainly lottery winners. Give me the item number on that bill of sale.'

Leon looked at it. 'SEM/ALB/4249.'

'OK.' Laura went over to the table and sat down at it, pulling the reading light closer and running her finger down the lists in front of her. She turned over several pages, and Leon could see the hope beginning to fade. At last she looked up, expressionlessly.

'Too bad,' said Leon. 'Would have been nice.'

'But it is nice,' she said. 'SEM/ALB/4249?'

'Yes.'

She beamed at him. 'Bingo!'

57

Laura was glad to have something positive to report to Hudson. It sugared the pill about Fielding. But he wasn't going to let that go, and she couldn't deny his doubts. The two hours' sleep she'd had before presenting herself in his office had helped, but not much. And she regretted the amphetamines she'd taken once she'd dragged herself awake again.

'There's no help from the CIA either,' Hudson was saying. 'There was a big cock-up when the army took the Château d'Uriel. OSS was supposed to take charge of the paperwork, but everything went up in smoke. At least, that's what they're telling us, and I see no reason why they should lie. Even they aren't stupid enough to hold back on anything that could help us. The shit storm isn't on the horizon, it's at the end of the street.'

'What's the strategy?'

'They're keeping the public quiet with more of the same: continued recession, double dip, worldwide crisis, long haul, all the usual crap – but if any more big concerns fail, it'll be the high-street banks, property . . . They're feeling the tremors already. No one's immune.' Sir Richard had gone so far, Laura noticed, as to loosen his tie.

'And Fielding?'

'Get her back. Better yet, if you find her, take her out first and ask questions later. The same goes for your precious Jack Marlow. I've had enough of his maverick tactics.'

'With respect, sir, he is in place in Barcelona –'

'Are you sure? You only have his word.'

'He's the only man who can pinpoint the map now.'

'That would surprise me. He isn't the only good agent we can field, and most of the rest of them know how to toe the line.'

'We've got a name.'

'Yes?'

'The purchaser of the map. He bought it along with a set of eighteenth-century books and some manuscripts by Verdaguer and Aribau.'

'Whoever they are.'

She ignored that. 'The collector's name is Oriol Guardiola. Or was. He died in 1959, but he was interested in keeping Catalan culture alive and he had a significant collection in his own private museum. He was a big industrialist. Chemicals. The Nationalists needed him, so they indulged him.'

'And you think the map's still there – in this private museum?'

'The museum does still exist. In a private house in Pedralbes, in the north of the city. Its trustees have kept it the same as it was when Guardiola died, but it's mainly used by researchers and experts. It's not really a public museum. So we have some hope.'

'Unless they've got there first.'

Laura bit her lip.

'Or unless Ms Fielding has led the Chevaliers to it,' Hudson continued.

'There is no way Fielding could have access to the material we've been working on. It all came to us courtesy of the Centro Nacional de Inteligencia in Madrid, via secure links and couriers, and all the information was locked down as soon as it was located. Dr Lopez saw to it.'

'In these days of the Inter-fucking-net, nothing is locked down.' Tie loosened *and* swearing. Laura was seeing a new Sir Richard.

'Luckily, none of this was ever transferred electronically.'

'I hope you're right. You're keeping communication with dear Jack to a minimum still, I hope?'

'Yes.' Good, Laura thought. The threat to take Marlow out was hot air – for now. 'We're taking the relevant information out personally. Today. He'll need back-up.'

'I hope you're right – that no one else could possibly have accessed the information you've been working on. Intercepted it in transit.'

'It's copper-bottomed.'

'Who are you sending?'

Laura was taken aback. 'I'm going myself.'

Hudson looked at her. 'No you're not.'

58

'The bastard,' Laura said, once she was back in Room 55, where Leon was waiting for her.

'You can't let this get to you,' he said. 'There isn't time.'

'I was determined to go on this mission. Now he tells me I have to stay here – at the helm.'

'That *is* your job now.'

'Didn't stop Jack when he was in my chair.'

Leon didn't answer that. Jack was an AAAAA-ranked field agent. And even he made mistakes. But he guessed Hudson had other reasons for clipping Laura's wings. She knew that, too –

'What Hudson really wants is to keep Jack and me apart – distinct.'

'Because you're too close.'

'That's what he thinks.' Laura let her words hang. 'If he cuts Jack loose, he'll have to do without me, too.'

'You know you can't do that. There's no such thing as resignation from your job.'

'Then I'll get myself reassigned. London bureau, maybe.'

'The doors of the gates to the temple, according to Humboldt – and if the place exists at all – will open close to the summer solstice – Midsummer's Day,' Leon reminded her.

'We've got to locate Fielding. What made her leave?'

'They were both in danger. She panicked and ran.'

'Doesn't sound like her. She abandoned Jack.'

'She knows he can look after himself. She'll make contact.'

'How?' Laura reached for the blue phone.

'What are you doing?'

'Obeying orders. Putting a team on to her.'

'Elimination?'

'That's what the man said.'

Leon put a hand on hers. 'Why don't you give her a day's grace?'

'Why?'

'Because she may still be valuable to us. If she thinks we've set the dogs on her –'

Laura sighed, and nodded. 'I'm in such deep shit anyway, a little more won't matter.'

'So who are they sending instead of you?' Leon asked.

The internal phone buzzed then. She picked it up, listened intently for a few seconds, then hung up.

'It's Hudson's office,' she said. 'He wants to see you.'

She watched him leave. She'd already guessed what that meant. Leon wasn't normally sent out on fieldwork, but he'd proved himself in the past and, in these circumstances, he was the best courier: he had the knowledge first hand, and his expertise would be valuable when they located the map in Oriol Guardiola's museum. *If* they located it.

She pushed the papers around her desk idly, not looking at them. Left here, she'd have little to do other than respond to reports, and they'd be few. She would have to mark time until Leon and Jack returned. This was the calm before the storm. But she wanted to be out there, and she wanted to be at Jack's side. Not just because of the feelings she had for him, and couldn't show; but also to watch his back. She was the only person who could do that effectively, she told herself, because she was the only person who had more than a professional interest in him. How self-sufficient was he, really? Wasn't he also a little lonely in his self-imposed isolation? Or didn't he mind solitude? Was it that which made him perfect for his job?

She shook her head. She knew his history, and she knew he wasn't a man who stood alone easily. And what about her? She had been tripped up once, but most of her life she had believed in her career and been driven by it. Now she knew there was something more to life – something outside her career that was more important. How, otherwise, could she be thinking about things like that at a time like this? But she was trapped. They were both trapped.

Time sorts everything out, she told herself; be patient. But, occasionally, time needs a little encouragement to do its job.

Leon had been gone a long time. But Hudson

respected him, and there were other aspects of their strategy he'd have to discuss with him. She wandered into his lab and nodded to the two technicians working on planning models for the isolation of the city of gold once it was located. Everything needed for a major operation, to be implemented within hours of the go-ahead, was in preparation, and more top-level talks were due to be held in Brasilia in a few days' time. Hudson would be flying out there the following day. The atmosphere in the lab was church-like, even monastic. The technicians worked with silent efficiency, almost part of the ranks of computers they controlled.

She left them to it and returned to her desk. Seldom had she found Room 55 so oppressive. She went back to shuffling the papers on her desk, as if she might find an answer there. All that came into her mind was another doubt, a doubt she'd been resisting but that would not go away: did she mistrust Natasha Fielding on purely professional grounds? Or was there another reason?

She sighed. She already knew the answer to that one.

Leon returned fifteen minutes later.

'You're going?' she said.

A nod from him confirmed it. 'You're coming too.'

She didn't know which hit her harder, relief or astonishment. 'What? I thought I was the last person –'

'He sees things differently now.'

Laura looked at him in open admiration. 'You're a magician! What did you say?'

'He came to the conclusion that the best person to follow leads to Natasha is you. You know the territory, the background and the enemy. That seemed to weigh more with him than keeping you and Jack apart.'

'So he still needs Jack?'

'Hudson's a pragmatist. He'll drop Jack only when he's sure he can get no more juice out of him.'

'I hope you're right.' She paused. 'Did he say anything about a possible leak?'

'He's worried.'

'Do you think he has cause to be?'

'We covered everything.'

But Leon knew what his boss was thinking. INTERSEC's own security systems were watertight; but when it came to dealing with outside agencies, they were on less certain ground. The Chevaliers had long tentacles and connections with Spain that went back centuries. If they had anybody in place within the Centro Nacional de Inteligencia, INTERSEC could still find themselves in a neck-and-neck race.

The Chevaliers might even be ahead of the game. They couldn't have knowledge of the carbon copy linking the map to Guardiola's museum, but there was no guarantee that a top copy didn't exist somewhere. One little piece of paper, Laura thought, and the whole world's fate might hang on it.

'Why do you think they attacked Jack?' she asked.

'They thought he had the map.'

'That means they're still looking. With luck, they still think that.'

'Then he'd better have covered his tracks.'
Laura grabbed her bag. 'Come on, let's go.'
She was out of the door before he had a chance to reach it.

59

Oriol Guardiola had never liked working in industrial chemicals, but that was the source of the money that had financed his passion. So he went dutifully to his office three days a week and oversaw the chloralkali process in his factory, the production of organofluorines and, latterly, polymers. The rest of his time he devoted to his collection. He had started with manuscripts, first editions, prints and drawings by Catalan poets and artists. As the twentieth century grew more industrialized and his company grew with it, so did his budget and his collection. But he remained conservative, traditionalist. He just spread his net a little wider, to cover Europe, and, later, the rest of the world; but he went on catching the same fish: manuscripts, first editions, prints and drawings. The only addition he made was maps, which began to have a fascination for him as his work obliged him to travel and he became acquainted with the world outside the narrow confines of his youth – Valencia, Barcelona, Girona and Perpignan.

His two marriages had been long-term disasters, between them taking up almost one third of his life. Once they were behind him, he decided he had learnt his lesson. He limited his social life to the occasional dinner with old friends, always male – and always at

Els Quatre Gats, where he had a standing reservation. Seldom were people invited to his large, rambling apartment on the two top floors of a turn-of-the-century building near the corner of Rambla de Catalunya and Aragó. There, he chose to spend most of his time with his collection, alone, content to read, listen to Schubert and mentally caress the thousands of items he'd amassed over thirty-five years.

One room at the centre of the Guardiola collection was now given over to maps. Some were framed, but the more expensive were housed in glass cases covered with velvet cloths to protect them from the light when he was not looking at them; others still were in leather portfolios bound with purple silk. His best examples were from the fifteenth and sixteenth centuries, the earliest by Martin Behaim – a rare sketch for the Africa on his famous globe; others by Waldseemüller and Gabriel de Vallseca. Guardiola also prized his Fernão Vaz Dourado, of the Mosquito Coast; a Christopher Saxton of the English county of Herefordshire; and a Lucas Waghenaer, of Galicia. But his most valued possession, though far from being the most expensive, was a map of *Amazonia Pars* by an unknown hand, showing signs of wear but made on sturdy parchment. He had no idea who had made it, and he'd bought it as part of a job lot the Nationalists sold him when 'rationalizing' the Catalan National Archive early in 1949.

There was something fascinating about the map. One day, he told himself, he would get to the bottom of whatever secret it seemed to be holding. But he never managed to do so. The four crudely drawn symbols, clearly by a hand other than the one that had made the map, seemed to hold both a promise and a threat. Guardiola, by nature unadventurous, was not a man to listen to such Sirens.

Seven years after he'd made the purchase, his apartment was no longer big enough to hold his collection. Books and papers barricaded the corridors and blocked the windows. His eccentric reputation had grown around town, and he was nicknamed Fafnir, after the dragon that guarded the legendary hoard of gold in Wagner's opera cycle. This gentle mockery, and the fact that he was getting old, prompted Guardiola to buy a substantial mansion in Pedralbes. The Museo Guardiola opened its doors on Wednesday 4 February 1959. On Thursday 22 October the same year, Oriol died, alone in bed, on his seventy-eighth birthday. His body wasn't discovered for a week but was then given a funeral worthy of such a major beneficiary to the city. He had built his pyramid, and he had taken care to set up a trust to manage the museum, with enough money to run it for a century. The trustees were careful to keep the substantial Catalan part of the collection under wraps until after the demise of Generalissimo Franco in 1975.

With the exception of occasional scholars, few visited it these days. Without Guardiola's endowment, indeed, the place would have closed years ago. The five attendants employed to watch over it during opening hours – which had never been altered and which were therefore totally uncongenial for modern visitors – never managed to fight off boredom for more than a few months, and so changed frequently. Only recently, when times were harder and employment of any kind attractive, had the keepers stayed in their posts longer: up to two years.

But the curator was dedicated. Enric Fabregas had worked his way up to the position over forty of his sixty-four years. He was well aware that this was not the career he had dreamed of, and that he would never now be director of the Prado, but he'd made the most of his mediocre talents and held off what little competition there'd been for his post with his talent as an archivist. There was nothing in the collection that hadn't been personally annotated by him, and he could pinpoint any item among the thousands gathered together over the years Guardiola had been active. Nothing had been added or taken away since he had arrived at the Museo. The collection was preserved in aspic, and he guarded it jealously. A pallid man, skin the colour of parchment, he lived with his bookish wife in an apartment on the top floor of the mansion that housed the collection.

But the museum had suffered under him. Inflation had taken its toll on the amount invested by the trustees for its maintenance, and this, coupled with Fabregas's natural conservatism, meant that computerization of the catalogue had never been undertaken, and that security was not as tight as it might have been. There was no CCTV except at the main entrance, and one watchman looked after the place at night. But, half forgotten as the museum was, none of that had mattered until now.

The first shock had been the visit itself – a visit not from the usual dusty academics Fabregas was used to receiving, with the grandiose and generally unhelpful condescension of a Renaissance pope, but from three informally dressed foreigners with an official warrant from the Spanish Security Service, no less. An auburn-haired, green-eyed woman and two men: a tall, bespectacled black guy in his forties and a taller white man who looked as if he might be their bodyguard. Only one of them, Dr Lopez, had any kind of academic title, and he was the one Fabregas took to be the senior member of the group.

He'd received them in his large, funereal office, whose furniture and decor had seen no change in sixty years, though the telephone was new. There wasn't even a computer. The only one in the museum sat on a table in his secretary's office along the corridor. The group was polite but insistent, and Fabregas found himself unable to fob them off with his usual 'Make an appointment with my secretary and come back in a week's time'. When he tried this, the younger man, the bodyguard, a dishevelled-looking fellow with unruly hair and hard, penetrating eyes, had gone beyond insistence and would have become downright rude if the woman, who looked the most intelligent of the three, hadn't restrained him. But, by then, Fabregas felt that his cosy, secure little world had been thoroughly breached, and he was scared. He knew exactly what they were looking for, and where to find it. One of the rare maps, not on display to the general public. No one had asked for it, and he himself had not looked at it, in years.

He bowed acquiescence, though his heart was resentful, instructed his secretary – a plump brunette in her forties – to serve the visitors coffee, and left them to enter the small room adjacent to his office. It was as well that they had come on a day when the museum was closed.

The second shock came when he unlocked the boxwood cabinet where the bound catalogues of the collection were kept. He'd been off sick for a day, after an inexplicable attack of food poisoning. He suspected that the source had been a dish of chipirones in a tapas bar he frequented nearby, though the owner had denied it. It had still been only a couple of days ago – on the previous Tuesday – that he'd last consulted them, but he could see at a glance that Volume XIII had been misplaced: it had been clumsily shoved back between XV and XVI. He took it down with trembling hands, placed it on a table and leafed through it to check the shelf mark he needed. MDL–MDCL/cart.*cat*.4249. His fastidious mind noted that the page had been roughly handled. There was a smudge on it, a dark stain, quite small, but glaringly obvious, partly obscuring the first neatly typed words on the page. There was also a fold in it, hastily smoothed back, but he would never have done such a thing, and he and his assistant, a bony young man whose fussiness surpassed his own, were the only two people to handle the catalogues. Where was his assistant? It occurred to Fabregas that he hadn't seen him since the day before. But his office was on the other side of the building, near the visitors' entrance, and they had regular meetings only twice a week.

The third shock he was in part prepared for, and he approached the indicated shelf in the temperature-controlled sub-basement (the temperature control a necessary technical innovation he had initiated) with trepidation.

It was as he'd both feared and expected. The niche between cart.*cat*.4248 and 4250 was empty.

60

Enric Fabregas's assistant had a gag in his mouth and a garotte around his neck. He'd been dead, Jack reckoned, less than twelve hours. They'd broken some of his fingers to make him talk. The desk drawer where he kept his set of museum keys was open, and the keys were gone.

Fabregas was slumped in a chair across the room, unable to speak. Nothing like this had ever happened to him. He had built a shelter around him all his life, but, in the end, it hadn't been bombproof.

'What shall I tell his parents?' was all he was able to say.

'Do you have any kind of back-up – anything that might help us?' asked Laura. 'Dr Fabregas, you've got to pull yourself together. You can have no idea how important this is.'

'Help us find whoever did this,' added Jack.

That stirred something in Fabregas. He made an effort to pull himself together, remembering that these people came with the authority of the Security Service, and said, 'Every item in the collection is either photographed or photocopied.'

'Then show us.'

'I'll come with you,' Laura said.

Left alone, Leon and Jack went through the other drawers of the desk and the filing cabinet in the room, but none yielded anything. The office was plain and modern: functional office furniture, not a trace of anything personal. The assistant did not have his own secretary. His window overlooked a tree in a small courtyard, beyond which was a blank wall. The window showed no sign of having been opened or tampered with and had a lock on its handle.

'Look at this,' Leon said suddenly.

Jack lifted the assistant's bloody hand from the blotter on which it rested. He had tried to scrawl something there.

'Can you read it?' he asked.

'Just the beginning of a word.'

'Something he overheard them say?'

'They must have strangled him before they went to get the map.'

'Not necessarily. They'd have checked first. They must have left him here with someone. Two people. Team of four. Two to get the map, two here – one to keep watch.'

'Possible.'

'Bern–' read Jack.

'Bern? Bernard? Bernardette?'

'Or a place.'

'Berne?'

'Here in town.'

'Possible.'

'A rendezvous?'

Two minutes later, Laura and Fabregas returned. By then, Jack had removed the sheet of blotting paper and rested the dead man's hand back on a clean sheet on the blotter. He turned to Fabregas:

'You may call the police after we have gone. But mention nothing of our visit.'

'I'll have enough explaining to do without that,' Fabregas replied, half to himself.

Back in their hired Seat Exeo, Jack huddled well down in the back seat. He hadn't been under threat since the attack two nights earlier, but breaking cover to visit the museum had been a risk, even with Leon and Laura as back-up. He partly opened the large-format photocopy of the map, and glanced at it.

'Let's get this back to base,' Laura said, taking the wheel. 'Don't want to be out in the open too long.'

'Hold on. Something else first. More important.'

'What could be more important?'

'Look at this.' Jack showed her the smudged word, written in blood on the blotting pad which he had brought with them.

'I don't know what it means,' she said. 'Part of a name?'

'Leon, look up hotels. We may still be in time. They may check what they've got here before they ship it out.'

Leon flipped open his laptop and sighed. 'Do you know how many hotels there are in Barcelona?'

'Just type in the letters.'

It took seconds. 'There's a hotel Catalonia Berna in Carrer Roger de Llúria. Corner of Consell de Cent.'

'You see? Let's get there. Now.'

The hotel, in the Eixample district, its exterior covered with distinctive neoclassical paintings, was in upheaval. It took a lot of arguing and a telephone call to Elena Blanco's office at the Centro de Inteligencia before they were let up to the room on the second floor.

A woman lay on the bed, a redhead, one neat bullet-hole in the middle of her forehead. The room was in chaos, with every sign of a violent struggle. There was a half-packed suitcase on a stand near the wardrobe.

'We found this,' the detective in charge told Jack. 'In her hand. Looks like it was torn off. Looks old.'

'When was she killed, would you say?'

The detective shrugged. 'Very recently. Within the last two hours. But too early to say for sure.'

Jack took the piece of paper from his hand and looked at it. Four crudely drawn symbols, part of one missing, left with the rest of the document the woman had been so desperately trying to hang on to. But Jack recognized them.

Just as he recognized the woman on the bed. He was looking at the face of Drita Agoli.

'You'll have to sign for that if you're taking it,' the detective said, nodding at the fragment of parchment Jack was still holding.

'Good luck with your investigation.'

'Is she known to you? Her passport's missing.'

'I've never seen her before.'

The detective looked at him and nodded, his resentment at the interference fading with the realization that he had come close to something way beyond his remit.

Laura drove them back to the short let Jack had taken in Gràcia. Once there, they studied the large-format photocopy Fabregas had given them.

'Is this it?' Leon said. 'Really *it*?'

They looked at the crooked lines and the annotations in spidery, all but indecipherable ink. But they could see the rivers, the thick forests, places marked where landings could be made, dangerous currents – all in detail, except for an area near the centre where the rivers and any tracks marked seemed to disappear into nothing.

'A part that isn't mapped?' Laura said.

'Maybe,' Jack replied thoughtfully.

'But the rest is so meticulous.'

'Perhaps he didn't have time. Perhaps it's an area they didn't explore. Look, there are a dozen crosses on the thing here, over to the west.'

'It's nowhere near any of the areas where Eldorado's been located on maps before,' said Laura. 'It's much further south.'

'It's something to go on,' mused Lopez.

'What do you mean?' asked Jack.

'I'm not sure – yet. But leave it with me.'

'Drita Agoli was one of the Chevaliers. They still don't have the map,' Jack said.

'But whoever does have it can make any number of copies, send it anywhere within minutes, and has probably done so,' said Laura.

'They don't have it all,' Jack said, delicately spreading the parchment left in Agoli's hand next to the photocopied version on the map Fabregas had given them.

61

It was a long night. After the carnage in Barcelona and the huge gear-shifts in their mission, Jack had too much on his mind for sleep to come easily. He had given up trying two hours ago, and now sat in an armchair in the living room of the apartment on the corner of Sutton Place and E57th Street, watching the lights of New York without really seeing them. His whiskey sat untouched in its glass on the table next to him, and his cigarette had burnt out in the ashtray, leaving a little wreath of blue smoke hanging in the air. Even the chess game he'd set out, with the intention of distracting himself with a problem or two he remembered from Velimirović and Valtonen, had failed to work its magic. The window was open, as it was warm even for June, and from far away the constant hum of the city came unheeded to his ears.

He was looking for answers which he was almost afraid to find. There had to have been a reason for Natasha's impatience; there had to be a reason why she'd disappeared – and he didn't think she'd fallen back into the hands of the Chevaliers. But they would be on her track, as they surely were on his. Which was why he was here, and not in his familiar downtown apartment, where he'd have dearly preferred to be.

Why had she abandoned him? She had made no attempt to make contact, which he *could* put down to caution; but he had still hoped she would. That was why he had not cut her number out of his cell phone or put a security block on it. He knew the risk he was taking but he also knew that she could still be useful. He told himself that was the only reason.

That she could take care of herself he had no doubt, but he wondered where she was and what her plans were. Was she working with others? That was another question. It would have taken a lot to remove Drita Agoli and get the map from her. She had clearly been about to fly out of Barcelona – but to where? There had been no plane tickets, no passport, nothing to indicate her plans. Had she herself still been loyal to the Chevaliers?

He came back to Natasha's sense of urgency. There was something there, some secret she had not shared with him. But why not? The only answer to that was the one he least wanted to face: that she was not on his side; that she had only been cooperating with him for as long as it was useful.

The armchair was too soft, too comfortable. It seemed to hold him in a disagreeable embrace. After the events of the last few days and the long flight home, during which they'd discussed the map and how to act on it, Laura had insisted that any plan of action must first be run past Hudson. Jack had to admit that she was right. If they were getting close now, they couldn't take a step without authorization from the highest levels.

And they'd have to be very careful about what hopes and expectations they raised.

The apartment, super secure, in a luxury block in one of the city's most exclusive quarters, hadn't been a victim of budget cuts, though the days of its usefulness in housing the most important Soviet defectors were long gone. Jack suspected that Sir Richard kept it on his books for his own occasional use. It had had to be redecorated and refurbished from top to bottom a couple of years earlier, after being home to a Colombian drugs baron turned informer for three months. He'd occupied it with his entire family, including five extremely spoilt children, who'd wreaked most of the havoc and damaged a Willem de Kooning from Hudson's collection almost beyond repair. It had been replaced by a reproduction of a large Dutch landscape in a heavy frame which sat well with the bland but expensive decor – soft-white walls, oatmeal Berber carpets and muted lighting – the apartment now exhibited.

Jack was uneasy here. He preferred some mark of humanity in a place. This apartment – six spacious rooms – felt to him like a luxury hotel, with a touch of mausoleum thrown in. He was also well aware that, while he was in the place, every move he made was being monitored by unseen mini-cameras and microphones.

He wondered how far Leon had got in deciphering the symbols on the map – if they *were* symbols; if they had any significance at all. Maybe they were just decoration? But the map hadn't been drawn for public consumption or admiration. The points of the compass were marked, but there was no ornate plate describing what the map showed: no dolphins or ships whipping up foam in the seas that abutted its coastlines, no cherubs holding up coats-of-arms in its corners.

Waiting. It was the time he hated most. And he knew in his gut there was little time for it. He knew that, soon, they would have to act on the map and follow the routes it indicated.

He showered and dressed, made coffee and settled down on a dining chair with an old biography of Sir Walter Raleigh by Eric Ecclestone:

> Even now, Raleigh did not wholly surrender to despair. Old, sick and broken as he was, he proposed to lead a fresh expedition in person to search out the elusive mine. But his followers lacked their leader's spirit. They were sceptical of the mine's existence . . .

What if Raleigh's companions had been right?

But that was a risk Jack couldn't afford to take. No one could pretend for much longer that the tidal wave that was towering over the world wasn't going to crash down on it soon.

He drank two cups of coffee without cream and smoked three or four cigarettes, abandoning the Raleigh biography – he could see the words on the page but failed to take any of them in – and, unable to settle, ranged the apartment like a caged animal. Natasha wouldn't leave his mind, and neither would the image of Drita Agoli, dead in the Berna Hotel.

It was 06h00 when the blue phone rang.

62

They met at the safe house out in Mount Vernon, which had become the operational centre after their return. Both Laura and Leon had travelled under guard from the apartments they'd been allocated, and Leon's family – Mia, Alvar and Lucia – were staying with friends in Brooklyn. That had been a security challenge that Mia had risen to with a calm and resourcefulness Leon had hardly dared hope for from his wife; but he knew from the few questions she'd asked that, after this, he would have to draw her far more into his confidence than he'd had to up until now. And he'd have other questions to answer, questions he put to himself: could he continue to run the risk of endangering his family; of damaging his marriage? But Hudson had insisted on ultra-secure measures being taken, now that, as he put it, 'the game's afoot'.

Jack only hoped that Hudson was right.

'The symbols weren't hard to decipher in the end,' Leon said. 'But their importance is a little harder to guess at.' He ran through the significance of the condor, the Dog Star, Sirius, and the constellations of Canis Major and Lepus.

'Everything points to a critical moment that affects the city of gold,' he went on. 'I've set up a PowerPoint model to show us all what I'm groping towards here. Let me show you.'

Laura and Jack watched the sequence of images as Leon continued. 'There are plenty of legends, from across the world, which indicate the existence of this kind of mechanism, and some, in fact, still exist, though none has ever been observed – at least, in any strictly scientific way – in our times. There are plenty of theories about the great pyramid at Giza, for example; and still more attaching to the Chaldeans and the Sumerians. The ziggurats of the Babylonians may well have been used by them as complex astronomical machines.'

'So, what are we saying?' Laura asked, her eyes intent on the screen.

'I'm saying that if we use the conjunction of these constellations and cross-refer the sun's path over the map reference – longitude and latitude data, that is, of where our map seems to indicate the city of gold to be – we get a precise moment in time when the sun's light hits an exactly pinpointed spot. That is where we will find the entrance to the temple.'

'And what mechanism are we talking about?' queried Jack.

'One that opens doors, I think. Or a gateway of some kind. Maybe even the way into a mineshaft,' Leon replied simply. Unlike Jack, he had slept like a baby for five hours after their flight. Afterwards, it had taken him another two hours of intense concentration to bring him to his conclusion. 'It also ties in with sun worship, which predates the Incas. They didn't appear until the thirteenth century. I think we may be looking at something way earlier than that.'

'This mechanism,' said Laura. 'Magnetic-field induced?'

'That could well be how the thing works. But if I'm right . . .'

'Well?'

'The timing is everything. This phenomenon takes place only once a year, maybe even only once every two or even five years. I have to do some more cross-checking on that, but two things are certain: it does happen, and we are on the verge of its happening. The sun will cross this precise point on the map on Midsummer's Day.'

'The twenty-fourth of June? But that's less than two weeks away.'

'Give or take. You have to allow for differentials over the four hundred years since the map was made – potential inaccuracies, of which I can find only minute examples, and a simple safety margin. But, within hours, at most, either side of midday. I think it will hit before noon, and on the day itself.'

'Jesus!' exclaimed Jack.

'And are we the only ones to know this?' Laura asked Leon.

'I don't know.'

'Why couldn't the doors just be blown open?' asked Jack.

'Have you seen the stonework the Incas were capable of? And how would anyone know what damage you might do to the mechanism if you used dynamite and failed? You might lock everything in for ever,' replied Leon.

Jack nodded. He was thinking again of Natasha's impatience. 'We can't assume that we are the only ones to know,' he said. 'Look at what's been happening. The timing of this whole operation is based on a build-up to *now*. That's why the Chevaliers panicked after they discovered they'd failed to secure the true map. And if they are getting any kind of financial funding from somewhere else, somewhere that maybe hopes to profit from a world financial meltdown –'

'A rogue state?' offered Laura.

'Maybe.'

'An unholy alliance? But the Chevaliers would never stick to any agreement once they had their hands on the gold.'

'If they get their hands on the gold, we won't be around to see what happens next.'

'I repeat: everything indicates that this place will be accessible only when the sun passes over and activates some kind of doorway,' said Leon. 'That is the only logical conclusion I can deduce from this material, these symbols.

'But there's something else that's interesting,' he continued. He pressed a key, and an image of the map, filling the whole one-by-two-metre screen, appeared. 'Here's the map. Now look at this.' He pressed another key, and two lines became visible: one red, one yellow.

They crossed the map and intersected at a point near its centre.

'Look where it lies,' he said.

'That's where the sunlight will pass?' Jack said.

'Precisely there.'

'We'd better pray for a clear day,' Jack said, only half flippantly.

'Are you certain your calculations are right?' asked Laura.

'I wouldn't be telling you this if I weren't.'

The three of them were silent. The lines crossed in the middle of the blank area of the map.

63

'We have one hope,' Jack said. 'The competition may know when – and they've had that advantage over us – but they don't know precisely where.'

'Nor do we,' said Hudson testily, 'if your lines cross in the middle of nowhere.' He tapped the copy of the map spread out on his desk.

'But we can fix the location.'

'You've still got to reach it – and through untracked jungle, as far as I can gather.' Sir Richard paused. 'But I hope you're right. This thing's beginning to hit globally. People are already taking to the streets in Caracas, Seoul, Rome, Madrid . . . The list goes on. London next; Paris maybe. We can't keep a lid on it any more.'

This was the last briefing before departure. In the last twenty-four hours, the ground had been covered again and again. There wasn't a speck of dust left unnoticed. They hoped. Sir Richard looked at his watch. 'You're scheduled to leave in two hours, Laura?'

'Check.'

'Good luck, then. Liaise via Dr Lopez, and only when necessary. Leave the torn corner of the original map with him – he'll need to do additional tests. And keep the GPS implant in your arm deactivated. We can't risk them locking on to that.'

'I took care of that before Barcelona,' she said.

'Good. Then make contact as soon as you've located the target. I'll deal with the heavy artillery to send in then. It's already in train. But we can't make a big move until we have absolute evidence. That'd blow the lid off the whole thing.' He stood to indicate that the meeting was over, and shook hands with both of them. 'You're really on your own now,' he said. 'Don't fail us.'

64

'In his good books again, am I?' Jack asked Laura as they made their way back to Room 55.

'I wouldn't bank on it.'

They'd returned briefly to HQ, which now had heightened security in place so that Leon, who'd remain behind to coordinate, needn't remain in the relative exile of Mount Vernon. No hostile activity had been detected around any of their apartments, which meant that, within another two days, Leon would be reunited with his family at his own home. But he wasn't looking forward to the conversation he'd have to have with Mia.

'Good at least that the Chevaliers aren't breathing down our necks here,' Laura reassured him.

'And bad,' Leon added. 'If they're leaving us alone, it means they don't think we have the map. They're after whoever took it from them.' He hesitated. 'If they haven't retrieved it already.'

They took the firm's Gulfstream G400 for the nine-hour flight to Manaus. Once they were airborne, the attendant brought Laura a sky-blue envelope, which she opened immediately, pulling out a black memory stick.

'What's that?'

'Homework.' She plugged the stick into the on-board computer and waited. 'Needed this to come to the plane separately. Security, obviously.'

'Of course.' Jack was already looking at the documents and photographs appearing on the screen. 'Background on the Chevaliers?'

'Yes.'

'New stuff?'

She nodded. 'I had Section 19 do some digging at the start of all this. Finally, we have results. It's OK, Hudson knows.'

'But I didn't.'

'That's right.'

'Why was I kept out of the loop?'

Laura looked defensive, and Jack could guess why. Hudson hadn't trusted him.

'No need,' Laura said. 'You know now.'

'This is about Natasha, isn't it?'

'We've been fooled before.'

'She isn't a double.'

'I've verified that. But you can't blame me for checking.'

'I could have saved you the time,' said Marlow, thinking: you haven't been through what we've been through together. But he didn't think further than that. 'And we may still need Natasha.'

'We're not dealing in gut feelings here, Jack. We're dealing in facts,' Laura said sharply, but she regretted her tone immediately. 'Either way, we'll track her down.'

'If the Chevaliers don't get to her first. We have to prevent that.'

'I think they have more important things to think about.'

He let her go on thinking that, and watched as she pressed a key. 'Look at these photographs.'

Jack recognized three of the four faces. 'Two of these people are dead. This one, I killed in Paris. The woman, we both know. This man was at my interrogation in Rio, and his name is Louvier. The fourth –'

But the fourth picture was out of focus, taken from a long distance away from the subject, who was apparently moving swiftly, from a building to a car. All you could tell was that it was a male, thick-set, bearded, probably not young.

'All Chevaliers, we think. We don't know their ranks. The dead man, Kristof Struna, was a heavy, a foot soldier, at the very most the equivalent of an NCO in their organization. Drita Agoli must have been pretty high-ranking, or she wouldn't have been entrusted with the mission in Barcelona. But the others . . .'

'Louvier was in charge in Rio. I'm pretty sure of that.'

'From the data Section 19 has dug up, he's near the top. But they don't think he's the head of the group. What's interesting is in the paperwork.' She pressed another key.

'Not much of it,' Jack said.

'Just a couple of intercepts. Stuff they thought they'd deleted. But there's enough to indicate that there may be some kind of division.'

'You mean a power struggle – *within* the Chevaliers?'

'From this, it looks like Louvier's got his eye on the crown,' Laura said.

Jack read through the two documents carefully. '"Wait until the right moment, but do nothing, absolutely nothing, until then." That could mean anything.'

'But worth bearing in mind.'

'Everything we know about the Chevaliers indicates their total dedication to a common cause.'

'Historically, yes. We live in less idealistic times.'

'Who's the other guy?'

'No data on him. But he's definitely connected.'

'You think someone from within the Chevaliers might have taken the map from Agoli?'

'It's possible.'

But Jack had other ideas.

65

No one was taking any chances. The Gulfstream was to stay at Manaus on standby. Only Wilson Trezza, the head of the Agência Brasileira de Inteligência, had been informed of their arrival. His closest aides had arranged for a black BMW X6M to be waiting for them at Eduardo Gomes airport. They took Santos Dumont, then the long Avenida do Turismo, before turning right on to Coronel Teixeira to reach the Manaus Tropical Hotel, a huge white, red-roofed edifice on the banks of the Amazon.

Outside, thirty degrees and humid. A slight breeze from the vast river bringing some relief. They unpacked in their double suite, two bedrooms separated by a small but elegant living area, and checked the kit they'd be taking.

'Rendezvous with the guides at 06h00 tomorrow,' Laura confirmed after a brief conversation on her secure cell phone.

Jack looked at his watch. 'Gives us twelve hours. Not much time for sightseeing. And to think I was hoping to take you to the opera.'

'Some other time.'

'It's beautiful, you know. Big crimson-and-white cake with a green-and-yellow dome. Not to be missed.'

'I've seen pictures. No way are we leaving the hotel. So enjoy.'

'It'll take two hours to go over this,' Jack said, indicating the kit. 'Champagne and pato no tucupi at eight?'

'I'll stick to the catfish.'

Laura knew Jack's lightheartedness was there to cover his tension. Inside, he was coiling the spring that would drive him along over the next – how long? In just over seven days they would be past the deadline. How far ahead of them were the Chevaliers, and how had they organized themselves?

'The Agência has arranged a light plane for the first two hundred kilometres.' Laura pointed at a modern map of the region they had spread out on the coffee table. 'Then, with luck, they'll helicopter us another thirty. Jump over the worst of the jungle approaches.'

'And after that we're on our own?'

'Yes.'

Jack didn't like the size of the operation. It was as small scale as it could be, but it would still draw attention. They had no choice if they were to keep everything as contained as possible, but he didn't like depending on the Agência, though he knew all the men involved had been top-level vetted.

They had no more information on the activities of the Chevaliers, and that disturbed him too. If they were going in to take possession of the city, they would be mounting a big operation. But if they had the resources, in the still-vast jungles of Amazonas, and they moved fast, they could keep it undercover. The USA couldn't possibly send a force into Brazil to counteract that without huge diplomatic upheavals, without blowing the lid off any containment of the Crisis.

He began to think they were faced with an impossible task.

And then his phone rang. He took one look at the number and went cold. Laura had already cast him a questioning look, but he shook his head at her and put a finger to his lips. He wouldn't be able to keep this from her, but he could find out what was going on first. He went out on to the balcony, where the heat hit him like a hammer. The shoreline of the great, sluggish river twinkled with lights, but he directed his gaze to the lush, tropical garden that fronted the hotel's entrance. Had he seen movement there, among the palms?

'Natasha!'

'Jack – listen. You've got to help me.' Her voice was desperate, imploring. It stopped the dozen questions that immediately crammed into his mind.

'Where are you?'

'Here.'

66

'I shook them off. I wouldn't have called you otherwise.' Natasha Fielding gulped down the glass of Cachaça Ypióca Laura had reluctantly fetched her. It had taken some very fast, persuasive explaining to get her into the hotel. She looked dishevelled, hunted; her linen jacket and trousers were dirty, and torn in places. She clung to the large leather shoulder bag she carried as if her life depended on it.

'I'm finished,' she said. 'I can't do this any more. I've got to hand over to you. Everything. I've been a fool. And they're not far behind me. Even though they think no one can stop them now, they want my death.'

'What's happened?' asked Jack.

'And how the hell did you find us?' added Laura angrily.

'I went back to New York. I knew you'd send people after me, but they weren't the only ones. But I had to get back. I wanted to make contact, but I couldn't. Louvier's on to me and I didn't dare break cover. I didn't want to compromise you.' She looked at Jack. 'I'm glad you're safe.'

'Never mind that,' Laura snapped. 'You've fucked our security now. Not that you haven't made it look like a joke anyway. Do you realize what your interference has –'

'I knew that if you had anything to go on, if there'd been any kind of back-up for the map at the Museo Guardiola, it would lead you here first. I hadn't a clue what to do, except that I knew that I would have to come here to Manaus, whatever else happened. This is the point of departure. They've been here already. They cannot be allowed to succeed.' A sudden rustling from the balcony made her stop and turn frightened eyes in its direction. But it was only the wind in the trees.

'I tracked you via your phone,' Natasha said simply. 'I knew you wouldn't have lost faith in me, Jack. Even after what I did.'

'Jesus,' said Laura. 'Block it now,' she said to Jack. '*Now!*'

'Already done.' But he was looking at Natasha. 'You've got it, haven't you?'

She nodded.

'Show me.'

Moving slowly – almost, it seemed, against her will – she unclasped her hands from the bag she held and laid it on the table. From it she drew the map and carefully unfolded it.

'Did you find the torn corner?' she asked.

'Yes.'

'I had to leave that hotel in a hurry. She wouldn't let go of it – she held on to it even after I had shot her. But it means you got there before the Chevaliers did.'

'But you remember what was on the torn corner?'

'Yes.'

'Do you know what the symbols mean?'

She nodded again. 'My father told me what they represent. The Brotherhood knew of the sun's power over the gates of the temple that guard the city of gold.'

'Then the Chevaliers know too.'

'Yes.'

'That was why you ran. After the attack. You knew the urgency, and you didn't tell me.'

'I had a mission too. I needed to fulfil it.' Her eyes were filled with the fire Jack had seen in them before.

'But you must have known you could never –'

'I didn't know that at all. I didn't think you would succeed. The Chevaliers had identified you, your organization. But we have to hurry now. They know all about the time limit too.'

'How could you possibly have believed you could stop them alone?'

Natasha gazed at the map. 'A little fish can slip through a big net. I didn't think beyond keeping the map from them.'

'Why didn't you destroy it?'

'I don't know. I couldn't. Look at it. Look at the secret it holds. Could *you* just throw that away? Besides, they will search for ever to find the city. They must be stopped now. Only by finding it first and destroying it – destroying the city – can we break their power for good.'

Jack and Laura were silent, but Jack was looking at the map with fresh eyes. Now that he saw the original, there was something there, he knew, something that was just beyond his grasp. Something . . .

'I've studied it,' Natasha said, as if reading his mind.

'I've spent days and nights looking at it, just as you are looking at it now. It cannot have been left incomplete. The blank part must have been filled in.'

'No one has ever been able to pinpoint Eldorado,' said Laura. 'The legend may live on, but belief in it has dwindled. What if all this is a massive delusion, begun by Sir Walter Raleigh and ending here? What if the Chevaliers themselves are chasing nothing but a wild dream?'

'You know we can't take that chance. The Chevaliers have invested millions in this, have gambled at the highest level –'

'So have rogue traders, so have all the people across history who've followed the tired old dream of money for nothing. Look at the banks in the run-up to 2008. Weren't they all after their own Eldorado? Isn't it all just a question of greed?'

'But our enemies want it for something else,' Natasha said. 'They want it to destroy us, by smashing the financial pillars on which all society is built, whether we like it or not. And by bringing their own brand of domination to the world. We can't rule out the possibility that they are already on their way. Drita Agoli had the map in her possession for long enough before I took it from her to have passed on the information in it. Even if it's incomplete, they're desperate to locate the city. From the scale, only the last few kilometres are blanked out. They may be desperate enough to take a chance.'

There was an uneasy pause. There *were* people – Park Avenue people – who'd found a kind of Eldorado already, reflected Jack. Who'd found it at a cost to everyone else, who'd found it and concentrated it within their small group, and always wanted more. He hadn't chosen this job in order to protect them. But the Chevaliers' remedy was no answer either, and he wouldn't be surprised if the people he was thinking of wouldn't survive them – might even join them; might even be behind them. And all the time he was looking at the parchment in front of him, willing its secret out of it. A glimmer of light appeared.

'Laura, think for a moment,' he said, not taking his eyes from the map, leaning closer to it and tracing invisible lines over the blank part with his finger. 'Think of our work. Think of how we cover our tracks.'

'What are you driving at?'

'We can make things disappear. We can make ourselves disappear. It gets harder and harder. Natasha traced me because I left a pathway open. But all the modern technology in the world, applied to this map, may have overlooked one thing.'

'I'm still lost,' said Laura, with growing impatience. But a light had dawned in Natasha's eyes.

'If you made a copy of this map, as we have done, it would show the blank part, and no one could reveal it to be anything but blank.'

'Yes.'

'But the original . . . If the map had been altered, or deliberately left incomplete, and then the important details were drawn in in such a way that only those privy to the secret could access them . . .'

Laura's lips parted in a cautious smile. 'You're joking.'

'Why not? People used it. People like us used it routinely until very recently. They wrote or drew in urine, lemon juice, milk, wine – semen, even. In fact, we still use it. Look at something as simple as UV marker pens. And remember that business with Rangzieb Ahmed in Britain a few years ago? The al-Qaeda notebook?'

'Christ,' said Laura.

'My near-namesake, Christopher Marlowe, worked for Sir Robert Cecil's espionage network. He was close to Raleigh,' Jack said.

'My father spoke of them,' said Natasha. 'They were among those fighting against the Chevaliers then, with my ancestor.'

'They wanted to keep the map but bury its secret within it. So they doctored it. They doctored it, but Raleigh must have had a key to it, which he later destroyed, to enable him to use it without giving away its secret,' Jack said.

'Let's try,' Laura said.

'But can it have survived this long? Will it still react?' said Natasha.

'If he used the right liquid.'

'Come on, then!'

Very gently, Laura held the map up. Jack brought the flame of his lighter close to the surface, taking infinite care not to bring it too close to the surface of the parchment. For a long time, nothing happened. They were about to give up when, suddenly, a few faint brown lines began to appear. They remained very faint, but they proliferated, until the empty space on the map became a network of tracks and lines which resolved itself into a series of pathways through forest, leading to the shore of a lake, at the western end of which was a small island.

Barely visible on the island, the map-maker had drawn a low hill, on which they could just discern some kind of tower.

67

Then they worked fast. They scanned the original map and enhanced it so that the faint lines on it became clearer, and Laura carefully traced Leon's coordinating lines on to it. They crossed at precisely the location of the tower.

'We'll use this. The original must go back to New York,' Laura decided. 'It's too dangerous to leave it exposed.'

'The scanned copy doesn't show the symbols,' Natasha said.

'But they *are* on the copy we have from the Museo Guardiola,' interjected Jack. 'We can use that as back-up. Unless –' He paused as a thought struck him.

'Unless?' questioned Laura.

'Unless we keep them to ourselves. We can't risk the Chevaliers having all the information, should the map fall into their hands.'

'It won't.'

'We can't take the chance. Natasha, your memory –'

'Yes?'

'Are you confident enough that you can carry those images clearly in your mind? You said you had a near-photographic memory.'

'I think so.'

'We must take a copy of the symbols,' said Laura. 'Keep them separate. We need them.'

'For what reason?'

'We may find out there is more to them than we've already learnt. Once we get there. In any case, if the map falls into the Chevaliers' hands, the game's as good as lost.'

'Natasha,' said Jack, 'do we need to take the map at all?'

'What do you mean?'

'Could you remember it? All of it?'

'That's crazy,' Laura objected.

Natasha hesitated, then said: 'Laura's right. I couldn't trust myself. We have to be sure.'

'But the symbols?'

'Yes.'

'Think carefully,' Laura said. 'They may mean more. They may be crucial.'

'I can remember them.'

'Then we don't take any record of them with us,' Jack decided. He looked at Laura. 'You'll have to go back to New York with the original.'

'What?'

'We can't trust anyone else. We've got to move fast. Natasha knows the score. I'll have to go on with her. Get the original back to Hudson, and he'll have all he needs to persuade the president to coordinate a strike force to come in after us. In the face of this, the Brazilian government will cooperate. But get them moving fast. I can't guarantee that I'll be able to contact you again. You'll have to persuade them to move *immediately*.'

Laura started to speak, but checked herself and nodded. 'I'll go back,' she agreed. 'Pity though, I was in the mood for a little adventure.' She looked at them hard, and tried to keep the disappointment out of her voice.

Half an hour later, Jack and Natasha watched from the balcony of the suite as the black Agência BMW purred away from the hotel's forecourt in the direction of the airport. Jack knew that Hudson's reaction to her return, and the fact that she'd authorized him to continue the mission with an outsider, would be mollified by the force of the circumstances and the arrival of the original map. He waited while Natasha took a shower and changed into the clothes Laura had left for her. Jack had noticed that the two women were more or less the same height and weight, the same physical type, but it still felt odd, seeing Natasha in Laura's clothes. The evening was well advanced by now. Neither felt like eating, but they settled for sandwiches and a couple of bottles of Serra da Graciosa mineral water. Alcohol should have been out completely, but –

'I think we should risk a little champagne,' Jack said. 'God knows when we'll get a chance to drink it again.'

So they added a half-bottle of Dom Pérignon to their room-service order. After they'd eaten, Jack took her through the kit they'd be taking with them, which had already been prepared by Laura. Light jungle survival gear, compasses, Vortex Razor binoculars, modern maps of the area, which, though not detailed enough, could be used as back-up, a small amount of plastic explosive, two Böker Toro hunting knives and three guns: a Remington 597 Collapsible and two handguns. Jack had decided to add a Taurus Tracker .44 revolver to his kit; he wasn't going to abandon his Glock and actually preferred it to the bigger pistol, but now he handed it to Natasha. They both had to be armed. Most important of all, a powerful miniaturized radio transmitter. He watched as Natasha laid it all out neatly before systematically repacking it into the two olive-green backpacks they would carry.

They were ready, and seven hours lay between them and their departure time.

'What if we run across them? What if they're there already?'

'If they're there, the only thing we can do is observe and get a message back.'

'But even if INTERSEC's ready to go the minute they get our message, they'll still be hours away.'

'The Brazilian Air Force has a base here. We'll use the Semtex to slow things down for the Chevaliers, if we get a chance to use it.'

'There's something else.'

'What?'

'My father told me of a tribe that protects the temple. A branch of the lost Akuntsu, he believed. They have always protected it. Raleigh and Humboldt knew of them. Who knows if they weren't responsible for the deaths of Brandau's party?'

They fell silent, and now the pressure began to

build. Now, the time would pass more quickly than they wanted it to. Now came the familiar wait before action when, Jack knew from long experience, you just want the whole thing over with, or, better yet, you wake up and find you've been dreaming it. He was trained to deal with this, but every time he was placed in this situation, he wondered why he'd chosen this path. He should have stayed in journalism, or in academic life. He'd be a professor by now, with a real home to live in, proper friends, maybe even a wife and children. But it was too late now, and a small nugget of self-awareness deep within him told him that this was the only choice he could have made. Jack couldn't deny or resist the excitement that went along with the dread, and that, more than anything, was what motivated him – more even than the sense that what he was protecting was worth all his efforts. He had questioned the validity of his job before, and the answers made him uneasy, because the longer he stayed in it, the more he wondered about the values of the status quo he defended.

He thought, not for the first time, of that line of Mercutio's from *Romeo and Juliet*: 'A plague on both your houses.'

But the issues were clear. Jack knew he was up against a group so old, so evil, so convinced of their right to warp the world to their ends, to shape it to conform to their damaged idealism, that he had to stop them if he could. Afterwards, the world could just go on going to hell in its own way. But no one had the right to control it to suit themselves. He took comfort in the thought that somehow – always – such ambitions came to dust.

'This is a pretty big suite,' said Natasha.

'Yes.'

'Have you tried the beds?'

'No.'

'I wonder which one you'd prefer?'

'Why don't you choose?'

She led him into one of the bedrooms. 'It's been a long time,' she said.

He still wondered about her, but she was undressing him now, her lips kissing his chest as she took off his shirt. Then her hands were busy with his belt. When she'd finished, he pulled the cotton sweater she was wearing over her head, and saw she was wearing nothing beneath it. He kissed her breasts softly.

'Darling, darling . . .'

'Oh *mon amour*.'

Her tanned skin was deliciously soft, and his hands caressed it, remembering. When they curled up in the bed together they did not make love at first, simply lay in each other's arms, taking comfort, until the urge became too strong. Then, her breathing became urgent, and her hands insistent. He responded quickly, gently, as their lips and tongues met, his hands on her thighs, her buttocks, and she slipped her body under him, pressing against him, guiding him into her before putting her arms around him to hold him there as she wrapped her legs around his lower back and he drove quietly and strongly against her.

Afterwards, he rolled back and lay by her side, close enough for the contours of their bodies to be touching as he put his arms around her and she curled close. They stayed like that, catching snatches of sleep, until, far too soon, the hours counted in the green light of the bedside clock slipped by, the dawn crept across the windows, and it was time . . .

They dressed rapidly. Natasha pulled on the khaki linen jacket and fatigue trousers Laura had left her, Jack a T-shirt, lightweight jeans and a soft leather blouson jacket, into whose inner pockets he dropped a compass and his binoculars.

Their kit was packed and ready. While Natasha was out of the room, Jack strapped a slim, polycarbon dagger to his left calf. He could reach down and over and get it out of its sheath in less than two seconds.

68

Davi Jurado and Marcos Geitoso finalized the checks on the Bell 206L-4, one of the two helicopters at the disposal of the Agência in Amazonas. The helicopter was parked some distance from the little wooden hut at the centre of the runway that had been cut out of the dense surrounding jungle, beneath a canopy of branches. No roads led to it. The only access was by foot – and that was all but impossible – and by air. They were waiting for the arrival of the old Beechcraft 95 that was bringing their passengers from Manaus.

Jurado and Geitoso were tough, lightly built men, each in his late thirties. Geitoso was from São Paulo originally, and Jurado, whose broad face with its high cheekbones bore the stamp of his Calapó ancestry, came from Manaus, but they went back a way, to 2007. They'd met as members of the Polícia Militar. They worked together in Rio for a while, and had been co-opted to BOPE, the Batalhão de Operações Policiais Especiais, for the Managuera district operation in 2011. Soon afterwards, each promoted to the rank of captain, they'd been approached by the Agência. Both trained in urban and jungle combat and survival programmes, both with helicopter pilot's licences, they had been valuable Agência officers for two years now, and were perfect for this assignment.

From the hut, they could hear the faint chatter of the four BOPE operatives stationed at the base who usually used the Bell for both routine and special Amazonas missions. This was a newish group, near the beginning of their two-week tour of duty, but they, too, knew the jungle that hemmed them in, and which, despite the devastation wrought on it over recent decades, still held enough secrets and mystery to be treated with respect.

Jurado slid the chopper's rear door closed and wiped the dew off it with his glove. 'About done,' he said.

'Shouldn't be long now. Back to the hut? Join the others? Time to change into flying kit anyway.'

'Buzz them first. Need two men back out to watch the machine.'

'Of course.' Geitoso activated his radio phone and spoke a few words into it.

Then they heard the distant hum of a light plane.

'They're early,' said Geitoso.

Jurado and Geitoso watched as the plane appeared in the early-morning sky above them, made one turn over the landing strip and came in to land.

But it wasn't a Beechcraft.

At the same time, the BOPE men emerged from the hut, shielding their eyes from the sun, looking up. Jurado yelled a warning to the officer in command of the post. The men grabbed their weapons and fanned out as the plane taxied towards them.

Two helmeted men in BOPE jungle fatigues emerged from the plane and made their way towards them.

The men were only a couple of feet away from Geitoso and Jurado when Jurado noticed that there was something wrong. The military fatigues the men were wearing bore no BOPE insignia.

'Marcos!' he yelled in warning, his hand going for his gun. The two men closed in fast, yelling themselves, the element of surprise gone. In an instant, the BOPE soldiers from the hut came running over. By then, Jurado was down. His attacker had plunged a long knife deep into the hollow of his neck below the jaw. Geitoso had had time to draw his pistol and get off three shots, killing Jurado's attacker before he could get back on to his feet and catching his companion in the thigh. He fired twice more before heading for the protection of the encircling trees, but he had scarcely reached the jungle's edge before five bullets had caught him in the legs and back. He plunged down into the undergrowth, dead before his head crashed on to the sodden leaves. Behind him, more men had emerged from the plane, machine guns blazing. The BOPE men were outnumbered and, though they fought hard, the battle was short.

Their attackers stripped the dead BOPE men of their jackets, then dragged the bodies into the forest and dumped them, along with the body of their own dead companion.

A last man emerged from the plane. He watched the aftermath of the operation impassively. It was a pity it hadn't been a perfectly clean kill, but it had gone ahead as planned, and the time frame was still in place. He looked at his watch. If the information in Manaus was correct – and he had no reason to doubt it – the Beechcraft would be arriving in an hour. His strategy had worked perfectly so far. Logistically, of course, it had been a nightmare, and expensive; but he had planned it all and pulled it off, and his cachet within his organization would rise: soon, his moment would come.

'Put the jackets on,' he ordered. 'Those that aren't damaged. They'll be looking for the right insignia. Now we can look like the real thing.' He turned to the two men under his command who would fly the helicopter. 'Your names are Davi Jurado and Marcos Geitoso,' he said, reading the name tags taken from the bodies of the two dead policemen. 'Clip these on to your jackets. Don't use Geitoso's jacket – if they see the holes in that, they'll think you've risen from the dead.'

'What about Ezquina? He's wounded.' The leader of the attack group had approached him.

'Get him on the plane, and get the plane out of here. *Fast!*' He would have preferred to kill the wounded man, but he didn't want to risk the loyalty of the mercenaries. The ten members of his attack group numbered six of his own men and four mercenaries. The mercenaries were being paid $150,000 each for this mission, and Ezquina was one of them. Now they would fly out with the plane, leaving the two replacement helicopter pilots and four men to play the roles of the BOPE operatives. They'd be retrieved later, but, in the meantime, the man didn't want tongues wagging back in Manaus, and they might do if he showed any sign of undue harshness. Unlike his men, the mercenaries were working just for the fee.

The man watched the plane take off and disappear towards the north. He gave final instructions to his remaining team, and settled down to wait.

69

'There it is,' the pilot said, and they saw the landing strip, a little brown scar in the green sea beneath them. 'The helicopter's camouflaged. To any outside observer, it's an ethnology research outpost for the Federal University.'

He brought the Beechcraft down lower, and circled once. They could see the little uniformed figures below, one waving the all-clear.

The plane made one more circle to regain height and then came in to land, bouncing across the stubble and coming to a halt near the hut. Several figures stood around it. The pilot kept his engines running as Jack and Natasha disembarked, then taxied away to the end of the runway as soon as they had done so. Moments later, the Beechcraft was airborne again.

A man wearing a BOPE lieutenant's uniform approached them, his face tense. He was flanked by two helmeted men also in BOPE uniforms, carrying two converted Madsen machine guns.

'Any problems?' Jack asked, immediately vigilant. Something was wrong here.

'We've had an alert, sir. From ABIN. It may be nothing, but the Agência reports activity in Manaus.'

Jack looked across to where the Bell helicopter had

been freed from its camouflage canopy. Its rotor blades were already turning, the crewmen already in their seats.

'It's a short flight from here. You'll have time to take stock when you reach your destination.' The lieutenant paused. 'Do you want any of my men to accompany you?'

'That won't be necessary,' Jack said. He barely had time to take stock of the situation, but if the Agência had sent an alert, as the lieutenant had said, they'd have to move fast. 'Briefing?'

'Just the alert. We'll radio information to the Bell as we get it.'

'No – keep security tight.'

'Certainly, sir.' The lieutenant saluted. 'Now, please hurry.' He fell back a pace or two, stopping as Jack and Natasha walked on towards the helicopter, ducking the rotor as they approached the open rear door. Then Jack saw the other passenger, lurking in the shadow of the passenger compartment. His hand went straight to his gun, but the two BOPE men had raised their machine guns. If they fired to kill now, they would risk hitting the helicopter, but not if they aimed low. That would be enough.

'Get in,' the lieutenant snarled, no longer polite.

Jack exchanged a look with Natasha, assessing the situation. They'd been trapped. But for some reason they hadn't been cut down immediately. Someone wanted them alive – for now. Grimly, he climbed into the Bell, Natasha following.

Their fellow passenger reached across and slid the

door shut as the helicopter rose into the air. He pulled their bags over on to the floor beside him and patted them down for arms, but casually, knowing that, even if he found any, they couldn't use them in a helicopter without bringing death to everyone on board.

He held a Ruger LCP in his lap. If he was careful, the man could use a little pistol like that on them without damaging the 'copter, thought Jack. But he'd already recognized his fellow traveller, who was looking at them both with the ghost of a smile.

'Good morning,' said Ambroise Louvier. 'I think you have something I've been looking for.'

Jack felt the hard surface of the polycarbon dagger against his calf. He could still win this. But right now, the Chevaliers had him in check. And if they searched him thoroughly once they'd landed, all his precautions, minimal as they were, would go to waste.

'You'll have to kill me to get the map,' Natasha said.

'Spare me the operatic gestures,' Louvier replied. 'Actually, I think we'll kill you *and* get the map.' He paused, his voice losing what pleasantness it had had. 'You have made life very difficult for us. We were fortunate that Ms Agoli was able to send enough detail of the location for us to set up a mobile operations centre close to where the city is. But you have caused us considerable delay.'

'And that's where we're going?' queried Jack.

'Of course.'

'Isn't that a waste of time? Why didn't you kill us back at the landing strip and take the map then?'

'I would happily have done so, but there is someone waiting at our destination who is quite insistent on saying goodbye to you both personally. And now – where is it?'

Jack nodded towards his pack, which was on the floor next to Louvier's feet.

'Jack – what the fuck are you doing?' Natasha said.

'Shut up,' said Louvier, and to Jack: 'Take it out for me.'

He obeyed. Natasha was about to say something else, seeing everything she'd worked for slip from her hands, but then something in Jack's eye told her that the game wasn't over yet.

He watched Louvier as the man unfolded the map carefully. But as soon as he had it in his hands the anger mounted in him.

'This is not the original,' he said, fury in his eyes.

'The original is safe.'

'And now you're going to tell me that this is an authentic copy!'

'Would I be carrying it if it wasn't? Or do you think I'd be putting my life at risk just to throw you on to a false trail?'

'People have done more stupid things.'

'Did Agoli tell you about the blank section? We have managed to break into it.'

Louvier's eyes focused on the area of the map Jack indicated. 'She did, and I see what you have done. But you could still be lying.'

'Do you have time to check? The original is out of

your reach, and it has the same information. Do you think you have any time to lose? You've probably lost the race already.'

Jack watched the anger and indecision appear on Louvier's face. He was weighing Jack's words.

'No one could have faked this in the time you've had,' Louvier began, but he was trying to convince himself.

'You've got us, but you know we're not working alone,' returned Jack. 'You know what you're up against. You've got to win this race or lose everything. It's your call.'

Louvier looked again at the map, re-tracking in his mind all the research, all the legends, all the documents he had studied, the Chevaliers d'Uriel had studied, to bring them to this moment. The map seemed to confirm them. And it was only a matter of days now before the sun's light would strike the doors. But still . . .

Jack watched his adversary's face closely. A plan began to take shape in his mind. But a lot depended on the situation he'd find when they landed.

And a lot more depended on Natasha.

70

The Bell came down in a large, cleared area of forest of well over three hectares near the bank of a river. Jack knew where they were: a location just on the edge of the blank area on the map. He could see from Natasha's face that she was thinking the same thing.

The place looked like a logging camp. There were two large wooden buildings, with a smaller one between them. The trees that had been felled were stacked at one end. A dozen armed men in green uniforms were gathered close to the helicopter, their guns ready.

They climbed out. The air was heavy and humid and the muddy ground showed traces of recent rain, though, now, the pale-blue sky above the canopy of trees was clear, and the sun had already begun to evaporate the moisture, so the air was filled with vapour. Under guard, Jack and Natasha followed Louvier the short distance to the central building, the only one with a crudely constructed veranda. The other two seemed to be barracks or storage rooms, and it was easy to see that all were temporary structures. The big doors of one stood open, and, within, Jack could see stacked piles of explosives. Near the stacks were two heavy trucks, and what looked like earth-moving equipment. At the far end of the clearing from the felled trees, about one hundred men in the same green uniforms were performing some kind of drill.

Leaving them waiting at the foot of the steps to the veranda, Louvier entered the hut with the map. They heard muffled voices, one once raised in anger, then what sounded like an explanation. Then silence.

It was like a piece of theatre. A few moments later, surrounded by a group of five aides, a thick-set man with ginger hair and a beard made his entrance on to the veranda. A man of around fifty. The map was in his hands. Jack now remembered having seen him briefly in the courtyard in Paris, and made the connection with the out-of-focus photograph Laura had shown him. But Natasha recognized him instantly, and shrank from him.

The man's lips drew back in the semblance of a smile. The eyes under the shaggy brows remained as hard as agate. 'Ms Fielding. What a great pleasure to see you again.' He let his gaze rest on her for a moment, appraising her, eating up her whole body with his eyes, before turning his attention to Jack. 'And you, of course, are Jack Marlow. Congratulations, Ambroise,' he said to Louvier. 'This will not go unrewarded.'

He turned to his entourage, who smiled and nodded their approval. He's holding court, Jack thought. The group surrounding the stout man were all male; all dressed in lightweight business suits and shirts, though they'd made the concession of abandoning ties; all were about the same age as the stout man; two wore glasses.

They looked out of place. All were uncomfortable in the heat, Jack could see that. Their leader, who'd chosen to wear a tailored, military uniform of sorts, had sweat marks under his arms and was failing to achieve the dignity he clearly sought. If this was the flower of the Chevaliers d'Uriel, Jack thought, God help the world if they succeeded.

But the man was enjoying his moment. 'You underestimated us,' he told Natasha. 'And you have done exactly what we wanted. Do you really think we would ever let you out of our sight – you, who tricked us of the key to all our endeavours? But now you will pay the price.'

'Who are you?' asked Jack.

'My name is James Topcliffe,' the man said, almost surprised by the question. 'Knight Commander of the Order of the Chevaliers d'Uriel. It is a pity you won't live to see the world reborn.'

'You've certainly got yourselves organized,' commented Jack.

'We are not amateurs,' replied Topcliffe boastfully. 'Do you think we didn't have everything planned, and in place, ready for this moment? This is a vast country. It's easy to operate in it without fear of detection. As soon as we had the information from Agoli, which, unfortunately for you, you were unable to stop, we set things in motion. Everything you see here has been brought in by helicopter and reassembled. We know we are not far from the goal, and nothing can stop us now.'

'Impressive. But this must have cost you a fortune.

Are you sure you'll be getting a good return on your investment?'

Topcliffe was about to reply, but Louvier whispered something to him then, and he waved an impatient hand. Six members of the armed guard still surrounding Jack and Natasha seized them and roughly manhandled them away from their audience with their leader. Behind the hut on the right was a windowless wooden annexe, sturdily built, out of the sun, close to the jungle's edge. Some kind of store room, with a heavy door, open now, chains and a padlock hanging from it. Within, Jack could see that someone had placed two wooden stools. Various carpentry tools hung from hooks on one wall: chisels, pliers, hammers, boxes of nails, and a saw. Thick wooden beams were stacked against the outside of the annexe. Big butcher's hooks were screwed into another short beam which ran across the ceiling, and two coils of thin nylon rope hung from them.

Jack knew they were unlikely to get out of this alive. Topcliffe may not have the time he would have liked to indulge in extensive torture, nor did he have the refinements of the instruments of pain in his collection, but his imagination and the contents of the tool room here would be more than enough to satisfy his appetite. The only hope was that Topcliffe's need to inflict pain would mean delay.

They were each being held by two guards. A fifth stood close with his machine-pistol ready. The sixth went into the annexe to unhook the lengths of rope. This was the only moment they'd have. Jack let himself go limp for a second, at the same time as his captors' attention was briefly distracted by their comrade's activity. He felt their grip slacken, and, in the split second before it tightened again, he wrested his right arm free and dived for the little dagger strapped to his left calf. In another second he had it in his hand, and drove it hard into the right eye of the guard on his left. He hit back with his right elbow and caught the other guard in the jaw, heard it crack, and winced with the pain of contact himself. The guard with the machine-pistol wheeled it round on him, but not quite fast enough. Jack rammed the polycarbon dagger into his neck, just above his shirt collar, pulling it out instantly and shoving the body back with his raised foot, at the same time reaching out and snatching the pistol from the man's hand. By now there was enough noise to have attracted the others. He fired a burst at the sixth guard, who was still standing in the doorway of the annexe with the ropes in his hand. It wasn't well aimed, as Jack was forced to use his left hand to shoot with, but the shots found their mark and the man fell back inside. The last two guards, the ones holding Natasha, had to release her in order to go for their own weapons. As they did so, Natasha, exchanging a lightning glance with Jack, understood, and dived into the trees only a metre away. Jack fired two short bursts, the gun unsteady in his left hand, but he was close enough to the remaining guards to cut them down. Not waiting to see whether his shots had been fatal, he plunged into the cover of the forest.

Six metres in, Natasha was waiting for him. He nodded to her and they made their way deeper into the jungle, stumbling over the uneven ground and undergrowth, weaving through the maze of trees until at last they reached a small clearing by a pool left by the recent rainfall, and stopped.

Jack listened intently, but apart from the sound of monkeys crashing away in panic through the canopy above them, they could hear nothing. When the noise the animals made had abated, there was only the murmur of the forest, the occasional call of a bird, the unending rustle of the trees. No sound of pursuit.

'They'll come after us,' Natasha said. 'They will.'

'No, they won't,' said Jack. 'They haven't time. They have the map now, and the coordinates they need. They have three or four days at most – according to our calculations – to get to the city, and they'll succeed only if they start now. They have been very lucky.'

'And what about us?'

Jack returned the dagger to its sheath. He was sweating hard. He stooped to the pool of water, splashing some on his face. Cautiously, he scooped some into his hand and tasted it.

'The water's OK. Drink a little.'

'What about us?' she repeated dully. 'We've lost. We're in the middle of nowhere, we don't have any idea which direction to take and, even if we did, we're hundreds of kilometres from help. We have no food, no supplies. We can't contact anyone –'

'Quiet,' said Jack. 'What we have is you – and this.' He drew the compass from his pocket and handed it to her while he checked the machine-pistol. It was a Steyr TMP, and its magazine was still more than half full. He ripped up a length of liana and used it to sling the gun across his back.

'I want you to concentrate,' he said when he had finished. 'We can't be more than five kilometres from the city, and we can get there much faster than they can. They can't use the helicopter, and they'll want to get explosives and as much of their back-up force there as soon as they can, to secure it. By now, Louvier at least will have put two and two together and realized that I wasn't bluffing. They know we have the original.'

'If Laura made it,' Natasha said.

Jack paused. 'Yes, if Laura made it.' There'd been nothing in Louvier's behaviour to indicate that she hadn't, but there was no way he could know for sure. On the other hand, it would take time for the US and Brazil to organize a task force, and he knew that as soon as the Chevaliers had access to the gold they would radio the news to their contacts worldwide and set in motion the *coup de grâce*. The whole financial world is a house built on sand. Markets and banks would founder, the Chevaliers would control world finances, and they could take their time in mining the riches of the city. They might not even need to do that. They might need only to sit on it, like the dragon, Fafnir. Its mere existence would be enough for them.

The clearing they were in was wide enough for them to take a bearing on the sun. Natasha checked the compass, letting its needle settle.

'I think I know where we are,' she said. 'Relative to their camp, we've come north. The sun was still in the east when we arrived.'

'Can you remember the map?' Jack asked, keeping his voice calm.

'I'm trying.'

'Concentrate.'

'We'll have to make our way further north from here,' she said. 'I can see the coordinates on the map, and the Chevaliers' camp is on the southern rim of the blank area we filled in. I remember the map now shows that the river makes a tight curve, doubles back on itself. The other side of the curve is where it feeds into the lake.'

'Thank Christ,' said Jack. They wouldn't have to retrace their steps and skirt the perimeter of the camp. By chance, they had set off in the right direction. But the enemy would know that. Pursuit was more likely and more imminent than he'd thought.

71

The jungle had not been kind to them. Nor had the mosquitoes. Nor had time.

It was trackless, confusing them at every turn and making them doubt the steadiness or the trustworthiness of the compass needle. The density of the canopy was claustrophobic. When they did discover a track, they became convinced that someone was following them, that they could hear footfalls and rustlings in the trees behind them, but whenever they stopped the sounds ceased as soon as did those they themselves made. Natasha spent hours without speaking, concentrating hard, and Marlow did not break their silence, though he sensed her increasing desperation.

It was the jungle that made them doubt themselves. Its constant rustling, its constant restlessness, unsettled them, and though they knew that the harsh and eerie calls and cries that broke the monotonous ripples and rushings of the leaves and the wind belonged to birds and harmless monkeys, the sounds still stabbed at their nerves. Creepers and roots snagged their feet with exhausting and infuriating regularity, whip-like branches slashed their faces and the edges of leaves cut their hands. They had to make an effort to rein in their impatience and to make slow, careful progress for fear of injury; even a sprained ankle could mean death out here. The gloom where they walked and stumbled along was so intense they felt as if they were walking along some green ocean floor. High above them, the sunlight seldom penetrated, except when clearings lay open to its harsh light.

Their clothes were drenched with sweat, and the sweat ran into their eyes and stung them. The insects danced perpetual attendance and would not let them rest for an instant. And that was how the whole of the first day passed, leaving them at the end hungry, exhausted, and thirsty, for they had passed no source of water since that first pool at the outset of their journey.

'It's not here. I can't remember any more,' Natasha said desperately, as the evening of the second day approached. During the second day they had gone on in the direction the compass indicated, but the maze of trees confused them, and it was next to impossible to relate the wilderness they were in to cold lines on a map, however accurately Natasha remembered them. With their increased bewilderment, her ability to focus her memory continued to weaken.

She was close to despair. 'And how the hell can we stop them even if we do get there?'

They bivouacked for the night in the dry hollow at the base of a huge tree by the side of a rivulet they came across, and which luckily accompanied them all day. So they had not gone thirsty, and they'd found fruit to feed themselves on, cut down with the polycarbon dagger, which was otherwise a pretty useless survival knife. They were reaching the limits of their endurance.

But when they woke the next day, cramped, and as weary as they'd ever been before, their hearts gave a rush and they were quickly on their feet as they realized what had awakened them.

Some distance away and hidden by the jungle, the noise of others: a large number of men, heading in the same direction.

Hope replaced despair, but along with it came an even greater sense of urgency.

'We'll shadow them,' Jack said.

'We must be very close now,' Natasha said. 'Closer than we thought. Jack, we must be very careful.'

'Of course.'

'Not just of the Chevaliers.' Natasha paused. 'Remember the tribe my father told me of.'

'They would have shown themselves by now. They would have attacked the Chevaliers' camp. They must have disappeared long ago.'

'In the camp, the Chevaliers could defend themselves easily, especially against the weapons the tribespeople have. But out here . . .'

'Even here, they'd be mad to attack against a force like that,' said Jack.

'They know the jungle. They have the element of total surprise. And in *their* eyes, *we'd* be desecrating the city too.'

'But they may not attack until they are absolutely sure we intend to get into it.'

'Can we take a chance on that?'

'What choice do we have?' Jack checked the Steyr machine-pistol. He hadn't been able to protect it from the humidity, but he'd have to take another chance on that. He prayed he wouldn't have to use it. 'If they turn on anyone, they'll turn on the Chevaliers first.'

'And pick us off afterwards? We're lost in this jungle, but to them it's Lexington Avenue or the Champs-Elysées.'

'Thinking like that doesn't help. Come on.'

Cautiously, they tracked the Chevaliers all that day, and, by the light of the setting sun, they came to the edge of the forest and gazed out on the lake. The island stood not fifty metres from the bank, joined to it by an ancient causeway which neither of them remembered from the map. The island was thickly wooded and, at its centre, on a low hill surrounded by trees that looked like worshippers but free of the plants they would have expected to see festooning it, a monolithic tower rose. Jack trained his binoculars on it. At its base, covered with primeval carvings, he could see an enormous double gateway of stone. As he watched, a flock of parakeets rose from the upper branches of a tree and flew past the tower to the right of it, their silhouettes caught in the embers of the sun setting behind it. He could not hear their cries, but it seemed to him that something had startled them.

72

The Chevaliers were setting up a makeshift camp. Hidden at the edge of the forest two hundred metres away, Jack watched them as they lit fires and made hasty preparations for the work ahead. There was a force of about fifty men, but he knew more would be following, with the explosives and the rest of their equipment, and would arrive soon, probably during the following morning. They would be just in time, for tomorrow was Midsummer's Day. He wondered what was happening in the greater world from which he was now cut off. Had the Chevaliers already acted, or would they wait until their triumph was certain? It seemed there was nothing he could do to stop them now. Once the gates opened, it would be finished. He had no resources. All he could do was pray, in the faint hope that INTERSEC had organized an intervention.

He imagined that the Chevaliers' manpower was hired – a force of mercenaries who had no idea of the true nature of this mission. But that didn't help him much. The men would have been well paid and they would ask no questions. They were a tool to be used and discarded the moment their usefulness was at an end. But they too would be tired and nervous, out here, far from any outside help. The desperate thought occurred to him that if he could find a way of sowing the seeds of panic among them, he might just be able to confuse their efforts. Well, if it came to it, that's what he would attempt. But he knew it would cost him his life, and Natasha hers, and almost certainly for nothing.

Whatever he did, he would leave it until the last possible moment. He waited for darkness to fall, waited until the fires of the camp burnt low.

'Come on,' he said to Natasha. 'We're going in closer.'

Staying well within the cover of the trees, they inched their way around the shore of the lake until they were within fifty metres of the camp. They didn't make a closer approach, because the Chevaliers would certainly have posted guards beyond the camp's perimeters, even here, in this sea devoid of any other humans. Jack wondered what Topcliffe thought had happened to them. Did he think the jungle had swallowed them? Or, when it was all over, would he try to seek them out? His fury now would be unbounded – but was his greed greater?

There was activity in the camp well before dawn, and Jack remembered what Leon Lopez had said.

'Up to now, we've been assuming that the sun will strike at midday,' Natasha said, watching the camp. 'But –'

Jack had picked up her thought. '– that's what we're *meant* to think? A kind of security precaution? Leon calculated that it might happen far earlier.'

'It's logical. As soon as the sun rises above the treetops in the east . . .'

'But do *they* know that?'

'We must get closer.'

'Wait!'

They were far nearer to the tower than they'd thought, and its rose-coloured stone was beginning to reveal itself in the growing light. Jack trained his binoculars on it. Now, the tower revealed itself to be a temple-like structure, its outer walls covered with dense carvings of birds and gods, and abstract shapes that might have been representations of galaxies. Suddenly, his attention was drawn to the carvings that ran across the giant lintel supporting the weight of stone above the gates. There was an ornate twisting design which he realized was a stylized representation of two snakes devouring each other, the mouths of each swallowing the other's tail. But, intermingled with the coils, and appearing in the same order as the scrawled symbols on the map, were those same symbols: Sirius, the condor, Canis Major and Lepus. Why were they there?

'Here!' He handed the binoculars to Natasha, pointing them out to her.

She looked at them hard and long before returning the binoculars to him, nodding in recognition of what she'd seen. 'But I've no idea why they're there, either,' she said, reading his thoughts. She took his hand, and gave him a smile that was curiously rueful.

At that moment they heard orders being barked from the direction of the camp. The light was growing stronger by the minute, and a group of men were lining up at the beginning of the causeway. Marlow recognized Louvier, Topcliffe and the men who'd surrounded the Knight Commander at the camp. All were now dressed in fatigues and wore hard hats equipped with torches. Their escort carried metal cases which, Jack guessed, contained explosives, picks, flares and ropes. One carried a powerful radio transmitter, but he would need to be in the open to operate it. Five of them carried lightweight assault rifles. Jack counted eighteen men in all.

'Advance party,' he said. 'Topcliffe wants to be first in.'

Above the tops of the dark-green trees to the east, the light grew stronger still, and red rays struck the upper reaches of the tower. The Chevaliers were already advancing along the causeway.

Behind them, those remaining in the camp were busying themselves with creating a greater clearing, preparing for the rest of their party.

Jack felt Natasha tense. She looked at him. Her eyes were dark.

'Forgive me.'

She released her hand from his and darted forward, weaving through the undergrowth and making for the edge of the trees. Once, she stumbled, but she quickly recovered and seemed then to dance over the rocky undergrowth, ducking skilfully beneath the hanging vines.

Jack was after her in an instant, and had almost reached her when he caught his foot in a tree root and sprawled forward. He shook himself free and forced himself to his feet, but the fall had sprained his ankle and it was minutes before he was able to limp down to the shoreline.

The Chevaliers had arrived at the gateway. They were dwarfed by it, looking up as the golden light crept down the tower towards them. He could see Natasha, halfway along the causeway now, unnoticed, moving fast and keeping low, pausing to take cover behind one of the great rocks that flanked it. Her gun was in her hand, but what could she do with it?

He looked up to see the sun's light strike the great lintel, and its carvings were thrown into deep relief. In that instant he understood what the symbols were, he understood what would happen after the doors had opened, he understood why the city of gold had kept its secret for so long. But Natasha was blinded by her mission, the mission that had been hammered into her from childhood, by a sense of duty she felt she owed to the Brotherhood's centuries of effort.

Would she think the same thing? And if she did, would she remember? Or had something snapped in her mind?

The men on the shore had seen her now. They were calling warnings, unslinging their guns. Jack realized there was one last thing he could do that might put an end to this. If Topcliffe could be panicked into thinking he was being attacked, he would rush into the temple as soon as the gates opened and then . . .

Jack was on the shore now, staggering forwards as he unslung the Steyr. He took aim at the first man he saw levelling his gun at Natasha, and, praying that the jungle hadn't affected it, pulled the trigger. The Steyr coughed and jolted then hammered out its deadly stream. Jack fell to the ground behind an outcrop of rock, yelling his warning to Natasha as he did so. She glanced back, but he knew his words had not reached her. She'd taken cover not ten metres from the Chevaliers.

The group by the gates stood undecided for a moment. Louvier seized Topcliffe by the arm, and the others surrounded them – but then the sun's rays passed below the lintel and on to the gates themselves.

For a moment, nothing happened, and then a faint quiver shook the ancient stonework. The gates began to move, in complete silence, opening inwards, and the sun's light followed into the darkness beyond, revealing a massive vestibule, pillared and decorated, in the midst of which a great stairway led downwards from an arch of mighty serpents. And all of it was gold, gold that shone like fire as it reflected the sun.

Jack managed to get off another burst before the Steyr jammed, and screamed his warning to Natasha once more. But there was no more gunfire. The men on the shore were watching, struck dumb as the temple revealed its secret and their leaders entered it. Jack could see Topcliffe, already at the head of the stairway, and Louvier, a pistol raised in his hand, close behind. He watched them, framed in the golden hallway, under the coiling archway, and for an instant everything slowed and his mind was suspended, hypnotized by the splendour and allure of what he saw. But he was quick to snap out of it. There were far more important things. 'Natasha!' he yelled, one last time. He had lost her among the rocks, but now he saw her dart forward again, through the great doors, slipping into the shadows behind them, as –

They had never fully opened, and, as soon as the sun's light had passed them, they closed. And they closed fast, silently. Jack could see the people inside turn, uncertain of what was happening, but before they could react the doors had closed, utterly, as if they had never been open, immuring those within until the next Midsummer's Day.

On the shore, there was panic, followed by fear. Several of the remaining men ran halfway along the causeway, unsure of what to do. At the same time, others came running along the shore in the direction Jack had fired from. He lay against the rock he'd sheltered behind, trying to unjam the gun. But as he cast an eye towards his attackers, they stopped, clutching at themselves, appearing to go into a frenzied dance. Beyond them, the same thing was happening to the other foot soldiers of the Chevaliers' doomed campaign.

The native guardians of the temple had known what would happen, known when to carry out their fatal attack. A hail of poisoned darts had fallen from the jungle on to those on whom the temple had not taken its own revenge.

Jack lay where he was until nightfall. Would Natasha have understood? Would she have realized that the symbols on the map, the symbols on the outer lintel, there as a reminder to those who knew the secret, were the key to getting out? In their greed to get in, the Chevaliers had never considered that the doors might close, as they had opened, on their own. But those who had built them had control over them and had designed a mechanism to open them from the inside. Would Natasha find a torch, a flare, in the darkness? Would she be able to find the corresponding symbols within the temple, on the inner columns supporting the lintel perhaps, and activate them?

He moved cautiously and raised his head at last. He had heard the tribespeople, seen some of them flitting like ghosts among the dead before melting into the jungle again, and he had sensed them move off in the direction of the Chevaliers' camp. But he'd still waited a long time before getting to his feet. Why he had been overlooked, or spared, he didn't know.

He looked at the silhouette of the tower rearing against the night sky. In the darkness, he could not distinguish the gates from the mass of the building.

He struggled to his feet, and, aching in every limb, made his way to the edge of the shore. He stopped and cupped water in his hands. He had never been so thirsty, or so tired.

73

The three big Chinooks – in a joint operation by the US Marines and the Brazilian Air Force at Manaus – flew in above the city of gold four hours after Jack had collapsed on the lake shore. A rescue team had been lowered, and was just in time to save him. Then they flew on to land at the Chevaliers' camp.

The bodies of the rest of the Chevaliers' force were scattered all over the artificial clearing. How many had died, how many had fled into the jungle, no one ever determined. The Marines deployed over the surrounding area, secured the temple island and the lake, and waited for the more substantial back-up force which, after lengthy negotiations, would be with them within three days. Meanwhile, Jack was transported back to Manaus, where the INTERSEC Gulfstream was waiting to take him home.

It was the Marines who radioed in the news, twenty-four hours after Jack had been taken to the special infirmary tucked away near Ridgewood, NJ, about thirty kilometres north-west of Manhattan.

After a meeting with Hudson in his office, Laura rejoined Leon in Room 55.

'Is he OK?' Leon asked anxiously, thinking the meeting might have concerned Jack.

She nodded. 'There's no change, but he's still stable. No reason to think he won't pull through.' She'd been planning to drive up to see him that afternoon, just to sit by his bed, hold his hand, will him to come back to them. Now, that would have to wait. Briefly, she filled Leon in:

'Colonel Draper has sent word of an explosion at the site,' she said.

'How big?'

'Not enormous, but it's done some quite heavy damage. It's brought the roof of the structure down, and that means the gates of the temple are blocked by masonry from within.' She paused. 'In other words, all access to the city has been blocked. It'll take a while, and massive machinery, to dig it out.'

'What do you think happened?'

'We'll have to wait until Jack can talk. But the safest guess is that they got in and were trapped. They must have taken explosives in with them, and they tried to blow their way out.'

Laura and Leon exchanged a glance.

Whatever had happened, the Chevaliers' plan had failed. Five days went by, and the tension on 24 June, from the White House to the Great Hall of the People, via Westminster, the Elysée Palace and the Kremlin, which had been at snapping point, gradually eased.

When the day itself had passed and no tremor announced the collapse of the dollar as the World Reserve Currency, there had been a lightning series of telephone calls between heads of state, their treasury and finance departments and the chiefs of the IMF and the leading world banks. Not a ripple of all this reached the press but, two days later, financial journalists were beginning to report an easing of the recent activity around gold, and a normalization of international market prices. A handful of big companies, two major merchant banks and one multinational had fallen victim to the recent 'gold plague', as the press chose to call it, but the ship wasn't holed below the waterline, Park Avenue soothed its ruffled feathers, and business shakily got back on track.

On 4 July, Laura was sitting at Jack's bedside in the room overlooking the gardens that surrounded the infirmary. He'd been conscious again for forty-eight hours, and at last the doctors had permitted her to visit.

She told him what had happened, and he filled in the gaps in her knowledge.

'I'll tell Hudson,' she said. 'You should get a citation.'

'Nobody got out?' he asked.

'If what you say is true, the Chevaliers are finished. Louvier and Topcliffe were the last big players. Section 19 has been doing some hoovering internationally, and all their major lieutenants were there with them. There's no trace, except for one or two isolated cells, and local security agencies are dealing with them.' She paused. 'No trace of any remnant of the Brotherhood either. I think this is one battle which can at last be consigned to history.'

'But nobody got out?' he asked again.

'No.'

'What'll happen to the site?'

'That's essentially for the US and Brazil to decide. They've kept the operation vague for the outside world. I shouldn't tell you this, but you, above all people, deserve to know. Hudson thinks that if the US–Brazil pact over this holds, it'll be best if the site is buried. Forgotten. No need for all that extra wealth. Just makes people greedy.'

'Someone will find out about it. What about the people behind the Chevaliers? The people who bankrolled them?'

Laura shrugged heavily. 'I don't think we'll ever know who they were. They'll have lost a lot of money, and they wouldn't want to draw attention to themselves over this. I doubt if the Chevaliers ever gave them the complete picture anyway.'

Jack nodded. 'Topcliffe was in it for himself. For his cause. I wonder if he really thought he was going to make the world a better place?'

'Whenever people like him crop up in the world, they always do think that. But they also like the power. And then they begin to think they're gods.'

'Yes.' His thoughts seemed to Laura to be drifting elsewhere.

'Anyone would have a hell of a job getting at the stuff now,' she said. 'It's as if it had never been.'

'Just as well.' Jack turned weary eyes to her, but she noticed a glint returning in their depths. 'Celebrating today?'

'I'd almost forgotten it was Independence Day. No. I'll go back to the apartment, open some wine, and try to finish *Les Misérables* – God, it's a marathon.'

'We'll do something together when I'm back on my feet.'

'Will we?' She looked at him, but there was a faraway look on his face. 'You're tired. I'll come back tomorrow.'

'Do that.'

She got up and left. He lay quietly for a moment, then turned his head to the window, his eyes on the green trees as their branches shook in a gentle wind.

But he was not looking at them. He was looking at someone in his mind.

'Natasha,' he said.